The Author at a book signing event in Hereford

FROM SHADOWS
.....TO A DARKER PLACE

About the Author

The author was born in the village of Ashbury, Oxfordshire. His early life was spent in nearby Watchfield – from where he attended Shrivenham Primary School and Faringdon Secondary Modern. Now retired, he was employed by MOD (Navy) and Boeing UK as a systems analyst.

Married to Lynn (nee Wilson), the couple initially lived in Swindon before moving to Brackley, Northamptonshire. Their current home is Melksham in Wiltshire. Alan and Lynn have two daughters – Kim and Nikki – and granddaughters Mistee and Mia.

Alan's interests include writing, poker and chess. He also enjoys the musical theatre and period drama. In the dim and distant past he once completed a London Marathon – but his sporting activities are now restricted to the golf course. He still suffers an occasional match at the Country Ground where Swindon Town FC was followed on a regular basis for twenty-five years.

Alan Barrett

FROM SHADOWS
.....TO A DARKER PLACE

Olympia Publishers
London

www.olympiapublishers.com
OLYMPIA PAPERBACK EDITION

A CIP catalogue record for this title is
available from the British Library.

ISBN: 978-1-84897-718-1

(Olympia Publishers is part of Ashwell Publishing Ltd)

This is a work of fiction.
Names, characters, places and incidents originate from the writer's imagination.
Any resemblance to actual persons, living or dead, is purely coincidental.

First published *in 2016*

Olympia Publishers
60 Cannon Street
London
EC4N 6NP

Printed in Great Britain

Dedication

Dedicated to my wife Lynn, and our forty-six years together.

Acknowledgements

Many thanks to Christine Thomson and Mary Blizzard for pointing out errors in my initial drafts – and to Richard Castle's eagle-eyed attention to detail during the proof-reading stages. I'm also indebted to Amy Fletcher for once again producing another eye-catching piece of 'SHADOWS' artwork.

Thank you to my wife Lynn, for providing the follow-up title to my first 'SHADOWS' novel.

And a final thanks to Zoe Hodgkinson – my Production Coordinator at Olympia – for all her help and expertise throughout the lengthy, but necessary, publishing process.

Also by the same Author

SHADOWS
ISNB: 978 184897 192 9

FOREWORD

North Downs and Surrey Hills:

Beneath his lightweight jogging suit the lone runner perspired profusely. A fierce summer sun had already heated the July morning to an energy sapping twenty-three degrees. Stretching out ahead of him was a single track road – bounded on both sides by dense, green hedging – the two arrow straight lines converging into a heat shimmer at their furthest point.

The road was on high ground. Intermittent gaps in the hedging revealed acres of rolling farmland, vast swathes of bright yellow flowering rapeseed touching the distant horizon. John Hendry slowed to a halt, breathing in the plant's heavy scent – a musky, sensual aroma that was almost overpowering. He stood looking at the view for several minutes before pushing on, gradually increasing his pace, embracing the body's discomfort.

Hendry's five-mile run was an integral part of a dedicated exercise regime – another of his passions being the pursuit of money. He'd played the stock markets on a small scale all his adult life, discovering that a conditioned body honed the mind; an essential requirement for studying hidden trends within the world's leading economies.

The unmarried thirty-five-year-old Dubliner settled back into a steady rhythmic stride, reflecting on his current situation. Hendry still found it difficult to believe that until quite recently he was routinely pursuing a career in forensics with the West Midlands Police. That way of life had suddenly and dramatically changed – a shady, but highly lucrative, business venture realising huge profits. His new-found situation would soon allow Hendry to move abroad, where there'd be opportunities to consolidate and increase the substantial windfall.

He was currently in the process of winding up his affairs in England. The cramped apartment rooms had been vacated several weeks ago, along with a hurried resignation from his police forensics post. Hendry would very shortly be living in an overseas tax haven – a full time speculator – building up blue-chip stock and trading in high-risk investments.

There were drawbacks though. Hendry couldn't tell family or friends about his future plans. Not yet anyway. He'd have to lie low for a while. Sever all contacts. The man from Dublin shrugged – a lifetime of wealth and privilege far outweighed what he was leaving behind.

Hendry smiled to himself. Those advantages would be fully exploited – the Irishman had discovered early in life that money was a powerful aphrodisiac. Although women appeared to find him attractive, the opposite sex showed considerably more interest when a high income status and profile was hinted at. To that end he'd indulged himself – a luxury purchase – his recently acquired Porsche-Carrera GT. The high performance car projected an overwhelming aura of money and male testosterone, a seemingly irresistible combination to those women who'd eased themselves down into the car's low-hung, soft leather passenger seating.

The most recent of Hendry's acquaintances to fall under the Porsche-Carrera's spell was one Ms Samantha Phillips – an impressionable twenty-year-old Personnel Assistant he'd met just days earlier. Ms Phillips was statuesque, extremely blonde, with a generous hour-glass figure that she would find difficult to reign-in as the years passed. The Irishman was due to meet her later that evening for dinner, and if he'd judged the signs correctly, Ms Phillips token resistance was nearing the point of collapse. Hendry felt the reassuring stirrings of an erection. Samantha Phillips continued to occupy his mind as he approached a stationary car, parked-up on the grass verge.

Hendry knew his cars, and the Bentley Continental Tourer looked out of place on the single-track road. He slowed to a walking pace. The car's bonnet was propped open. His gaze lingered on the hiked-up skirt and bare legs of a young woman who was stooped over the Bentley's engine. As Hendry drew level with the vehicle a pair of green, almond-shaped eyes turned to look directly at him. The woman's cropped black hair complemented a light, olive-coloured skin – stretched taut over prominent cheekbones.

The Dubliner switched on his most engaging smile and nodded towards the car. *'Unusual for one of these to experience problems,'* he said to the woman.

She stood to one side. *'I don't have trouble before.'*

Her fractured, heavily accented English added to Hendry's curiosity. Eastern Europe possibly. *'I'll check the basics for you,'* he offered. *'That's about the extent of my expertise.'*

'You can fix?' The woman frowned as she searched for the right words. *'Is not easy for me. My phone have trouble.'*

Hendry nodded. *'The signal's not good up here.'* He stooped beneath the car's bonnet and tugged at the battery's connections.

'I have to repay for your help,' the woman said.

'I'm sure there's some sort of arrangement we could arrive at,' the Dubliner murmured to himself. It went quiet. *'Where are you headed?'* he asked. The woman didn't reply. Hendry glanced to his side and saw that she'd moved away. The Irishman sensed someone behind him. He turned around.

A man stood in front of him – tall, slim, the face smooth and lightly tanned – irregular flecks of grey peppering his short dark hair. The cream linen suit he wore looked hand-made, a pair of dark glasses protected his eyes against the sun's rays. He smiled at the Dubliner through thin, colourless lips, arms folded nonchalantly across his chest. The man's demeanour carried an implied threat. Hendry was immediately wary.

'You are a rare creature of habit, Mr Hendry.' The man's English was near perfect, just a trace of accent. *'Your routines have proved very convenient for us.'*

Hendry's concern rose another notch. Now he felt intimidated.

The man spoke again. *'Allow me to introduce myself. Ilyad Medzev. I am the project's executive co-ordinator.'*

'Project?' Hendry snapped. *'What bloody project?'*

The man ignored his question. He directed Hendry's attention back towards the woman. *'My chauffeur you've already met. May I also introduce my personal bodyguard?'* A figure emerged from behind the Bentley and stood next to it. *'This is Golem.'*

Hendry stared. The co-ordinator's bodyguard was a throw-back to pre-history. On either side of his squat, barrel-shaped body a pair of extended arms hung down to his knees, the wide forehead dominated a flat, elongated skull. He was dressed completely in black, his thin roll-neck sweater stretched across a muscular chest and torso.

'If you're familiar with The Bible,' Medzev said, *'you'll be aware that it refers to a golem as being an incomplete substance with limited intelligence. One who carries out his orders immediately and without question.'*

Hendry's eyes remained on the bodyguard.

Ilyad Medzev smiled. *'If I ordered Golem to put a loaded gun into his mouth and told him to pull the trigger he would do so instantly.'*

Golem bowed his head towards the co-ordinator. *'Of course, master.'*

Medzev looked fondly at his bodyguard. *'When Golem came into my ownership ten years ago I had to name him. I consider the choice very apt. Would you not agree, Mr Hendry?'*

The Irishman didn't offer any reply.

'We are aware of your current circumstances,' Medzev continued. *'A temporary suite of rooms at the Hilton Hotel and your possessions locked away in self-storage units.'* He held out a hand towards the Irishman. *'I will take your keys. We know that you carry them on your person.'*

Hendry's brain raced. This was obviously to do with his newly acquired wealth. The recent business venture would have upset certain organisations and attracted the interest of others. The Dubliner didn't

16

move. He made no attempt to reach into the zipped pocket of his jogging suit for his keys.

Medzev nodded. *'As you wish. It can be dealt with at a later juncture.'* He gestured towards the Bentley. *'And now you are required to accompany us on a short journey. Please get into the car.'*

Hendry's eyes darted from side to side, looking for an escape route. He eyed a gap in the hedge.

'I'd advise against it.' The man's voice sounded unconcerned. *'Golem is deceptively fast, and his physical attributes would enable him to incapacitate you in seconds.'*

The bodyguard nodded enthusiastically, an idiotic smile exposing large, yellow teeth. Hendry was accustomed to making instant decisions. He spun around and sprinted toward the hedge. A bullet buzzed angrily past his ear, thudding into the grass bank. He froze.

'Face me!' a voice instructed. *'Slowly!'*

Hendry turned.

The woman chauffeur stood with her legs braced, arms fully extended – she held a small pistol in both hands, the gun's silencer pointing directly at him. Working the firearm's chamber release mechanism she ejected an empty bullet case onto the road. A thin feather of acrid-smelling smoke hung in mid-air, unable to escape the humid atmosphere. She stooped to retrieve the empty casing, her eyes never leaving Hendry's face.

The co-ordinator's voice cut in, clipped, impatient. *'There are limits to my good nature, Mr Hendry. Move to the car's front passenger door and step inside.'*

The incident had shaken Hendry. His legs lacked substance. He was barely able to reach the open door and lower himself inside. The door was immediately closed. There was movement behind him, a sensation of cold metal at the back of his neck. *'No more heroics, Mr Hendry,'* the man said to him. *'Please fasten your seat belt.'* The pressure to his neck was reinforced.

Hendry sat and stared through the windscreen. A wave of nausea hit him. He had to swallow hard, forcing down a surge of vomit. The woman chauffeur's movements were brisk and efficient. She lowered the car's bonnet and walked around to the driver's open door, sliding into the seat alongside him. Hendry risked a sideways glance. The woman's face remained impassive as she immediately fired-up the Bentley's engine. A short time later they were travelling back along the same stretch of road that Hendry had covered minutes previously.

He risked a question. *'Am I allowed to ask what this is about?'*

'Not yet,' the man replied. There was a rustle of cellophane and Hendry felt a sharp pinprick to the side of his neck. He lapsed into unconsciousness.

The Bentley headed away from London – eating up the miles as it continued along a pre-arranged route of back roads and country lanes. After a journey of over three hours the Bentley slowed, turning left into a narrow, semi-concealed entrance. An uneven, pot-holed surface jolted the car's occupants – causing Hendry to stir. He opened his eyes. It took a moment to recall where he was and what had happened.

'Welcome back, Mr Hendry,' the co-ordinator said from behind him. *'Your timing is once again impeccable.'*

It was still light outside. Hendry glanced at the Bentley's dashboard panel – a small circular clock indicated it was three o'clock. They slowed to a halt. Someone exited the car. Moments later his door was pulled open and the bodyguard waved a handgun, motioning him to step outside. Hendry was still feeling slightly groggy but tried to take in his surroundings. It might be important. The house they'd drawn up outside was substantial, imposing – its large garden untended and overgrown. He looked over his shoulder. The driveway must have measured over a hundred yards in length, and there didn't appear to be any other houses in the near vicinity.

Ilyad Medzev – if that was the man's name – brushed past him, striding briskly up to the building's weathered front door. It swung open to his touch and he disappeared inside.

Golem prodded Hendry forward, pushing the short gun-barrel into his back. Both men stepped through the open doorway. Hendry was manoeuvred across an expanse of dry, cracked linoleum, towards a bare wooden staircase. Golem followed him as they slowly ascended to a small landing above. It wasn't quite as gloomy here – two recessed windows shedding some light. To Hendry's left was an open door. He was motioned inside. A key turned in the lock behind him. Hendry began to shake, probably an after-effect of the drug. It took several minutes before he was able to take in his surroundings. The room they'd locked him in was small, dingy, badly in need of decoration. A thread-bare carpet, its original pattern unrecognisable, covered the floor.

He crossed to a large, sash window and tried to push aside the retaining clip, but it was either locked or jammed. The Irishman leant forward to peer outside – looking down a sheer drop of at least fifty feet. He turned back around. In the room's far corner was a narrow divan stacked with blankets and pillows – the only other items of note being a small square table and two hard-backed chairs. To his immediate left was a curtained recess. Hendry pulled the flimsy, grubby material to one side. Just a small kitchenette. He stepped inside. The Irishman pulled open a small drawer and sorted through various items of cutlery. He picked out a double-sided slicing knife. Another spasm of nausea swept over him. He had to lie down. Hendry returned to the other room and slipped his knife under a pillow, before lying out full length on the narrow bed. He didn't intend to fall asleep.

CHAPTER 1

Birmingham High Street: Friday 14th October 2011: 10.30 a.m.

Crosby rustled his way through the newspaper – earthquakes in Japan, piracy and kidnap on the high seas, civil unrest in North Africa – and the back pages were already beginning to escalate coverage of next year's London Olympics. The fifty-nine-year-old ex-detective looked up to make sure that his wife was still out on the shop floor somewhere. It would have been a surprise to see her just yet – they'd only been inside the store for two hours.

Situated in Birmingham's High Street, the department store and its lay-out suited them both. On this particular morning he'd parked himself in the store's on-site café with a newspaper whilst his wife browsed and shopped – an exercise that had always tested Crosby's patience. As the practice hadn't become any more acceptable to him since his retirement – and because his wife didn't drive – a compromise was eventually arrived at. He would find a convenient place to wait, somewhere close-by, and they'd meet up at some point for lunch. It seemed to work for them.

As the ex-detective reached for his half-empty coffee mug he caught the eye of a young woman sitting five tables away. She smiled across at him. Crosby couldn't place her but he nodded back anyway – one of those faces you recognise but can't put a name to. Bloody annoying. Maybe his ability of being able to instantly pull a file from memory was finally diminishing.

Crosby retreated behind his newspaper – the woman's identity continuing to gnaw at him. He began to subconsciously trawl back through past investigations *'Shit!'* Crosby straightened in his chair. It was Lucy. Robert Milner's daughter.

Memories of four years ago flooded back. A remote Welsh hill farm – Lucy staked and tethered inside one of the outbuildings. Lucy's mother, hysterical and screaming outside. Robert Milner, unloading the contents of a double-barrelled shotgun into his mouth. Crosby could still see remnants of skull and brain scattered across the farm's concrete yard.

Robert Milner wasn't the only casualty to be air-lifted away by helicopter that night. Lucy's step-father Henry Roberts, and twenty-year-old rookie PC Peter Stewart, also left *Dryffed's Farm* in grey, plastic body-bags – the bloody climax to a six-week murder investigation.

Detective Inspector Crosby, as he was back then, had witnessed the shootings – fortunate to escape with his life. Subsequent repercussions from the flawed investigation were major factors in his decision to take early retirement.

He peered over the top of his newspaper to find Lucy Roberts still looking across at him. It was little wonder that Crosby hadn't recognised her initially – she'd lost weight – and the time spent in prison had turned her hair white. An image of Lucy's late father flashed into the ex-detective's subconscious. He shrugged off an involuntary shiver.

As Lucy had originally been sent down for a term of five years, she was presumably out on early release. Crosby would have given her life, but an astute barrister had somehow convinced a jury that her role in the six-week killing spree was minimal – and Lucy's performance in the witness box had been worthy of a Hollywood Oscar.

'Fuck!' he mouthed to himself. She was on her feet and walking towards him, attracting a lot of interest from male customers. The cropped white hair, angular features, and tall, slim build gave her a remote, almost android-like appearance – strikingly attractive – and far removed from the young, elfin-faced, dark-haired student who'd stood in the dock of Birmingham's Crown Court less than four years ago.

'Detective Inspector Crosby?'

He folded the newspaper slowly before looking up.

'I thought it was you.' Lucy extended a thin, almost skeletal hand for him to shake.

He ignored it.

Lucy didn't seem at all put out by Crosby's deliberate snub. *'Are you still at Studwell? With the CID there?'* She was well spoken. Her voice light.

'I'm retired.'

'Surely not.' The woman laughed. *'You don't look old enough.'*

Crosby didn't join in her laughter. The ex-detective had been one of the officers responsible for Lucy being imprisoned. He wondered where this bizarre encounter was heading.

She sat down in a chair opposite. *'May I join you?'* The smile Lucy offered him looked genuine enough but it didn't reach her eyes. She leant back, deliberately taking her time to cross a pair of long, slender legs. *'It's been a while since we last saw each other.'*

Crosby didn't reply.

'Three years and ninety five days to be precise,' Lucy's voice now had a slight edge to it, *'but then I did get to spend a lot of time in my cell looking at the calendar.'*

Crosby needed to cut this short. *'Was there something, Lucy? I am expecting my wife for lunch.'*

Lucy's smile returned. She inclined her head towards the shop floor. *'I was talking to your wife earlier. Doreen isn't it? I do so admire people who can chat quite openly to complete strangers,'* she paused, *'about all manner of things.'*

The intimidation wasn't even subtle. Crosby suppressed his anger. *'I'd appreciate you not approaching members of my family. The Sixfields investigation makes it inappropriate. But I'm sure you're aware of that.'*

'We were just talking, Inspector.' Lucy's face assumed an expression of innocence. *'There was nothing sinister intended.'*

'My wife and I are not alike,' the ex-detective said sharply. *'I don't do social bloody chit-chat. Just what is it you want?'*

Lucy held up her hands. *'I actually came over to apologise. My behaviour three years ago was extremely irresponsible.'*

'Irresponsible!' Crosby hissed. *'Two of my colleagues lost their lives because of your actions.'* He leant forward across the table. *'You personally arranged to have six people murdered on the Sixfields estate. It instigated a full-scale riot.'*

Lucy shook her head. *'I was only eighteen. My step-father's influence and the promise of money put me in a bad place.'*

'The only bad place was inside your head,' Crosby said brusquely. *'I doubt that's changed.'*

'I've paid for my mistakes.'

'You've paid fuck all!' The ex-detective's voice was louder than he intended. *'A life sentence wouldn't have been long enough for what you did.'*

Customers at nearby tables began to glance in their direction. Lucy lowered her eyes. Crosby pushed his face in close. *'And don't play that little girl lost routine,'* he said. *'It's fucking wasted on me. Your only regret was the operation didn't work out as planned.'*

Lucy's features hardened. Her eyes snapped wide-open. Crosby had witnessed the same intense look on her late father's face – and Robert Milner hadn't been a well man – his depression and mental health issues were significant factors during the Sixfields investigation.

Lucy's attention was diverted. The moment passed. She waved to someone across the room, beckoning them over. Crosby followed her eye-line. The figure striding towards them was at least six foot tall – broad-shouldered – dressed in a white, open-necked man's shirt and dark trousers. As the newcomer approached them Crosby could see that it was a woman. The detective in him automatically filed away a description. It was an unattractive face, hard, devoid of any make-up. The short brown hair, complete with side-parting, added to a look of undisguised masculinity. She was also a lot older than Lucy. Probably mid-thirties.

On reaching their table the woman planted herself directly in front of Crosby's chair. *'Is this him?'* A trace of Lancashire in the accent.

Lucy nodded. *'Inspector. I'd like you to meet Rose Cavendish.'*

Professional instincts warned Crosby that the new arrival was trouble. She continued to stare at him. It was rude. Bloody annoying. The ex-detective inclined his head slightly. *'Ms Cavendish,'* he said, deliberately stretching out the woman's title. *'I would appreciate you not standing over me.'*

Lucy motioned for her to stand back. The woman did so reluctantly, but remained standing.

'Rose was a prison warder at Foston Hall,' Lucy said. *'She took a personal interest in my welfare during the time I had to spend there.'*

Crosby couldn't help himself. *'I imagine she'd have made that a priority.'*

Cavendish bunched one of her hands into a fist. *'Don't fucking push it, copper!'*

The ex-detective gained some satisfaction from it. At least he was annoying her now.

'A lot of inmates were keen to befriend me,' Lucy continued, looking fondly at the older woman. *'Rose made sure they kept their distance. After my release she left the prison service and we set up home together.'*

'It was fortunate you found one another.' Crosby's face remained expressionless. *'Too many people go through life without ever finding their soul-mate.'*

Cavendish placed two large hands on the table-top as she pushed her face into Crosby's. *'I've told you once!'* she warned him. *'Watch your mouth! Lucy's vulnerable. And the reason I'm still having to protect her is because of people like you. Your investigation framed her when there was no one else left to take the blame.'*

The woman was too close again. Crosby stood up. *'If she's managed to convince you of that, Ms Cavendish, I'd be very concerned about your future together. Lucy's father discharged a double-*

barrelled shotgun into the roof of his mouth because of what she did to him. Ask her about that.'

Lucy smiled and shook her head. *'Rose and I have no secrets, Inspector. We are very much in love.'* She reached across and laid a hand on the older woman's arm. *'Your stories and half-truths won't alter how we feel about each other.'*

'I hope all this trust includes the fact that you shot your own brother.'

Lucy's face hardened. *'We both know that isn't true, Inspector. My father accused me of that after his mind had gone. The man would have been certified insane if he hadn't killed himself.'*

Crosby had heard enough. *'I hope you'll be very happy together then.'* He turned to leave.

'Our meeting was not a coincidence, Inspector,' Lucy said to him. *'There's an urgent matter we need to discuss.'*

'Urgent?' Crosby said impatiently. Rose Cavendish reversed one of the chairs and sat with a leg straddled either side of it, looking directly across at him. Lucy leant back, her arms folded. *'Dryffed's Farm and the surrounding area was processed as a murder site,'* she said, *'but Scenes-of-Crime didn't report any major finds or discoveries.'*

The ex-detective shrugged. *'And your point is what exactly?'*

'There was a large cache of narcotics hidden on the farm.'

Crosby's eyes narrowed.

'Heroin,' Lucy said. *'Ninety per-cent pure. A street value in excess of three hundred million pounds sterling.'*

'Three hundred million!' Crosby was genuinely taken aback.

'Don't look so surprised,' Lucy said. *'You knew what was planned for Sixfields. It needed at least that amount for the syndicate to kick-start another drugs network within the estate.'*

Crosby resumed his seat. *'There was no indication that you'd stockpiled everything before-hand,'* the ex-detective said. *'We assumed the drugs would have been procured after the riots.'*

If the Sixfields operation had gone to plan both Lucy and her step-father, Henry Roberts, would have been heavily involved in the supply and distribution of narcotics throughout the entire estate. It was only at the tail-end of their investigation that Crosby had become aware of what the syndicate intended. *Dryffed's Farm* obviously made an ideal storage site – the property located just over the border in Wales – only an hour's drive from Henry Roberts' country estate in Oswestry.

'The merchandise was shrink-wrapped in airtight containers,' Lucy continued, 'along with a substantial amount of cash. I returned there last week to make sure everything was still in place.'

Crosby shrugged. 'And why are you telling me this?' he asked. 'I could go straight to the authorities with it.'

Lucy ignored him. 'The concealment's empty,' she said. 'It's been cleaned out.' A short silence. Crosby couldn't immediately work out the implications. 'So what exactly do you want from me?' he asked. 'Sympathy? Technically it's theft. You could always inform the police.'

Cavendish jabbed the ex-detective's arm with her forefinger. 'Shut the fuck up and listen!'

Lucy pulled a small notebook from her pocket. 'On the night my step-father was killed you were left alone at the farm for at least an hour.'

'Apart from three dead bodies,' Crosby replied. 'And there was you of course. Tethered to a post in the barn.'

Lucy turned a page. 'It was recorded at my trial that Detective Constable Taylor went back down the mountain to get help.' She looked across at him. 'Whilst you remained at the farm.'

'I'm rapidly tiring of our reunion,' Crosby said. 'Is there a point to all of this?'

Lucy glanced down at her notebook again. 'When Detective Constable Taylor left you behind at the farm she stated that my step-father was still alive.'

'Barely,' Crosby replied. 'Your father had just unloaded both barrels of a shotgun into your step-father's back before he killed himself.'

'Only my step-father and I knew where those drugs were hidden,' Lucy said. 'No one could have found that concealment by chance. Henry must have told you where it was before he died.'

Crosby laughed. 'Why the hell would he do that?'

Lucy didn't laugh along with him. 'How the fuck do I know! He was dying. You could have forced it out of him.'

'I didn't know there was any bloody heroin stored at the farm!'

'Didn't you?'

'What the hell's that supposed to mean?' Crosby was beginning to raise his voice again.

'I recently collected some papers that my father-in-law left in a safety deposit box.'

'And?'

'Henry was meticulous in scheduling and resourcing every one of his operations,' Lucy replied. 'He had contingency plans for every possible situation. There was even a document concerning you.'

Crosby frowned. A frisson of concern.

'The document was dated three weeks prior to my father-in-law's death.' Lucy was eying him closely. 'It refers to the possibility of re-locating our heroin stock. Apparently a Detective Inspector Crosby had come into information that there were drugs hidden on the farm.'

Crosby straightened in his chair.

'It also goes on to say that you did not share this information with the Major Investigation Unit.'

'That's bollocks!' Crosby was angry now. 'I hadn't heard of Dryffed's Farm until the day your father-in-law drove us up there.'

Lucy ignored it. 'We've had someone check-out your expenditure over the past three years,' she said. 'New car. A Mediterranean cruise. Your home improvements. A tidy investment tucked away for the grandson.'

27

'*I retired.*' Crosby stood up. '*It comes with a decent lump sum and pension. And I'm done with this conversation.*'

'*Sit down!*' Rose Cavendish instructed. '*We've not finished yet.*'

'*Yes we bloody well have,*' Crosby said. '*You need to consider why the goods were moved without your knowledge. It sounds as if step-daddy no longer considered you part of his operation.*'

Lucy shook her head. '*He didn't re-locate anything. The heroin was still there when Henry and my mother left for the Caribbean. They returned a day before he was killed at the farm.*'

Crosby looked at both women in turn. '*So I'm supposed to have cradled a dying man in my arms as he rambled deliriously about treasure trove in secret hiding places.*'

Cavendish interrupted him. '*You're not convincing anyone,*' she said. '*You knew that Dryffed's Farm was being used to store the heroin. And there was plenty of time to shift it all after the site had been processed.*'

Crosby shook his head. He nodded at Lucy's notebook. '*I suggest you trawl through your notes again. If I'm the prime suspect then you're in for a big disappointment. I think step-daddy's contingency plan to shift it all is your best option.*'

'*We won't be looking for anyone else,*' Lucy said.

'*I wish you luck then.*' The ex-detective made to leave again.

Rose Cavendish was on her feet and blocked his way. When Crosby tried to push her aside he found himself full length on the floor with an arm twisted up around his back. A member of staff at the café counter quickly picked up a phone.

Three years of retirement had seen Crosby lose a lot of his fitness. He struggled for breath as Cavendish continued to lock his arm. Lucy was at his ear. '*I will have what remains of my three hundred million, Inspector. We'll then discuss how you intend to repay the balance.*' Cavendish's pressure on his arm eased. Both women stood up. '*If the necessary arrangements aren't made,*' Lucy added, '*then your grandson becomes a focus of attention. Consider this a warning. We will speak again.'*

A uniformed, over-weight security guard hurried into the café, brushing past Roberts and Cavendish as the two women left. He went straight across to speak with the counter assistant. His appearance and general demeanour didn't fill the ex-detective with any confidence. Crosby hauled himself back into his chair. *'Shit!'* he mouthed to no one in particular. Although shaken by what had happened he didn't want the incident pursued. Lucy's accusation needed evaluating. And the threat against his grandson had to be taken seriously. He knew what Lucy Roberts was capable of.

The security guard eventually made his way across to Crosby's table. *'Is everything OK with you, Sir?'*

'I'm fine,' the ex-detective answered brusquely.

'I've been told that a female customer pushed you to the floor.'

Crosby thought he detected a slight mocking in the guard's voice. *'I slipped,'* he said. *'She was helping me up.'*

The security guard looked unsure. *'It needs to be logged. I'll check to see if she's still in-store. If you remain at your table I'll come back and take some details.'* He unclipped a small radio from his belt and spoke into it before leaving the café's seated area.

'Jesus Christ!' the ex-detective muttered aloud.

'And why are you calling on the son of our Lord?' his wife enquired brightly. She deposited several carrier bags in an adjacent chair before sitting down next to him. *'Have I been too long? Or has something in the newspaper annoyed you?'*

'I'm fine,' Crosby loosened his collar. *'It's too bloody warm in these places. If the damned heating was turned down they could save enough to serve their coffee at a reasonable price.'*

'Are we staying here for lunch?' his wife asked, *'or is that over-priced as well?'*

Crosby was already standing. *'We'll find a pub somewhere. I've been sitting here all bloody morning.'* He picked up two carrier bags and made for the café's exit.

'We still have to call in at the chemist,' his wife called after him. *'I think we've run out of your happy pills.'*

Crosby wasn't listening, his mind elsewhere. He had some serious thinking to do. Old practices and instincts had been stirred. A case not quite closed. He could do without it though. The two women would be in contact again – three hundred million pounds was a lot of money – and the threat to his grandson had been a genuine one.

CHAPTER 2

Sunday morning at number ten Hawthorne Rise had assumed a familiar, well-ordered routine over recent years. The sequence of events hardly varied. After breakfast, whilst Crosby retired with the newspapers, his wife busied herself throughout their three-bedroom detached house – ensuring it was fit to receive visitors. This despite the fact that every room had been thoroughly serviced only two days previously.

At precisely eleven o'clock, and usually after Crosby had drifted into an un-scheduled nap, a call of *'Frank!'* would signal the start of preparations for lunch. Crosby's responsibility was to prepare the vegetables – his wife insisted that he made a contribution.

The family arrived at eleven-thirty. Michael, their son, was cast in the same mould as his father, tall, slightly overweight, thinning sandy hair – wearing clothes that looked more comfortable than fashionable. Angela, their daughter-in-law, was five years younger than Michael, a complete opposite in all respects – petite, pencil slim, smart designer labels, and an outgoing personality to match. Crosby had always thought them a most unlikely couple, but several years later they were still together, and seemingly very happy. Michael hadn't followed the family tradition of a career in the police force – his business was insurance brokering – and although Angela spoke of returning to work at some point in the future she currently remained a full-time housewife.

The young couple were accompanied by their five-year-old son Jack – a high-octane, excess of energy who only operated in fast forward. Crosby could always rely on Sunday night for a solid eight hours sleep after seeing his grandson off the premises.

Jack was the centre of Doreen Crosby's universe. She doted on him. And due to Michael's inability to remain conscious at the first sight of blood, she'd even been present to witness her grandson's birth. Throughout the ensuing five years their special bonding had continued to build – Jack spending nights at Hawthorne Rise from an early age.

Whilst Doreen Crosby and her daughter-in-law added finishing touches to their Sunday roast, the five-year-old was escorted to a nearby park and local play-area. His enthusiasm for the playground's apparatus could only be described as reckless, with scant regard for the site's health and safety warning notices. A previous visit had resulted in Crosby trying to retrieve his grandson from halfway-up a rope climbing-frame – both of them having to be helped down during the subsequent rescue operation.

On this particular morning the play-area was virtually deserted – temperatures were down into single figures and a stiff breeze added to the chill factor. Although a partially filled paddling pool was not on the agenda today, it had taken several minutes of patient negotiation to steer Jack in another direction. Both men retired to a nearby wooden bench, waiting for Jack to tire himself out on the spring-loaded, yellow rocking horse. Crosby's attention wandered – urgent, muffled shouts drifted across from an adjoining park – a local, Sunday morning football match in progress.

The ex-detective focused on a couple in long dark coats, walking their dog around the park's perimeter. They stopped to look in his direction. A sliver of white hair flashed briefly in the weak, mid-October sunshine.

Crosby was immediately on his feet.

Michael looked up at him. *'Something wrong, Dad?'*

'Touch of cramp.' The ex-detective rubbed at his calf. *'I'll have to walk it off.'*

'You could gate-crash the football,' Michael said good-naturedly. *'Show them some of your old step-overs.'* He turned his attention back to Jack's exertions on top of the yellow rocking horse.

The ex-detective made his way up a slight, grassy incline. *'Where you going, Gramps?'* Jack called after him. Crosby waved a hand but kept his eye on the two figures – still over a hundred yards away – drifting in the opposite direction. He neared the football pitch, its players charging up and down a muddy, well-worn strip without too much guile or purpose. Small knots of spectators had stretched themselves out along the touch-line, shouting encouragement to their teams. Crosby's attention remained on the couple and their dog as they disappeared behind a single storey, prefabricated block – changing rooms for both the home team and their visitors.

When he reached the building and walked around to its rear there was no one in sight – a full to overflowing car park but the couple had disappeared. Crosby walked up and down several lines of vehicles. None of them occupied. He made his way back around the building to find Lucy and her partner facing him. As Crosby approached them a small Cairn terrier strained at its leash, snapping at the ex-detective's ankle. He flicked out a foot.

'Do that again,' Rose Cavendish warned him, *'and I'll be kicking you.'*

'Keep the bloody dog under control then!'

Lucy interrupted. *'We don't have time for this,'* she said to the ex-detective. *'You've had two days to consider our problem.'*

'I don't have a problem,' Crosby replied, *'but I am considering a call to the police.'*

'You're only considering it, Inspector?' Lucy pushed a pair of over-sized dark glasses up onto her forehead. *'That tells me you do have concerns.'*

A prolonged outburst from spectators behind them caused the Cairn terrier to yap and strain at its leash again. *'We don't have all day,'* Lucy said.

Crosby saw little point in being overly hostile or un-cooperative. He needed to clear this up – finish it – unpredictable genes passed down from a mentally unstable Robert Milner was not something the ex-detective wanted to deal with in his retirement.

'*I didn't take your merchandise.*' Crosby lifted his shoulders. '*How do we get around this? Details of my bank account?*'

'*We're not interested in your local fucking Barclays,*' Cavendish replied. '*How about a Swiss numbered account? An ex-CID officer would know how to money launder the odd few million.*'

'*And that's reflected in my lifestyle is it?*'

'*Even a policeman with your limited intelligence would only siphon it off in small chunks,*' Cavendish said.

Crosby's initial good intentions were fast disappearing. Rose Cavendish was getting under his skin again. He pointed to the older woman. '*I'm not doing this while she remains here.*'

Lucy ignored it. '*There's another interested party. The Sixfields shipment originated from a South American cartel. They only received part payment at the time of delivery.*'

Crosby had been on the point of leaving. It stopped him. '*And why wasn't this mentioned last Friday? What game are we playing now, Lucy?*'

'*It's no game,*' the younger woman said. '*They want their money.*'

'*Why wasn't the shipment paid for up front?*'

'*We didn't have that sort of money,*' Lucy said. '*You know what we had planned. A Sixfields narcotics retail chain would have paid off outstanding balances.*'

'*What about the wholesalers?*' Crosby asked.

'*We were the wholesalers,*' Lucy said impatiently. '*This was a major overseas cartel importing direct into the UK.*'

'*Organisations like that don't write off large investments,*' Crosby said.

'*I know how they fucking operate!*' Lucy snapped. '*I dealt with them often enough.*' She quickly brought her outburst under control. '*It didn't get written off. They think the original shipment is still intact.*'

'*Why would they think that?*'

'After my arrest I got word out the heroin was recoverable.'

'You didn't tell them where it was hidden?'

'And see my share of the profits disappear.'

'Three years is a long time to wait.'

'They didn't have a choice.' Lucy shrugged. 'I was safe enough in prison. The heroin could just sit there appreciating in value.'

'Have they been in touch since you were released?' Crosby asked.

'Indirectly.'

'What have you told them?'

'That I'm in the process of recovering their stock.'

'How long have they given you?'

'I need to provide samples from the shipment before next weekend.' Lucy's voice betrayed the hint of a tremor.

Crosby couldn't be sure. She might be acting. He wasn't totally convinced the drugs cartel existed. 'None of this makes any difference,' the ex-detective said. 'Your father-in-law was misinformed. I had no prior knowledge of where these drugs were hidden.'

'If my father-in-law was wrong about you,' Lucy continued, 'I want to know who is responsible. You need to come up with a name. Have a word with ex-colleagues. Use your old contacts.'

'Why would I do that?'

'If you don't,' Lucy said. 'I'll pass details of your family to the cartel.'

Crosby realised this wasn't going away. The expected threat didn't make it any easier to deal with. Handling Lucy was a problem he could possibly manage. To be on the wrong side of an international drugs supplier was another situation altogether. He couldn't take the risk of just ignoring it. 'I'm still in touch with officers from the original investigation. If I make some enquiries will you leave my family out of this?'

'That depends on what you come up with.'

'He's stalling,' Cavendish said. 'The bastard knows something. I don't trust him.'

35

'We don't have a choice,' Lucy replied.

'Does your mother still own the farm?' Crosby asked.

'She sold it after my father-in-law's estate was sorted out.'

'Are you in contact with her?'

'We're not here to discuss my mother.'

'Has it occurred to you that she knew there were drugs hidden at the farm?'

'Not possible.'

'Your father-in-law could have told her about them.'

Lucy shook her head. *'It wasn't that sort of relationship. He didn't involve her in his business operations.'*

'But you can't be sure.'

'I'm fucking sure!' Lucy said sharply. *'We can leave my mother out of this. I no longer see the woman.'*

Crosby was surprised at the hostile reaction. Lucy's relationship with her mother had obviously broken down since the trial. Penny Roberts was certainly not an easy woman to deal with. Crosby had interviewed her twice during the Sixfields investigation, and on both occasions she'd been rude, arrogant and dismissive. The woman was high maintenance – someone who considered that other people existed to serve her personal needs – both husbands had been selected because of their social standing and the income they generated. When Robert Milner lost his job, and his way in life, he was quickly replaced by husband number two. Although there was no evidence to suggest that Penny Roberts had been personally involved with the Sixfields operation, it wouldn't have surprised Crosby to learn that she knew what was taking place. He needed to speak with her. See if she was aware of the hidden drugs.

'Where exactly on the farm is this concealment?' he asked Lucy.

Rose Cavendish answered for her. *'You know where the fucking concealment is because you cleaned it out.'*

'You've got a week,' Lucy said to the ex-detective. 'If your contacts and ex-colleagues don't come up with some answers I'm taking you and your family down with me.'

A final, shrill blast from the referee's whistle brought play to an end. Lucy pulled the dark glasses down over her eyes. 'You know from past experience that I don't make idle threats, Inspector.' She turned away towards the car park. Crosby watched her leave. Rose Cavendish deliberately brushed past the ex-detective, allowing her over-excited terrier to launch another attack on his turn-ups.

'Rose!' Lucy shouted back at her partner.

Cavendish pulled sharply on the dog's lead. Threads of material hung from the terrier's mouth as it was hauled away from Crosby's trouser leg. 'I know you're fucking responsible,' the older woman said to him, 'and I'm less patient than Lucy.' She held the ex-detective's gaze for a few seconds before turning away. Crosby tracked the women's progress back towards a white Renault Laguna. He jotted down its registration number as the vehicle filtered out into a stream of nearby passing traffic.

Crosby made his way slowly past the muddy, churned-up football pitch, back towards the playground. His instincts were telling him to get in touch with the police. He dismissed it. The situation was unpredictable. If there was an overseas supplier shadowing Lucy then she would be frightened. Scared shitless probably. Any contact by the police and she might immediately pass his name to whoever was representing the cartel.

Crosby would have to follow it up. Lucy was looking for someone to shift the blame onto and he'd been presented as her only option. He had to do some digging – ask a few questions – find something to convince her the missing heroin was nothing to do with him. 'Fuck!' Crosby said out aloud. Where the hell had all this suddenly come from?

'Watch this, Gramps!' Crosby had arrived back at the play-area. He looked up to see Jack launch himself head-first down a children's slide. The ex-detective suppressed a spasm of unease. Neither Lucy nor her overseas drugs cartel would have little hesitation in making Jack a target if there were three hundred million pounds involved.

A burst of musical wind chimes sounded from deep within his jacket pocket, an annoying ring-tone that he'd never got around to changing. The smart-phone had been a recent birthday present but he only employed the mobile's telephone and texting facilities – its additional technology completely wasted on him. *'Yes!'* he barked irritably into the mobile's receiver.

'Mr Happy's lunch will be on the table in thirty minutes,' Doreen Crosby said in his ear. She didn't wait for a reply. Both men set about persuading an un-cooperative Jack away from the slide – eventually managing to usher him towards the playground's exit gate.

Crosby was noticeably quiet on their way back to Hawthorne Rise, glancing into parked vehicles, looking at the faces of passers-by. *'Not very talkative this morning, Dad,'* Michael said. His father shrugged it off, blaming a lack of sleep from the previous night.

Doreen Crosby eyed the state of her husband's torn trousers as she answered the front door to them. *'You sometimes have to wonder who the child is,'* his wife commented. She turned to her grandson, sweeping him up in a huge bear hug. At five years old he was street-wise enough to endure his grandmother's lengthy embrace. There'd be a treat on offer to compensate. *'No sweets before lunch, Jack,'* his mother warned. Grandmother and grandson disappeared into the kitchen with a conspiratorial arm around each other. *'Is it chocolate, Nan?'* the boy asked in a loud whisper.

They sat down for lunch in the dining room at two o'clock – meals on a tray in front of the television were not an option in Doreen Crosby's house. At any other time the ex-detective's attention would have been totally focused on his wife's sirloin of beef and speciality red onion gravy – but today he needed to steer the conversation towards his grandson's welfare and safety.

After a calorie-laden dessert of raspberry crumble and clotted cream his wife asked Jack whether he was enjoying the swimming lessons his school had organised. It gave Crosby the opening he was looking for. *'Where does Jack go for these lessons?'* the ex-detective asked his daughter-in-law.

'The school has an arrangement with a sports and leisure centre in Odbourne,' she replied. *'It's only half a mile from the school.'*

'Who supervises them?'

'Teachers,' Angela replied, *'with the help of their playground assistants.'*

'Aren't these assistants just trained to monitor children within school grounds?' Crosby asked.

His daughter-in-law raised her eye-brows. *'Possibly. Why do you ask?'*

'I was interested.' Crosby shrugged. *'The lack of security in schools and hospitals is all over the news again.'*

'Our headmistress is very aware of her responsibilities.'

'I'm sure she is.' Crosby changed tack. *'What about at home? That footpath running along the bottom of your garden must be a safety issue when Jack's playing outside.'*

'The garden's perfectly safe.' Angela frowned. *'I'm very conscientious about monitoring Jack when he's out there.'*

'Something bothering you, Dad?' Michael asked.

'Whatever's got into you, Frank?' his wife interjected. *'You're annoying our visitors.'*

'Sorry!' Crosby held up his hands. *'Just ignore me. We old people worry about our grandchildren.'*

'I think you're the one we need to be concerned about,' his wife said sharply. *'You turn up here for lunch with your trousers ripped to shreds. Hardly say a word throughout the meal. Then you start interviewing Angela about her son's safety.'* Doreen Crosby sniffed and gave her husband a look. *'You retired from the CID three years ago.'*

'These things can't be ignored.' Crosby turned to his daughter-in-law. 'If you ever have a problem with running Jack to school just get in touch with me. I'd rather you did that than have one of these young mothers take him. Most of them just wander along the street tapping their damn smart phones. They haven't a clue as to where the kids are.'

His daughter-in-law shook her head in amusement. 'Thanks for the offer, Dad. I may take you up on it one of these mornings.'

'And I'll thank you to mind your language in front of our grandson,' Doreen Crosby warned her husband. 'If you've finished interrogating the suspect perhaps you can attend to stacking the dishwasher.' She turned to her grandson. 'We'll be sending Mr Grumpy to bed without any supper tonight if his behaviour doesn't improve.'

The five-year-old laughed enthusiastically, highly amused that his grandfather might be punished. 'You could put him on the naughty step, Nan.'

'What an excellent idea, Jack.' Crosby was subjected to another look from his wife.

He shouldn't have pursued it. Crosby had wanted to warn his family to be on their guard without causing undue alarm. All he'd done was annoy them. He glanced across at Jack, traces of raspberry filling still smeared around the five-year-old's mouth. Crosby tried to ignore the premonition that was tightening his gut.

Their Sunday routine continued in the lounge. Jack was allowed access to the TV remote, flicking expertly between his preferences of 'Tiny Pops' and 'CBeebies'. The adults, apart from Crosby, dozed on and off in the comfort of their armchairs. He remained awake. A lot on his mind.

CHAPTER 3

Odbourne Primary School: Monday 17ᵗʰ October 2011: 8.45 a.m.

Crosby's finger jabbed a button set into the driver's door. His window closed. The decibel count from over two hundred and fifty excitable children, compressed into an enclosed play-ground, was beginning to grate on his ears.

Odbourne had first opened its doors to pupils back in the early seventies. The Church of England Primary School was responsible for the education of five to eleven-years-olds within its limited catchment area. A ten-acre site accommodated five teaching blocks, the main assembly hall, administrative offices and a sizeable playing field.

Crosby had parked away from the school's designated dropping-off area. He watched his daughter-in-law arrive in her 4x4 Fiat Panda – which seemed to spend most of its time sat on their driveway. Why she needed a 4x4 for the school run remained a mystery to him. After delivering Jack into the playground area his daughter-in-law returned to her car, leaving almost immediately.

The ex-detective tracked his grandson as he ran across to join a group of other children. Satisfied that Jack was safe within school confines he turned his attention to the arrival and departure of other vehicles outside Odbourne's entrance gates. Some of the drivers remained for a short while – watching to see their children safely inside school grounds. None of the parked-up cars raised his suspicions. He scanned the surrounding area. Nothing untoward. A piercing whistle cut through the din. All movement within the playground came to an abrupt halt and silence descended. A second whistle saw the children being manoeuvred into straight, regimented lines. The third and final whistle sent them marching off towards their individual classrooms – headed by teachers who looked as if they'd only just left school themselves.

Crosby waited until the playground had emptied before digging out his mobile. He scrolled down a list of contacts before activating one of the numbers. *'DC Taylor,'* a voice announced in his ear. *'Studwell CID.'*

'Grace,' the ex-detective replied, *'Frank Crosby here. Is it possible to meet up?'*

A slight hesitation. *'I'm really snowed under today, Frank. Will it keep?'*

'Ten minutes of your time? I wouldn't ask if it wasn't important.'

Taylor relented. *'We'll have to meet here. I'll leave word at the main gate.'*

'Ten o'clock OK with you?' Crosby asked.

'Drive around to the CID annex,' Taylor replied. *'Wait for me there.'*

'Appreciate it, Grace. See you shortly.'

Crosby disconnected the call. Grace Taylor had been one of his DC's during the Sixfields investigation - a third-generation Jamaican whose grandparents had arrived on Britain's shores in the late fifties. She'd nearly lost her life at *Dryffed's Farm*, partly due to an error of judgement on Crosby's part. Although it had tested their working relationship they still kept in touch with each other after his retirement.

The ex-detective clipped his seat belt into place and fired up the car's engine. It might be a long day. There were at least three other people he needed to call on. His wife would be under the impression he was camped out on a damp, muddy riverbank somewhere – fishing rods and angling gear had been packed into the Mondeo's boot at seven o'clock that morning.

Crosby waited for a blue transit van to pass before pulling out behind it. His intention was to return at three o'clock that afternoon – when Odbourne would re-open its gates and return all of the pupils back into their parents care. That was his intention anyway.

Crosby's Mondeo slowed to a halt in front of the red and white hooped security pole. He looked beyond the entrance barrier – Studwell's eighteenth-century, red brick edifice dominating his eye-line. The police station was located approximately twenty miles north-west of Birmingham's city centre, serving as a headquarters for the area's regional policing unit. Its three-storey residence was home to over two hundred regular officers, an administrative department, and the local community's support personnel.

A slow-moving blue serge uniform emerged from an internal kiosk. Crosby slid open his window. *'Morning, John.'*

'Good Morning, Inspector.'

Whenever Crosby had occasion to re-visit Studwell he was usually addressed by his old rank – a courtesy appreciated by the ex-detective. John Harris was a familiar face, the security guard having worked at Studwell for a number of years. He handed the ex-detective a large, plastic, temporary car pass. Crosby propped it against the inside of his windscreen.

'I'll see to the barrier for you,' Harris said.

'Anything to sign?'

'All sorted, Sir. DC Taylor rang through earlier.'

'How's that daughter of yours?' Crosby asked. *'Poppy isn't it?'*

'She's at university now,' the guard said. *'It's costing me a bloody fortune.'*

Crosby would have offered some meaningless words of sympathy, but John Harris was already trudging back to his kiosk. A few seconds later the red and white barrier jerked skywards. Crosby eased his Mondeo over a set of traffic calming humps – carefully observing a twenty-mile-an-hour speed limit as he made his way around the site.

After finding a space in Studwell's rear car park he looked across at the familiar CID Annex. It remained largely unaltered. Crosby's memories of his time there were mixed – a fifteen-year spell had culminated in a Major Investigation Unit posting that saw him promoted to the rank of detective inspector. The resulting Sixfields enquiry had been Crosby's penultimate case, a particularly traumatic one, and now Lucy Roberts' re-appearance was threatening to resurrect it. His eyes swept the car park. A maroon Jaguar XJ6 coupé caught his eye. He recognised it immediately, the vehicle evoking more unpleasant memories.

At ten o'clock precisely DC Grace Taylor emerged from the annex's rear door. Crosby allowed his gaze to linger. The policewoman wore a chunky roll-neck sweater and close fitting blue denim jeans – her slim, lithe figure was something else that hadn't changed since his time at Studwell. He flashed the Mondeo's headlights and Taylor hurried across. Opening the front passenger door she slid into the seat beside him.

Crosby indicated the Jaguar. *'Rees-Bramley?'*

Taylor nodded. *'Detective Superintendent Rees-Bramley now. He's based at Lloyd House.'* She looked across at him. *'Will you be taking the opportunity to call in on him?'*

Crosby smiled. Oliver Rees-Bramley had been his Chief Inspector and Senior Investigating Officer during the Sixfields case – a fast-tracked university graduate who had joined CID direct from one of the Oxford colleges. Crosby hadn't been enamoured with his SIO's rule-book management techniques, and Rees-Bramley didn't appreciate Crosby's old-fashioned maverick approach. They hadn't seen eye to eye and didn't part on the best of terms. Grace Taylor was well aware of their previous working relationship.

'It's a disgrace that you've not made detective sergeant yet,' Crosby said.

Taylor's mouth compressed a fraction. *'It's still a man's world,'* she replied. *'The old boy's network is alive and well. Rees-Bramley only has to shake hands at a few social gatherings to find himself another rung up the ladder.'*

The ex-detective felt her bitterness. He didn't pursue it.

Taylor checked her watch. *'I really am busy this morning, Frank.'*

'It's about Lucy Roberts and Dryffed's Farm,' the ex-detective said.

'What about them? I know Lucy was released a couple of weeks ago.'

The ex-detective raised his eyebrows. *'Keeping an eye on her?'*

'It flashed up on our radar.' Taylor shrugged. *'A routine notification.'*

'Lucy contacted me a couple of days ago,' Crosby said.

It was Taylor's turn to look surprised. *'Why would she do that?'*

Crosby paused. He wasn't sure how much to divulge. The policewoman picked up on it. *'Come on, Frank. There's no point in holding anything back. It's obviously important.'*

The ex-detective nodded. *'Off the record?'*

'If that's what you want.'

Crosby shifted in his seat. *'Dryffed's Farm was being used to stockpile heroin at the time of our Sixfields investigation. The drugs remained undiscovered.'*

Taylor frowned. *'They must have been well hidden. Scenes-of-Crime would have swept the place with a fine-tooth comb.'*

'The heroin had a street value in excess of three hundred million.' Crosby said.

'Bloody hell!'

'When Lucy went back there to recover it after her release everything had disappeared.'

'Why would she get in touch with you?' Taylor asked.

'I'm supposed to be involved in some way,' Crosby replied. *'She's convinced her father-in-law told me where the drugs were hidden.'*

'When was this supposed to have happened?'

'That night at the farm. After you left to get help.'

'The man wasn't in any fit state to communicate anything.' Taylor paused. *'Was he?'*

Crosby shook his head. *'Lucy's desperate.'* He leant forward to activate his wipers as a fine drizzle began to fall on the Mondeo's windscreen. *'There's a South American drugs cartel involved. They've been patiently waiting to find out what happened to their investment.'*

'Christ! Have you contacted the anti-narcotics squad?'

'It's complicated.' Crosby switched off his wipers. *'I've been given a week to come up with some answers.'*

'Why in the hell would you do that?' the policewoman asked.

'Lucy's threatened to pass details of my family to this overseas cartel.'

Taylor shook her head. *'You can't get involved with this, Frank. These are not reasonable people. And why are you speaking to me about it?'*

'Has Lucy tried to get in touch with you since her release?'

'Is there any reason why she would?'

'We were both at the farm that night.'

It took a moment to register. *'What the hell's that supposed to mean? What are you implying?'*

'Sorry.' Crosby rubbed a hand across his forehead. *'I'm not implying anything. I'd just like to give them something. Point Lucy in a different direction.'*

Taylor sat back. She still looked angry.

'I don't suppose there's been any developments in the past three years?' Crosby asked.

'The case was closed,' Taylor said. *'A drugs seizure worth that amount would be good PR for anti-narcotics. Why keep it quiet?'*

Crosby stared through his windscreen into the distance. *'I just need something to steer it away from me.'*

Taylor laid a hand on his arm. *'I'll ask around for you. I have to go, Frank.'* She reached for the door release.

'You'll be keeping this to yourself?' Crosby reminded her.

'And what if something happens to your family in the meantime?'

'I'm dealing with it.'

'Your choice then. My advice is to report it.' Taylor pushed open the car door but didn't immediately step outside. 'There was something. You remember Paul Berne?'

Crosby nodded. The ex-detective remembered him very well. DC Paul Berne was originally North London. He'd transferred in from the Met with an attitude problem. A bit of a Jack the Lad with lofty opinions about himself. His success with women had probably annoyed Crosby the most – a gift the ex-detective had never been blessed with.

'You were continually having to fend him off as I recall,' Crosby said.

Taylor dismissed it. 'Paul was harmless enough. He just assumed that any female who rejected his advances had to be a lesbian. It then became a personal challenge for him.'

'Is he still with CID?'

'Resigned a couple of years ago.' Taylor remained half-out of the car. 'He set up his own detective agency. We met by chance in Birmingham last week.'

Crosby's antenna twitched. The ex-detective's previous life had always taught him to be wary of chance meetings.

'It was odd really,' the policewoman continued. 'After starting off by reminiscing about old cases he brought it around to the Dryffed's Farm investigation.'

'In what way?'

'I had to cut him short,' Taylor replied. 'The whole conversation was getting tedious. I told him his chat up lines needed polishing and said my goodbyes. Do you think there's something in it?'

Crosby shrugged. 'I'll pay him a visit.'

'You're getting too old for all of this, Frank.'

'I'd have to agree with you.'

Taylor left. Crosby didn't immediately start the Mondeo's engine. He watched the policewoman hurry back across the car park and tap a code into the building's external security pad. She pushed open the door – turning to give Crosby a final wave before disappearing inside.

The ex-detective continued to stare through his windscreen. Taylor's advice would be ignored. Paul Berne's interest needed checking out. Another name on his list was Penny Roberts – and that particular meeting would have to be approached with extreme care. The light drizzle turned into something heavier, obscuring his view. Crosby didn't notice. He continued to sit in the car.

Odbourne Primary School: Monday 17th October 2011: 3.00 p.m.

Three o'clock in the afternoon saw groups of young mothers gathered into their various cliques outside Odbourne's school gates. Chaos temporarily reigned as two hundred and fifty over-excited pupils were regurgitated back into the school playground. The children were quickly re-united with their parents or escorted to a waiting school bus.

Parked across from Odbourne's entrance, the occupants of one particular vehicle didn't seem in any hurry to leave. An outstretched hand opened the passenger-side glove compartment to retrieve a small pair of field glasses. The magnified images of a young mother and her son were tracked from the playground to a light-grey 4x4 Fiat Panda. After strapping the blond-haired child into a booster seat his mother moved around to the driver's door. She climbed inside. Several more minutes elapsed before the Fiat eventually accelerated away. The watching car immediately pulled out behind them, maintaining a respectable distance between both vehicles.

CHAPTER 4

Weston Heath: Birmingham: Monday 17th October 2011: 7.00 p.m.

Of the forty-five suburbs that surround Birmingham's inner city, the outlying district of Weston Heath would not be considered its most affluent. Initially created from Birmingham's post war re-building programme, its original pristine state had fallen into steady decline over the years. *'Shabby, Genteel'* might best describe it now – slightly down-market in nature – but still attempting to project an outward appearance of respectability.

Crosby was in Weston Heath's north-west sector. He'd located the *Four Bells* public house among a network of dingy back-streets and small terraced houses. The pub didn't look particularly inviting – not even the inadequate street lighting could disguise a down-at-heel, slightly seedy-looking establishment. A large white arrow, painted half-way up its front-facing wall, pointed towards a rear car park. Crosby eased the Mondeo through an adjacent stone archway. His headlights picked out two parked vehicles as he drove into a vacant space. Switching everything off he sat in total darkness – a grey October day had lost its light about six o'clock that afternoon. Crosby ran through the outcome of his previous rendezvous. The meeting hadn't been particularly fruitful. He'd also missed a surveillance outside Odbourne school. The detective in him wasn't happy about it.

After waiting several minutes to ensure that no one had been following he exited the Mondeo – walking back around to the *Four Bells* front entrance. He unlatched a low wooden door and stepped into what was presumably the main bar. It was dimly lit. An unpleasant mix of stale beer and tobacco fumes filled the air – an aroma that must have permanently ingrained itself into the pub's fixtures and fittings over the years. A faded, worn carpet complemented strips of discoloured peeling wallpaper that lined the room's walls. Half-a-dozen stained, chipped wooden tables added to the interior's run down appearance. There were no flashing slot machines, no music, and hardly any customers – two elderly patrons, still wearing coats, sat just inside the door. They looked up suspiciously at Crosby's entrance before returning their attention to a pair of half-empty pint glasses.

'*Over here, Frank!*' Crosby turned to a far corner of the room. Ian Brown's lean, wiry frame emerged from the gloom. The Scot's long, thin face was unshaven. He wore a white grubby tee-shirt and loose-fitting jogging bottoms. Crosby shook the outstretched hand. '*Thanks for seeing me at such short notice, Ian,*' he said. '*You didn't mind me ringing the office?*'

Brown waved a hand. '*No problem, laddie. Sit yourself down.*' The voice was that of a smoker – deep, gravelly. '*What you having?*'

'*Better make it a shandy. I'm driving.*'

Brown viewed the ex-detective with some suspicion. '*Ladies tipple it is then.*'

Crosby half-smiled. His preference was for a light Beaujolais these days, but he suspected a *Four Bells* wine list might prove difficult to locate. The Scot certainly wouldn't appreciate having to ask for it. Crosby watched Ian Brown order their drinks – the two of them had become well acquainted over past years – working together on a number of cases out of Studwell. Ian Brown was a Scenes-of-Crime officer, blunt and forthright in his views. These were usually expressed in the language of his roots – a gritty, unfashionable district in the suburbs of Glasgow.

Brown carried a small tray back to their table. It included two pints of bitter and what looked like a double-Scotch. He quickly deposited Crosby's shandy on top of a stained, cardboard beer-mat, as if anxious to disassociate himself with it.

'*This your local?*' Crosby asked.

'*Aye.*' Brown lifted one of the pint glasses and drained a generous measure. '*Reminds me of somewhere I used to drink back in Glasgow.*' The Scot took a pack of cigarettes from his pocket and extracted one.

The ex-detective raised his eyebrows.

Brown flicked a lighter at his cigarette. *'There's not much passing trade here. We all said bollocks to the anti-smoking laws and just carried on.'* He pulled hard at his cigarette before flicking ash to the floor.

Crosby looked around him. *'You didn't keep the spittoons?'*

Brown's natural morose expression didn't alter. It was difficult to tell whether the remark had registered. Crosby found the tin of small cigars he'd fallen back on since his recent encounters with Lucy. *'I've started on these again,'* he said. *'My chest's reminding me why I gave them up in the first place.'*

The Scot nodded as he took a swallow of Scotch. *'I was coughing up a lot of shite earlier this year. Couldn't stop. I gave those e-cigarette sticks a try.'*

'Any good?'

Brown dragged in a lungful smoke. *'It stopped me coughing. You're just sucking in flavoured water vapour.'*

'Where is it then?'

The Scenes-of-Crime officer grimaced. *'I couldn't get on with them. They didn't hit the back of the throat.'* He barked out a rare laugh. *'The 'Authentic Thai Fanny' flavour was OK until I got a pubic hair caught between my teeth.'*

Brown's attempted humour was delivered with a straight face. A good sign though. The ex-detective was quite happy for him to increase his alcohol intake and continue talking. A relaxed Ian Brown would be more likely to confide any information he might have heard about *Dryffed's Farm*. Crosby glanced around the room again. *'Most public houses have changed a bit since our day,'* he said.

'Aye,' Brown agreed. *'Not for the better. They've all been turned into glorified bloody restaurants now. I blame these television cookery programmes.'*

'You don't watch them?'

Brown snorted. *'All the bloody TV chefs are either gay or foreign. Probably both. If they're not cooking pots of snails, it's tossing bloody salad leaves. If you come across one of them in his restaurant these days he's probably fucking lost.'*

Crosby ignored the rant. *'Do they serve food in here?'* he asked. *'I had to skip lunch this afternoon.'*

'Aye,' the Scot nodded. *'Pickled eggs and crisps behind the bar. A choice of flavours.'*

'I'll wait.' Crosby lit the cigar he'd been holding.

'Cheers then.' Brown lifted his half-empty glass of bitter and swallowed the remainder of its contents. He put down the glass and looked across at Crosby. *'Retirement suiting you?'*

Crosby shrugged. *'Plenty of fishing. The odd round of golf.'*

Brown turned down the corners of his mouth. *'Never seen the point of either. How's the wife? Doreen wasn't it?'*

'She's OK,' Crosby replied. *'You still not married?'*

'I've thought about it,' Brown said. *'My old drinking partner back in Glasgow acquired one of these mail order brides from the Philippines.'*

'How's that working out?'

'He told me she doesn't nag. Makes sure the fridge is well stocked with beer. Never argues or asks for money. Doesn't get a headache at bedtime.' Brown sniffed. *'What do you reckon?'*

Crosby nodded. *'Sounds like an investment.'*

'Can't see it, laddie.' The Glaswegian screwed up his face. *'Sounds too good to be true. Has to be a catch somewhere.'*

Crosby needed to move the conversation on. *'You still with the West Midlands?'*

'Aye.' The Scot started on his second bitter. *'Workload's increased. Not the pay.'*

'Who's your Head of Department now?' Crosby asked.

'*John Carmichael retired last year.*' Brown's face showed a degree of displeasure. '*We acquired a bloody schoolboy with several degrees in Computing Science.*'

'*It's the way forward.*'

'*I'm a Sellotape and tweezers man,*' Brown said. '*All this latest bloody technology is beyond me.*'

'*It can be difficult.*' Crosby tried to sound sympathetic.

'*We seem to get issued with new bloody kit every other day,*' Brown complained. '*I haven't got a fucking clue how to use half of it. They had to give me a written warning last week.*'

'*What about?*'

'*The Head asked me why I wasn't making full use of a Mobile Digital Forensic Toolkit we'd all been issued with.*'

'*You had a written warning for that?*'

'*Not exactly,*' the Scot replied. '*I told him they could stuff an electronic mouth-organ up my ass but it wouldn't necessarily mean I'd be able to fart out the National Anthem on it.*'

Crosby stubbed out his cigar. '*I could see why he might be annoyed.*'

Brown picked up his Scotch and downed the amber liquid. He leant back, folded his arms and looked across the table at Crosby. '*We finished with all this small talk then, Frank? I've not seen you in three years. What's this about?*'

'*Dryffed's Farm,*' the ex-detective replied. It was pointless trying to broach the subject indirectly.

Brown didn't need to search his memory. '*Not your finest hour laddie. You were lucky to come out of that one alive. Three dead bodies wasn't it?*'

'*I had a visit from Lucy Roberts three days ago,*' the ex-detective said. '*She's just been released.*'

Ian Brown threw his head back and laughed out loud. '*Another fucking lunatic back on the streets. What was she looking for? A character reference?*'

'She's acquired a female live-in soul mate,' the ex-detective said. *'An ex-prison officer from Foston Hall.'*

'Fuck me!' Brown barked out another laugh. *'Lucy Roberts a carpet muncher. I might have to re-visit that one tonight.'*

'She left three hundred million pounds of heroin stashed away at Dryffed's Farm.'

It caused the Scot to straighten. *'Fuck's sake! Are you being serious?'*

'She went back to collect her investment last week. It had disappeared.'

The Scot frowned. *'Why didn't Scenes-of-Crime find anything? They'd have been swarming all over that place.'*

'It must have been hidden away from the farm.'

Brown shrugged. *'Serves the bitch right. Two police officers died because of her.'*

'I'm Lucy's number one suspect,' Crosby said.

Ian Brown raised his eyebrows.

'According to papers left by her father-in-law I had prior knowledge of these hidden drugs.'

'Have you seen these papers?'

'No.'

Brown shook his head. *'The woman's barking. Same as her old man. Did you tell her to piss off?'*

'It gets complicated,' Crosby replied. *'There's a South American drugs cartel involved. They imported the heroin and were never paid off. They've been waiting for Lucy's release and their money. She's threatened to pass on my name to them.'*

A short silence. Crosby had the Scot's attention. *'It needs taking to the police, Frank.'*

'I can't risk that yet,' Crosby replied. *'My family are also being threatened.'*

Brown looked towards the door. His manner had changed. *'We're not talking about local ass-wipes here, Frank, dealing out shite on a street-corner. What if you've been tailed?'*

'I wasn't followed.'

The Scenes-of-Crime officer didn't look happy. He shifted in his seat. *'What the fuck do you want from me anyway?'*

'Just a few questions.'

Another short silence. The Scot nodded. *'You were OK, Frank,'* he said. *'We used to rub along. What do you want to know?'*

'Your department assisted in the processing of Dryffed's Farm.'

'It was minimal,' Brown replied. *'Scenes-of-Crime in Wales wanted some on-site advice and continuity with regard to the murders in Sixfields.'*

'Were you sent there?'

The Scot shook his head. *'Managed to side-step it.'* He reached for another cigarette. *'Didn't fancy being stuck half-way up a Welsh mountain in the middle of winter.'*

'Do you know who they sent?'

'I think it was John Hendry,' Brown replied. *'Did you ever work together?'*

'Don't recall him,' Crosby said. *'I know it's been four years but he may have picked up on some rumour or gossip that didn't get into the official report.'*

The Scot nodded. *'I'll try to get an address or telephone number for him. He left us a while back. And there's someone I drink with in the drugs squad,'* Brown added. *'He may have heard something.'*

'Appreciate it.'

'There'd better not be any comeback on this, Frank,' the Scot warned. *'I lead a quiet life and mind my own business.'*

'Understood.' Crosby reached for his mobile. *'Do you want to exchange numbers?'*

'No I fucking don't!' Brown said. *'I'll sleep easier if I'm not on your list of contacts. Just write it down.'*

The ex-detective retrieved his notebook from a jacket pocket. He jotted down his number and tore out the page. Brown reached across the table for it.

Crosby glanced down at his watch. *'I've an hour's drive, Ian. I'll have to make a move.'*

'You'll not be forgetting who's in the chair,' Brown reminded him.

Crosby nodded. *'Bitter and a Scotch chaser wasn't it?'*

'Very generous of you,' the Scot replied. *'It was a double.'*

Crosby made his way to the bar. A bored-looking, unshaven landlord fixed his drinks without entering into conversation. The ex-detective took them back to Brown's table. *'You'll let me know within the next couple of days?'* he asked.

'Aye.' Ian Brown picked up his whisky. *'I'll check it out first thing.'* Crosby left him to it. The Scotch had disappeared before he reached the door.

Crosby stood for several minutes just inside the *Four Bells* car park entrance. His antenna didn't pick up anything untoward. After pulling out from the car park he pointed his Mondeo in the direction of home. It was impossible to switch off – an over-active mind forcing him to run through what had to be done tomorrow.

CHAPTER 5

Odbourne Primary School: Tuesday 18th October 2011: 8.50 a.m.

Tuesday morning saw Crosby keeping vigil outside Odbourne school again. He'd arrived home at nine o'clock last night. After a late supper with his wife the ex-detective had disappeared into his study – citing paperwork and emails he had to deal with. The next hour had been spent cutting, pasting and inscribing two lengths of white plastic card – which he'd then trimmed and shaved to fit inside an old CID wallet.

Crosby reached across to open his glove compartment. He pulled out the CID wallet and flipped it open to reveal a photograph of himself above the name of Detective Inspector Colin Martin. Opposite his photograph was a replica West Midlands Police badge. The false ID obviously wouldn't stand up to detailed scrutiny but ought to satisfy a cursory glance.

Angela's Fiat Panda arrived outside the school gates. He watched a re-run of yesterday's routine as his daughter-in-law chaperoned young Jack into the playground. When Angela returned to her 4x4 she was accompanied by a tall, slim, individual, smartly dressed in a suit and tie. The man was clearly older than his daughter-in-law. Crosby watched them leave together in Angela's car. Probably nothing. She was just giving someone a lift home. A friend? Maybe an affair? It wouldn't have totally surprised him. The fact that her companion looked foreign was more of a concern. He would have to follow it up.

Crosby's mobile ring-tone cut in. He picked up the phone from his passenger seat and pushed the receive button *'Yes?'* A brief message. Crosby disconnected the call. He pulled his notebook from a jacket pocket and scribbled down an address. Ian Brown had something for him that he didn't want to discuss over the phone.

A series of whistles emptied the playground. Crosby slipped his fake ID into an inside pocket – well aware of the consequences if caught in possession. He'd read somewhere that retired police officers from certain USA states were allowed to retain and use their old warrant cards – a practice that would have been very useful to him over the next few days. *'God bless America,'* Crosby muttered. He started the Mondeo's engine.

Reddington Library: Tuesday 18th October 2011: 11.00 a.m.

Two hours later saw Crosby logged into one of three computer terminals inside Reddington's local library. It was a rare visit for the ex-detective. Throughout his retirement, Crosby's wife had diligently renewed her husband's library card every year. *'And why do I bother?'* she'd often ask him. *'A lot of the smaller libraries are closing down because of people like you.'* Crosby could only agree with her. *'It's the same with your bus pass,'* his wife usually added. *'That never sees the light of day either.'* Again the ex-detective had no argument. If there was one thing he detested more than shopping it would be waiting around in a bus queue.

Crosby's primary reason for being in the library was to plough through web-sites – and he couldn't do that at home because his wife had already detected there was something going on. She'd taken to following him around the house – checking on what he was doing – asking questions about his numerous fishing trips. *'Is it another woman?'* was one accusation.

'I'd like to have the bloody energy,' he'd muttered to himself.

Reddington library was not busy. Apart from the ex-detective there were only two other patrons. An elderly pensioner slept in one of the room's easy chairs – two newspapers spread across his knees. A middle-aged woman prowled the crime thriller section.

There was only one librarian on duty. The name badge affixed to a thick, grey cardigan identified her as *'Mary'* – an intense woman of short stature and indeterminate age – her wispy hair scraped back into a loose bun. She seemed incapable of remaining in one place for more than a few minutes, nervous bird-like movements taking her on frequent tours of the library's interior. As Crosby was not one of her regulars the librarian had initially approached him to offer her services. *'Computers can be a little daunting for our generation. Is there anything I can help you with?'*

Crosby wasn't in the mood for well-meaning intentions. *'I'd imagine a master's degree in computing science should see me through anything too complicated.'* The woman had quickly retreated to the safety of her desk.

When Crosby had returned to trawling through the media coverage from four years ago there was plenty to keep him occupied. Sixfields and *Dryffed's Farm* had been an editor's dream – the remote farmhouse murders – a marauding serial killer – the estate's night of rioting – drug conflicts and gang warfare. It was little wonder the story had remained front page news for several weeks. When Lucy Roberts' trial finally opened, the newspapers were able to inflate their circulation figures all over again.

Crosby spent over four hours in the library. He read every single media report written during that period. Not one of the articles hinted at concealed drugs in association with *Dryffed's Farm*. There was no reference to anything of note during the intervening years either. Crosby wasn't particularly surprised – he'd still been a serving CID officer at Studwell ten months after the case had closed and would have surely heard about any subsequent developments. At two o'clock Crosby gave it up and logged off his machine. The librarian smiled across at him as he made to leave. *'A successful morning?'* she enquired.

'Appreciate the use of your facilities,' Crosby answered. He quickly picked up his notebook and headed for the library's exit – forestalling any attempt by *'Mary'* to engage him for a second time.

Later that day the ex-detective found himself in a noisy, crowded, fast-food outlet on the outskirts of Sixfields. Crosby wasn't happy. He found the atmosphere oppressive – a smell of hot cooking oil hung thick in the air – an excess of customers reducing his oxygen intake to uncomfortable levels. The ex-detective was wedged into a small corner-table, nursing his cardboard cup of lukewarm coffee and waiting for Ian Brown to arrive. Crosby had driven straight from the library and missed out on lunch again. His taste-buds weren't tempted by what the outlet's colourful menu-board had to offer. He checked his watch. Ian Brown was late. The Scenes-of-Crime officer had suggested a five o'clock rendezvous at the fast-food outlet as he was currently processing a nearby crime scene in Sixfields. Crosby yawned and stretched out a cramped right leg, his foot sliding unchecked along the floor's greasy surface.

The Scot pushed his way through a crowded entrance at five-thirty. He raised a hand in Crosby's direction but headed straight for the service counter. Twenty minutes later he squeezed into the chair opposite Crosby, his tray filled with two boxes of deep fried chicken pieces, large fries, and a tall, carbonated drink.

'I know,' Brown acknowledged. *'I'm late. Remember those good old days.'*

Crosby couldn't really object. The Scot was doing him a favour.

Brown re-arranged the contents of his tray and eyed it appreciatively. *'Bloody starving. I've had nothing since breakfast.'*

'How's your cholesterol levels?' Crosby enquired.

'My fucking arteries, laddie!' the Scot replied. He sucked meat from his first chicken bone and groaned in pleasure. A globule of slow-moving grease eased its way down past his chin and dripped onto a grubby, white shirt. Crosby waited patiently as the Scot noisily reduced the contents of his tray. Brown dropped a final chicken bone back into the cardboard box and drained what was left in his paper cup. He

belched appreciatively, before looking up to scan the crowded tables. A group of teenage schoolgirls in the far corner caught his eye. *'Fuck's sake! Look at that lot. Skirts up to their chuffs and still at bloody school.'* He shook his head. *'It's the lads I feel sorry for. Poor buggers are caught like rabbits in a headlight.'*

Crosby wanted to press Brown about the purpose of their meeting but the Scot hadn't finished yet. *'How's a fifteen-year-old supposed to concentrate on his equations when there's a push-up bra sat opposite poking his eye out?'*

The ex-detective felt obliged to offer a comment. *'Girls develop at a younger age these days.'*

'Aye,' the Scot agreed. *'Too bloody right they do. Schoolgirls in my day wore a woolly vest with nothing much to fill it.'* Brown's morose expression was of someone who felt as if he'd missed out during his formative years.

'No schoolboy romance for you then?'

'Just childhood fantasies, laddie,' the Scot replied. *'Miss Page's tits were the centre of my universe. I never missed one of her lessons.'*

'Don't want to push you, Ian,' Crosby said, *'but was it John Hendry they sent to Dryffed's Farm?'*

'It was.' The Scenes-of-Crime officer swung back around to face him, his voice business-like. *'He resigned three months after his attachment in Wales and then just vanished apparently.'*

Crosby's antenna twitched. *'Vanished?'*

'I spoke to a colleague who was friendly with him at the time,' Brown said. *'They used to drink together. He tried to get in touch with Hendry afterwards. Nothing. He'd vacated his flat in Birmingham, discontinued his telephone numbers and email addresses, disappeared from all his old haunts.'*

'Who is this ex-colleague?'

'Nigel Stanhope.'

'I'll talk to him.'

Brown shrugged. *'Up to you. Not sure he'll have anything to add.'*

'What reason did Hendry give for resigning?'

'Something about a family crisis.'

'Do you have any background on him?'

The Scot reached into his jacket pocket. He unfolded a sheet of typed A4 and read from it. *'Thirty years old. Irish. Born and raised in Dublin's Temple Bar district. Achieved a Bachelor's Degree in DNA and Forensic Science from Dublin's City University and was subsequently employed for two years by The Garda in their Forensic Science Laboratory. He came to us after a spell working for the RUC in Belfast.'*

'That's a lot of information.'

'Someone in Personnel owed me a favour.' Brown slid the sheet of paper across to Crosby. *'I've included all the relevant stuff from his file and what Nigel Stanhope told me about him. There's his last known address, old telephone numbers, and pubs he used to drink in.'* The Scot pointed out a name. *'Terry Halloran. A contact neighbour of Hendry's from the flat above. He had no family here. Might be useful.'*

Crosby picked up the typed sheet. *'Thanks Ian. I owe you.'*

The Scenes-of-Crime officer sat back and folded his arms. *'I've added something else,'* he said. *'There was a whisper at the time about Hendry having links to certain associations.'*

'What associations?'

'The Real IRA was mentioned.'

'Bloody hell!' Crosby was well aware of the Real IRA – a paramilitary organisation who'd taken up the fight to unite Ireland after the Provisional IRA had called for a final ceasefire prior to the Good Friday agreement. The terrorist group had been responsible for a number of bombing and shooting incidents in Northern Ireland since then.

'Was there any basis to these rumours?'

'*All of the necessary security checks would have been carried out on him.*' Brown shrugged. '*I'm just passing it on.*'

The ex-detective nodded and stood up. '*Thanks again, Ian. I'll not take up any more of your time.*'

'*I hope it's of some use.*'

Crosby stretched out a hand.

The Scot didn't immediately shake it. '*I've made a nuisance of myself, Frank. Poking around in the office and asking questions.*' He paused. '*If there's a possibility that drug cartels and terrorist groups are involved with all of this?*' Brown left his question hanging in the air.

'*Not the sort of contacts you'd want on your Facebook page,*' Crosby said.

'*It's nothing personal, laddie.*' Brown reached up to shake the ex-detective's hand. '*As I said yesterday. We rubbed along OK. I wish you luck.*'

Crosby turned and made his way towards the exit, unaware that his progress was being monitored from another table. The ex-detective's mind was on other things, working through what Ian Brown had told him. Tracing John Hendry would mean he'd have to call in favours from old contacts – those who had access to HMRC and DWP government databases. A former colleague attached to the West Midlands counter-terrorism unit might also be able to help out. The ex-detective's own enquiries would have to continue with the use of his fake warrant card.

CHAPTER 6

Officially compiled statistical reviews can be an all-consuming passion for certain types of individual. And within their wide range of subject matter they would undoubtedly be aware that Birmingham has the largest Irish population per capita in the UK. Crosby had chanced across that particular fact when checking background information about the city's *Digbeth* area – a sector popularly referred to as Birmingham's Irish Quarter. John Hendry's last known address had been tagged with a *Digbeth* postcode.

Crosby's intention to trace the Irishman through HMRC and DWP sources had met with little success. Although he'd managed to get in touch with old contacts the previous evening they were both aware of his retirement, neither of them willing to check for any recent activity concerning John Hendry. It was the reason for Crosby's presence in a multi-storey car park close to Birmingham's re-developed coach station. Earlier that morning the ex-detective's wife had watched him set off for yet another day's fishing, still suspicious about his behaviour. He'd had to sneak trousers and a jacket into his waterproof rucksack – an outfit in which Detective Inspector Martin would be able to conduct his day's business.

Crosby exited the Mondeo and crossed to a pre-paid car parking machine – slotting in the necessary coinage for a two-hour stay. He returned to drop his parking ticket onto the Mondeo's windscreen ledge, leaning across to collect a white plastic carrier-bag from his front passenger seat. The bag contained items purchased from a local charity shop – two coffee mugs, several pens, some dog-eared paperbacks, and a second-hand pair of scuffed trainers.

As Crosby had already changed into the jacket and trousers *en route* he locked his car and descended a nearby flight of concrete steps

– emerging at street level into a crisp, sunny, October morning. According to his street-map he estimated a fifteen-minute walk to Beaumont Way. Crosby turned left towards it – checking the fake warrant card was still secure in his jacket pocket.

The area he walked through was fairly busy for the time of day. Crosby stopped at a small convenience store, emerging five minutes later with a newspaper tucked underneath his arm. The stocky well-built figure, wearing a black leather jacket and baseball cap, hadn't moved on. He'd been with Crosby since the car park. The ex-detective continued his journey – occasionally stopping to browse a shop window – but always keeping the leather jacket in his peripheral vision. It remained a constant fifty yards behind him.

He reached Beaumont Way, a tree-lined avenue of semi-detached three-storey town houses, set far enough back from the road to retain a degree of privacy. Crosby stopped to consult the street-map again, checking behind him. The leather jacket was no longer in view. Crosby increased his pace to a brisk walk.

Ten minutes later he stood outside the substantial and imposing structure that was number thirty-nine Beaumont Way. A pair of Victorian bay-fronted windows, either side of an extended stone porch, accentuated the building's overall dimensions. Crosby nudged open a rusting, wrought-iron gate. The front garden had not been well maintained – spindly vegetation forcing its way up through gaps in the pathway's crumbling concrete. A perimeter of dense, unruly hedgerow was keeping several broken fence panels upright. The front door looked solid enough.

Crosby had been able to confirm beforehand that Terry Halloran was still resident at the address. There were three name-plates alongside an external intercom box. Halloran's name-plate indicated the top floor flat. *'It bloody well would be!'* Crosby muttered. The ex-detective liked to have an escape route. He pushed the intercom button next to Terry Halloran's name-plate and waited. Nothing. He pushed the button again, holding it down this time.

'What!' The disembodied voice sounded annoyed.

Crosby lowered his head to the intercom. *'Terry Halloran?'*

'Do you know what fucking time it is?'

'I'm an ex-colleague of John Hendry,' Crosby answered. *'We worked together in forensics.'*

No response.

'I have some of his belongings,' Crosby pressed, *'from the office.'*

'John left your place over three years ago.' Halloran's reply was indistinct. Crosby had to keep his ear to the intercom.

'Our department was recently re-furbished,' the ex-detective said. *'These items have only just come to light. I thought you might still be in touch with him.'*

'And why would you think that?'

'John gave your name to our Personnel Department as a contact when he lived here.'

'Well he doesn't live here any more.' Halloran's annoyance rose another notch. *'If the stuff had any value he'd have taken it with him.'*

'It's just bits and pieces,' the ex-detective persisted. *'There's a pair of trainers, two coffee mugs, and some old paperbacks.'*

'Try a charity shop.'

'I was hoping you might have an address for him.' Crosby kept his tone upbeat. *'It's been a while since we last saw each other.'*

'I told you.' The voice now sounded aggressive. *'He moved on. Now why don't you do the same and fuck off!'*

Crosby spoke a little louder into the intercom. *'We also found a roll of bank notes in one of the coffee mugs.'*

A distinct pause. *'How much?'* Halloran responded.

'I'm not sure exactly. About three hundred pounds.'

Another pause. A loud buzz as the door-lock was remotely de-activated. Crosby pushed through into an unfurnished hallway that smelt of damp, rotting vegetation. There were no windows, the interior unlit and gloomy. A closed door to his left was obviously the ground floor flat. He moved across rough concrete flooring – towards a flight of bare wooden stairs that led up to the next level. He ascended them slowly, to a small landing above. It wasn't quite as gloomy here – a small recessed window shedding some light. Halfway up the second flight of stairs he heard the front door open below him. *'What the fuck now!'* Crosby muttered to himself.

He waited on the stairs. An ongoing silence. Maybe it was the ground floor tenant. Crosby waited a few moments longer before continuing on up towards Halloran's flat. He reached the top floor. There was a closed door directly in front of him. He stepped forward and rapped his knuckles against it.

The door cracked open – a sliver of face appearing in the narrow gap. Several moments elapsed as Crosby was checked over. A number of security chains were disengaged before the door was fully opened.

Ian Brown hadn't told him that Terry Halloran was a woman. It could have been deliberate. The Scot's sense of humour was an acquired taste.

Ms Halloran was a dyed blonde, blowsy and full figured – her thin, grubby, towelling bathrobe displaying a generous cleavage. Crosby judged the woman's tired, worn face to be in its late thirties. She had a pasty white skin, dark circles underneath dull, listless eyes. Possible signs of a regular heroin user.

Halloran nodded at the carrier bag he was holding. *'Is that John's stuff?'* A voice that had been indistinct through the intercom now identified its roots in Southern Ireland. Crosby handed over his bag and the woman rummaged through it. *'You said there was money.'*

'There is.' The ex-detective patted his jacket pocket. *'Can we do this inside?'*

'You give me the money and I'll make sure he gets it.'

'I did say earlier that it would be nice to see John again.' Crosby's voice remained casual. *'Are you still in touch with him?'*

'I already had this conversation with someone else he used to work with.'

'Who was that?'

'Can't remember.' Halloran regarded him suspiciously. *'You the fucking law?'*

Crosby ignored it. *'If you don't know of John's whereabouts there seems little point in handing his money over.'*

The woman's eyes narrowed. *'I know someone who can pass it on.'*

'Do you have their address?' Crosby asked. *'A contact number?'*

Halloran realised at this point there'd be no money forthcoming. *'You're just wasting my fucking time. Piss off!'* She went to shut the door. Crosby stretched out a foot to prevent her closing it and shoved the woman backwards. She stumbled and fell. He stepped inside the flat and reached into his jacket pocket to retrieve Inspector Martin's fake warrant card – flipping the wallet open before quickly closing it again.

The woman struggled to her feet. *'I fucking well knew it!'*

Crosby closed the door behind him. Halloran had not yet drawn back the curtains at her sitting room window. In a gloomy half-light the room looked a mess. It certainly hadn't been cleaned recently. There were several empty bottles of cider standing on Halloran's low coffee table. The remains of a take-away meal had been left to coagulate in two foil cartons. An overflowing ashtray and its smell of stale cigarette smoke permeated throughout. Crosby scanned the room for evidence of syringes or spoons. There was nothing in open view. Halloran planted both hands on her ample hips and fronted up to him. *'I want to see your fucking search warrant.'*

'I'm not carrying out a search.'

'And I'm not answering any more fucking questions!'

'Is the landlord aware that your flat is being used for the purposes of prostitution?' Crosby's accusation was an educated guess.

Halloran's eyes flashed.

'Well?'

'I don't bring my clients back here.'

'So the landlord isn't aware of what you do for a living?'

'Like he'd give a toss.'

'We could always ask him.'

The woman hesitated.

'I want to know all about your ex-neighbour,' Crosby said.

'John told me he was going back home.' Halloran's tone and body language was less aggressive now.

'And where would home be?'

'Dublin.'

'And you haven't seen or heard from him since?'

'We weren't that close,' the woman replied.

'You spent time with each other though.'

'Drinking mainly.' Halloran shrugged. *'The occasional screw when he was drunk. We were company for each other. Nothing serious. Why are the police interested in him?'*

'You indicated a third party,' Crosby said. *'Someone who's in touch with him.'*

'There isn't anyone. I wanted the money.'

Crosby thought she was lying. *'And that's all you know?'*

'Yes.'

The ex-detective stepped forward and grabbed a fistful of Halloran's hair. Twisting it round in his hand he forced the prostitute backwards – slamming her hard into a wall. It was out of character for him. The safety of his grandson had been keeping Crosby awake at night. A half-winded Halloran struggled to catch her breath. *'I don't do freebies, love.'* The bravado was forced. Crosby's actions had frightened her.

He pushed a forearm against Halloran's prominent Adam's apple and held it there. She made small choking sounds, trying to drag in air. Crosby put his mouth to her ear. *'Ms Halloran. Your well being is of little concern to me. I might just crush your larynx if you don't give me a name.'* The ex-detective pushed harder. When Halloran's eyes started to roll he relaxed his grip. She sucked in lungful's of air. Crosby gave her time to recover. *'Well?'*

'Patrick Mandleway,' Halloran gasped.

Crosby stepped away. 'And this Patrick Mandleway would know where Hendry is now?'

The woman nodded. 'Probably. He knew John from way back. When they both lived in Dublin.'

'And where can I find him?'

Halloran's chest heaved. 'I don't believe you are the fucking law.'

'Not my concern. Where can I find him?' the ex-detective repeated.

'Lamb and Flag.' The woman rubbed her throat. 'Oakley Street.'

'If that's not genuine I will be back.'

'Bastard!' the prostitute spat at him.

'When necessary.' Crosby had already crossed to the apartment's door. He opened it. A thin-faced man, wearing faded jeans and an old green fleece, blocked the ex-detective's exit. He fixed Crosby with pale blue eyes – a contrasting growth of dark stubble framed his sunken cheeks. The man continued to lean nonchalantly against Halloran's door-frame, arms folded, making no attempt to move out of Crosby's way. 'I heard raised voices, Terry.' His accent was also Irish – but from the North – a harsh brogue that echoed around the landing's narrow confines. Thirty years out on the street had taught Crosby to classify individuals at first sight. He instinctively knew the man was dangerous.

'Would this gentleman's presence be causing you some distress, Terry?' the Irishman asked.

'A misunderstanding, Michael. I'm fine.'

'A misunderstanding is it,' he said. 'And this misunderstanding? It's been resolved?'

'It has, Michael. It has.' Terry Halloran's eyes darted between Crosby and the Irishman.

'And is your visitor leaving us now?'

'He is, Michael. He is.'

'*That's grand now.*' Since his arrival the man's eyes hadn't once left Crosby's face. '*And shall you be wanting me to escort this gentleman from the premises?*'

'*I don't want any trouble, Michael,*' Halloran said. '*He's CID.*'

The Irishman didn't look particularly concerned. '*An officer of the law is it,*' he said softly. '*And does the law carry identification with him?*'

Crosby produced his fake warrant card.

The man barely glanced at it. '*I'll be sure to remember your face, Inspector.*'

'*Move away from the door.*' Crosby had found his voice again. It sounded more confident than he was feeling. '*If you continue to obstruct me I will have to call for assistance.*'

The Irishman smiled. '*I deal with empty threats on a regular basis, Inspector.*' He unzipped his fleece, allowing Crosby to glimpse a handgun stuffed into the waistband of his jeans.

'*Michael!*' Terry Halloran said sharply.

The man looked disappointed. '*You've made my acquaintance on a good day, Inspector.*' He stood reluctantly to one side. '*I have a lot of bad days. My advice would be to take the nature of your business elsewhere.*'

Crosby wasn't slow to leave Halloran's apartment. The Irishman's intimidation and manner suggested links with heavyweight organisations.

Once outside, the ex-detective felt for his emergency ration of small cigars. Crosby's hand shook as he thumbed his lighter – the encounter had un-nerved him. Christ knows who else was involved in all of this. Crosby pulled hard on his cigar. A visit to the *Lamb and Flag* public house might not be advisable today. What he really needed to do was pass everything onto Lucy – hope it was enough to divert her attention elsewhere.

Crosby ground out the half-smoked cigar beneath the heel of his shoe. After exiting number thirty-nine's front garden he began to re-trace his steps back towards the multi-storey car park – aware that his leather-jacketed companion from earlier had picked him up again. It certainly wasn't the Irishman from Terry Halloran's flat.

At the next corner Crosby turned into a shop doorway – waiting for the tail to catch him up. It didn't happen. Crosby waited five minutes. His pursuer had either seen enough or realised the ex-detective was onto him. It was another unwelcome development – the interest in him escalating – and that in turn would focus yet more attention on his family.

CHAPTER 7

Odbourne Primary School: Thursday 20th October 2011: 8.50 a.m.

Crosby watched the playground slowly empty – orderly crocodile lines of children filing obediently into class for another day. He reached for the Mondeo's ignition key. A thirty-five-year police career had accustomed him to routinely monitor situations where absolutely nothing occurred.

Rose Cavendish suddenly materialised in front of his windscreen. At the same time Lucy Roberts opened the front-passenger door and slid into the seat beside him. Crosby cut his engine. He was annoyed at not seeing them approach – but their appearance wasn't entirely unexpected – they'd given him a week to come up with something. Lucy waited until her partner had walked around to the driver's rear-door and climbed in behind them.

'*Well?*' the younger woman asked.

'*I've got a name,*' Crosby answered. '*John Hendry. A former Scenes-of-Crime officer. He resigned from the Department only three months after carrying out detached forensic duties at Dryffed's Farm.*'

'*Doesn't mean anything,*' Lucy said dismissively. '*Where is this John Hendry now?*'

'*He's disappeared,*' Crosby replied, '*and no one's been able to contact him since.*'

'*That's fucking convenient!*' Cavendish said.

'*I've been in touch with a couple of old contacts from HMRC and DWP.*' Crosby embellished the non-information he'd received. '*There's been no recorded activity for Hendry within the last two years.*'

Cavendish interrupted again. '*And what the fuck are we supposed to do with that?*'

Crosby ignored her. He retrieved an envelope from his jacket pocket and handed it to Lucy. *That's some background information on him.* She took out the sheet of A4 that Ian Brown had given to the ex-detective and quickly scanned through its content. *The Real IRA?*

A splinter group of the Provisional IRA, Crosby replied. *They would certainly be interested in the proceeds of a three hundred million pound drugs haul.*

I know who they fucking are! Is Hendry a member of this organisation?

It would seem likely, Crosby answered. *I'd need more time to confirm it.*

You're running out of time. Where do you think this John Hendry is now?

Dublin probably.

I'll pass the information on, Lucy said.

What about me? Crosby asked.

You need to keep asking questions.

He's given us nothing, Rose Cavendish said from behind them. Crosby turned to her. *I've just given you a fucking name!*

Lucy opened the front-passenger door. *And I told you that we'll pass it on.* Crosby reached across to stop her leaving. Rose Cavendish leant forward and wrapped a muscular fore-arm around the ex-detective's neck. He struggled to free himself but the older woman's hold on him was vice-like.

Cavendish waited for her partner to leave the car before loosening her arm-lock from around Crosby's neck. When the ex-detective tried to open his door she made a fist of her right hand – driving all four knuckles into the protruding bone behind Crosby's ear. The pain was excruciating. It disorientated him. *I'm running out of patience with you, copper.* The woman's voice seemed to be reaching him through a long tunnel. *You're just giving us the fucking run around.* Cavendish grabbed a handful of the ex-detective's hair and pulled his head back. *I'm not Lucy. I'll be doing something about it.*

Crosby's rear-door slammed shut. By the time he'd recovered his senses both women had returned to their car, which was already accelerating away past Odbourne's school gates.

Crosby slumped back in his seat. A wave of nausea followed the initial shock and pain. He was in no fit state to go after them. *'Shit!'* Now there'd be bruising to explain away. That certainly wouldn't escape his wife's powers of detection.

Although the ex-detective had dealt with a great many aggressive and unpredictable women throughout his police career, he'd never once felt like inflicting serious injury on any of them. Rose Cavendish might prove to be an exception. This was the second time that Crosby had experienced the woman's brute strength. He was sure there'd be further physical confrontation to deal with.

His nausea gradually subsided, the throbbing behind his ear eased to a dull ache, but he didn't immediately leave. A requirement that had implanted itself a few days ago re-appeared. It wouldn't go away. There'd be consequences however.

Crosby continued to sit in the car for another five minutes before coming to a decision. After clipping his seat belt into place he turned the Mondeo's engine over and pulled away, heading towards the Sixfields Community Housing Estate.

Sixfields Housing Estate: Thursday 20th October 2011: 10.30 a.m.

Crosby's Mondeo entered the eastern sector of Sixfields after an hour's drive. It flicked a number of switches in the ex-detective's memory – none of them particularly pleasant. Of the numerous investigations carried out during his long CID career, a good many of them had taken place within the five square miles of Sixfields. It was the estate's full-scale riot and its string of brutal serial killings that had hastened Crosby into an early retirement.

Although he hadn't returned to Sixfields during the intervening years it was still the same depressing vista – row upon row of featureless, nondescript housing – stretched out in a continuous grey blur. The occasional well-maintained property intermittently presented itself, but they were few and far between, looking conspicuous and out of place in their surroundings. Crosby had no doubt that anti-social behaviour, gang warfare, and drug related problems were still rife on the estate – inevitable in an under-privileged community that housed over ninety thousand inhabitants.

As his Mondeo climbed the slight rise towards ParkGate's Shopping Centre he couldn't resist a glance at number sixty-nine Silver Street. An image of Robert Milner, and the shadows that haunted a troubled mind, tugged more snapshot memories from Crosby's subconscious. The ex-detective turned to look at a stretch of park-land opposite. It was where Donald, a twenty-five-year-old with Downs-syndrome, used to walk his overweight Labrador. The pair had been inseparable.

When Robert Milner was alive he had regularly protected Donald against the prejudice and hatred meted out by local resident gangs – but he hadn't been able to prevent an attack on Donald's Labrador. The animal had sustained fatal injuries from a vicious kicking carried out by one particular gang member. Crosby had subsequently witnessed both Robert Milner's and Donald's anguish. He'd never forgotten it. A figure appeared on the stretch of park-land. It looked like Donald. Crosby thought briefly about stopping but continued on.

The ex-detective arrived at ParkGate's main entrance and turned left into a large, rundown car park. He navigated his way carefully around its numerous pot-holes before coasting to a halt. There didn't seem to be any marked parking spaces. Crosby switched off his engine. In the car park's far corner, approximately thirty yards away, stood a thick-set, stocky male. He wore a black leather jerkin and loose-fitting jeans. The man detached himself from a wall he'd been leaning against and looked across in Crosby's direction. A small knot of hooded figures who'd been gathered around the man drifted casually away.

Zamir Veseli had already been warned by his spotters of an unfamiliar vehicle entering the car park. A well-rehearsed and practiced routine saw the dealer's stock of cannabis bags and heroin twists transferred to his teenage runners, who quickly left the immediate area on their BMX hybrid-styled bikes.

The ex-detective opened his car door and stepped out, aware that Veseli was watching him. Crosby knew the dealer well – a regular informant of his over several years. The ex-detective was also acquainted with Veseli's early life – a violent childhood past that had left the dealer both mentally and physically scarred. Crosby understood the man's anger and grief.

Zamir Veseli was ethnic Albanian, a refugee from the Kosovo conflict of thirteen years ago. Arriving in the UK through a British Red Cross re-settlement programme, the ten-year-old had been relocated to Sixfields along with hundreds of other Kosovan refugees. He was ideal recruitment material for those elements who controlled his adopted neighbourhood.

After living through months of hostile Serbian brutality the ten-year-old boy found a relative haven of peace and opportunity in Sixfields – merging comfortably into the ways of its local gang culture. Veseli initially worked as a runner and spotter for neighbourhood street dealers, slowly climbing the estate's hierarchies. He eventually built up his own network of pitches, controlling them with ruthless efficiency. The twenty-three-year-old Kosovan had found a comfortable niche in life. He wasn't about to give it up – successfully resisting all attempts at repatriation back to his homeland.

Crosby's slightly ponderous gait gradually closed the distance between them. Veseli's dark, swarthy features, suspicious at first, were slowly transformed into a genuine smile of recognition. *'Sergeant Frank!'* The dealer beamed – his teeth a contrasting white against an olive skin and coarse black hair. *'You come back to me.'* He still retained the harsh, flat tone of his Slavic upbringing.

'Hello, Zamir.'

Veseli reproached him. *'I not see Sergeant Frank so much.'*

'I got promoted,' Crosby said.

'I know that,' the Albanian nodded. *'Then you retire. But you always Sergeant Frank to me.'*

The ex-detective looked around him *'Business still good, Zamir?'* he asked.

'Is OK.' The Kosovan shrugged. *'You come to buy?'*

'Yes.'

The dealer's smile grew wider. *'Zamir's special weed is good for old people. You get much relax.'*

Crosby shook his head. *'I want a small handgun.'*

Veseli's smile disappeared. His eyes narrowed. *'You not fuck with me, Sergeant Frank?'*

'I'm serious.'

'What is your purpose?'

'That's my business.'

'You good policeman, Sergeant Frank. Zamir is disappointed.'

'I disappoint myself,' Crosby said. *'Can you get me the gun?'*

'OK. OK.' The Kosovan shrugged. *'I get you gun. Is fine with me. Line up all fucking world for what I care. We kill everybody. I help you.'*

Veseli's mood was changed. The ex-detective's request had triggered memories. Crosby was aware of what they were. At ten years of age the young boy had watched a local Serbian militia unit enter his village. Whole families were rounded up. The Serbian militia forced them to dig out a shallow pit and then lined-up everyone alongside it. Watching from a nearby hiding place the young boy had to witness his parents, grand-parents, two brothers and a sister, being raked with automatic machine-gun fire. He watched them topple headlong into their makeshift grave – where any survivors were summarily executed with a single bullet to the head.

Veseli had once told Crosby that he still woke every night, drenched in a cold sweat, screaming for his lost family. It was little wonder the young Kosovan had no regard for human life. *'I make many addicts,'* he could often be heard to boast. *'It fuck up all the family.'*

The small number of Serbian refugees that remained in Sixfields knew to give Zamir Veseli a wide berth. When the rage descended on him he would go hunting for them. Any that were unlucky enough to cross his path were beaten to within an inch of their life. *'I never kill them, Sergeant Frank,'* he'd said to Crosby. *'They have to live. I need to kick the shit out of them again. Is a good feeling.'*

Veseli had never been prosecuted for any of the attacks. None of his victims would testify against him. And because most of the Serbs that he hospitalised were also dealers the police showed little interest. It meant one less criminal out on the streets to deal with – temporarily at least.

'What you want?' Veseli asked. *'I get you anything but submachine gun. Is bad memories for me.'*

'I've told you what I want,' Crosby said. *'A small handgun. Semi-automatic.'*

The dealer considered his request. *'I have Walther PPK,'* he answered. *'They make in Germany. Very reliable.'*

'How much?'

'You would like new?'

'Well I don't want one that's bloody traceable!'

Veseli held up a hand. *'I can do.'* The dealer pulled a battered old tobacco tin from his pocket. Crosby waited for him to calculate the maximum amount of profit that he could squeeze from their transaction. *'Two thousand then,'* the Kosovan pitched.

'One thousand,' Crosby countered.

Veseli laughed. *'I like we haggle, Sergeant Frank. One thousand and half.'* He deliberately placed a loosely packed marijuana roll between his lips and flicked a lighter at it. The dried cannabis flared as Veseli sucked in smoke from the burning leaf.

'Twelve hundred,' Crosby said. *'I can go elsewhere.'*

'I make no money, Sergeant Frank.' Veseli's smile indicated otherwise. *'But we shake. You old friend.'* The dealer stretched out a hand.

Crosby declined it. *'We were never friends.'*

The Kosovan didn't look offended. *'I understand. Is difficult for you.'*

'I want a fitted silencer and ammunition,' the ex-detective added.

'A PPK clip have eight rounds,' Veseli said.

'I'll give you an extra fifty for the silencer and a full magazine.'

'A hundred,' the Kosovan countered.

Crosby wanted to leave. *'OK.'*

'You drive hard bargain, Sergeant Frank.' Veseli ground out the cannabis stub beneath his heel. *'You come back tomorrow. We finish our business.'*

Crosby turned. He began walking back to his car. A smell of food drifted across the car park – ParkGate's two fast-food outlets were racking up production from their commercial deep fryers. It reminded him that he'd skipped breakfast. A ParkGate burger didn't appeal however. The ex-detective turned up his collar as a light drizzle began to fall. He couldn't remember feeling more miserable or depressed than he did at this moment in time.

'You bring your plastic card, Sergeant Frank.' Veseli called after him. *'I have machine now.'*

Crosby didn't join in the dealer's laughter, continuing on towards his car. He looked around him, checking the car park for CCTV cameras. There didn't appear to be any – and Veseli seemed comfortable enough conducting his day-to-day business there. CCTV elsewhere in Sixfields might cause problems at a later date. He couldn't concern himself with it at the moment. There were other, more pressing matters.

Crosby left ParkGate, heading for the estate's nearest exit point. He still needed to speak with a number of people who had direct access to *Dryffed's Farm* at the time – Lucy Roberts' mother being one of them. The ex-detective wasn't fully convinced about her not being involved in the drugs network intended for Sixfields – she'd still been married to Lucy's father-in-law back then. It was time for Crosby to pay her a visit and renew old acquaintances.

Time wasn't on his side however – he'd had to use someone to locate the woman and dig out some current background on her. She hadn't been difficult to find. Crosby's investigator was able to point him in the direction of an impressive looking company web-site. *'Aquileia Catering.'* The former Penny Roberts had apparently married again – her husband an Anglo-Italian businessman who owned the company. Crosby wasn't surprised about the marriage. Penny Zardelli's previous husbands were selected on the size of their income. The ex-detective was in no doubt that her latest tryst had been entered into for the same reason. She was listed on the web-site as *Aquileia Catering's* executive director.

A face-to-face with Penny Zardelli would mean Crosby having to visit the south coast. It certainly wasn't a trip he'd look forward to. The tenor of their previous encounters could be described as frosty, even hostile on occasions. He glanced at the Mondeo's dashboard clock. Eleven o'clock. The south coast would have to wait until tomorrow. Paul Berne, however, was operating his private detective agency from a lot closer to home – and according to DC Grace Taylor he'd been showing a recent interest in the events that had taken place at *Dryffed's Farm.*

He was killing time in the café of a large department store – close to Birmingham's city centre. The store's central heating raged at full blast and Crosby was extremely warm. He'd finished lunch – bland, over-priced cheese sandwiches and a small pot of weak tea. Crosby contemplated the fact that it was only six days ago, inside a similar store, that Lucy and Rose Cavendish had disrupted his retirement. The ex-detective again questioned why he was continuing with this. Was it because of the threat to his family that pushed him on? Maybe he was subconsciously enjoying the investigation. What if he just sat back and let events run their course? It was possible that Lucy's drug syndicate had already tracked down the elusive John Hendry. The pessimist in him said probably not.

Crosby forced down the last of his lukewarm tea and made ready to leave. As an ex-detective he had to exhaust all lines of enquiry – and Paul Berne's *'PB Investigations'* were located just around the corner in Gower Street. Crosby returned the café's complimentary tabloid to its wall rack. There hadn't been a single page where the coming London Olympics didn't feature in one form or another. At least it was giving the newspaper's well-endowed page three models a chance to express their art in a variety of Olympic sporting poses.

After finally escaping the department store's oppressive heating system he stood outside its main entrance doors – routinely checking the manner and behaviour of everyone in view. Nobody caught his eye. The ex-detective's paranoia was growing. A man had followed him into the store's toilets earlier and Crosby had been unable to empty his bladder – not until the man had zipped himself up and left.

Crosby found number seventy-eight Gower Street wedged in-between a hairdressing salon and an estate agent's office. The narrow, two-storey building was fronted by a reinforced frosted-glass door – *'PB Investigations'* engraved across it in large italic lettering. Crosby opened the door and stepped inside.

The private investigator's reception office was small and sparsely furnished – two easy chairs and a low coffee-table stacked with old magazines in the far corner – an office desk, swivel chair and filing cabinet to his left. There was no one manning the desk. All four walls were painted neutral beige in colour, a large framed certificate hung strategically from one of the walls. Crosby moved across to take a closer look at it. The certificate, issued by the Association of British Investigators, indicated that Paul Berne was an accredited member of their organisation and had apparently satisfied all requirements with regard to its award. The commendation's prominent display position was obviously intended to impress clients with its degree of authenticity. Crosby was aware the profession of a private detective was neither regulated nor licenced in the UK.

A black leather jacket, thrown casually across one of the easy chairs, caught his eye. It was too much of a coincidence. *'Anybody home?'* Crosby called out, his voice sounding un-naturally loud in the small office.

An inner door opened. A shaven-headed, white male emerged into the reception area. He was stocky, well-built, broad muscular shoulders supporting a thick, short neck. Crosby's wife would have taken an immediate dislike to him – *'never trust anyone with small eyes set too close together'* – one of her many standby character assessments.

The man hesitated. He looked momentarily unsure – further confirmation to Crosby that it was the tail who had followed him to Beaumont Street yesterday. His face looked familiar though. Crosby knew him from somewhere else. *'Yes?'* The man had recovered from his initial confusion.

'I'm an old colleague of Paul Berne's,' Crosby said. *'Is he in? There's a matter I'd like to discuss with him.'*

'He's at lunch.' The voice was brash, arrogant. *'Won't be back for an hour or more.'*

'I'll wait,' Crosby said. *'Are you an associate of Paul's?'*

'I work for Mr Berne. What do you want to see him about?'

'A private matter.'

The man compressed his lips into a thin line. He held Crosby's gaze. The street door opened. A slim, attractive looking girl, wearing a short black skirt and white blouse, stepped inside. About eighteen years old, Crosby surmised. A name-badge identified her as Emma Devonshire. She half-smiled in Crosby's direction but didn't acknowledge the other man's presence. Her body language suggested a tension between them. She crossed to the office's reception desk and sat down. Switching on a small laptop the girl lowered her head to concentrate on its screen.

'This gentleman's waiting to see Mr Berne,' the man said brusquely. He disappeared back into his office. Crosby found one of the easy chairs. A silence ensued as he sat and waited. Emma Devonshire was obviously not one for polite small talk. *'Have you worked here long?'* Crosby asked. The girl lifted her head. *'Five days,'* she replied in a marked, West Midlands accent.

'Do you enjoy it?'

'It's OK.' The response was stilted, monotone.

'Quite an exciting profession though,' Crosby persisted. *'You must get a lot of interesting cases.'*

'I can't really say.' She glanced towards the inner office door.

'Mr Berne's colleague,' Crosby said. *'He didn't give me his name.'*

The girl lowered her voice. *'It's Mr Alcott.'* She leant in towards her screen. *'You'll excuse me. I need to finish this.'*

Now Crosby remembered him. Police Constable Derek Alcott. An ex-metropolitan police traffic officer. Crosby recalled the man's court case. At his trial he was accused of forcing vulnerable females into having sex with him by promising not to report their motoring offences. Alcott and his co-driver employed a variety of threats to coerce victims – ranging from points on licences to falsifying breathalyser read-outs. There were also rumours of physical attacks carried out on those women who refused to comply. Alcott's conviction and subsequent sentence was based on the evidence of just one witness – other victims being too frightened or ashamed to testify.

He was described in court as a dangerous, sexual predator – sent down for a total of three years and dismissed from his post. The judge in his summing up of Alcott said – *'You believed it was your given right to take advantage of vulnerable women alone in their vehicles. The fact that these attacks were carried out from a position of trust makes this crime even more abominable. I have no hesitation in passing this custodial sentence upon you.'*

Crosby presumed that Paul Berne knew Alcott from his time with The Met in London. Berne had always been an over-confident, sharp operator, but Crosby was still surprised that he'd employ someone with Derek Alcott's background and track record.

Paul Berne breezed through the door of *PB Investigations* at two o'clock. *'Frank! What brings you here?'* The surprise in his voice didn't sound genuine. Alcott had obviously been able to warn his employer that Crosby was waiting for him.

There were changes in Berne's appearance. It was more than three years since Crosby had been his supervising officer, and during that time the private investigator's hair colouring had turned grey. *'Shit!'* Crosby had a sudden flashback. Was it Paul Berne he'd seen with his daughter-in-law outside Odbourne school last Tuesday morning? The man's face had been in profile. Surely he was older.

'Is there somewhere we can talk in private?' Crosby asked.

'Sure. Come on through to my office.'

Crosby followed him. The room they stepped into seemed small. That was probably due to Derek Alcott's considerable bulk – his six-foot frame wedged in behind the office's one desk. *'Would you mind, Derek?'* Berne asked. *'This is my old DI from Studwell. He's looking to have a word in private.'*

Alcott didn't reply. He manoeuvred himself around the desk, looking long and hard at Crosby before leaving. Paul Berne pushed the office door to, but didn't close it completely. He edged past Crosby to sit in Alcott's vacated chair. The ex-detective remained standing. Berne looked up at him. *'Yes, Frank? What can I do for you, mate?'*

Crosby was annoyed that his former DC had deliberately addressed him in familiar terms. It was intentional and disrespectful. Their previous working relationship had been a formal one and not overly friendly. *'I want to know who employed your agency to follow me around.'*

The pause was minimal. Berne realised there was little point in denying it. *'You know I can't disclose that sort of information, Frank. I'd be compromising client confidentiality.'*

Crosby stepped forward and placed both hands on Berne's desk. He leant in towards him. *'I suggest you make a fucking exception in this instance. My family's been threatened and I want to know who's responsible.'*

The door behind him was pushed open with some force. Crosby turned. Derek Alcott had obviously been listening outside. The former traffic officer fronted up to Crosby, jabbing him in the chest with his forefinger. *'You're fucking retired! You don't come in here telling us what to do.'* The man's features were flushed and ugly. *'I used to take orders from a wanker like you. I never did get the chance to shove his rank up his ass.'*

Paul Berne was quickly to his feet. *'It's fine, Derek.'* He stretched out a hand. *'Frank and I are OK. I was just explaining our code of practice to him. We understand each other now.'*

Crosby didn't find it particularly warm inside the small room but Alcott was perspiring heavily. Two half-circles of sweat had formed around both armpits – dark shadows of perspiration against his white tee-shirt. He was obviously finding great difficulty in trying to restrain himself. It took another few moments for the situation to pass. Alcott eventually unclenched both his fists and backed out of the office. Crosby began to breathe a little easier. *'The man's a bloody psychopath,'* he said to Berne. *'Why the hell are you employing him? He was barely able to control himself.'*

'*Derek's all right.*' The private investigator waved a hand and sat down. '*He's been misrepresented.*' Berne's face told a different story. He'd also been taken aback at Alcott's outburst.

'*Misrepresented!*' Crosby couldn't believe what he was hearing. '*Jesus Christ! What's that supposed to mean? The man's a convicted rapist. He physically intimidated lone women motorists. Don't tell me you didn't know.*'

Berne looked uncomfortable. '*Those women consented to having sex with him,*' he replied. '*And the GBH was never proved. His bark's worse than his bite.*'

Crosby shook his head. '*Are you frightened of him? Does he have something on you?*'

Berne's forced laugh sounded uneasy. He leant back in his chair. '*Now you're just being delusional, Frank. Tell you what I'll do. As you're an old colleague I can have a word with my clients. Put your concerns to them.*'

'*How about I put my concerns to the police,*' Crosby said.

Berne shrugged. '*Which you're perfectly at liberty to do.*'

'*I presume it's Lucy Roberts employing your services?*'

Paul Berne stood up from behind his desk. '*If there's nothing else then, Frank?*' He stretched out a hand. Crosby ignored it, turning to leave. It was perhaps fortunate that he hadn't yet taken delivery of his handgun. There'd have been a temptation to threaten the private investigator with it.

'*Leave me alone!*' Emma Devonshire's voice – loud, distressed, from the outer office. It took Crosby a couple of strides to pull open the door. Paul Berne followed him. The girl was out of her chair, looking flushed and upset. Alcott stood close-by. He smirked at the ex-detective.

'*The man needs taking to a vet,*' Crosby said to Berne. '*He's trouble.*'

'*I need a word, Derek.*' Paul Berne stepped back into his office. Alcott followed him, locking eyes with Crosby as he passed the ex-detective. Emma Devonshire was visibly shaking. She turned away from Crosby as he headed for the agency's outer door.

Hawthorne Rise: Thursday 20th October 2011: 7.15 p.m.

Crosby was restless. He fidgeted, manoeuvring himself into yet another position on the couch. Doreen Crosby lost patience. His wife had settled down to an evening of television and didn't appreciate having it disrupted. She turned to face him. *'What in God's name is the matter with you, Frank? We had the same performance last night.'*

'I'm fine.'

'You're not fine,' his wife said. *'You acted like this during major investigations. There's something going on.'*

Crosby didn't respond.

His wife persisted. *'Talk to me, Frank.'*

Crosby was half-tempted to confide in her. He dismissed it. If she was told about a possible threat to the family it would be one more problem to deal with. There were enough of those already. *'It's just a migraine developing,'* he said. *'I'll take something for it.'*

His wife continued to press him. *'We never see each other lately. I don't believe you're spending all this time away on fishing trips.'* She pushed a button on her remote. The television screen went blank. *'We'll just sit here until you tell me what's going on.'*

Crosby was forced to concoct something. *'I've been offered an opportunity in a business venture. There's been a couple of meetings.'*

A pause. His wife didn't look convinced. *'What sort of business?'*

'An ex-colleague is looking to set up a private security firm.' Crosby knew he was digging a hole for himself. *'There might be some part-time consultancy in it for me.'*

'Why all the secrecy?'

'*You wouldn't have approved,*' Crosby said, '*and it's only a proposal at the moment. There was little point in telling you about something that might not happen.*'

'*What's the name of this ex-colleague?*'

'*You wouldn't know him.*'

'*Try me.*'

'*John Trevvers,*' Crosby said off the top of his head.

'*Have you just made that up?*'

'*What the hell's that supposed to mean?*'

'*I don't know yet.*' His wife turned the television back on. '*You're hiding something though.*'

Crosby stood up. '*I'll have to take something for this migraine.*'

'*We've been married for over thirty-five years,*' his wife called after him. '*I know when you're not telling the truth.*'

'*So does a bloody lie detector machine,*' the ex-detective muttered as he left, '*but you can switch those off.*'

Crosby retired to the bedroom. He couldn't settle. Too many thoughts crowding in on him. Doreen Crosby switched off the programme she'd been watching, unable to concentrate on it. Her husband didn't look well. He'd lost weight. And it wasn't caused by a non-existent business venture either. She closed her eyes. The days of having to worry about him leaving the house should have stopped after his retirement.

CHAPTER 8

Hawthorne Rise: Friday 21st *October 2011: 6.30 a.m.*

Crosby closed and locked the front door quietly behind him. It was early. After their conversation last night he'd wanted to leave before his wife was up and about. He glanced at a patchy, barely lit sky – sunrise was still over an hour away. At least the late-night forecast hadn't threatened rain for his drive to the south-coast today. He sniffed the air. Mild for late October. They'd have to pay for it at some point.

Inside the Mondeo he clamped his sat-nav into place. A recommended route had been pre-programmed and stored in the device overnight. Although he'd come to rely on it more and more recently the ex-detective still wasn't a total convert – annoyed at having spent too many years mastering the now obsolete art of reading a road map. All he did now was listen to a back-seat driver who directed him unerringly and efficiently to the correct destination. Crosby muttered under his breath as the sat-nav's screen burst into life. He tapped all the necessary icons to display a small, colourful map. *'At the end of the road turn left,'* a disembodied female voice intoned. Crosby muttered again as he slipped the Mondeo's clutch. Motoring shouldn't be this easy.

Doreen Crosby watched from an upstairs window as her husband reversed from their drive. She stood there long after his tail-lights had disappeared around the top-corner.

It took three and a half-hours, via the M5 and A358 as instructed, for Crosby to arrive at his south-coast destination. The journey had been accurately predicted to within three minutes. He reached forward to switch off his electronic receiver, returning its space-age technology back into the black hole it had materialised from.

Most of Crosby's long journey to Weymouth had been taken up with deciding how he should approach and conduct his meeting with the abrasive Mrs Zardelli. Lucy's mother rode rough-shod over those people she considered beneath her – an impatient woman – one who took for granted her privileged circumstances and position in life.

Penny Zardelli was forty-two years old at the time of his Sixfields investigation. She looked much younger. Men were attracted to her finely sculpted features and eye-catching figure – assets that Mrs Zardelli had made good use of over the years. Crosby hadn't seen her since Lucy's trial – but it sounded as if she'd moved on from the trauma suffered at *Dryffed's Farm.* According to the information that Crosby had been given, her latest acquisition was one Enrico Zardelli – a forty-three-year-old self-made millionaire who held both UK and Italian passports.

Crosby had asked his investigator to check out the man's history and background - a line of enquiry that might have some relevance. The investigator had been very thorough. Enrico Zardelli's paternal grandfather was Sicilian – a conscript farm labourer who saw out World War II from his prisoner of war camp in the south-west of England. After VE day he elected to remain in Britain, marrying a local girl from the small market town of Bridgwater in Somerset. Their only child was a son - Tomas Zardelli - the father of Enrico.

The young Enrico Zardelli had initially trained as a chef, but he was ambitious, and at the age of thirty-one had formed *Aquileia Catering.* The business currently served five-star hotels and specialised in providing culinary requirements for high-order corporate functions. Probably due to his business commitments the Anglo-Italian had somehow managed to evade any long-term relationships – that was until he met the former Penny Roberts. Crosby could easily imagine the woman using all necessary means at her disposal to deprive Zardelli of his bachelor status.

Aquileia Catering had recently seen a spectacular rise in its fortunes – to the point where Enrico Zardelli was apparently considering a flotation on the London Stock Exchange. Last year's tax returns indicated an annual turnover in excess of ten million pounds.

The turnaround in his then modest business and its small profit margins was two years ago – when substantial capital had been injected into *Aquileia's* operating budget. It also coincided with the year of Enrico Zardelli's marriage to Lucy's mother.

Crosby had pressed his investigator as to where *Aquileia's* investment capital might have been raised. *'The money was transferred and filtered through numerous layers. Almost impossible to identify its original source.'* Crosby's investigator had also pointed out a five million pound ocean-going yacht that was currently moored in Weymouth's harbour marina. An asset far in excess of the company's present standing.

Aquileia Catering's area of operations stretched all along the south coast – and Penny Zardelli was certainly hands-on in her current husband's business – another reason why Crosby believed that she was aware of the drug smuggling activities at *Dryffed's Farm*. Mrs Zardelli's position as *Aquileia Catering's* executive director indicated she was responsible for its day-to-day running, an appointment presumably sanctioned by her husband. Crosby thought the title over-stated in a private company of its size. The woman's ego had probably insisted on it.

Enrico Zardelli's company had landed some high-profile tenders recently – including corporate hospitality and concession stands for next year's Olympic sailing events in Portland. Because of *Aquileia Catering's* Olympic commitments, much of Penny Zardelli's time was being spent at their head office – its premises located close to Weymouth's town centre. Crosby's information indicated she would be in office today – a journey of about an hour from her luxury mansion in Poole's exclusive Sandbank development – the area referred to by locals as millionaire's row.

Crosby was slow to open the car door, his body stiff after the long drive. He stepped outside. A chilly sea breeze carried the unmistakeable scent of salt and iodine. Crosby took a couple of deep breaths, stretching and rotating his lower back. He'd chosen to park near the Pavilion Theatre on Weymouth's old pier – far enough away from the town centre and *Aquileia Catering's* head office. Opposite him was *Condor's* cross channel ferry port. One of their high-speed catamarans was currently in the process of being loaded with cars and passengers destined for the channel islands of Jersey and Guernsey.

He glanced at his watch. Ten o'clock. A slow walk along the esplanade and into town should find *Aquileia's* executive director at her desk. Whatever other qualities were necessary for her post the redoubtable Mrs Zardelli would certainly have no problem in adopting an executive director's ruthless streak. Crosby had experience of it.

He headed out of the car park and made his way along the south-facing sea front. As he neared Weymouth's iconic, one hundred-year-old Jubilee Clock it evoked memories of a day from his previous life, sitting with Doreen and son Michael on the beach. A hot uncomfortable afternoon – trapped in a corporation deck-chair and perspiring heavily – tiny grains of sand finding their way into the skin's hidden folds and creases. He automatically glanced up towards the resort's north-east headland – seeking out their old Pontins holiday hotel above Bowleaze Cove. The Spanish-styled modernistic hotel built in 1937 was now Grade II listed – still a prominent landmark just below the coastal walkway – and still retaining its colourful Mediterranean blue and white façade. Crosby had read somewhere that Saudi Arabian investors now owned the hotel. An image ran through his mind of a guest being given twenty lashes in the hotel gardens for smuggling in alcohol. On another occasion the thought might have brought a smile to his face.

Crosby waited for a gap to appear in slow moving traffic. He hurried across the sea-front road, cutting through a side-street that divided two large Victorian hotels. Ten minutes later he was standing outside the offices of *Aquileia Catering* – a modern, split-level terracotta-bricked building flanked by two white flagpoles. The green, white and red tricolore of Italy fluttered alongside a Union Jack in the stiff breeze. *Aquileia's* own distinctive logo, a full-sized butler's figure wearing the traditional white gloves and long tail-coat, had been tastefully etched into a smoked-glass entrance door.

The small car park was divided into approximately twenty parking slots – half of which were occupied. An expensive-looking silver BMW 3 Series Convertible sat in the space reserved for *Aquileia Catering's* executive director. Penny Zardelli was in office. Crosby jotted down the BMW's number plate.

He pushed through the smoked-glass door. *Aquileia's* reception area was designed to impress prospective clients – spacious, airy, and thickly carpeted. Several items of minimalistic, designer furniture had been strategically positioned around the room. A light airborne scent was provided by six vases of freshly cut flowers. The glossy framed photographs on view appeared to be of functions that *Aquileia Catering* had previously hosted.

A smartly dressed receptionist, crisp white top and pencil-slim black skirt, looked up from behind a glass-topped desk. She pasted an enquiring smile onto her face. *'Good Morning, Sir. How may I help you?'*

'I'm here to see Mrs Zardelli.'

The receptionist glanced down at her computer screen, tapping several buttons on the machine's keyboard. *'Are you expected? I don't seem to have any appointments in her diary for this morning.'*

'I'm sure she'll see me.'

The receptionist looked unsure. She reached for one of her telephones. *'Who shall I say is calling, Sir?'*

Crosby moved across to a door marked *Executive Director.* He knocked once and opened it. Penny Zardelli was sitting behind a large, solid oak desk. She looked up, her annoyance clearly evident. Outwardly she hadn't changed. The vivid blue eyes, stylishly cropped short black hair, high prominent cheekbones, the same unlined elfin-shaped face. Crosby was sure that her character and personality wouldn't have altered a great deal either. A tailored black business suit, offset by several items of white gold jewellery, completed the look of a highly efficient, professional businesswoman.

'Mrs Zardelli,' Crosby said. 'It's been a while since we last met. You'll no doubt remember me from our investigation into the events that occurred at Sixfields and Dryffed's Farm.'

If Penny Zardelli was surprised at his appearance it didn't show. She leant back in her chair. 'PC Plod,' the executive director said to him. 'How could I forget you? Your inept blundering is forever etched in my memory.'

An anxious-looking receptionist had made it to the doorway. Penny Zardelli waved a dismissive hand in her direction before turning back to the ex-detective. 'Crosby wasn't it? Detective Inspector? Shouldn't you have been put out to grass by now?'

He ignored it. The woman's acerbic manner hadn't altered. 'You must be extremely busy, Mrs Zardelli.' Crosby sat down in the chair opposite. 'I appreciate you agreeing to see me at such short notice.'

'I did not agree to see you,' the executive director said, 'and I did not invite you to sit down.'

Crosby remained in his chair. 'Mrs Zardelli.....' he began.

'It's Ms Zardelli,' the executive director said. 'What exactly is it you want, Inspector?'

'I mentioned the Sixfields investigation earlier,' Crosby replied. 'We've had to re-open our files on it. There's been a development concerning Dryffed's Farm.'

The executive director hesitated. 'What bloody development! All of that happened over three years ago. The case was closed.'

Crosby had noted her hesitation.

Penny Zardelli's voice rose. 'Why hasn't anyone been in touch with me about this?'

'I'm getting in touch with you,' Crosby said.

The woman's face hardened. 'Don't get bloody smart, Inspector. I have a certain amount of influence in these parts.'

Crosby didn't mind the woman losing her poise. She was more likely to let something slip. *'It's just a few routine questions,'* he continued. *'We'd like to know of anyone who showed an interest in Dryffed's Farm after your previous husband died.'*

'How the hell would I know who showed an interest?' Penny Zardelli's manufactured, middle-class accent resonated around the office. *'Dryffed's was sold as part of Henry's estate. I didn't have anything to do with it.'*

'Who purchased the farm?' Crosby continued to antagonise her. He already knew who the current owners were.

Penny Zardelli's eyes narrowed. *'You're supposed to be a bloody detective for Christ's sake! Aren't you aware of who bought it?'* She reached for her telephone. *'I've had enough of this. I'm not putting up with your moronic behaviour for a second time.'*

'I appreciate my visit brings back unpleasant memories.' Crosby was unconcerned about her making the call. He had something in reserve. *'I understand you suffered a breakdown because of the events that took place at Dryffed's Farm.'*

Penny Zardelli finished punching in numbers on the telephone's key-pad and leant back in her chair. *'I have never suffered a breakdown in my life, Inspector. That's the domain of weak, emotional women with no back-bone.'* She flicked him a look from beneath her eyebrows. *'You attempted these mind games with me over three years ago. They didn't work then and they certainly won't work now.'*

Crosby heard a faint answering voice coming from Penny Zardelli's telephone. The ex-detective leant forward. *'I received a visit from your daughter six days ago.'*

Penny Zardelli didn't reply to the voice on her phone. She slowly replaced the receiver. *'Lucy's been released?'*

Crosby nodded.

'How was she?' A less confrontational tone.

'Your daughter's not been to see you?' Crosby knew she hadn't.

'No.' The woman's eyes dropped. '*She also refused my applications to visit her at Foston Hall.*'

Crosby had the woman's Achilles' heel. He allowed a lengthening silence to continue.

'*Did Lucy mention me?*' Penny Zardelli's prickly exterior had temporarily disappeared.

The ex-detective shook his head. '*Your daughter's concern was for a missing cache of drugs. They were hidden at Dryffed's Farm over three years ago by Lucy and your previous husband.*'

Another extended silence.

'*He and your daughter were using the farm to stockpile heroin intended for Sixfields.*' Crosby paused. '*Were you aware of this concealment?*'

'*You know full well I was cleared of having any involvement in Henry's criminal activities.*'

'*That wasn't the question,*' Crosby said. '*Did you know about the concealment?*'

'*No I bloody well didn't!*' The executive director had recovered herself, but wasn't reaching for the telephone. She frowned. '*Why would my daughter approach the police about missing drugs that she'd helped to store?*'

Crosby ignored it. '*Was there any particular reason for Lucy refusing your applications to visit her at Foston Hall?*'

'*I saw my daughter there once.*' Penny Zardelli sat back in her chair. '*Lucy told me she'd formed some sort of relationship with a female prison officer. I wasn't very understanding about it.*'

The ex-detective nodded. '*Rose Cavendish.*'

'*You know of her?*' Penny Zardelli grimaced. '*A gross woman. She was wearing a man's suit when I met her.*'

Crosby was surprised. '*You've met?*'

'*She came to see me with a message from my daughter,*' the executive director replied. '*Lucy didn't want me to visit her at the prison again.*'

97

'You've not seen Cavendish since?' Crosby asked.

'No!' Penny Zardelli replied, *'and I don't wish to. God knows what sort of dysfunctional family spawns an individual like that. She obviously took advantage of my daughter's vulnerability. I should have reported the relationship.'*

'Why didn't you?'

Penny Zardelli shrugged. *'I wanted my daughter protected. At least the woman was looking after her.'*

They were interrupted by a knock at the door. Through it stepped a tall, slim figure, his face smooth and lightly tanned, the prominent, aquiline nose betraying Italian origins. A scattering of grey flecks peppered his short dark hair. The tailored charcoal suit he wore looked expensive.

'Is everything OK, darling?' the man asked. *'I called in to brief you about the Bedbury Hotel development. Hannah was just telling me that your visitor was unnecessarily insistent about seeing you.'* He glanced at Crosby. It wasn't a friendly look. *'If there's a problem concerning Aquileia Catering,'* the man said to him, *'I am the company's owner. Enrico Zardelli.'* He remained in the doorway.

Crosby was treading a thin line. He didn't want the added complication of having to speak with Penny Zardelli's husband. *'It was just a routine matter, Sir.'* The ex-detective stood. *'I was about to leave.'* Enrico Zardelli made no attempt to move aside. Crosby had to brush past him as he exited the office and stepped through into *Aquileia*'s reception area. Penny Zardelli's husband watched the ex-detective's departure before turning to his wife.

'Inspector Crosby,' she said. *'West Midlands CID. We met in a previous life.'*

'I know he's the bloody law,' her husband said sharply. *'What did he want? I won't have our Olympic contracts screwed because of problems with the police.'*

Penny Zardelli compressed her lips. *'I'd appreciate you not talking to me like that. He was just covering old ground about Lucy and Henry's part in the Sixfields riot. The police have launched another enquiry into it.'*

'Will there be any more visits?'

'I don't think so,' the executive director said. She paused. *'He also told me that Lucy's been released.'*

Enrico Zardelli frowned. *'She's out? Is it a problem for us?'*

'No.'

'Make sure she stays away,' Aquileia's owner warned his wife. *'I don't want her causing any trouble here.'*

Penny Zardelli's face flushed. *'I've worked bloody hard to help build this business up,'* she said. *'I'm not about to let it go under because of something that happened over three years ago.'*

Her husband didn't look convinced. *'I don't want this company's name linked with that shit hole you used to live in. Just keep on top of it.'*

'You know full well that I didn't live there.'

'Your first husband did.'

Penny Zardelli bit down on her intended reply. She began to sort through a file of paperwork. *Aquileia's* owner turned to leave. *'I'll be working from home this afternoon if you need me.'* He closed the door behind him.

'Yes, darling,' Penny Zardelli murmured. *'I assume the Bedbury Hotel briefing wasn't that important.'* Enrico was proving more difficult to manipulate than previous husbands. She'd have to bide her time – there was little point in compromising *Aquileia's* current situation. Penny Zardelli sat back in her chair. The detective's visit might be a problem however.

Crosby was already outside, making his way through *Aquileia's* car park. He passed a Rolls-Royce Phantom Coupé, parked at an angle across two spaces. A uniformed chauffeur was leant nonchalantly against the car, closely tracking the ex-detective's progress. Crosby returned his look. He presumed it was Enrico Zardelli's driver – a squat, swarthy-looking individual with flat, brown eyes. Despite his uniformed jacket the man's heavily muscled upper-body strength was clearly evident. He'd obviously been employed for more than just chauffeuring duties. Crosby nodded as he walked past. It wasn't acknowledged. Up close the ex-detective could see a heavily pitted face with old acne scars – thick, coarse, greasy hair protruded from beneath a peaked, grey cap. Crosby felt the man's eyes remain on his back as he exited the car park.

Once out of view the ex-detective stopped to jot down Enrico Zardelli's licence-plate number. Twenty minutes later he'd retraced his steps back to the Pavilion Theatre car park. Crosby glanced at his watch. Eleven o'clock. He decided against an early lunch – and by eleven-thirty the efficient sat-nav lady had delivered him back onto the A37. An estimated arrival time of two-thirty was showing in the screen's bottom right-hand corner.

If nothing else had been achieved today the ex-detective could pass onto Lucy Roberts and Rose Cavendish that *Aquileia Catering* was a possibility with regard to the missing drugs. Lucy may have severed all contact with her mother since *Foston Hall*, but the recent substantial capital pumped into Enrico Zardelli's company might cause her to get back in touch. His visit this morning had been a calculated risk. Impersonating a serving officer and using the false-id would undoubtedly catch up with him at some point. Had today been worth it? Time would tell.

Three hours later and Crosby was still picking his way through events and information from the past ten days. He forced himself to leave it alone. His mind had reached saturation point. He leant forward to switch on the car radio.

At two o'clock precisely the station's hourly news bulletin was announced. Their lead item reported that a five-year-old boy had gone missing, possibly abducted, from a school in the West Midlands. Crosby was only half-listening. The female newsreader continued. Something registered in the ex-detective's subconscious. Did she say *'Odbourne Primary School?'* Crosby's delayed reaction slammed on the brakes and his Mondeo skidded to a halt – laying down two thick ribbons of dark rubber on the road's tarmac. A car travelling fifty yards behind did well to swerve around the ex-detective's sudden stop.

Crosby's hand shook as he fumbled to switch on his mobile. *'Shit!'* No signal. He felt nauseous. An acid bile rose in his throat. He revved the Mondeo's engine dangerously high and accelerated away – Michael and Angela's home was only fifteen minutes from his current position. Within ten seconds Crosby was breaking the speed limit. All he could see was his grandson's face staring back at him through the windscreen. A dull chest pain accompanied the nausea. It continued all the way to his son and daughter-in-law's home in the village of Little Wintermore.

Crosby screeched the Mondeo to a halt outside their four-bedroom detached house. He left his car door swinging open and rushed up the drive – falling into the hallway through an unlocked front door. Crosby stopped to catch his breath. Someone was crying. In the kitchen. He forced himself towards the door-way. *'Hello, Gramps,'* his grandson said.

The relief that Crosby felt was almost physical – like an electrical surge running through him. His daughter-in-law sat at the kitchen table, both arms around her son. Doreen Crosby was standing next to them, her hand on Angela's shoulder. Jack appeared to be fine. The look that Crosby received from his wife did not indicate she was pleased to see him. *'I heard snatches on the car radio,'* he said. *'What's happened?'*

'I've left you messages.' His wife's tone was icy. *'Your phone's been switched off. A boy's missing from Jack's school.'*

Crosby picked up his grandson. He held the boy close. Angela stood up, her eyes red-rimmed. *'I'll take Jack to his room. I need to speak with him. He doesn't understand what's going on.'* Crosby gave his grandson a final hug and put him down. Angela took the boy's hand.

Doreen Crosby waited until they'd both left. *'It's young Billy Lucas,'* she said to her husband. *'He was taken from outside the school. His mother's frantic. The poor woman's had to be sedated.'*

Crosby knew immediately what had happened. Billy Lucas was the image of his grandson. He slumped into a chair. *'I need to speak with Michael.'*

'I rang him,' his wife said. *'He's on his way home.'* Doreen Crosby went across to close the kitchen door before sitting down opposite her husband. *'You know something,'* she said accusingly. *'What is it?'*

'Now's not the right time,' he answered.

'When is the right bloody time?' she hissed at him. *'A child's just been abducted for Christ's sake!'*

'I need to speak with Michael first.'

'You can bloody well speak to me!'

Crosby hesitated. *'It might concern our family.'*

His wife climbed slowly to her feet. *'Does this have something to do with Jack?'*

Crosby couldn't look her in the eye.

'I'm telling you, Frank,' his wife warned. *'If you're involved in something that's threatening the safety of our grandson this marriage will not survive it.'*

He tried to take her hand. *'We'll talk later.'*

'Yes we bloody will!' Doreen Crosby snatched her hand back. She fixed him with another scathing look before stalking from the room. Crosby allowed a few moments for his emotions to subside before leaving the house to wait outside. He'd only been sat in his car for a few minutes when Michael pulled up sharply alongside. Crosby's window was already down. *'In here, Michael.'* His son opened the Mondeo's passenger-side door and slid in alongside him. *'Mum called. A class-mate of Jack's has been abducted from the school.'*

Crosby nodded. *'I think Jack was the intended victim.'*

'What!' Michael's face drained of colour.

Crosby didn't have much time. Not for what he had in mind. *'It goes back to the Sixfields investigation four years ago. I'm being targeted about a cache of drugs that were hidden at Dryffed's Farm.'*

His son didn't reply, still trying to take in the news that Jack was somehow involved. Crosby spoke quickly. *'Lucy Roberts and her step-father had stockpiled the drugs there for distribution in Sixfields. Lucy's just been released from prison.'* His words were running into each other. *'When she went back to the farm a few days ago her inheritance had disappeared.'*

Michael finally found his voice. *'What's all that got to do with the abduction from Jack's school?'*

'Lucy is in possession of a document from her step-father that implied I knew where the drugs were hidden.' Crosby paused. *'She's accused me of removing them.'*

Michael turned to look at him. *'And did you?'*

'Did I what for Christ's sake?'

'Did you know there were drugs hidden on the farm?'

Crosby was genuinely stunned. *'No I bloody didn't!'*

'I'm struggling with this,' Michael said. *'Are you saying that Lucy Roberts intended to kidnap Jack? To get at you?'*

'It's more complicated than that,' Crosby replied. *'The shipment was originally supplied by a South American drugs cartel who were not paid at the time. They might be responsible for the abduction.'*

'Jesus Christ!' Michael shook his head. *'How long have you known about this?'*

'Lucy contacted me a week ago.'

'Have you spoken to the police?'

'I threatened to,' Crosby replied, *'but Lucy said she would pass my name to whoever's representing the cartel over here. I was given a few days to come up with some answers.'*

'Is there a possibility the abduction could be just a coincidence?'

'I doubt it.'

'Then someone's not bothered to wait.'

103

'It looks likely.' Crosby winced. The pain in his chest had returned.

There was an extended silence. Michael stared through the windscreen. *'Have you managed to find out who was responsible for taking these drugs?'*

'Not exactly.'

'What the bloody hell's that supposed to mean?'

'I've been making enquiries,' Crosby said. *'There may be others involved.'*

'Others?'

'You don't really need to know the details.'

'Yes I bloody well do!'

Crosby had wanted to avoid this. He knew what Michael's reaction would be.

'Well?' his son persisted.

The ex-detective gave a resigned shrug. *'There's a number of possibilities,'* he said. *'An IRA splinter group. A business on the south coast. The Italian Mafia. A former Scenes-of-Crime officer.'* Crosby waited for the outburst.

'Jesus Christ!' Michael turned to face him again. *'Can you hear yourself? Calmly reeling off all these organisations. This is not part of my world.'*

'Neither is it mine!' Crosby snapped. *'None of this is my fault.'*

Michael shook his head. *'What about this poor kid that's been abducted. The police will have to be informed that Lucy Roberts might be responsible.'*

'They'll know,' Crosby answered. *'I unofficially sounded out an ex-colleague with all of this a few days ago. She'll have heard the news and passed it on somehow.'*

'You're sure about that?'

'Positive!'

'And will this ex-colleague include your name?'

'I don't think she'd include either of our names,' Crosby said. *'It would have repercussions for both of us.'*

'And what if it's not Lucy Roberts?' Michael asked. *'Where does that leave us?'*

'We could take it to the police,' Crosby said. *'They might offer us protection.'*

'And they might not,' Michael was quick to answer. *'Are we supposed to just carry on with this hanging over us?'*

'You can't.'

'What then?'

'I think you should take the whole family away.'

Michael's head came up. *'Are you serious?'*

'These organisations are ruthless,' Crosby said. *'It won't end here if we're a target for them.'*

'And where the hell are we supposed to go?'

'I know a place on the Isle of Wight.'

Michael nodded. *'A bloody safe house.'*

'The police no longer use it,' Crosby said. *'I know the couple there. They'd help me.'*

'And when is this supposed to happen?'

'Tonight.'

Michael shook his head. *'That's not possible.'*

'You make it possible. They will try again.'

Michael glanced up at his son's bedroom window. *'How long are we supposed to stay at this place?'*

'Until it's safe to come home,' Crosby replied. *'Any communication will have to be minimal. I'll pass messages through my contact. We can't use our mobiles.'*

Michael looked unsure. *'I don't know.'*

'You don't have a choice.' Crosby pushed a little harder. *'I'll fix everything up this afternoon. You'll stay in a hotel overnight. There'll be a hire car parked outside tomorrow morning. I can pick up your Volvo from the hotel if you leave me a spare set of keys.'*

'And you can arrange all of this today?'

Crosby nodded. *'I'll book an early ferry crossing. You'll be travelling under assumed names. I can give you all the details later this evening.'*

'Angela will need to be persuaded.'

'Tell her what the alternative is.'

'Will mum be coming with us?' his son asked.

Crosby pinched the bridge of his nose. Now he felt a headache developing. *'You'll need to speak with her. She won't listen to me. I don't want any of the family left here.'*

'What about you?'

'I'll have to stay here and see it through.'

'I'm not happy about it.'

'Whereas I'm bloody ecstatic,' the ex-detective said. *'You need to pack now and drive over to Hawthorne Rise. I'll have made the arrangements by then and your mother can pick up what she needs.'*

Michael opened the car door. He turned to look at his father. *'I can't believe you've put us in this situation.'*

'I'm not responsible for the bloody situation!' Crosby snapped back at him.

'You never are.' His son left, slamming the car door forcibly behind him. Crosby punched the heel of his fist into the car's dashboard fascia. It probably hurt. He didn't feel it. The Mondeo's engine was turned-over and gunned with some venom as Crosby reversed out into the road at speed.

Aquileia Catering: Weymouth: Friday 21st October 2011: 6.00 p.m.

Penny Zardelli was still at her desk. The sun had set some fifteen minutes ago. It was now dark outside. Hannah Lewis knocked on the executive director's door and looked in. *'I'm just about to leave, Ms Zardelli. Is there anything else you require?'*

'*I don't think so, Hannah.*' The executive director glanced at her watch. '*Has everyone else left?*'

'*Yes,*' the receptionist replied. '*Would you like me to switch off the lights out here?*'

'*You can leave them on. I'll be another hour or so yet.*'

'*What about the alarm system?*'

'*I'll see to it,*' the executive director answered impatiently. She turned back to her computer screen.

'*Goodnight then.*' The receptionist pulled a face as she left.

Penny Zardelli waved a hand. She didn't bother to look up. Shortly afterwards, *Aquileia Catering's* outer door clicked shut as Hannah Lewis left the building. A few moments later her small Fiesta was reversed from its parking slot, the car's headlights momentarily sweeping across Penny Zardelli's half-open blinds. The executive director didn't notice. She continued to work quietly at her desk.

A wall-clock ticked around to six-fifteen. '*Shit!*' the executive director swore. Her office had suddenly been plunged into darkness. It was only two months previously the whole area had suffered a similar loss of power. She stood up from her computer. The room was pitch-black. '*Shit!*' she repeated with even more feeling. It was vital the half-completed spread sheets were available for a meeting tomorrow morning.

Her eyes gradually adjusted to the darkness. Illumination from a nearby street lamp slowly filtered its way through the half-open blinds, providing a dim, shadowy light. *Aquileia's* executive director felt her way across towards the office door, continuing to swear intermittently and loudly at whoever was responsible for the loss of power. She frowned. It suddenly registered that the street lamp outside was still working. An involuntary shiver was dismissed. *Aquileia's* wiring system had obviously short-circuited somewhere and activated one of the trip switches. She made her way carefully through a gloomy reception area towards the building's main fuse box.

Penny Zardelli instinctively sensed movement coming from behind her, unable to react quickly enough. A gloved hand clamped itself over her mouth and nose. She struggled to draw breath, the distinctive smell of kid-leather filling her nostrils. *'Don't move a fucking muscle!'* The man's voice was deep, muffled. *'It's razor sharp, with a needle point.'* Penny Zardelli could feel the thin length of blade, cold against the front of her throat. *'I'll remove my hand,'* the voice said from behind her. *'If you scream then your vocal chords will be severed. Is that fucking clear?'*

Penny Zardelli could hardly breathe. She nodded. The gloved hand was removed. It took a few moments for *Aquileia's* executive director to suck in enough air to get her breathing under control. She began to shake. A forearm wrapped itself around Penny Zardelli's neck. The thin-bladed knife was removed from her throat. A brief pause. She felt the knife's point underneath her skirt, gently caressing an inner thigh. It slid further up between her legs. She tensed. *'Easy now,'* the man said. His breathing quickened. He allowed the knife's tip to play around the woman's genital area, scraping it lightly against the material of her tights and panties. The man laughed. He returned the knife to her throat. *'Your visitor earlier. What was the nature of his business?'*

'I've had three appointments today.' Penny Zardelli was recovering from her initial shock. He was asking questions. Think ahead. Don't panic. Keep him talking.

'Don't get too fucking cute,' the voice hissed in her ear. *'Your last caller. What did he want?'* His knife pressed a little harder against her Adam's apple.

'Detective Inspector Crosby. West Midlands Police.'

The man grasped Penny Zardelli's hair and pulled it back hard, laying her throat wide open. *'I didn't fucking ask who it was! Final warning. My patience is running out.'*

Penny Zardelli had stalled as far as she dare. *'I previously owned a holiday farm in Wales. My ex-husband and my daughter were* responsible for stockpiling heroin there to supply a nearby housing estate. The police investigation cleared me of any involvement in the operation they were running.'

'I'm listening,' the man said.

Aquileia's executive director sensed her attacker knew most of this already. He wanted more information about the missing heroin. She had to gain his confidence. 'My daughter was recently released from prison. When she went to recover drugs that had been left hidden at the farm they'd disappeared. Lucy made contact with this Detective Inspector Crosby about it.'

'Why would your daughter contact the police about missing drugs that she was responsible for storing in the first place?'

'I don't know. He wouldn't tell me.'

'What does your daughter say?'

'I haven't spoken to her for three years,' the executive director replied. 'We do not have a close relationship. I don't know where she is.'

The knife's point deliberately nicked Penny Zardelli's ear lobe, drawing a pinprick of blood. 'Are you responsible for the missing heroin?'

'I've already told you.' Penny Zardelli tried to pull her head back. 'I was cleared of any involvement in their operation. They acted alone. My daughter hasn't confronted me about it because she knows that I wasn't told anything.'

Several seconds elapsed as the man seemed to consider Penny Zardelli's answer. She held her breath. A telephone rang. 'Leave it!' he instructed. Penny Zardelli waited for Aquileia's answering device to cut in. The ringing continued for a few seconds before it stopped. Hannah had obviously forgotten to activate the system. 'That will be my husband,' she said. 'He knows I'm still at work.'

The man didn't seem overly concerned. Penny Zardelli felt his free hand work up underneath her blouse. 'I wouldn't like to think our meeting has been a complete waste of time,' he said. Adrenalin and fear pumped through the executive director in equal measures. She could feel his erection pushing against her from behind. Try to keep calm. The man eased up her bra. *'Nice tits.'* He laughed, squeezing a nipple between his thumb and forefinger. She winced.

'On your back!' the man instructed.

'We have money in the safe. I'll open it for you.'

'On your fucking back!' The voice louder, insistent.

There was little point in resisting. She lowered herself down to the floor. *'I won't report it. You don't have to hurt me. Our business would be affected by any adverse publicity.'*

'Shut up!' The man dropped to his knees, the knife remaining in contact with Penny Zardelli's throat. It was the first time she'd had to face him. Only his eyes and mouth were visible, through slits cut into a woollen balaclava. He pulled up her skirt.

'Fuck you!' she hissed.

The man laughed again. *'You don't mind if we skip the fore-play. I'm on a tight schedule.'* He hooked the knife's point into Penny Zardelli's tights and ripped them apart. Pulling at the waistband of her panties he sliced through its thin material before returning his knife to the woman's throat. After unzipping himself the man freed his erect penis and straddled across her in a kneeling position.

'I want you to use something,' Penny Zardelli said to him.

The man waved a condom in front of her face. *'A boy scout. We always come prepared.'* He tore at the wrapper with his teeth.

Penny Zardelli turned her head.

'Put it on!' the man instructed.

She hesitated.

'Put the fucking thing on!' he said, raising his voice. *'I don't want my DNA swimming around inside you.'*

Penny Zardelli felt for the tip of his erection and rolled the condom over it. *'Done that a few times have you?'* he said. The knife remained at her throat. He used his other hand to force the woman open. She winced. *'You're hurting me.'* He lowered himself, pushing his erection hard into her. It didn't take him long to approach a climax. His breathing became more ragged as his thrusts quickened. *'You're probably enjoying this more than me.'* The man's voice was thick and laboured in Penny Zardelli's ear.

'Hurry up and finish will you,' she said.

Penny Zardelli's apparent indifference caused him to orgasm. He ejaculated abruptly, collapsing on top of her. The man groaned for several seconds as his genital muscles continued to contract. She bore his weight with difficulty, remaining completely still, apprehensive and unsure as to what might happen next. The man stood up. He didn't bother to remove his condom, casually tucking away the semi-erect penis and zipping up his trousers. Penny Zardelli's pulse raced as the man looked down on her. *'You don't move for thirty minutes,'* he said. *'I'll be watching from outside. Do you understand?'* She nodded.

The man left in a matter of seconds. Penny Zardelli remained where she was, controlling her breathing, relieved to be alive. She turned her head towards the glass entrance doors. A shadowy outline stood outside. *Aquileia's* executive director focused her attention on the silhouette. It didn't move. Ten minutes passed. As she considered edging across towards her receptionist's telephone the figure suddenly disappeared. Penny Zardelli forced herself to move. Although there was no sound of a car starting up she sensed that he'd gone. Managing to crawl on her hands and knees towards the outer door she reached up and activated its lock. Still unable to raise herself upright she remained on all fours, making it into the reception area's small washroom. Leaning over the toilet bowl, *Aquileia's* executive director splattered a stream of vomit into the water below.

She slumped back against the wall in a sitting position, rivulets of cold perspiration running down her face and neck. A few minutes elapsed. Penny Zardelli recovered sufficiently enough to haul herself up. On very unsteady legs she made her way across to the building's fuse box and pushed all of its switches back to their *'On'* position.

Light flooded *Aquileia's* interior, allowing Penny Zardelli to find her way back through the reception area.

Once inside her office she crossed to a mobile drinks trolley and poured herself a large cognac. After downing the brandy in one swallow she poured another. Penny Zardelli was still trembling and feeling nauseous – not because she'd been assaulted and raped – that was just a physical act. She had often used detached, unemotional sex as a means to an end in the past. What Penny Zardelli couldn't deal with at this moment was the fact that many rapes also result in the victim's murder. She gradually regained control of herself. *Aquileia's* executive director had always prided herself on being able to deal with any situation. She opened the lid on a box of long thin cigars and lit one up, dragging its acrid smoke deep into her lungs before downing the second glass of brandy.

Ten minutes later and Penny Zardelli's emotions had turned to anger. She reached down to remove her ripped tights and underwear. The soiled garments were stuffed into a plastic carrier bag displaying the *Aquileia Catering* logo. There were decisions to make. She would not be reporting her rape to the police. It was out of the question. Some of their Olympic contracts were still being finalised, and *Aquileia Catering* would quickly find itself out of favour at the first sign of sensationalist newspaper headlines. Penny Zardelli's husband would also remain unaware of the assault – that could become far too complicated. The rape would be dealt with however.

Aquileia's executive director first rang her husband. He didn't seem overly concerned that she'd be late home. She punched in another number. It was answered almost immediately. *'Giorgio? It's Ms Zardelli. Does my husband require your services this evening?'*

'No, Signora.' The voice was rough, uncultured.

'I want to see you in my office at seven o'clock.' Penny Zardelli replaced the phone without waiting for an answer. She picked up a small, discreet business card from her desk. It had been taken from the man's pocket at his point of climax. She slipped the card into a desk

drawer. What Penny Zardelli really craved for at this moment was a hot bath and an hour to soak in it. She'd have to make do with the office shower however, before returning to her half-completed spreadsheets. *Aquileia's* executive director had never been a woman to allow emotion or feelings get in the way of life's practicalities. She may have just been used by some inbred degenerate to sexually relieve himself, but that wouldn't be allowed to compromise or interfere with *Aquileia Catering's* ongoing business and future reputation. And she'd also sleep tonight. Strength of character had always been her mainstay in life.

Friday 21ˢᵗ October 2011: 6.30 p.m.

On a cold afternoon, after another never-ending school day, his bedroom was a familiar, welcoming haven. The five-year-old loved its bright, colourful wallpaper – *Spiderman* and *The Hulk* looking down on him as he watched television from the small rocking chair – a birthday present from his grandparents.

Billy wasn't in his bedroom tonight. He was in a room without carpet, the walls bare and undecorated. It was cold, unfriendly, and he hadn't eaten. His mum always allowed him milk and biscuits before tea – not that Billy could have managed them in his current state – he was more frightened than hungry – and in urgent need of a toilet. The boy couldn't move either. After being thrown onto a lumpy mattress earlier that afternoon both his feet and hands had been tied together. Billy had stopped trying to free himself over an hour ago – the effort too painful – a thin, knotted cord biting deeper into his skin every time he tried to pull it apart.

As darkness fell beyond a curtainless window the five-year-old became ever more terrified. There was no light in his room. He began to see dark shapes and shadows dancing on the walls – disappearing then re-appearing in several different forms. Billy pulled a grubby blanket up and over himself as best he could. It wasn't like his warm, familiar duvet at home. The blanket made his arms itch. It also had a funny smell.

The five-year-old's confused, immature mind couldn't work out if he'd be in trouble. Although Billy had been warned by his mum not to talk with strangers, there'd also been numerous instructions telling him not to disobey any of his teachers. It had been difficult. The woman who approached him in the playground said she was Miss Jones, a new teacher. But she was also a stranger. The new teacher told him that his mother was waiting in their car outside the school gates. Billy did think it was a little odd. He usually caught the school bus home. The teacher was insistent however, and his mum had told him never to answer back. All that Billy could remember about Miss Jones now was the long blonde hair, and a scarf she'd held over her mouth because of the cold. That was what she'd told him anyway.

Billy didn't know what he could do to make everything right. Tears began rolling down his cheeks. They blurred his vision. Whenever the five-year-old was upset he always reached for Snowy – a constant bed-time companion for as long as he could remember. Snowy was his polar bear, the familiar white furry coat always a comfort in times of upset. Henrietta, the family's excitable golden Labrador, would also be wondering where he was. She usually lay outside his bedroom, scratching and whining, because Billy often closed the door on her. The five-year-old wished Henrietta was outside his door now. He could hear raised voices coming up through the floorboards from downstairs. Billy couldn't shut them out.

'Do we have to?'

'There's no fucking choice!'

'I had my face covered.'

'The little bastard might still recognise you.'

'Well, I'm not doing it.'

'Well someone's got to fucking do it! We can't risk keeping him here.'

114

Billy managed to pull the thin blanket over his head. The voices were indistinct now, but he knew they were still talking about him, and they'd been using bad words. The boy automatically reached out for Snowy – before realising he wasn't there. Billy cried out for his mum.

'*Shut the fuck up!*' someone shouted loudly from downstairs.

It made him wet the bed. Now he'd be in trouble for that as well. As he continued to lie there the warmth of his pee soon turned cold. It made him shiver. Billy started to cry again. He huddled deeper into the blanket and pretended to be at home in his bedroom.

Aquileia Catering: Weymouth: Friday 21st October 2011: 7.00 p.m.

Penny Zardelli heard the car as it turned into *Aquileia Catering's* car park. She left her chair and crossed to the window. Through the blind's semi-open slats she watched Giorgio Messina exit her husband's Rolls-Royce. *Aquileia's* executive director went through to the reception area and unlocked its outer door. Messina stood in front of her. He made no move to step inside, awaiting further instruction from Penny Zardelli.

'*Don't just bloody stand there,*' she said impatiently.

'*Si, Signora.*' Messina stepped cautiously inside. The man took off his chauffeur's cap as he'd been taught. He twisted it nervously in both hands as *Aquileia's* executive director looked him up and down.

Giorgio Messina was from peasant Sicilian stock, his hulking physique hewn from generations of fishermen and farm labourers. Enrico Zardelli had brought him across to the UK three years ago – '*a distant relative,*' he'd told his wife. '*I take care of my family. He can handle cars and speaks a passable amount of English.*' Penny Zardelli knew the man was hired muscle, employed to sort out problems that required a physical presence. She was not privy to what these problems were. *Aquileia's* executive director had been told it was an aspect of the business that didn't concern her.

115

'There's a situation I need you to deal with.' Penny Zardelli's tone was brusque. She'd fully recovered from the assault on her. *'My husband is to have no knowledge of it. Do you understand?'*

'Signora?' Messina looked confused. The Sicilian didn't usually take orders from his employer's wife.

'Don't look so bloody vacant.' Penny Zardelli dispensed with any preamble. *'A man broke into the building less than an hour ago and raped me.'*

The chauffeur wasn't sure he'd heard correctly. *'Raped you, Signora?'*

'Jesus Christ!' the executive director said. *'I don't have the time to repeat myself. It isn't bloody difficult. I've just been raped. Do you understand?'*

The Sicilian flinched. *'Si, Signora.'* His face suggested he didn't understand at all. This was not how a woman behaved after she'd been raped.

'There are a number of tasks I wish you to carry out in relation to this,' Penny Zardelli said.

Messina frowned. *'Scusi, Signora?'*

'I need your help to track this man down.'

The chauffeur looked hesitant. His manner indicated it was not something he wanted to be involved in. *'We speak with your husband, Signora.'*

'Give me bloody strength!' Aquileia's executive director took a step closer to the Sicilian. *'I repeat,'* she said. *'My husband will not be told anything about this. Neither will the police be informed.'*

Messina didn't trust himself to answer.

'Any negative publicity,' Penny Zardelli continued, *'would have an adverse effect on this company. You and I will deal with the situation.'*

'Me, Signora?'

'You, Giorgio.' *Aquileia's* executive director passed the small business card to him. *'I believe the man who attacked me worked for this company.'*

'I'm not sure what you want of me, Signora.'

'I've checked out their website,' Penny Zardelli said to him. *'They are a small operation. I want a report on all their staff. It should be fairly straightforward to identify who was responsible for raping me.'*

'I can do that, Signora.'

'I shall then require you to kill him and dispose of the body.'

'Kill him?' It took the Sicilian by surprise. He shook his head. *'Is not possible, Signora.'*

'Jesus Christ!' the executive director snapped at him. *'I know what you do for my husband. Your job description includes dealing with awkward customers. I doubt that involves polite conversation over long business lunches.'*

'I give this man a beating for you, Signora.'

'You'll do as I say.' Penny Zardelli waved a hand at him. *'Your country virtually invented the family code of honour. We're just putting an animal down. It's not bloody difficult.'*

Messina tried again. *'Is a matter for the polizia, Signora.'* His voice betrayed a twinge of desperation.

'This is becoming tiresome, Giorgio,' Penny Zardelli said, *'and it's making me angry. Do not mention the bloody police again. Our Olympic contracts will not be put in jeopardy because some low life used me to physically relieve himself.'*

Messina looked thoroughly unhappy. *'I cannot do this thing, Signora.'*

'I will explain to my husband that you are assisting me in a marketing exercise,' the executive director said briskly. *'You will be well paid.'*

'I already have money, Signora.'

Penny Zardelli didn't want to take this elsewhere. Had she chosen wrongly? *Aquileia's* executive director appraised him. She was used to getting her own way. *'If this man is disposed of,'* Penny Zardelli said. *'I am willing to pay for the service by having sex with you.'*

The Sicilian wasn't sure he'd heard correctly. *'I do not understand, Signora.'*

'Again you don't understand.' The executive director shook her head. *'I am offering to fuck with you, Giorgio. Does your rustic, peasant dialect need a translation for that?'*

Messina hesitated. He looked even more desperate. The chauffeur's eyes darted around the reception area, as if a trap was being set for him. *'Someone is here, Signora. I think you test me.'*

'It's not a fucking test, Giorgio! There's no one else here.'

The Sicilian still looked unsure. He was tempted though. A physical coupling with *Aquileia's* executive director was an image that Messina had often fantasised about. Penny Zardelli saw the hesitation. *'You will be paid in advance,'* she said. *'It will occur only once. At a time and place of my choosing. Are you absolutely clear as to what has been agreed?'*

Giorgio Messina nodded, although he couldn't actually recall agreeing to anything. The executive director turned and headed back towards her office. *'You will wait here until I'm ready to leave,'* she instructed.

'Si, Signora.' Messina felt a stirring as he watched her cross the room. It wasn't the first time that he'd experienced an erection after being in the same room as his employer's wife.

The Italian lowered himself into a nearby chair, still not entirely clear about the situation he found himself in. The woman said she'd just been raped and was offering to pay for his services by having sex with him. He shook his head. It wasn't like this back in the remote fishing village he came from. Messina studied the small printed business card he'd been given, laboriously reading aloud each word.

Crosby paced his kitchen floor. All the arrangements had been completed on-line over an hour ago but his family were still not here. He wanted them away from Little Wintermore as soon as possible and into their hotel. The ex-detective continued to pace, willing their arrival, unable to settle. He'd telephoned Michael twice now – who'd reacted impatiently to his calls. Crosby moved across to the kitchen window. *'Where the bloody hell are you?'*

He had to wait another ten minutes before his son's Volvo appeared around the cul-de-sac's top corner. Crosby hurried from the kitchen to let them in. His wife was first through the door. She swept past without acknowledging him. There were no words of greeting from his son and daughter-in-law either. At least his grandson was smiling up at him. *'We're going on holiday, Gramps,'* Jack said. *'Are you coming with us?'*

Crosby picked him up. *'I'm too busy. We'll go somewhere in the summer.'*

'You've retired,' Jack replied. *'My dad said you're on one long holiday anyway.'*

The ex-detective put his grandson back down. *'And you're becoming far too smart.'* They went through to the lounge. A chocolate biscuit was mentioned. Angela took her son's hand and they disappeared into the kitchen. Doreen Crosby shot her husband another look before going upstairs. Crosby ushered his son through to their conservatory. He picked up an A4-sized manila envelope from the table and passed it to him.

'All your instructions are in there,' the ex-detective said. *'Ferry arrangements. Names you'll be travelling under. Car hire details. Location of the safe house. Hotel reservations for tonight.'*

Michael took the envelope. He handed over spare keys to the house and his Volvo. *'I'll pick up your car from the hotel tomorrow,'*

Crosby said. *'Have you cleared everything at work and with the school?'*

'Yes.' Michael opened the envelope and took out two sheets of printed instructions. *'How long is this situation likely to last?'*

'A couple of weeks.' The answer lacked conviction.

'You don't know then.' Michael began to read through the instructions.

Crosby pointed to a name. *'This man will meet you at the safe house. All contact is to be through him. He will let you know when it's safe to return home.'*

'And if something happens to you?' Michael asked.

'It won't,' Crosby replied.

Michael didn't bother to stay and argue the point. Crosby followed him through into the lounge. His wife was struggling half-way down the stairs with two suitcases. *'Do you want a hand with those?'* he asked.

'No!'

'Go ahead and break your bloody neck then,' Crosby muttered to himself.

His wife completed the final few stairs and handed both suitcases to her son. When Angela and Jack re-joined them from the kitchen they all made their way outside. Michael wasted no time in getting his family into the Volvo. *'See you, Gramps,'* Jack said as he was being strapped into his car-seat. No one else spoke. Michael quickly reversed off the drive.

A huge weight lifted from Crosby's shoulders as he watched the car exit Hawthorne Rise. The relief was almost physical. Just one other thing that needed sorting out tonight. He went back inside the house to pick up his car keys – re-emerging a few minutes later. An Audi Quattro entered the cul-de-sac at speed – pulling up in a squeal of brakes behind his Mondeo. DC Grace Taylor stormed from her car and marched up the drive towards Crosby. *'What the hell's going on, Frank?'*

'I've been expecting you,' the ex-detective replied. 'Shall we do this inside?'

'Are you alone?'

'Yes.'

Grace Taylor walked straight past him and into the house. Crosby followed. He was getting pissed off with people just brushing past him. Taylor was waiting for him in the lounge. 'Do you want to sit down?' Crosby asked.

'No I don't want to bloody well sit down!'

Grace Taylor was angry, almost shouting. 'You came to see me about Lucy Roberts. The woman was threatening your family because of drugs that were taken from Dryffed's Farm.'

'Yes.' Crosby would have to let her anger run its course.

'Now a five-year-old boy has been abducted from your grandson's school.'

'Yes.'

'Too much of a bloody coincidence!'

'I don't think it's a coincidence,' Crosby replied.

Taylor pointed a finger at him. 'There's a child's life in danger. What have you done about it?'

'I've had someone making background checks.'

'I'm not talking about fucking background checks, Frank!'

'If you'd let me finish,' Crosby said. 'He was able to trace Lucy's current address from her car registration. It came through this afternoon.'

'And you've passed this to the police?'

'Yes.'

'Anonymously I suppose.'

'There's still a few public telephone boxes around.'

'Still not good enough, Frank.' The policewoman's anger continued. 'They should have been alerted about the possibility of this when Lucy first made contact with you.'

'I told you what she was threatening,' Crosby answered. 'You agreed to keep quiet about it.'

Grace Taylor's eyes snapped open. 'Don't you dare try to pass your fucking guilt onto me. I told you not to handle this yourself.'

The remark had been unnecessary. Crosby held up both hands. 'I shouldn't have said that. It's an impossible situation. I'm just trying to protect my family.'

'And now there's another family suffering.'

Crosby moved across to the settee. He had to sit down. 'This shouldn't have happened. Lucy said she'd give me a week.'

'Well it has bloody happened,' the policewoman said, 'and you'd better hope they find this poor kid alive.'

'Have they put together a specialist abduction team yet?'

Grace Taylor nodded. 'I've also passed Lucy's name to them.'

'I thought you would.'

'I've managed to keep our names out of it,' Taylor said.

'I appreciate that.'

The policewoman looked down at him. 'It wasn't done for your benefit, Frank. I'm also in big trouble if they find out I had prior knowledge of this.'

'What if Lucy wasn't responsible?' Crosby said. 'This drugs syndicate may have taken matters into their own hands.'

'All the more reason for you not to have been involved in the first place.' Taylor shook her head. 'I had a shotgun levelled at me four years ago because you made an error of judgement. I hope this isn't another.' She slumped down on the settee next to him. 'It's a bloody mess.' A short silence ensued. Crosby sensed the policewoman's anger was subsiding. She turned to look at him. 'You helped me a lot when we worked together, Frank. I've never forgotten it. But this shouldn't have happened.'

'I didn't intend to personally involve you,' Crosby said.

The policewoman shrugged. *'It's not your fault. I don't know what I'd have done in your position. But if anything happens to this child will you be able to live with it?'*

Crosby's head dropped. *'Probably not.'* He began to massage one side of his forehead.

'You don't look well,' the policewoman said sympathetically. *'Your health's suffering.'* She moved closer to him, laying a hand on his arm. *'I don't want this to affect our friendship.'*

Crosby put his hand over hers. Taylor misinterpreted it. She reached around the back of his neck and drew him closer. He pulled back.

'Jesus Christ!' The policewoman was immediately to her feet. *'What the fuck am I doing?'*

'It's OK, Grace.'

'It's not OK. I'm fucking embarrassed!'

'You were just being supportive. It's fine. Forget about it.'

Taylor walked towards the door. *'I'm leaving.'*

Crosby was slow to his feet. Taylor was already in her car by the time he made it outside. She wasted no time in reversing off the drive. He watched her *Quattro* disappear around the cul-de-sac's far corner. *'Shit!'* the ex-detective muttered. Another bloody complication to deal with. Only his initial surprise had made him pull away in the first place. Probably just as well. If it hadn't been for his current state of mind he would have found it difficult to turn down what might have followed.

As Crosby went back to lock his front door he felt a spot of rain. It increased to a steady drizzle during the course of his thirty-mile journey to Oxley village. By the time he'd reached his destination a howling wind was driving the rain almost horizontal. Crosby spotted flashing blue lights from high ground just outside the village. He immediately stopped and parked-up. After looking down on the scene for several minutes he three-point turned his Mondeo across the narrow road and headed back towards Hawthorne Rise.

Crosby had wanted to make sure the Renault Laguna's address was being investigated – but if Lucy Roberts and Rose Cavendish were responsible for the abduction of Billy Lucas then it was unlikely they would be still be around. He questioned the logic of them taking the schoolboy. It made little or no sense. Had they been forced into passing on his name already? Crosby couldn't focus on it – the guilt he felt for Billy Lucas was clouding his mind, continuing to weigh heavily on him.

CHAPTER 9

Saturday 22nd October 2011: 5.00 a.m.

They came for him at five o'clock in the morning. Billy had cried himself into a fitful sleep last night, but he was frightened again now. They untied his feet and hands, then gagged and blindfolded him. The five-year-old tried to tell them he'd wet the bed. They ignored him. His slight frame was no weight at all – easy enough to man-handle down the stairs and out into a bitterly cold morning. Billy was stood down. He shivered in just his school uniform. A car door was opened and the boy shoved unceremoniously inside – made to lay full length across the back seat. Two blankets were thrown over the top of him. After its doors were slammed shut the vehicle started almost immediately. Both sets of wipers were flicked on to clear light, overnight rain from the windscreen. Billy lay quietly in the back, unable to move, his heart thumping. He knew something bad was about to happen.

The journey lasted about twenty minutes. *'We can do it here,'* Billy heard one of them say. When the car slowed to a halt he tried to curl himself into a tight ball. It made little difference. He was dragged from the back seat and thrown out, his head striking the ground. The impact dazed him. His teeth began to chatter. Several minutes ticked by as he waited for something to happen. When it became too cold for him to lay there any longer the five-year-old cautiously pulled at his gag and pushed up the blindfold. He slowly opened his eyes.

Billy found himself stretched out on a wet pavement, in a shallow puddle, his blue school jumper and grey trousers thoroughly soaked. Although it was still dark, the hazy, orange glow from a nearby street lamp provided enough light to tell the boy he was in unfamiliar surroundings. His first instinct was to run, but in what direction. Billy looked about him. There were bright lights in the distance and he was naturally drawn towards them.

Minutes later he was at the entrance to a shopping precinct. The boy recognised some of its shops. He tried with difficulty to recall previous trips there. Had they walked? Was it by car? Last night's ordeal had fogged his memory. As he wandered aimlessly, the injury to his head began to throb. A few early morning passers-by started to appear. They were giving him odd looks. When someone approached him he broke into a run. Billy had learnt his lesson that all strangers should be avoided. A woman watched him leave the precinct. She reached into a coat pocket for her mobile.

The five-year-old continued running until he couldn't draw breath. A quick glance behind told him that no one was following. He looked around. Instinct must have guided him to the housing estate he found himself in. That was John Dulman's home, one of his friends from school. It gave Billy renewed energy, taking him into the next street and more familiar territory. Ten minutes later the boy was looking at his own house. A police car parked outside told him he was likely to be in big trouble though.

Billy reached his front door and pushed open the letterbox. *'Mum!'* he shouted through it. Henrietta started to bark as the boy waited. A woman with blonde hair opened the door. Another stranger. It almost made Billy turn and start running again. Then his Mum came flying down the stairs and wrapped both her arms around him. She was shouting and crying at the same time. *'Where have you been? Are you hurt?'* The blonde-haired woman was talking into her mobile. *'Am I in trouble?'* Billy wanted to know. The woman tried to prise his Mum away, saying something about his clothes.

Then someone opened the kitchen door and Henrietta raced out at full speed, knocking him backwards. Billy just lay there, allowing the dog to lick his face all over. More people appeared in the hallway. He buried his face deep into Henrietta's fur. Billy's mother dropped to her knees and wrapped her arms around both of them.

A distinctly unfriendly dawn broke over the island's east coast a few minutes before seven o'clock. Its murky, dismal light revealed ragged cloud formations, racing each other at breakneck speed across a fragmented sky. Three figures, balanced precariously on a cliff edge, faced out into Alum Bay. The buffeting force-eight gale tore and whipped at their night attire as they waited. Clearly visible, four hundred feet below them, was a familiar, iconic landmark – 'The Needles' – its three distinctive chalk stacks rising up steeply from a heavy Atlantic swell. Another figure, male, stood a little way back from the cliff edge. A black scarf covered his lower face. He wore blood-stained army fatigues, an Uzi submachine gun dangled from his left hip. Alongside him stood a small boy, barefoot, wearing thin, cotton pyjamas.

'*Walk forward,*' the gunman barked at the three figures.

Crosby's grandson looked up at the man. '*They'll fall,*' he said.

The man in army fatigues pulled down his black scarf to reveal himself as Zamir Veseli. '*I also watch my family die,*' he replied. '*I was ten years old.*'

'*I'm only five,*' said Jack.

The Kosovan nodded and smiled. '*Will make you a man.*' Veseli casually lifted his submachine gun and pointed it directly at the boy's family. He turned to wink at Jack – unleashing a full magazine of nine millimetre cartridges at the rate of six hundred rounds-per-minute. The automatic gunfire was muted, almost noiseless, instantly snatched away by the wind and swept out to sea.

Veseli took the five-year-old's hand. They both stepped forward, able to watch all three bodies cartwheel and somersault their way through the air. In a matter of seconds the boy's family had smashed into a line of rocks directly below him, at over one hundred miles-an-hour.

'*See,*' the gunman said. '*They feel no pain now.*'

'But they're dead,' Jack said.

The Kosovan shrugged. *'Is life.'*

Veseli snapped another magazine into the Uzi's pistol grip, before swinging it back around towards the boy. *'Sorry, Jack,'* he said. *'Is not my fault.'* The submachine gun chattered its death rattle once more. Veseli dropped his weapon next to the small, lifeless body, tears running down both his cheeks. *'See what you did!'* he shouted up at the sky. *'See what you fucking did!'*

Crosby woke with a start, continuing to scream abuse at the ceiling above him. It took the ex-detective a few moments to stop shouting. He gradually came to. The nightmare only served to remind him that his family were still at risk. Crosby attempted to stand. He'd fallen asleep in a chair at his landing window because of noises outside – something or someone waking him just after two o'clock in the morning. He'd dragged a chair to his landing and monitored the cul-de-sac for visitors, falling asleep in the process.

The ex-detective unravelled his body in easy stages – fighting the stiffness – forcing himself into an upright position. He leant forward against the window ledge to look out on Hawthorne Rise, its collection of near identical properties taking gradual shape in the early dawn. Nothing untoward. Crosby moved across to the bathroom for a much-needed shower. After dressing he headed downstairs, flicked a switch on the kettle and dropped two tea-bags into his mug. A slice of bread still sat in the toaster from yesterday morning – his appetite almost non-existent now. Crosby took the mug of tea through to his conservatory and turned on a small radio. At eight o'clock the station announced its hourly news bulletin. *'Good morning. This is Colin Berry with the BBC news at eight o'clock. Our main headlines. A five-year-old boy abducted from outside his school yesterday morning has been found safe and well.'* Crosby was immediately out of his chair to turn up the volume. *'Initial reports indicate the boy returned to his family home at five-thirty this morning. A statement from West Midlands Police is expected later today.'*

Crosby took a deep breath and slowly exhaled. *'Thank Christ for that!'* he said out loud. It lifted him. The relief was huge. It renewed his energy levels, gave him the incentive to leave immediately and continue his enquiries. There were still people to be checked out – one of them being the agent-caretaker who'd been employed to look after *Dryffed's Farm* in-between holiday lets. It would mean a trip to Wales at some point. The boy's safe return added an extra zip to Crosby's movements. He switched off his radio and headed for the front door.

An hour later and Crosby was deep inside the Sixfields Housing Estate again, pulling into ParkGate's run down shopping centre. He manoeuvred his Mondeo into the same parking slot he'd occupied on Thursday morning. Zamir Veseli had not yet arrived at his trading post. Crosby sat back and waited.

He watched a steady stream of estate residents using the nearby walk-through into ParkGate's shopping area. Most of those that passed him were young mothers – blank unsmiling faces – already weighed down by life and the children trailing in their wake. One particular girl looked no more than eighteen years of age. She struggled past him, manoeuvring a baby's pushchair with one hand, two toddlers clinging to her coat. It was a depressing, isolated scene. Crosby felt her hopelessness.

Zamir Veseli arrived with his BMX outriders at ten o'clock. He spotted the ex-detective immediately but didn't acknowledge him, his eyes sweeping the car park for unexpected visitors. Crosby allowed a few minutes before getting out of his car. The Kosovan looked up at Crosby's approach. *'Sergeant Frank! We finish our business this fine morning.'*

Crosby nodded.

The dealer snapped his fingers. One of Veseli's young runners free-wheeled across to Crosby. He looked about ten years old. The boy withdrew a folded square of thin, black cloth from inside his zipped top. Veseli's fingers snapped again. A pungent smell of light machine oil filled the air as his runner unfolded the square of black cloth. A

Walther PPK handgun was held up for the ex-detective's inspection. Veseli waved a hand. *'You look, Sergeant Frank. Is not used.'*

Crosby gave the handgun a cursory glance. He nodded. The firearm was re-folded back into its square of black cloth and handed over to him. He stuffed it into a jacket pocket. Veseli beckoned another BMX rider forward. A thin, plastic carrier-bag was unhooked from his handlebars and passed to the ex-detective. Veseli pointed at the carrier-bag. *'I have for you ammunition and silencer.'* Crosby reached inside his jacket and pulled out a brown padded envelope. He handed it to the BMX rider who ferried it across to Veseli.

'You make plenty trips to hole in wall, Sergeant Frank.' The Kosovan took out a thick wad of notes and inspected them.

'They're not marked,' Crosby said.

'You make joke with me, Sergeant Frank.' The dealer grinned. *'Is not funny for you I think.'*

'Count it!'

'I don't check.' Veseli stuffed the padded envelope inside his leather jerkin. *'You honourable man,'* he paused, *'but now I have to worry you not use this gun before.'*

'I know how to use the bloody gun!' Crosby snapped. Although he'd not had to carry one during his career, the ex-detective's voluntary attendance at hands-on training courses meant he was familiar with firearms and their usage.

Veseli shrugged. *'Is your fucking business then.'* The dealer signalled his followers. He turned back to Crosby. *'We leave now. I have a new Sergeant Frank. He tell me bloody drug police here later.'* The Kosovan grinned. *'Is fucking disgrace. I try to make honest living and they treat me like bloody criminal.'*

Crosby wasn't in the mood to share his humour. *'Have you noticed an excess of heroin flooding Sixfields within the last two or three years?'* he asked.

'What you mean excess?' The dealer's eyes had narrowed.

'Don't play bloody games with me, Zamir,' Crosby said impatiently. 'You know full well what I mean.'

Veseli frowned. 'Why you ask, Sergeant Frank?'

'Have you?'

'No.'

'Are you sure?'

'I fucking sure!' The Kosovan looked puzzled. 'If I have information I would give you. It would be like good old times again.'

'I don't recall any,' Crosby said.

Veseli laughed. He raised a departing hand. 'We maybe meet again, Sergeant Frank. Do some more business.' A loose, protective cordon of BMX riders formed around him as he left.

Crosby walked back to his Mondeo, opened its boot, and dropped the carrier bag inside. He made his way across to ParkGate's shopping area. The occasional cigar that he used to enjoy had turned into a regular habit. His stock was running low.

He returned ten minutes later to find a group of six black youths leaning casually against his car. They looked cloned – lean, rangy, all of them wearing low-slung jeans and hooded tops. 'We your neighbourhood watch,' one of them announced. 'Just minding your wheels, man. A lot of anti-social shit happen on this estate. Give us a bad name, innit.' The play-acting and phoney-accented dialogue was clearly meant to intimidate.

Crosby waited.

'Shit!' the same youth said. 'See what happened? Probation officer done turned me into a model fucking citizen.'

Crosby presumed this was the alpha male ring leader. His attempt at humour was greeted with loud sniggering from the others. It persuaded him to offer more of the same. He took a black, slouch beret from his back-pocket and began to wring it with both hands. 'I dun pick yo cotton, Massa. Where my grits'n'cornbread now?' It drew more laughter. Crosby smiled along with them as he moved towards his car. Three of the youths blocked his route. One of them placed a hand on top of the Mondeo's wing mirror, testing its strength. Alpha male returned the beret to his pocket. *'We've been looking after your fucking car.'* The fake pseudo-rap accent had disappeared. *'You'll be wanting to show your appreciation.'*

'In what way exactly?' Crosby enquired.

'You're a funny man.' The ring-leader dropped an arm to reveal the blade-end of a knife concealed up his sleeve. He snapped his fingers at the ex-detective. *'Wallet!'*

Crosby nodded. *'I don't normally carry a lot of cash with me. What is your hourly rate?'* he asked politely.

The gang leader allowed more of his knife to show. *'This is how it works dumb fuck. We take your plastic. You give us the numbers. One of my brothers will collect our fee from the cash point. We can jaw some 'til he gets back.'*

'And how much do you intend to withdraw for your services?' Crosby asked.

The gang-leader pulled his knife out into open view. *'Just give up the fucking card, man!'* Crosby casually reached into his jacket pocket. He pulled out the square of black cloth, and began to slowly unfold it.

The group leant forward. Crosby allowed them a clear, uninterrupted view of his handgun before picking it up. He released the weapon's safety locking mechanism.

A short silence. All of the gang members edged slowly away, continuing to face him as they backed off. Crosby took a step forward. The group turned and ran, sprinting towards the car park's nearest exit point. *'It's not loaded,'* he called after them.

Crosby's hand trembled slightly as he re-folded the black cloth around his handgun. He retrieved the recently purchased tin of small cigars from a jacket pocket and lit one up.

CHAPTER 10

The intercom buzzer woke her. As she'd injected twice last night, it took a few moments for the senses to unscramble and re-connect. Terry Halloran eventually decided it was probably Saturday. She turned over and glanced at her bedside clock. Eleven-thirty. The thirty-nine-year-old prostitute had arrived home earlier that morning – another eight-to-one stint at her regular pitch in Morris Avenue.

Business had been quiet – a scarcity of customers due to the weather – even her minder hadn't bothered to show up. Those punters who did brave the elements had been serviced in the back seat of their cars. She drew the line at having her bare ass backed up against a damp wall in the pouring rain.

Halloran's intercom buzzer sounded again. *'Fuck Off!'* she shouted at it. The intrusive, high-pitched buzzing continued. Halloran grimaced as she climbed from her bed – aches and pains from late night exertions were taking longer to shake off these days. She went through to her lounge and pushed the intercom button. *'Who is it?'*

'Brian Thomson,' a tinny voice responded.

The woman groaned as she recalled one of her tricks from last night – a nondescript little man who couldn't maintain his erection after they'd climbed into the back of his car. *'It'll be the wife's fault,'* he'd explained. *'She prefers to travel in the back-seat when I'm driving. It's affecting my performance. I can feel her presence.'*

'It's a sight fucking more than I can feel, Brian,' the prostitute had told him. *'Where are you hiding it?'*

Thomson hadn't seemed offended. *'Is there somewhere indoors you can take me?'* he'd asked.

'Not tonight, Brian,' she'd told him. Halloran only entertained a few trusted clients inside her flat. Business had been slow however.

Customers thin on the ground. She'd compromised. *'I can book you in for a consultation tomorrow morning. Twelve o'clock. It'll cost you another twenty on top of the street price.'*

Brian Thomson seemed happy enough with the arrangement so she'd given him the address of her flat. He looked harmless enough. It was easy money. She had an expensive habit to support and there was always the chance he'd become one of her regular clients.

Halloran spoke into the intercom. *'You're early, Brian. I need time to prepare myself.'*

A slight pause. *'Will you take long?'*

'A fucking sight longer than you,' the prostitute muttered. *'I'll be ten minutes, Brian,'* she shouted into the intercom. Terry Halloran sighed and went to relieve a full bladder, her heavy, pendulous breasts swinging in unison as she shuffled into the bathroom. Halloran sat on her toilet, contemplating another week-end shift in Morris Avenue. It did nothing to lift the spirits. She rinsed her hands in a small hand basin. *'Wouldn't want the little runt to catch anything.'* There was no humour in her remark.

Back in the bedroom Terry Halloran appraised her naked body in a full-length mirror. The hour-glass figure was beginning to spread. She sighed again – a growing realisation that her earning capacity from working the streets had a limited future. It was becoming more difficult to maintain the illusion. Thicker make-up. The bleached hair. A heavier perfume to mask lingering odours. And for those paying customers who visited her flat, the de-foliation of a greying pubic bush had become a regular, necessary chore.

The woman continued with her routine preparations. She rooted out the half-used tube of K-Y Jelly from her scuffed street-bag and squeezed out a generous amount – rubbing the non-greasy lube deep into her vagina. After rummaging through an underwear drawer she pulled on a pair of black panties and squeezed into a 38D lacy bra. Her make-up from last night was removed and re-applied – just lipstick and mascara. Brian Thomson's attention would presumably be focused elsewhere. What Terry Halloran really craved for at this moment were the contents of two small twists hidden in the recesses of her street-bag. She resisted it. That would be for later – to get her through another late-night shift on Morris Avenue.

The prostitute's thoughts strayed to her deceased parents. It was happening more and more recently. They never had found out what their little girl did for a living. Would it have made a difference? They'd been good to her. She hadn't repaid them. All too late now of course. If she found it difficult to blot them from her mind, when the pain became too acute, there was always another bag of white powder to dull the senses.

Halloran contemplated wearing last night's outfit – a short skirt, low-top and thigh-length white plastic boots. On closer inspection of the garments she decided against it. One excited punter had ejaculated over her as she'd been about to roll on his condom. The prostitute settled on her bathrobe, leaving it loosely tied, to show plenty of cleavage. An application of feminine deodorant spray, a dusting of talcum powder between her legs, and Halloran was ready for whatever Brian Thomson had in mind.

Her intercom sounded again. *'Jesus Christ!'* the prostitute muttered. *'He's fucking eager.'* She was OK with it, wanting him primed, unloaded, and on his way. Halloran went back through to her lounge and released the outside door lock. *'Top of the stairs, Brian.'*

His knock on the door moments later was tentative. She moved across to open it. Brian Thomson stood nervously in front of her. A short, balding man – the fuzz of ginger moustache on his upper lip twitching furiously. He carried a re-usable canvas shopping bag.

'What have you got in there, Brian?'

He looked anxious. *'It's the wife's shoes. I wanted you to wear them.'*

'Fucking hell!' the prostitute murmured under her breath. She opened the door wide and ushered him inside. *'Go and sit yourself down.'* Thomson walked hesitantly across the room to a small settee

and lowered himself onto it. Halloran followed. She leant over him – allowing Thomson to view her black lace bra and the deep cleavage. He sat upright, the canvas shopping bag perched on top of his knees, a darting tongue moistened thin colourless lips.

Terry Halloran wanted this over with. *'What's it to be then, Brian,'* the prostitute asked him. *'I do a straight for thirty-five pounds. That's either standing up or with me on top. You can have fully dressed or just bra and pants,'* she recited in a bored monotone. *'In the buff is five pounds extra, doggy style another ten, and an oral will cost you thirty. I'll entertain all other reasonable suggestions but I no longer take it up the rear-end.'*

Brian Thomson's eyes flicked from the woman's ample breasts to her face and then back again.

'What's it to be then, tiger?' the prostitute asked.

'I could tie your hands to the bedpost,' Thomson blurted out.

'No you fucking well couldn't!' Halloran was quick to reply. *'I'll be having a word with your wife if you don't behave.'*

Thomson let out a high-pitched giggle. *'I'll pay extra for it,'* he said.

The prostitute hesitated. *'How much extra?'*

Thomson took out his wallet and extracted two fifty-pound notes.

Halloran was tempted. *'You can loop a couple of scarves around my wrists,'* she said. *'Just loose though. Not tied.'*

Thomson nodded. He wiped a bead of moisture from his moustache.

Halloran took the money. *'Come on through then, stud.'* Brian Thomson stood up. She cupped the front of his trousers with her hand. *'Bloody hell, Brian. You'll have to get more excited than that or we'll be here until next fucking Christmas.'* Thomson giggled again. Halloran sighed and led her client from the sitting room, thinking it might be hard work to wrap this one up early.

In her bedroom the prostitute retrieved two, thin, chiffon scarves from a dressing table drawer. She handed them to Thomson before lying on the bed and holding out both wrists towards him. He was immediately at the woman's side, leaning forward to snap the bracelet from a pair of handcuffs around Halloran's left wrist. The other half he clipped to a metal bed-post behind her. It happened in an instant. The prostitute was momentarily stunned. It took her a few seconds to realise what he'd done. *'That's not funny, Brian. Take these fucking things off or I'll scream the place down.'*

Thomson reached across and stuffed one of the chiffon scarves into Halloran's mouth. Her eyes widened. She was frightened now, and tried to tear out the scarf with her free hand. The man was too quick. He grabbed her wrist and knotted the second scarf around it – tying the thin material securely to Halloran's other bed-post.

She kicked out at him. The man grabbed her legs, pinning them underneath an arm. He reached down for a length of cord from his shopping bag and tied one of her ankles to a corner of the lower bedrail – viciously tightening the cord's knot. Thomson yanked her other foot across to the bedrail's adjacent corner and secured it with a second length of cord. He straightened up to survey his work. Halloran's feet were already beginning to turn a pale, unhealthy blue, as the restricted blood flow took effect.

Thomson slowly opened a small pen-knife and pulled the woman's robe apart. He used the knife to slice through Halloran's flimsy underwear, ripping the shredded lace free of her naked body. She could only lay on her back, completely exposed, watching him – both legs spread wide apart and her arms stretched taut to the bed-posts behind.

The man looked down into Terry Halloran's face, savouring the abject terror reflected in her eyes. He unzipped his trousers – in complete control now – able to maintain the erection he couldn't achieve last night. Thomson snapped on a pair of blue surgical gloves. Terry Halloran desperately shook her head, trying to force the chiffon scarf from her mouth. The man pulled another piece of thin cord from his canvas bag, winding it around both hands. He climbed up onto the bed and sat astride Halloran, holding the shortened cord directly in front of her face.

The prostitute bucked and writhed beneath Thomson's weight. He stroked her hair. *'Hush now,'* he said softly. *'It's your time.'* Thomson slipped the cord behind Terry Halloran's neck, pulling both ends across the front of her Adam's apple. His wrists were surprisingly strong for a slight man and the silk cord gradually disappeared into a fold of skin around Halloran's neck. She tried to cry out - the sounds ineffectual – delicate bone structures around her larynx already cracking and splintering as Thomson continued to tighten the ligature. Terry Halloran desperately tried to suck in oxygen through her damaged airways – but when the flow of blood to her brain was eventually cut off she lay very still, all signs of life extinguished.

Thomson gradually regained control of his ragged, heavy breathing. He leant forward to take one of the dead woman's nipples in his teeth, biting completely through its soft tissue. Retrieving the bloodied nipple from his mouth he placed it reverently into a small plastic container within the cloth-bag. Thomson's penis was still erect. He held it between the woman's two breasts and proceeded to masturbate into her cleavage. On completion of his orgasm he dismounted and zipped himself back up.

The handcuffs and lengths of cord were removed. Thomson took a large sponge from his canvas bag and soaked it with hot water from the bathroom. He slowly and carefully sponged away all traces of ejaculation and blood from the woman's body – using a small towel to dry her afterwards. Another towel was used to wipe down the bed-post surfaces, rails, and surrounding areas. Thomson then double-checked that everything had been returned to his canvas bag, including the two fifty-pound notes. He turned his attention to Halloran's lifeless body, inspecting it for any tell-tale traces that might have been missed. She stared back at him. Pinpricks of blood dotted the whites of her eyes. An extended tongue poked from between swollen lips. Thomson frowned at the ugliness of her face in death. He took the two chiffon scarves and fashioned them into a large bow, fixing it into the prostitute's dyed, blonde hair.

Thomson studied her afresh. Still something missing. Taking out his pen-knife he cut two bloody V's into each of Halloran's cheeks and sliced away the tip of her nose. Thomson had read that Whitechapel's Jack the Ripper had performed a similar facial adornment on his fourth victim. He stood back and nodded with satisfaction at the result. Halloran's face reminded him of a favourite doll that he used to mutilate in his childhood. The woman ought to be sat up though, looking directly at anyone entering the bedroom. He propped her body into a sitting position, fussing over the robe, re-arranging it to expose Halloran's missing nipple.

Brian Thomson lingered – admiring his handiwork – reluctant to leave her bedside. He took one final look, committing the scene to memory, eventually crossing to the bedroom door. It was only after exiting Terry Halloran's flat did he strip the blue surgical gloves from his hands.

CHAPTER 11

Hawthorne Rise: Sunday 23rd October 2011: 3.00 a.m.

Something woke him. It was the second night in a row. Probably his unreliable sixth sense again. Crosby rolled across to his bedside drawer – the *Walther* handgun and ammunition clip located beneath a layer of socks and underwear. He checked to make sure the weapon's safety de-cocking lever was in place before getting out of bed.

It felt cold. Pulling on his old, threadbare dressing gown he went through to the landing and peered out of its window. Not a good light. There were two street-lamps in Hawthorne Rise but only one of them appeared to be working. Crosby yawned, still half-asleep. The cul-de-sac looked quiet and deserted. As he thought about returning to his bed a pair of headlights materialised, crawling slowly around the estate's top corner. It brought him to his senses. He was fully awake now. The vehicle coasted to a halt sixty yards away. Its lights were immediately extinguished. Crosby eased the gun and ammunition clip from his dressing gown pocket and waited. He could just about make out the shape of a car and where it had pulled up.

Several minutes passed. Crosby detected movement. A dark figure passed through some patchy light shadow and headed directly towards his house – about thirty yards away and closing. The ex-detective suppressed an adrenalin surge. He snapped his ammunition magazine into place and released the handgun's safety mechanism. The metallic rattle of his firearm being made operational was loud in the confined space. Pulling the top slider back with his thumb and forefinger he allowed it to release forward, stripping a cartridge from the ammunition clip and seating its bullet in the *Walther's* firing chamber. *'Shit!'* he muttered. The gun's silencer was still in his bedside drawer. Too late now.

He watched the figure pass beneath him. Crosby held his breath, waiting for sounds of breaking and entering from downstairs. Minutes passed – another movement – someone at the rear of his Mondeo. Almost immediately the figure straightened and hurried away. He remained at his landing window. An engine started-up and a pair of headlights blazed into life. The vehicle reversed slowly from the cul-de-sac, eventually disappearing from view. Crosby realised he'd been holding his breath. He exhaled, ejecting the live cartridge from its firing chamber. His hands were shaking. He waited for them to quieten before pushing the *Walther's* safety mechanism back into place. Crosby stood up. Now he was being targeted at home. In his frustration the ex-detective lashed out at an adjacent wall, managing to graze all of his knuckles. It didn't help.

He slotted the live cartridge back into its magazine holder and went back to bed. An inspection of the Mondeo would have to wait until first light. He wouldn't sleep though. When dawn broke just before seven o'clock the ex-detective was immediately out of his bed, flicking open the window blind slats. A bank of multi-layered dark storm clouds hung low in the sky. They threatened a wet morning.

Crosby dressed quickly and went downstairs. His first priority was the Mondeo. Collecting a heavy-duty torch from his hall-table the ex-detective opened his front door and stepped outside. As he did so the storm broke with some violence. The Mondeo still had to be checked. Crosby hadn't ruled out the possibility of a car bomb.

He moved immediately to the Mondeo's rear. With the heavy, driving rain literally bouncing off his back he lowered himself down onto all fours – angling his torch upwards and running its beam along the car's underside. Nothing untoward. No trailing wires. Now he had to lie full length on his back and ease himself underneath the Mondeo's boot. Almost immediately his torch picked out a small, matchbox-sized object, tucked in close to one of the rear wheel-arches.

Crosby knew instantly what it was. Stretching out an arm, he gained a purchase with his thumb and forefinger, tugging at the object's magnetic force-field. It eventually gave up the struggle and dropped into his hand. The ex-detective didn't have to examine it too closely – a GPS vehicle tracking system that could monitor and pinpoint his Mondeo's whereabouts twenty-four hours a day. Was someone hoping he'd lead them to where the missing drugs were? Crosby replaced the device – its magnetised surface re-clamping itself firmly to his car's underside. He didn't want anyone alerted to the fact it had been found. Not yet anyway.

On returning to the house he quickly stripped off his wet clothes and changed into dry ones. He was ready to leave. Breakfast could wait. Thirty-five years as a police officer had accustomed his digestive system to eating on the hoof. A bacon roll and hot coffee out on the road would suffice at some point that morning.

It had stopped raining. The ex-detective directed his Mondeo in the direction of where Lucy and her partner had set up home. He'd heard nothing from the two women since their encounter outside his grandson's school four days ago. Had they disappeared before the police were able to question them? Were they still at their rented property? If Lucy had been responsible for taking the boy she was far too smart not to have established an alibi – and all the police had to go on were the two anonymous tip-offs from Grace Taylor and himself. He wouldn't contact the policewoman to ask about the enquiry's progress. It wasn't an option currently. Her visit to Hawthorne Rise had probably compromised their relationship.

After the Mondeo had wound its way around Staffordshire's narrow country lanes for an hour, a plain, black and white sign welcomed careful drivers to the village of Oxley. It was quiet. Still early. Crosby drove slowly along the village's only thoroughfare, careful to observe a thirty miles-per-hour speed limit. The layout and composition was similar to countless other villages throughout the English countryside – a centuries old church – the village green – dwellings that ranged from small period cottages to pockets of modern, new-build properties. He passed a tired-looking community hall, just along from the *Rose & Crown* public house. There was even a village duck pond – green-headed mallards paddling aimlessly across its murky looking surface water. Crosby logged the village's detail. It might be important.

His Mondeo reached a simple, black granite cross, commemorating Oxley's dead from the two great wars – a time when men lived in one community for the whole of their lives. It was different now. The villages were also home to new money – recent arrivals co-existing uneasily with older surviving locals.

Endwell Cottage was on the village outskirts. Crosby slowed, half-expecting to find a police presence. The cottage was roadside, a stone-wall façade, partially obscured by climbing wisteria and honeysuckle vine. *'Idyllic,'* the ex-detective muttered. He stopped his Mondeo outside. It looked deserted – no sign of movement behind the small, curtainless windows. Crosby re-engaged his clutch and moved on. Twenty yards past the cottage was open farm-land, hundreds of acres planted with corn maize – a sea of leafy stalks and tassels stretching away into the distance. Crosby parked his Mondeo in a recessed gateway and walked back along the narrow pavement to Rose and Lucy's rented accommodation, peering through a small leaded window into what must have been the sitting room. A grand-father clock stood in the far corner. It was difficult to make out any other detail. Crosby rapped his knuckles on the weathered oak door. It opened almost immediately, taking Crosby by surprise. He certainly didn't expect to see Rose Cavendish standing there.

The ex-prison officer was dressed in a white blouse and tight-fitting skirt – her feet squeezed into a pair of strapless, low-heeled sandals. The hair was now blonde, longer than he last remembered it. She was also wearing make-up – a pale lipstick, blue eye-shadow, a light dusting of powder blush on her cheeks. It was certainly a more feminine-looking Rose Cavendish – although there was no disguising the heavy lantern jaw and broad shoulders. She was the first to speak. *'Can I help?'* Still a trace of Lancashire accent – but her voice lighter,

143

more friendly, the body language non-threatening. It threw Crosby. He hesitated.

The woman laughed. *'I've managed to confuse you. It's my sister Rose who lives here. We look similar but dress differently.'* Crosby was still floundering. The woman held out a hand. *'Sam Cavendish. I'm staying here for a few days.'*

Crosby shook her extended hand. *'James Gilroy,'* he responded, the first name that came into his head. *'A neighbour. I didn't know that Rose had a sister.'*

'She doesn't,' Sam Cavendish replied. *'I'm her twin brother.'*

Crosby searched for a suitable response. He could only come up with, *'You're her brother?'*

Cavendish laughed again. *'I may not be your stereotypical male of the species, Mr Gilroy. And you're probably not over-run with them in Oxley. But even you must be aware of what a transvestite is.'*

The ex-detective still hadn't overcome his initial surprise. He smiled, trying to retain a casual tone. *'Oxley was liberated some years ago. We're actually quite a broad-minded community.'*

'Really?' Cavendish raised her eyebrows. *'My sister told me quite recently that a number of your so called broad-minded residents are openly hostile to the fact that she lives here with another woman.'*

Crosby wasn't sure if he was expected to respond.

The transvestite shrugged and smiled. *'It's OK, Mr Gilroy. She tends to find these bigots quite amusing.'*

'You must have been subjected to similar prejudice,' Crosby said.

The transvestite shrugged. *'It's something you get used to. We'll see how liberated Oxley is when I totter into the village pub wearing my six-inch stilettos.'*

Crosby needed to switch the conversation. *'I wondered if there was any news of Lucy and Rose. I haven't seen them for days.'*

Sam Cavendish regarded him. *'As a close neighbour you would know what's been happening.'*

'When the police turned up,' Crosby replied, 'there was obviously speculation. I didn't know how much you were aware of.'

'I'm aware of it all!' The transvestite's eyes flashed for a split second. 'My family were hounded by the police immediately after it happened.' Cavendish's northern geniality seemed to have temporarily deserted him. 'It's ridiculous of course. There is absolutely no way that Rose would be involved in the abduction of a schoolboy. She adores children.'

Crosby didn't offer an opinion. 'Have you been interviewed by the police?'

'Interrogated would be the term I'd use,' Cavendish replied. 'Three of them turned up mob-handed at my parents' home last Thursday. They're just putting on a show for the media.'

'And where is home?'

'Rochdale,' the transvestite answered. 'I'm staying here until this misunderstanding has been sorted out. Rose and Lucy must have taken off somewhere before all of this blew up. They'll be in touch once they discover the police want to interview them.'

'The story's been all over the news,' Crosby pointed out.

'Which also reported the abducted child's safe return,' Cavendish replied sharply.

'Your sister's not answering her mobile then?' the ex-detective casually enquired.

Cavendish's eyes narrowed. 'They're obviously somewhere that doesn't have a signal. You have a very inquisitive nature, Mr Gilroy.'

'I'm just a concerned neighbour.'

'Back in Rochdale we'd call it poking our nose in,' Cavendish said. 'The police were asking similar questions.'

'My apologies.' Crosby held up his hands. 'I've outstayed my welcome. It's a difficult time for you.'

'I appreciate your concern,' Cavendish said. She hesitated. 'How well do you know Rose's partner?'

'I don't know either of them that well.' Crosby shrugged. 'They only moved in a short while ago. Why do you ask?'

Sam Cavendish shook his head. 'No particular reason.' He made to close the door. 'It's nice to have made your acquaintance, Mr Gilroy.'

'Likewise.' Crosby waved a departing hand. 'I hope you get some good news soon.' The door closed firmly behind him.

Back in his car the ex-detective mulled over of Sam Cavendish's arrival and its implications. Although Billy Lucas had returned home safely he was surprised there'd been no police presence at the cottage. A background check on Cavendish's family wouldn't go amiss. He'd put the call through to his source later. A muffled ring-tone sounded from within the confines of his jacket pocket. Crosby retrieved the mobile and pushed its 'Receive' button. 'Yes!'

'Frank?' It was Ian Brown's voice. He sounded unusually upbeat. 'I enjoyed our wee dram together last week. We should do it again, laddie.'

'I was thinking exactly the same thing,' Crosby replied in a similar manner. 'When are you free?'

'I'm busy for the next couple of days,' Brown said. 'How about Wednesday night?'

'Same place as last time?' the ex-detective asked.

'I'll confirm it tomorrow.' Brown disconnected the call.

Crosby dropped the mobile back into his jacket pocket. 'What the hell now?' he muttered to himself. Ian Brown certainly didn't want to meet him for a social get-together. The Scenes-of-Crimes officer had warned Crosby that he was on his own after their last meeting. The Scot's cheerful tone and lack of message content also indicated he was concerned about their mobile conversations being monitored. Crosby started the car. He'd take the long way home. His intruder's tracking device might attract a travelling companion on the journey back to Hawthorne Rise.

CHAPTER 12

The Scenes-of-Crime officer terminated his call to Frank Crosby and ground out a half-smoked cigarette beneath the heel of his shoe. He slipped the mobile into a trouser pocket and turned back towards an unmarked, Ford Transit van. He opened its rear-doors.

Inside the vehicle was a stack of white hooded, forensic coverall suits. Brown stripped protective cling-film wrap from one of the suits before stepping into it. He sorted through an over-sized holdall – packed full of shoe covers, disposable latex gloves, and other assorted items. The Scot found what he was looking for and slammed shut both rear doors of the van. Picking up his case of forensic equipment he made his way along Beaumont Street's pavement – towards three squad cars, a West Midlands NHS ambulance, and a coroner's funeral hearse.

Outside number thirty-nine a bored-looking police constable stood sentry duty – his bright yellow tabard lighting up the gloom of a grey morning. *'Top flat,'* he said to Ian Brown. The Scenes-of-Crime officer pushed open a small, wrought-iron gate and made his way along the garden's narrow concrete path. Another uniformed PC, stationed in front of the building's open front door, waved him around a barrier of yellow and black plastic warning tape – *'POLICE CRIME SCENE - DO NOT CROSS'* The Scot glanced across at three adjacent name-plates. One of them identified Terry Halloran as the building's top floor resident.

Brown had received the urgent, priority call about forty minutes ago – a local prostitute murdered inside her flat. A Major Investigation Unit had already been assembled and its senior officers appointed. As he was on duty call that week-end the Scot had been summoned to carry out forensic processing inside the victim's flat and its

147

surrounding area. The Beaumont Street address was too much of a coincidence. His first instinct had been to get in touch with Frank Crosby. It was only a few days ago that he'd passed Terry Halloran's name and address to the ex-detective.

Inside number thirty-nine's dingy hallway the Scenes-of-Crime officer lowered his box of equipment to the floor, slipped on a pair of plastic shoe covers, and headed towards an adjacent flight of stairs. He eventually made it to the top floor landing, stopping to wipe a thin film of perspiration from his forehead. The combination of thirty cigarettes a day and hauling his forensic equipment up two flights of stairs had winded him.

The flat door was wide open. He could see Detective Chief Inspector Jack Gould in conversation with one of his team. The DCI was an experienced Senior Investigating Officer – a local man from the West Bromwich area. Ian Brown had investigated crime scenes with him before. It was a comfortable working relationship. The Scot picked up his case of forensic equipment again and stepped inside. DCI Gould walked across to him. *'Pathologist's been waiting for you, Ian. He's anxious to get some photographs of this woman's injuries.'*

'Not likely to get up and wander off is she?' Brown remarked. *'Who's the pathologist?'*

Gould nodded towards an internal door. *'Dr Carter. He's in the bedroom.'*

Brown made a face.

'That's not all the bad news,' Gould said.

'Oh aye?'

'We'll need to watch procedures this morning,' the detective warned. *'There's a high-ranking officer on his way to monitor proceedings.'*

Brown raised an eyebrow. *'Who's that?'*

'Detective Superintendent Rees-Bramley.'

The SOCO's head jerked up. *'You're joking! I thought the little runt had been shunted off to HQ.'*

'He's back to ruffle our feathers.'

'That's all I fucking need!' The Scot grimaced. 'Rees-Bramley stuffed up my crack all day.'

'It gets worse.'

Brown shook his head. 'Unlikely.'

'He's bringing a guest with him,' the detective continued. 'Some smart-ass at Lloyd House came up with the idea of a personnel exchange programme.'

The SOCO looked wary. 'An exchange with who?'

'New York Police Department.'

'He's bringing a Yank with him?'

Gould nodded. 'Lieutenant Bradley Thorburn III. The superintendent thought this morning would be an ideal opportunity for him to look at how West Midlands conduct a murder investigation.'

'So when are they due?'

'Any time now.'

The Scot shook his head. 'Two pricks up my ass instead of one.'

'If it's any consolation,' Gould said, 'I'll probably get more grief than you.'

Ian Brown nodded towards the bedroom. 'I'd better crack on. The good doctor will be getting impatient. It doesn't take much to annoy him.'

'I'd like something early doors,' the DCI called after him. 'There's a VIP to impress.' Brown waved a hand in reply as he made his way towards the bedroom door.

Dr John Carter, his bald pate gleaming under the four hundred watt arc-lamp, was standing over a double-bed, engrossed in his work. Terry Halloran sat propped-up against the bed's headrest, her eyes vacant, wide open, the face stiff and distorted. She was draped in a grubby-looking white bathrobe that had been pulled apart to expose the woman's grey, wiry bush and a mutilated breast.

'*Morning,*' the Scot said to her, as she continued to stare directly at him. Brown lowered his case to the floor. '*Morning, Doc,*' he said to the pathologist.

Carter didn't look up. '*Traffic a problem?*'

'*Nose to tail,*' Brown answered.

'*Unusual for a Sunday morning,*' the forensic pathologist said.

'*Asshole!*' Brown muttered under his breath, mindful that Carter was his senior officer during their assignment.

The pathologist removed a thermometer from deep within Terry Halloran's rectum and tapped some figures into his electronic notebook. '*You're aware that we have high-profile visitors this morning,*' he said.

Brown nodded. '*Aye. Batman and fucking Robin.*'

'*I don't want any inappropriate behaviour or bad language while they're here, Ian,*' the pathologist warned. '*We're both aware of how exacting the superintendent can be.*'

'*It's time I retired,*' Brown answered. '*You were just left to get on with it when the top brass were all Freemasons. Now we have to put up with all these bloody fast-tracked university schoolboys doing everything by the book.*'

Carter wasn't listening. He'd already turned his attention back to taking swabs from Terry Halloran's body. Brown pulled on a pair of latex gloves and opened his forensics case. '*Where do you want me to start?*'

'*Photographs,*' Carter replied. '*There's a circular wound around the victim's neck. Bruising to her wrists. Mutilation to the face. One of her breasts has suffered major trauma.*'

The Scot took a closer look. '*She certainly pissed off somebody.*' He set about putting together his Nikon Coolpix digital camera. The camera's design allowed him to mount it on a microscope, recording magnified images of wounds and trace evidence. Brown moved closer to the bed. Terry Halloran continued to watch him. '*Is she still in a state of Rigor?*' the Scot asked.

Carter nodded. *'The larger muscles are just starting to relax. Time of death would have been yesterday morning. Sometime after nine o'clock.'*

Ian Brown ran an experienced eye over the bedding and bathrobe, checking for visible signs of trace evidence left by the killer. All stray fibres and hair strands would have to be lifted and bagged for subsequent laboratory analysis. *'Anything under her nails?'* he asked Carter.

'I haven't taken any scrapings yet,' the pathologist replied.

'Sexual abuse?'

'Not to her lower body.' Carter indicated the woman's mutilated breast. *'That's not a clean cut. He's bitten through her nipple.'*

'He?'

The pathologist nodded. *'Point taken.'*

Brown connected an ISO flash control system to his camera and located a fully charged battery pack from his case. He flipped open a compartment lid on the Nikon and snapped the battery pack into place. After a couple of adjustments to his camera settings he leant in towards Halloran's neck and fired off several flashes. *'Ligature strangling?'* he asked.

'Looks like it,' the pathologist answered. He waited whilst Brown spent the next few minutes photographing Halloran's body from several different angles. There was a sudden flurry of activity and voices coming from the next room. Carter looked up. Ian Brown continued loading images into the Nikon's memory chip. A curt voice from the open doorway. *'Doctor Carter? It's been a while.'*

Ian Brown lowered his camera and sneaked a sideways glance. The newcomer's short, slight figure was impeccably dressed – a three-piece pinstriped suit that looked hand-made. Detective Superintendent Oliver Rees-Bramley didn't do *'off the peg'*. His university crested silk tie was dark-blue in colour.

John Carter had almost come to attention. Although an experienced physician in his own field the pathologist's previous experience of Rees-Bramley seemed to be un-nerving him. *'Jesus Christ!'* Brown muttered. *'You'll be dropping into a fucking curtsy next.'*

The superintendent stepped into Halloran's bedroom. He was followed by an imposing individual dressed in dark, casual trousers and an open-necked shirt. The man was black. Very tall. Intelligent, inquiring eyes. Both men wore protective overshoes. Halloran stared openly at her new visitors. They didn't return the woman's interest in them.

Rees-Bramley addressed John Carter. *'I'd like you to meet Lieutenant Thorburn from the New York Police Department,'* he said. *'The lieutenant is with us for several weeks to gain an insight into how the West Midlands operate.'* The superintendent's short, clipped accent resonated sharply in the small bedroom.

'A pleasure to meet you, Sir.' The American hoisted a hand in greeting. *'Don't let me keep you from your work.'*

Ian Brown put the American in his mid-thirties. The accent was smoother, less raucous than a typical New Yorker. John Carter remained standing at Halloran's bedside. The pathologist looked unsure as to whether he should continue with his work.

'So what do we have here?' Rees-Bramley asked him.

'Looks like a dead fucking body to me,' Brown muttered inwardly.

'A probable ligature strangling,' Carter said to the detective superintendent. *'It also appears that both wrists were restrained in some way.'*

Rees-Bramley nodded. *'Handcuffs?'*

The pathologist shrugged. *'Possibly. A full autopsy will confirm it.'*

'Possibly?' Rees-Bramley smiled thinly. *'An opinion too early in proceedings was never your forté, Doctor Carter.'*

The pathologist didn't reply. Rees-Bramley switched his attention to the Scenes-of-Crime officer. *'Mr Brown, isn't it?'*

'Aye.'

'We've also worked together in the past I seem to remember.'

'It's forever etched in my memory, Sir,' the Glaswegian said.

One of the detective superintendent's facial muscles twitched. 'And what has our victim offered up for evaluation?'

'Nothing at first glance, Sir,' the Scot answered. 'It looks a very professional job.'

'Professional?' Rees-Bramley frowned. 'According to DCI Gould's initial enquiries the woman is a local prostitute. Surely one of her deranged customers is a more likely explanation.'

'I'm probably not the best person to ask, Sir,' Brown said. 'You'd be better off running that one past a detective.'

Rees-Bramley's facial muscle twitched again. He gave the Scot a long hard look. The NYPD officer had been watching their exchanges with a bemused smile on his face. 'We weren't introduced,' he said. 'Brad Thorburn.'

'Ian Brown,' the Scot replied. 'I trust your visit over here is proving useful. How do we measure up this side of the pond?'

'I got nothing but admiration for you guys,' Thorburn replied, 'but everyone's permanently hard wired into their jobs. I keep telling the Super he works too hard. Some recreation and leisure time wouldn't go amiss.'

'I'm sure the superintendent has arranged one or two social nights out on the town for you both,' Brown said innocently.

Rees-Bramley's face remained straight. Thorburn smiled broadly. 'I have promised Oliver that we'll hit a nightclub together before I return home.'

The detective superintendent looked even more stony-faced. Brown wasn't sure if it was because the American had referred to him as Oliver, or whether it was the thought of visiting a nightclub. Probably both. Rees-Bramley put a stop to the exchanges. 'I suggest we continue this in the other room with our Senior Investigating Officer.'

DCI Gould had obviously been listening. He appeared in the doorway. *'I'll need to speak with Doctor Carter, Sir.'*

'I'm sure your detective sergeant is perfectly capable of liaising with him,' Rees-Bramley said to the DCI. *'I require you to run through your procedures to date for the benefit of Lieutenant Thorburn.'*

'Yes, Sir.' DCI Gould half-raised his eyebrows in Ian Brown's direction.

Rees-Bramley had already turned his attention back to the pathologist. *'A copy of your autopsy report would be appreciated, Doctor. Shall we say tomorrow morning?'*

'It should be ready by then,' the pathologist replied.

'I would have thought so.' Rees-Bramley turned on his heel. *'If you're ready, Lieutenant Thorburn?'*

The American nodded towards Brown and Carter. *'Thank you for your time, gentlemen. Most enlightening.'*

'Don't keep the superintendent out too late,' Ian Brown advised. *'He can be tetchy first thing if he doesn't get his full eight hours.'*

'A pleasure meeting you, Mr Brown.' Thorburn followed Rees-Bramley through to the sitting room. DCI Gould trailed after both of them.

John Carter glanced across at the Scenes-of-Crime officer. *'Was there any need for that?'*

'The man's a prick!' Brown said.

Rees-Bramley had continued through Halloran's sitting room and out onto the landing. He waited for the other two officers to join him. *'A rough diamond your Mr Brown,'* the American said.

'He's Scottish,' Rees-Bramley replied, as if further explanation was unnecessary. *'DCI Gould will give us a brief run through of the procedures covered this morning.'*

Gould nodded. *'Yes Sir. Paramedics initially confirmed the woman's death. As our victim obviously died in suspicious circumstances the Coroner's Office was informed and the crime scene secured. A Senior Investigating Officer was then appointed and his* team assembled. *Scenes-of-Crime and a Home Office pathologist are already on-site and carrying out preliminary investigations. Our victim has been identified as one Terry Halloran. She was a known local prostitute who lived alone in the rented flat.'*

'I assume it's too early for suspects?'

'Yes, Sir.'

'Who discovered the body?' Rees-Bramley asked.

'Another local prostitute.' DCI Gould referred to his pocketbook. *'Gabriela Eminescu. Rumanian. Doesn't look any more than seventeen. She worked the same area as our victim. When Halloran didn't turn up last night she called around this morning to check on her. Raised the alarm when there was no answer.'*

'Where is she now?'

'One of my team is taking a statement.'

'Have you spoken to her?'

Gould nodded. *'Briefly. She's very distressed.'*

'Did she have anything useful to say?'

The DCI shook his head. *'Not a great deal. We may need an interpreter. Her English is limited.'*

'She can probably speak it better than you,' Rees-Bramley said. *'Put some pressure on her. These street-walkers never offer up anything voluntarily. And check her immigration status.'*

'Yes, Sir.' The DCI knew from previous encounters that sympathy was not an emotion Rees-Bramley had a lot of time for.

'There's two other flats in the house.'

'Both tenants were at home yesterday,' Gould replied. *'We'll be talking to them shortly.'*

'I'd like Lieutenant Thorburn and myself to sit in,' Rees-Bramley said. *'Inform me when you're ready to proceed. What about Halloran's pimp?'*

'We're still trying to establish who that is.'

'Have you contacted her landlord?'

'On his way.'

'Door to door enquiries?'

'Already under way, Sir.'

'Lieutenant Thorburn may have questions for you at some point,' Rees-Bramley said. *'He's been acquainting himself with a copy of the Senior Investigating Officer's handbook.'*

'A fascinating read,' the American added, his face expressionless.

Rees-Bramley turned and made his way down the first flight of stairs. Lieutenant Thorburn didn't immediately follow. *'And after we finish here,'* the American said to Gould, *'your superintendent's briefing me on how to foster good relations with staff and colleagues.'*

The DCI merely nodded, unsure as to whether their American visitor had been joking.

CHAPTER 13

Derek Alcott exited the offices of *PB Investigations* and stepped out into Gower Street. It felt chilly. A cold October sun had disappeared over an hour ago. He checked the time. Paul Berne had given him a surveillance job for tonight but there were still three hours to kill. These would be spent at the nearby *Horse and Plough* – a convenient and regular watering hole after his working day.

Alcott automatically checked out passing females. The former metropolitan police officer was an habitual sexual predator who stalked his quarry over a wide area – the *Horse and Plough* being one of his more favoured hunting grounds. It offered cut price drinks, an all-day menu, and a choice of vulnerable, unattached women who ate alone. They would be Derek Alcott's initial choice of prey. An easy target. If none were readily available then alternatives would be sought elsewhere – and forcibly persuaded into eventual submission if necessary. He quite enjoyed the ones who resisted. It made the pursuit and conquest more enjoyable. Alcott's pulse quickened, anticipating the hunt. He lifted his face skywards to sniff at the cold night air, like an animal detecting a scent trail.

Inside the *Horse and Plough* he watched his first lager being drawn into a long glass. The young barman set it down in front of him. Alcott waited, allowing droplets of condensation to form and run down the outside of his glass, anticipating the lager's first hit. He picked up the glass and drained half its contents in one swallow. Alcott turned to survey the room. Most of its tables were occupied. The private investigator scanned faces, checking that none of his previous conquests were there tonight. In a dimly-lit corner, eating alone, was a dark-haired woman, attractive, mid-thirties. Alcott continued to monitor her. The woman glanced up and caught him looking. She smiled briefly in his direction before dropping her eyes.

'Bingo!' the Londoner muttered. Now she had to be landed.

Alcott waited for the woman to finish her meal before making his move. He turned to the young barman. *'Lady on her own. In the far corner. What's she drinking?'*

'Pinot Grigio,' the youth replied immediately.

Alcott nodded. *'A large glass of it then.'*

Moments later he was at the woman's table, carrying a fresh pint of lager and the glass of Pinot Grigio. *'I apologise in advance,'* Alcott said. *'I'm not in the habit of doing this but it looked as if you were about to order another drink.'*

The woman studied him. *'Do I know you?'* she asked.

'Guy Marshall.' The private detective switched on his most disarming smile.

'Well, Mr Marshall,' the woman said. *'I'm not in the habit of allowing a complete stranger to buy me drinks. Your intrusion is not welcome.'*

'Ouch!' Derek Alcott placed the glass in front of her and held up both hands. *'I can only apologise again. Please accept the wine with my compliments.'* He backed away. *'Now we'll see who's playing hard to fucking get,'* the Londoner muttered.

'Mr Marshall,' the woman called after him. *'That was rude and offhand.'* She gestured to a chair opposite. *'You caught me off guard.'*

'Hook, line and fucking sinker,' Alcott murmured, turning back to the table. His instincts hadn't let him down. He thrust out a hand.

'Jayne Tindall,' the woman replied, accepting his handshake.

Alcott eased himself into the proffered chair. An absence of rings, wedding or otherwise, had already been noted. *'Did you enjoy your meal?'* he asked.

'I'm ashamed to admit that I eat out far too often.' The woman shrugged. *'There's not a lot of enjoyment in cooking for one.'*

'You're not in a relationship?'

Jayne Tindall regarded him quizzically. *'You have a very direct manner, Mr Marshall.'*

'It has been pointed out,' the private detective replied. *'One of my many faults.'*

'I'm not sure why I would be telling you this,' Jayne Tindall said, *'but in answer to your question I've just come out of a relationship. How about you?'*

'A confirmed bachelor I'm afraid.' Alcott spread his hands. *'Not by choice. I'm still waiting to be snapped up.'*

Jayne Tindall arched her eyebrows and laughed. *'I suspect that's not true. Men seem to enjoy their single status far more than women.'*

'It becomes less enjoyable after a certain age.'

The woman didn't look convinced. *'So how do you pass your bachelor evenings?'* she asked.

'It's back to an empty flat tonight. A few hours in front of the television.' Alcott had slipped into a well-practiced routine of polite conversation. *'Are you going on somewhere?'*

Jayne Tindall shook her head. *'My evening will consist of a half-finished novel and my poetry.'*

'Poetry?'

'I've been writing for more years than I care to remember.' Tindall self-consciously brushed non-existent crumbs from the table in front of her. *'Inadequately I'm afraid. But the enjoyment it brings justifies any end results.'*

Alcott made an effort to look enthusiastic. *'I'm impressed. Do you allow others to see your work?'*

'There's a collection of poetry and verse being published shortly,' Tindall replied. *'Two of my poems are to be included.'*

'Really!' Alcott raised his eyebrows. *'A published author.'*

'Hardly that.' Tindall shrugged. *'It's small budget and all very low-key.'*

'Even so,' the private investigator said. *'It's quite an achievement. You must be pleased with yourself.'*

'I am,' Tindall nodded. *'It's given me the incentive to complete other poems I've been working on. Unfortunately my PC crashed three days ago and I can't get to them.'*

'What's the problem?' Alcott casually picked up his glass. *'I'm in the IT business. I may be able to help.'*

The woman relaxed back in her chair, completely at ease now. *'You fix computers?'*

'Software mainly.' The private detective took a swallow of lager. *'I can replace components and tweak circuitry if necessary however.'*

'Well mine's completely locked up,' Jayne Tindall said. *'As it's quite ancient and non-portable I've had to arrange a home call. The technician's let me down twice already though.'*

Alcott spread his hands. *'I could give it a quick MOT if you're agreeable. Satisfaction guaranteed or your money back.'*

'I should probably invest in a new laptop,' Tindall said. *'The model I have must be technically obsolete.'*

'Have you backed up all your files to a separate storage device?' the private detective asked.

Jayne Tindall turned down the corners of her mouth. *'One of those things I never got around to.'*

'We'd need to recover what's on the hard disc then.'

The woman looked unsure. *'I shouldn't impose.'*

'It's up to you.'

'I'd pay of course.'

'You can take me out to dinner,' Alcott replied smoothly.

'I am lost without it. When would you be able to take a look?'

Derek Alcott smiled. He was almost there. *'How about tonight? Where do you live?'*

'I have a flat just around the corner,' Tindall answered. *'It's convenient for work. A local estate agent.'*

Alcott shrugged. *'I could walk you home. We'll see what the problem is.'*

'It's very good of you.'

'*All sorted then.*' Alcott picked up his glass. '*We'll finish these and make a move.*'

Jayne Tindall also picked up her glass. She leant back to cross a pair of long, slender legs. '*It's fortunate I decided to call in here this evening.*'

Alcott smiled broadly. '*My lucky night as well.*' His attention strayed to where the woman's skirt had ridden up.

Jayne Tindall finished her wine before standing. '*I just need to freshen up.*'

Alcott also stood. The woman raised her eyebrows. '*A gentleman as well.*'

'*You might change your fucking mind about that,*' the private investigator murmured to himself as he watched Jayne Tindall ease her trim figure through the maze of closely packed tables. Derek Alcott sat back down, anticipating the conclusion of his evening. Would she put up any resistance? He didn't really know at this stage. Not that it would make any difference to the outcome.

Ten minutes later the couple were standing outside. As they began to stroll slowly along Gower Street the private investigator took her hand. She didn't pull it away. They'd only walked a short distance when Jayne Tindall stopped outside an estate agent's window. She indicated the flat above. '*I told you it was convenient for work.*'

'*No excuse for being late in the mornings then,*' Alcott remarked. He was anxious for them to get inside.

The flat's entrance was through an adjacent door, next to the office's large display window. Jayne Tindall fumbled in a small black handbag for her keys. She slotted one of them into a Yale-lock and pushed the door open, switching on an inside light. Alcott followed her up a narrow staircase, his eyes fixated on the sway of her hips as she continued ahead of him. They reached a small landing, prompting the woman to select another key. A few seconds later and they were standing inside her flat. Jayne Tindall motioned him towards a small settee. '*Would you like a drink?*' she asked.

161

Alcott was impatient now. He already felt himself fully aroused. *'I'd prefer something else.'* The private investigator pulled her close. She didn't resist. They kissed for several seconds. He tried to slide his hand up the inside of her thigh. *'No!'* She pulled away from him. *'That's too fast.'*

Alcott went after her. *'I'm not here to play fucking kiss chase.'* The woman backed further away from him. *'I want you to leave.'*

'Bitch!' Alcott lunged across the room. He raised his arm and back-handed the woman across a cheek bone. The resounding crack left an ugly weal to her face. Alcott's face was a mask. He grabbed the woman's hair. *'This is what happens to fucking prick teasers.'*

A bedroom door opened behind him. He spun around.

Penny Zardelli stepped into the room, a frown on her face. *'And I always thought that trapping wild animals was a difficult business.'*

Alcott looked totally confused, the hunting lust still reflected in his eyes. *'Who the fuck are you?'*

Aquileia's executive director circled slowly around him. *'Take your time, Mr Alcott. I'm sure it will come back to you. A recent day trip to the seaside possibly?'*

Now he remembered her. His eyes darted between both women, the aggression in him gradually receding. *'What the fuck are you doing here?'*

'To administer a great deal of pain and suffering.' Penny Zardelli stopped in front of him. *'I'm afraid we'll have to disrupt your intended plans for the evening.'*

'We?'

Aquileia's executive director folded her arms. *'My companion and I will be administering a brand of justice that's long overdue.'*

'What the fuck are you talking about?' Alcott looked unsure though. The woman had an air of assurance about her. *'Are you about to give me a good kicking then? Or will the pair of you be shagging me into submission?'* His voice sounded more bravado than confident.

'*A sense of humour, Mr Alcott.*' Penny Zardelli's smile didn't reach her eyes. '*You'll do well to retain that during the course of our evening together.*'

Alcott made for the door. '*Out of my fucking way!*'

Penny Zardelli moved in front of him.

The private investigator raised his hand.

Another person stepped through from the bedroom. Giorgio Messina's physique and stature was an intimidating presence. It filled the room. A long stiletto knife, loosely held in his right hand, added to the threat.

Alcott had faced enough hostility during his years with the metropolitan police to be capable of handling most situations. The man confronting him looked a different proposition however. Instinct and experience warned the Londoner he was in trouble. Penny Zardelli seemed to read his thoughts. '*I would have to agree with you, Mr Alcott. Any kind of resistance is likely to result in more suffering.*' He didn't look at her. His attention fixed on the stiletto that Giorgio Messina was transferring from hand to hand.

Aquileia's executive director turned towards the woman who called herself Jayne Tindall. '*There will be an additional payment on top of our agreed fee.*' Penny Zardelli's voice was clipped, business-like. '*It will compensate for the physical assault.*'

The woman shrugged. '*I've had worse.*' She touched the angry, red weal across her cheekbone and looked across at Alcott. '*A pity I can't stay to watch.*'

Penny Zardelli nodded. '*I'm quite looking forward to it myself.*'

The woman picked up her bag and left. *Aquileia's* executive director closed the door behind her. Alcott had re-focused on Giorgio Messina. The Sicilian was moving slowly towards him, weaving small circles in the air with his long-bladed knife. Alcott snatched up a nearby cushion and dropped into a low crouch. Both legs buckled underneath him as Penny Zardelli cracked a solid, rubber cosh to the back of his head. He wobbled, half-stunned, managing to remain on his feet. Messina stepped in close, straight-arming a fist to the Londoner's jaw. He was unconscious before the floor came up to meet him.

When Alcott next opened his eyes he found himself lying full length on a bed, both arms stretched behind him, hands tied to the bed's metal framework. He felt nauseous. His head throbbed. A gag of thin material, tightly knotted, had forced Alcott's mouth wide open. Penny Zardelli and her Sicilian chauffeur stood over his naked body.

Aquileia's executive director checked her wrist watch. *'You were unconscious for five minutes, Mr Alcott. One of Giorgio's many skills is the ability to concuss someone for a specific amount of time.'* She reached down to check the private investigator's gag was securely in place. *'We don't want to alarm passers-by. Your pain will be intense.'* Alcott's eyes darted wildly about him. He was fully recovered now.

Penny Zardelli began to pace, lightly smacking the rubber cosh into the palm of her hand. *'I hope you're frightened, Mr Alcott. You have every reason to be. Your Neanderthal behaviour is about to catch up with you.'* She viewed his prostrate figure. *'Your castration is a favoured option. Giorgio is extremely proficient with his blades.'* The woman shrugged. *'There's no immediate hurry. We have other surprises planned.'*

The private investigator arched and twisted, desperately trying to free his hands. *Aquileia's* executive director eyed him dispassionately. *'Your turn to struggle, Mr Alcott. How does it feel to be a victim?'*

Alcott lashed out with his legs. Penny Zardelli stepped in close to him, bringing her rubber cosh down hard onto the bone of Alcott's left knee. He screamed in silent agony. She brought it down several more times. It stopped him struggling.

Aquileia's executive director stepped back, eyes wide open, trembling slightly, her breathing ragged. She gradually regained some composure. *'My chauffeur and I recently concluded a joint business transaction. It emerged from our time together that Giorgio admitted to being bisexual. A surprisingly high percentage of men are apparently.' Aquileia's* executive director snapped her fingers. Messina nodded. He began to remove his clothing.

Penny Zardelli turned back to the private investigator. *'You are about to be raped, Mr Alcott. Brutally I'm afraid. I doubt you'll appreciate the irony of your situation.'*

Messina interrupted. *'Signora.'* The Sicilian had completely undressed. He was fully erect. *'I am ready.'*

Aquileia's executive director appraised him. *'Indeed you are, Giorgio.'* She stepped to one side. *'Will you be using any protection?'*

'I take my chances, Signora.'

'Would Mr Alcott appreciate some form of lubrication?'

'It would be less painful for him.'

Penny Zardelli smiled. *'I think not then.'* She indicated for the chauffeur to continue. Messina climbed onto the bed and forced Alcott's legs apart. The private investigator offered no resistance as he was forcibly penetrated. There was little fight left in him.

Penny Zardelli retreated to a nearby chair. She watched closely and with some interest as the Sicilian proceeded to savagely rape his victim. After the Sicilian had climaxed he immediately withdrew and looked across at *Aquileia's* executive director for approval. She nodded. Messina climbed from the bed. He picked up his clothes and disappeared into the flat's bathroom.

Penny Zardelli stood up from her chair. *'My only concern was that you might enjoy the experience, Mr Alcott. Clearly you didn't. A satisfying outcome.'*

Derek Alcott regarded her with dull, vacant eyes. Penny Zardelli walked over to the bed. She leant forward and spat into his face. He didn't react. The woman stepped back. *'When my chauffeur returns your gag will be removed. You will then tell me who has engaged your agency to ask questions about Dryffed's Farm. I advise you not to be difficult. Giorgio is highly skilled in the art of inflicting pain.'*

The bathroom door opened and Messina re-appeared. Penny Zardelli waved her chauffeur towards the bed. *'Remove his gag.'*

'*Si, Signora.*'

Aquileia's executive director resumed her chair. *'In practical terms we'll have to reject the option of having you castrated, Mr Alcott.'* She paused. *'Which is a great pity. I'm afraid the evening will conclude in your permanent demise however.'*

There was still no reaction from the private investigator. Derek Alcott appeared comatose, as if resigned to what was in store for him.

CHAPTER 14

A grey Honda Civic had been constant in his rear-view mirror for two miles now – keeping its distance but maintaining contact. The car had picked him up not long after he'd pulled out of Hawthorne Rise. Crosby needed to confront whoever was tailing him. He took a sharp left, delaying until the last moment. The Honda Civic remained with him.

When he had initially set off that morning his intention was to visit *PB Investigations* again. Despite Paul Berne's promise to get back in touch with him there'd been no call. If the agency had been employed to investigate *Dryffed's* missing drugs then he needed to know who had retained their services. Crosby glanced into his rear-view mirror again. A further confrontation with *PB Investigations* would have to wait. His immediate concern was the Honda Civic, still behind him, still maintaining close contact.

Another two miles elapsed. He passed a sign for *Lendlebury Airfield.* Up until a few years ago the old World War II aerodrome had been used by a local gliding club. When that particular enterprise went into liquidation it left the site abandoned and deserted. Recently, amid rumours of a major re-development scheme, security fencing had been reinforced around the airfield's perimeter. Crosby knew where at least two semi-concealed entrances were located however. He headed towards the nearest of them.

Accelerating his Mondeo through the next set of traffic lights, then taking an immediate right, he increased speed along what was now a single track country road. Minutes later he pulled hard on the steering wheel and veered sharply to his left, disappearing through a narrow overgrown entrance into *Lendlebury* airfield.

The Mondeo bumped across a stretch of grassy, uneven terrain. His nearest point of cover was an old, corrugated Nissen Hut – its iconic, half-cylindrical shape covered in a bright orange rust. Crosby drove around to the building's far side, cut his engine, and flipped open the car's glove compartment. He leant forward to retrieve his handgun and silencer – aware this was the second time he'd reached for its protection. Crosby quickly inserted the *Walther's* magazine clip and stepped out of his car. A buffeting wind swept across *Lendlebury's* wide open spaces. It whipped at his thinning, sandy hair. The Honda still hadn't appeared. Even if the vehicle tracking system wasn't responsible for the car following him it wouldn't take long for his pursuer to find the airfield's semi-concealed entrance.

He didn't waste any time, hurrying towards the old Nissen Hut – a structure originally manufactured for use during the First World War. They were a rare sight now. Crosby estimated this particular construction to be at least sixty feet long, with windows and a wooden entrance door cut into its corrugated steel sheeting.

The door was locked. Crosby tested its strength with his shoulder, the thin wooden panel bowing under his weight. He stood back to give himself room, driving the heel and sole of his shoe into where the lock was positioned. It buckled and gave way, allowing the door to swing inward on its hinges. Crosby stepped into an airless musty interior, a gloomy half-light. He could just about make out a long, narrow, central corridor – giving access to several partitioned spaces along the hut's length.

Crosby heard the sound of a vehicle pulling up outside. He moved further along the corridor, tucking himself out of sight behind a partitioned section. The seconds ticked by. Silence. He could hear his heart thumping. Someone stepped through the open doorway. Crosby tried to control his breathing as he screwed the *Walther's* silencer into place. Hesitant, faltering footsteps began to advance along the corridor towards him. He reached down with his left hand to release the handgun's safety mechanism; impossible to muffle the noise it made in his enclosed space.

'*Frank!*' A familiar, rasping, Glaswegian accent echoed along the hut's corridor. '*Where the fuck are you?*' It threw Crosby. What the hell was Ian Brown playing at? He stepped out from behind his partitioned space. The Scenes-of-Crimes officer stood in front of him. There was just enough light filtering through the row of small window openings for them to see each other.

'*Jesus Christ!*' Brown took a step back when he looked at what the ex-detective was pointing at him. '*Is that a fucking gun?*'

'*You're bloody lucky I didn't use it.*' Crosby de-activated the *Walther* and unscrewed its silencer, slipping them both into his pocket. '*What the hell are you following me for?*'

Ian Brown exhaled loudly as he watched the gun disappear. '*I'm still looking after your fucking interests, laddie. Why the hell did you turn in here?*'

'*Why!*' The ex-detective's adrenalin surge had left him angry. '*Your car on my tail might be a good bloody reason. What did you think I was doing? Checking out where I'd stored the missing drugs?*'

'*It did cross my mind.*'

The remark did nothing to curb Crosby's anger. He raised his voice. '*You followed me for over four miles. Why the bloody hell didn't you flash your headlights or something?*'

'*I had to make sure there was no one tailing us.*'

'*Why didn't you just ring if you're so bloody paranoid? Or wait to meet me as arranged?*'

'*Which would have put me at fucking risk!*' The Scot was beginning to match Crosby's anger. '*You're probably being monitored and followed.*'

'*You've chased me halfway across a bloody airfield to tell me something I already know?*'

'You ungrateful shit!' Brown snapped at the ex-detective. *'I'm trying to do you another favour here. I should just fucking well leave you to it.'*

Both men drew breath. Crosby realised they'd been shouting into each other's faces. The ex-detective backed off. *'This isn't your fault,'* he said to Brown. *'I shouldn't be taking it out on you.'*

'No you fucking well shouldn't!'

There was a short silence.

'The threat to my family escalated,' Crosby said. *'Someone tried to abduct my grandson from his school. We were lucky this time. They took the wrong child.'*

'Jesus Christ! I saw that. The kid who was snatched last week?'

Crosby nodded. *'I'm under a lot of strain.'*

Brown indicated the ex-detective's pocket. *'You fucking well must be if you're carrying a gun around. Where did you get it?'*

'Doesn't matter.'

'Bloody hell, Frank.' The Scot shook his head. *'I told you last week this could get nasty.'*

'It can't get much worse.'

'It just fucking has!'

Crosby's head lifted.

'Did you get to call on Terry Halloran?' the Scot asked.

'A week ago. I think she knows something.'

'She knows fuck all now,' Brown said to him. *'You've obviously not seen any news over the weekend.'*

'Not had time.'

'She's been strangled. At her flat in Beaumont Street.'

It took Crosby a split second to take in what the Scot had said. *'Murdered?'*

'Well I don't think she throttled herself.'

'Shit!' The news of Terry Halloran's death had taken Crosby aback. *'It might be a coincidence.'*

'And we both know that's not fucking likely.'

'Have the police confirmed it as a murder?'

'Ligature strangling,' Brown replied. 'She'd also been re-arranged and displayed afterwards for effect.'

'That sounds more like a deranged psychopath.'

The Scot shook his head. 'Intended to mislead. She was taken out professionally.'

'What are you basing that on?'

'I've just spent two fucking days sweeping the place,' Brown replied. 'It was clean. Too bloody clean. Nothing on the body or in her flat. This wasn't down to some punter she picked up off the street.'

'Who's leading the investigation?'

'Jack Gould.'

Crosby nodded. 'I know him. Have they come up with anything yet?'

'Fuck all at the moment,' Brown replied. 'Did any of Halloran's neighbours clock you?'

'One of them did.'

'You're in deep shite, laddie.' The Scot shook his head. 'My advice is to let CID know you were there. What happens if you're identified without coming forward?'

'I'll take my chances. I don't think this particular neighbour would involve himself in a police investigation.' Crosby had to lean against one of the partitions, a wave of tiredness sweeping over him.

'All of this implicates me,' Brown said. 'I gave you that address. What the fuck happens now?'

'I'm close to getting some answers,' Crosby replied. 'I just need a few more days.'

'Are you still being pressurised by Lucy Roberts?'

'She's disappeared. Along with her live-in companion.'

Ian Brown raised his eyebrows. 'The cartel got to her?'

'It's a possibility,' Crosby answered. 'She may have gone to ground because of the police. I anonymously passed her name and address to them after the schoolboy's abduction.'

171

'Lucy lifted the kid?'

Crosby shook his head. *'I honestly don't know.'*

'How did you find out where she was living?'

'Through her car registration.'

'Have you been there?'

'It's how I found out they'd both disappeared,' Crosby replied. *'Rose Cavendish's twin brother was there. He's turned up to find out what's going on.'*

'Twin brother?'

Crosby nodded. *'He's legit. I've had someone check him out.'*

'Was he able to help?'

'Only if I needed advice on how to walk in high heels,' the ex-detective replied. *'He answered the door wearing a skirt and make-up.'*

'Fuck me!' A rare smile split the Scot's cheerless features. *'And his sister's a doughnut grinder. They must have had fun growing up together.'*

'Not your average family unit,' Crosby agreed.

'Bloody confusing if you were half pissed and met them on a night out.' Brown chuckled. *'You wouldn't know whether to talk about football or enquire about a shag.'*

Crosby didn't bother trying to interpret the logic of Brown's thought processes.

'What else have you managed to turn up?' the Scot asked.

Crosby shrugged. *'There's a private detective agency asking questions,'* he said. *'And Lucy's mother could have known about the drugs. She used to own Dryffed's Farm before it was sold. A lot of money was ploughed into her new husband's company not long afterwards.'*

'I remember her,' the Scenes-of-Crime officer said. *'Penny Roberts. Married to Lucy's step-father.'*

'*Penny Zardelli now,*' Crosby answered. '*Her husband's family originated from Italy. South American drug cartels and Italian organised crime are in bed with each other all over Western Europe.*'

'*What about John Hendry? Did you manage to find out where he's disappeared to?*'

'*I'm still trying to trace his whereabouts,*' the ex-detective replied. '*He could be back in Ireland.*'

There was a noise from outside the hut. Both men lifted their heads, straining to pick up the sound. It became louder. An approaching vehicle. Brown panicked. '*I fucking knew it! We've been followed.*' He stepped into one of the partitioned spaces. Crosby followed him. They waited. Just the wind howling now. Two minutes passed.

The sound of a car door opening and closing. Crosby's hand wrapped itself firmly around the *Walther's* grip in his pocket. '*You stay here,*' he whispered, peering around the partition's corner.

'*Where are you going?*' Brown hissed at him. '*I want that fucking gun next to me.*'

Someone stepped into the hut. '*Falcon Security Services,*' a silhouetted figure called out. '*Identify yourself.*'

Crosby gauged the figure's stance and body language. It looked more wary than threatening. '*I represent Axebury Developments,*' the ex-detective shouted back. '*We're here on a site visit.*' He stepped out into the hut's central aisle and moved slowly forward, watching for any sudden movement, ready to take cover in in one of the adjoining partitions. The security guard, if that's what he was, remained at the door. Crosby gradually closed the gap between them, gripping the handgun in his jacket pocket. The security guard still looked wary. '*I've called for back-up,*' he warned, indicating the personal radio clipped to his tunic. '*I wasn't told about any site visit.*'

'*My apologies.*' Crosby relaxed slightly as he reached the guard. '*Our company recently made a bid for the airfield. We were carrying out an initial recce this morning.'* He nodded towards the door. *'That was already forced. We were checking there was no one inside.'*

'We?'

'My colleague and I.' The ex-detective smiled and raised his eyebrows. *'He frightens easily.'* Crosby shouted back down the hut's length. *'You can come out now.'*

Ian Brown eventually appeared from the gloom – ashen-faced – his attention fixed on the security guard. All three men made their way outside. Crosby remained a couple of paces behind. He took out his mobile. *'I'm ringing our head office. You should have been informed about the visit.'*

The security guard appeared satisfied, returning to his vehicle. Ian Brown had also reached his car and was already inside it. The look he gave Crosby told the ex-detective there'd be no protracted farewells.

CHAPTER 15

Oxley Village: Thursday 27th October 2011: 07.45 a.m.

He glanced at the illuminated digital display on his dashboard. Five minutes until sunrise. It would be hidden under a blanket of thick, grey cloud this morning. Crosby pulled onto the grass verge and parked-up on top of a slight rise, looking down on the village of Oxley. He was paying another visit to *Endwell Cottage,* the early morning call deliberate. If Rose and Lucy had not yet returned to the cottage he wanted to catch Sam Cavendish in residence and off-guard; the transvestite may have received news of his sister's whereabouts. Crosby was still looking for a breakthrough. His delayed visit to *PB Investigations* yesterday had drawn a blank – the agency's door locked against him. A glance through their outside window had confirmed an empty reception room. On returning to his car he'd found a folded sheet of notepaper tucked underneath one of the windscreen wipers. Its simple message was blunt enough – *'WE WILL TRY AGAIN'*

Crosby pushed a button and slid open the driver's window. He found his tin of small cigars and thumbed a lighter at one of them. The ex-detective had skipped breakfast again that morning. Just a black coffee. He was aware of some weight loss but had no appetite. Crosby dragged more of the acrid smoke into his lungs.

His attention wandered to the village below, enough light to make out some detail now. At the bottom of the hill was *St Mary's* – Oxley's picturesque eleventh century Norman church. Although the ex-detective wouldn't claim to be a particularly religious person he appreciated the peace and solitude that being inside a church could offer – somewhere to gather his thoughts and focus on day-to-day problems.

Crosby wasn't unfamiliar with the church and its history. He and his wife had visited *St Mary's* on a previous occasion. According to notices inside the church, a place of worship had originally been established on the site by invading Anglo-Saxons in the fifth century. Most of Crosby's previous visit had been spent in the churchyard's cemetery – his wife rooting among weathered headstones – searching out the name of a distant relative. One of Doreen Crosby's interests was the compilation of their family's ancestry charts; a hobby the ex-detective had helped her with after his retirement.

A sudden flash of colour in Crosby's peripheral vision interrupted his thoughts. It startled him. His head swivelled. He was surprised to see a small yellow canary, in amongst the twigs and prickly thorns of an adjacent hedgerow. The canary looked cold and miserable, balanced precariously on a thin branch, trying to keep out of view. Others had spotted its presence however. A number of black shapes swooped from the sky – agitated and noisy – their anger focused on the small bird.

Crosby recognised the wild birds as Carrion Crows, a distinctive purple, metallic sheen to their bodies and wings. He opened his car door in an attempt to scare them off, but only succeeded in causing the small, frightened canary to take flight. The crows immediately gave chase. It was a very uneven contest. A series of high-pitched distress calls ended in an explosion of yellow feathers as one crow hit the domesticated bird in mid-flight. It fell to ground, directly in front of Crosby's car. Not content with their kill, the crows descended on the canary's lifeless corpse, tearing and stabbing at it with their beaks. All they left behind were wispy traces of bloodied, yellow feathers, glued to a dark stain left on the road. Their vicious attack was over in seconds.

The crows wheeled away, cawing in noisy triumph, opening out distinctive splayed wing-tips to circle overhead. They eventually retreated to their high roost – a line of bare poplars sited along one side of the church's graveyard. Apart from an occasional flutter of wings the brooding black shapes remained static, continuing to hold a watching brief from the poplars' topmost branches.

The incident had unsettled Crosby, doing little to improve his current mood. He glanced at the Mondeo's dashboard again. Eight o'clock. Time to wake up Sam Cavendish. A BMW convertible passed his nearside window at speed. He managed to catch most of the registration number as it continued down towards *St Mary's* church. The vehicle triggered a flashback. *Aquileia Catering's* car park.

Crosby reached into a jacket pocket and retrieved his notebook. He flipped through several pages to find the registration numbers recorded in Weymouth. There was a match. What the hell was Penny Zardelli's BMW doing in Oxley? Crosby could only think she'd also managed to trace the address of where Lucy had been living. He looked up in time to see the BMW's brake lights illuminate as it turned into *St Mary's* small car park. The ex-detective frowned. What reason would she have for visiting the church?

Looking down from his vantage point he watched two people emerge from the BMW. A man and woman. Crosby couldn't identify either of them from his current position, but the woman certainly carried herself with a self-assurance he would have associated with Penny Zardelli.

The ex-detective watched as both figures made their way up a path towards *St Mary's* entrance porch, the pair of them disappearing from view around an adjacent corner. If it was Penny Zardelli visiting the churchyard he wanted to know why. It crossed his mind that *St Mary's* might be a possible hiding place for the missing drugs. Ten minutes passed. He'd move in a little closer – to make sure it was *Aquileia's* executive director when she eventually returned to the car park. Crosby started his engine, easing the Mondeo a little further down the slope before parking-up again.

Another ten minutes passed before the two figures re-appeared. One of them was certainly Penny Zardelli. The hulking physique ambling alongside looked like her husband's chauffeur. Crosby had last seen him in *Aquileia Catering's* car park, leaning against his employer's Rolls-Royce Phantom Coupé. The ex-detective briefly thought about confronting them. He decided against it.

Penny Zardelli's BMW was expertly reversed and manoeuvred out of *St Mary's* car park. Crosby watched it disappear in the direction of Oxley village. After checking the road was clear he coasted his Mondeo down into the empty car park. He immediately left his car – heading up a wide cobbled pathway towards the church. Crosby by-passed *St Mary's* studded, oak entrance door, hugged the church's south wall, and made his way around to the building's rear. On his right were older burial plots – crumbling, tilted headstones – most of them sunk half-way into the ground. Their chiselled lettering was difficult to read, the stonemason's work no longer sharply edged, defaced by time and the weather.

Crosby reached a stone-buttressed corner at the church's rear. Its headstones and burial mounds were more recent here, one of the graves covered in wreaths and cellophane wrapped flowers. To his left, beyond the cemetery's boundary fence, was a three-storey, grey-bricked house – *St Mary's* old rectory – a Victorian, gothic styled building constructed for Oxley's resident clergy. As a home it didn't look particularly welcoming, the exterior cold, austere, its thick walls inset with small, curtainless windows. On his last visit here someone had told him about local rumours of a strange presence within. The ex-detective's cynicism put that one down to Borley Rectory – reputed to have been the most haunted house in England.

Crosby's eyes swept the building's bleak exterior. It looked un-inhabited. Not surprising in today's economic climate – where the present generation of vicars and rectors might be expected to oversee and administer at least two different parishes. The ex-detective lifted his gaze to a distant stretch of high ground, towards another historic relic from the village's past – Oxley's ancient hanging gallows – perfectly silhouetted against the grey skyline. Crosby's attention fixed on a figure dangling from the structure, both hands tied behind its back, the head angled to one side from a noose looped around its neck.

'That be Hangman's Hill,' a voice shouted across at him.

The ex-detective turned towards a far corner of the churchyard, to where a final resting place was being prepared for one of Oxley's recently departed. Alongside a small, mechanical excavator, surrounded by mounds of piled-up earth, was the lanky figure of a youth leaning nonchalantly on his spade.

Crosby made his way over. The gravedigger watched him approach – small darting eyes – a sly look to his face. Crosby estimated the youth to be around nineteen years of age. His features were sharply defined – angular – sparse ginger stubble and a rash of pimples competing for the limited amount of space on his receding chin. He wore mud-covered blue overalls and a greasy woollen hat, pulled down low over his ears.

On Crosby's arrival the young gravedigger planted his spade into a mound of earth. He grinned at the ex-detective, exposing small, discoloured teeth. *'Our vicar man calls it a gibbet.'* The youth looked over Crosby's shoulder towards the old gallows. *'He told me stories about what they used to do up there.'*

'There's someone hanging from your gibbet,' Crosby pointed out.

'It's where they used to string up highwaymen.' The youth grinned again. *'Left 'em swinging, 'til all their meat dropped off.'*

Crosby nodded. *'They obviously forgot to take the last one down.'*

The gravedigger seemed amused by his comment. He lapsed into an oddly effeminate fit of giggling. *'It's only a Guy Fawkes, mister. Me and Arthur Coombes hung it up there for a laugh.'*

'I'm guessing that Oxley has little to offer you in the way of entertainment.'

Crosby's remark didn't seem to register. *'My name's Tom Dedberry,'* he volunteered. *'I'm the village gravedigger.'*

'And Dedberry's your name is it?' Crosby enquired. *'Or does Arthur Coombes call you that for a laugh as well?'*

The youth wrinkled his brow. *'Eh?'*

179

'Doesn't matter. How long have you been working here, Tom?' the ex-detective asked.

'Since I left school,' Dedberry replied. 'Vicar man tells me I'm lucky to have a job.'

'I'd have to agree with him,' Crosby said. 'Do you live here in Oxley, Tom?'

The youth nodded enthusiastically. 'All my family do. Have done for years.'

'Most of them married to each other presumably,' Crosby muttered to himself. He gestured towards the freshly dug grave. 'Do you see yourself continuing in this line of work?'

'I shan't always be doin' this.' The youth looked put out. 'Rod Stewart used to be a gravedigger you know. I got plans.'

'You sing in a band then?'

Dedberry shook his head and frowned. 'No.'

Crosby regarded the youth – not entirely sure who was humouring who. 'There was a man and woman here,' the ex-detective said. 'They've just left. Where did they go?'

An artful look crossed Dedberry's face. 'They went back to the car park I think.'

Crosby smiled. 'Are we still playing games, Tom?'

'What?'

'Not that bloody silly are we.' The ex-detective reached into a jacket pocket and took out his wallet. He slowly extracted a five-pound note. 'Did you see what part of the churchyard they went to?'

'Might have.'

'I can easily find out another way.' Crosby proffered the note.

Dedberry stretched out a mud-caked hand for it. He jerked his head towards St Mary's rectory. 'They were lookin' at them row of graves over by the old house.' He turned to the mechanical excavator's cabin, tucking away his five-pound note into a small glove compartment. It drew Crosby's attention to a powerful looking air rifle lying across the operator's seat. *'That looks as if it needs a licence,'* he said, nodding towards the weapon. *'What size calibre is it?'*

'The vicar man give it me for shootin' vermin.' Dedberry picked up the rifle, swinging it around in Crosby's direction.

The ex-detective flinched. He raised his voice. *'Point that bloody thing somewhere else will you!'*

Dedberry laughed. *'You looks nervous, Mister.'* The gravedigger took aim at a nearby tree. *'I kills squirrel with it. The vicar man tells me they're a bloody nuisance. Strips the bark off all our trees.'* He tapped his airgun. *'This sorts the buggers out. Rips a pellet right through 'em. I see's to the rats with it as well.'*

Crosby was still eying the rifle. *'Put the bloody thing down! It might be loaded.'*

The gravedigger broke open his airgun and looked inside. He feigned surprise. *'Who put that bugger in there?'*

Crosby held the youth's gaze, waiting for him to lay the rifle down. Dedberry grinned, eventually dropping it back into the excavator's cabin. Crosby turned on his heel and headed towards *St Mary's* rectory house. Although he didn't look back the ex-detective was aware of Dedberry watching him.

A row of headstones ran alongside *St Mary's* rectory fence – the dates on them indicating burials carried out within the last five years. Crosby walked slowly past, reading the gilt-edged inscriptions. A name jumped out. It physically jolted him.

ROBERT JAMES MILNER.
Now you can rest in peace. February 1968 - March 2007

Robert Milner's name brought back into sharp focus the horrific sequence of events at *Dryffed's Farm* yet again – especially the memory of Milner jamming both barrels of a shotgun up into his mouth and blowing his head apart.

Crosby hadn't realised that Oxley village was where Penny Zardelli had buried her first husband. The ex-detective did know from questioning Robert Milner during their Sixfields investigation that he and his family had once lived out in the country – until a series of cost-cutting initiatives found the ex-financier surplus to requirements at his Birmingham office. If Milner's children previously lived in Oxley it probably explained why Lucy had rented a property in the village when setting up home with Rose Cavendish.

He glanced instinctively at the adjacent grave. Crosby wasn't entirely surprised to see a headstone bearing the name of Robert Milner's son. Stephen had also been killed during the Sixfields investigation – he'd become a liability within the drug smuggling operation that his father-in-law was running. Stephen had probably been executed by his sister Lucy. This was the character of woman that Crosby had dealt with four years ago. She wouldn't have changed.

Crosby remained at both graves, turning over the development. Was Oxley village a key to all this? Why would it be? There was a logical enough reason for all of Robert Milner's family to be congregated here in one form or another. It was probably just the *Dryffed's Farm* connection preying on his mind again.

A flicker of movement caused him to look up. It had come from above his eye-line. The old rectory. Crosby scanned its exterior. Nothing. He didn't immediately turn away, his attention concentrated on the building's upper storey. At one of the bedroom windows a face appeared, its features indistinct, looking directly down at him. The image was fleeting. It disappeared, replaced by a handwritten message pushed up against the pane of glass – uneven, scrawled lettering – just large enough for Crosby to make out the words *'HELP ME'*. That also vanished, leaving him to stare at the reflection of an empty window.

The ex-detective's cynicism favoured a prank – another of Tom Dedberry's associates – maybe the same one who thought that hanging *Guy Fawkes* from Oxley's gibbet had a certain warped appeal. *'Shit!'* He'd have to check it out though, which would put the visit to *Endwell*

Cottage and Sam Cavendish further behind schedule. Crosby looked over his shoulder to see if the young gravedigger had been watching. Dedberry wasn't in view, his position blocked out by the church's nearside corner.

Crosby looked back up at the window. No one there. He briefly considered returning to the car park. There was a torch and his *Walther* tucked away in the Mondeo's glove compartment. He decided against it, enough time had been wasted already. After making his way through an adjacent garden gate he took a narrow gravelled path up to the rectory's front door.

The house looked even more inhospitable close-to – its downstairs windows hadn't been cleaned in a while and the front door's faded paintwork was peeling away in strips. Crosby attempted to twist the solid, pitted brass door-knob. It wouldn't budge. He didn't bother to knock. Moving across to a nearby window the ex-detective peered inside. Possibly the sitting room. It was difficult to tell – the interior light virtually non-existent.

Walking around to the rear of the house he found a wide expanse of lawn, stretching away to merge with surrounding farm and meadowland. The rectory's garden had been well maintained – more so than the house – its grass recently cut and flowerbeds tended. Probably the gravedigger's work. Crosby edged his way along the building's rear wall, reaching a pair of white PVC French doors. They looked to be a recent addition, out of character with its nineteenth century surround. He pushed down on one of the door handles. It didn't resist.

Crosby stepped cautiously into a large hall and reception area, the stone-flagged flooring cold beneath his feet. A gloomy half-light made it difficult to see. He paused, sniffing at a dry, musty atmosphere, trying to gauge whether his intrusion had alerted anyone. There were only background noises – the old rectory creaking and groaning – as if stretching itself after a long night's sleep. Crosby listened for sounds of movement above him. Nothing. He clicked a nearby wall switch. It didn't produce any light. *'Bollocks!'* The torch would have been useful.

A door on his right had been left ajar. Crosby walked across to it. Inside the room a number of white dust sheets had been spread around, covering what looked like heavy, solid furniture. All of the walls were bare, devoid of any decoration. Above him, running the whole length of a high ceiling, were two supporting dark oak beams.

Crosby turned and went back into the reception hall. In front of him a flight of un-carpeted stairs wound their way up towards the gloom of a first-floor landing. Crosby moved across to the staircase. His weight on the first step caused it to creak and echo in the silence. He waited. The noise didn't appear to attract anyone's attention.

He continued slowly up a dozen more steps, making it to the first-floor landing. There were three doors, probably bedrooms, all closed against him. Crosby paused. The landing had no outside windows. It was almost completely dark here. There was another flight of stairs, leading to an upper storey. Only the staircase's first three steps were visible to him.

A floorboard creaked – different to the other sounds – caused by someone moving across the floor above him. He bit down on an impulse to call out. His sixth sense advised him it wasn't friendly. The movement stopped. Tiny hairs on the back of Crosby's neck began to rise. He shouldn't be here. *'Bit fucking late now!'* Three years of retirement told him he probably wasn't in shape to deal with this.

Another floorboard creaked. There was someone coming down the stairs. Crosby flattened himself against the wall, trying to peer up through several layers of darkness. It happened very quickly. A shadow came out of the gloom and lunged towards him. There was the dull glint of an extended blade. Crosby's reflexes took him two paces back – but the landing's top stair was misjudged. As the ex-detective fell he curled his body into a tight ball, rolling and bumping at speed down the short staircase. He was vaguely aware of his assailant falling down the stairs alongside him. As the stone floor came rushing up to meet them both the ex-detective thrust out a protective hand, his wrist buckling under impact. Although disorientated by the fall he instinctively rolled over onto one side, sensing his attacker close-by. Crosby felt the knife's blade slash past him. Metal scraped against stone and a shower of sparks lit up the darkness.

The impact to his wrist hadn't registered immediately but now it kicked in, a sharp pain shooting up his arm. Crosby lay spread-eagled, incapable of further movement, the injured wrist making him an easy target. He anticipated the knife's hit and pushed out a hand to shield himself. Nothing happened. When the ex-detective looked up he found a face peering down at him through the gloom. *'Very undignified,'* Penny Zardelli remarked. The chauffeur stood next to her. He was keeping a vice-like grip on Sam Cavendish. Crosby struggled to his feet.

'You've lost that detective's ability to keep a low profile, Inspector.' Penny Zardelli stood with arms folded. *'We passed your car earlier.'* She nodded at Crosby's attacker. *'Do you know her?'*

The transvestite was wearing a thick woollen sweater over black leggings. A blonde wig had somehow remained in place. An application of heavy make-up completed the spectacle. *'It's a him,'* Crosby replied.

'Is it really.' *Aquileia's* executive director turned to face Cavendish. *'And what's the name of this unfortunate misfit?'*

'Sam Cavendish,' Crosby answered. *'Rose's twin brother.'*

Penny Zardelli looked more intrigued than surprised. *'A slight family resemblance I suppose. Although he does look more attractive than his sister. Wouldn't you agree, Inspector?'*

Crosby didn't reply. He was more concerned with the pain in his wrist. *Aquileia's* executive director slowly circled the transvestite. *'He obviously intended for you to join St Mary's permanent residents here in the cemetry,'* she said. *'Any particular reason for that?'*

'I've no idea.' The ex-detective shrugged. 'We've only met once before. At Lucy's cottage. He's here to find out what's happened to his sister.'

Penny Zardelli stopped pacing. 'Who seems to have disappeared along with my daughter.' She looked at Cavendish again. 'The cottage appears empty. Where are they?'

No reply.

'And your reason for attacking a police officer during the course of his duties?'

The transvestite just glared at her. There was no sign of the friendly, genial character that Crosby had encountered last week. Penny Zardelli sighed. 'Tiresome and unnecessary. Another interrogation for Giorgio to amuse himself with.' She turned her attention back to Crosby. 'I presume your visit here also concerns my daughter, Inspector?'

'I told you last week,' the ex-detective said. 'I'm investigating a missing cache of drugs from Dryffed's Farm.'

'So you did.' Penny Zardelli's frown was an exaggerated one. 'And on whose authority would that be? My enquiries indicate that you retired three years ago.'

Crosby wasn't that surprised. At this moment he didn't particularly care either. The fall had badly shaken him and his wrist was becoming increasingly painful. There seemed little point in continuing the pretence. 'Your daughter's being threatened by a drugs cartel because of the missing heroin,' he said. 'They weren't paid for the original shipment and Lucy claims I'm responsible for its disappearance.'

'And are you?'

'Your daughter's desperate,' Crosby replied, 'and because of that she's threatened my family.'

'The abducted schoolboy?'

'Yes.'

'The police have questioned me about that.' Penny Zardelli showed some hesitation. 'I don't believe my daughter is capable of kidnapping a child.'

Crosby wanted to point out Lucy's past history and the resulting prison sentence. He steered away from it. 'Your daughter's not well, Ms Zardelli. I believe the situation has affected her mind.'

Penny Zardelli's head lifted abruptly. 'Lucy's father suffered from chronic depression and mental health issues. Are you suggesting my daughter has inherited them?'

Crosby left her question hanging.

'Lucy is suffering from acute stress,' Aquileia's executive director said sharply. 'It's not surprising. She's been an innocent victim in all of this from the outset. My second husband exploited a young girl's naivety to coerce her into his drug smuggling operation. Rose Cavendish took advantage of my daughter's age and vulnerability in Foston Hall. The woman remains a continuing influence on her.'

'I'm the only victim here, Ms Zardelli,' Crosby said. 'My family should not be expected to suffer as a result of your daughter's self-inflicted situation.'

Aquileia's executive director waved a dismissive hand. 'Your family's circumstances are of little concern to me. The only reason I have not reported your impersonation of a police officer to the authorities is because it would serve no useful purpose at this point. As you and I both need to establish Lucy's current whereabouts we may be able to help each other.' Penny Zardelli looked towards Cavendish. 'At the moment, however, it would appear that this oddity offers us the best chance of providing some answers.'

'I should question him now, Signora?' Giorgio Messina asked, his muscled forearm still wrapped around the transvestite's neck.

'Probably not,' Penny Zardelli replied. 'He may need persuading. Somewhere you won't be disturbed.'

'I can't be a party to that,' Crosby said.

Penny Zardelli regarded the ex-detective. *'You are in no position to dictate anything. Your views are irrelevant. And are you really that concerned?'*

She had a point. Crosby wasn't entirely sure what his objections were anyway. They were interrupted. Cavendish had somehow managed to free himself and a scuffle broke out. The transvestite threw several wild punches at Messina before the Sicilian stepped in close to him and short-armed an uppercut to Cavendish's chin. Penny Zardelli eyed the spread-eagled transvestite with a look of disdain. *'How long will he be out?'* she asked her chauffeur.

'Ten minutes, Signora.'

'You'd better check upstairs,' the woman instructed. *'His sister might be hiding out up there with Lucy.'*

Messina made his way towards the staircase. *'I'd like to know if they're here,'* Crosby said.

'You'll leave!' the woman instructed. *'I'll consider passing on anything that's relevant.'* Crosby offered no argument. The pain from his wrist was becoming almost unbearable. He needed medical attention and painkillers.

On leaving the rectory he tried to open his tin of cigars one-handed, eventually having to give up on it. In the churchyard he looked across to where Tom Dedberry had been working. His mechanical excavator was still there but the young gravedigger wasn't. Crosby made it to the car. He found his mobile and managed to switch it on. There was voicemail. *'It's Grace,'* the voice said in his ear. *'I may have something for you. Don't ring me. I'll be in touch.'*

Crosby switched off his phone. What now? At least she was talking to him. He examined his wrist, which had begun to swell alarmingly. He'd have to find the nearest *Accident and Emergency Department.* Crosby wasn't leaving just yet however. He needed to know whether Lucy and her partner had been hiding out in the rectory. It was only when Penny Zardelli and her chauffeur came into view, propping up a groggy Sam Cavendish, did the ex-detective start up his Mondeo and move off.

CHAPTER 16

Birmingham City Centre: Friday 28th October 2011: 8.00 p.m.

Detective Constable Grace Taylor was thinking about the message she'd left with Frank Crosby yesterday. She hadn't been able to call on him in person – an awkwardness still lingering from last Friday's visit to Hawthorne Rise. And where had that suddenly come from? There'd certainly been no sexual chemistry between them previously. Or had there? Was she embarrassed because of the move she'd made on him or because he'd rejected her advances? And why leave a message to indicate she had information for him? Was there some advantage in telling him what she'd discovered? Probably not, but Taylor still retained a degree of affection and loyalty towards her old boss. She didn't like to see him suffering. The situation he found himself in wasn't his fault.

Someone who Grace Taylor certainly didn't feel any loyalty towards was the West Midlands Police Force. There'd been an anger building within her for some time now, a bitterness about still holding the rank of detective constable at this point in her career. Although she'd passed written and practical examinations with consummate ease, the rank of sergeant had been denied on two separate occasions now – promotion board members failing to spot her potential during the final interview stage. She'd convinced herself that prejudice against women still existed within the force, that equal opportunity quotas for female officers were not being maintained.

As Taylor watched less capable male officers promoted ahead of her the deep-rooted sense of injustice had continued to grow. She'd become disillusioned – lost enthusiasm and focus for the job – given a lot of thought to resigning her position. The frustration that Taylor felt had resulted in her acting out of character. When Frank Crosby initially asked for help about a missing cache of heroin she'd carried out some unofficial off-duty enquiries – coming across information that suggested a possible connection between the missing drugs, a murdered prostitute, and the abducted schoolboy. Now the policewoman had to decide how she would present her findings. What Taylor really wanted to do was publicly embarrass the West Midlands Police, reveal how she'd managed to uncover what other detectives in the Department hadn't picked up. Not just yet though. There were still loose ends to tie-up and confirm. But she was very close now.

Taylor pushed it to the back of her mind. She was on a night out. The policewoman relaxed and leant back, sipping at a dry white Chablis, savouring its aromatic flavour. She returned her long-stemmed wine glass back onto the crisp, white tablecloth, taking in more of her surroundings. Attentive waiters glided effortlessly between diners, their movement complementing the room's subdued lighting and unobtrusive background music. Taylor reached for a leather-bound menu and flicked through its heavy, embossed pages. An exorbitant price list confirmed the establishment's stellar reputation. It didn't concern her. She wasn't paying.

A tall, well-built figure approached the table. Grace Taylor looked up, switching on what she considered was a welcoming smile. As to whether it was genuine or not, even she wasn't sure at this stage of the evening.

'Hi.' Lieutenant Bradley Thorburn III wore a well-cut, light-grey suit, its colour in marked contrast to his dark skin. He stood before her, like an errant schoolboy waiting to be reprimanded. Taylor thought it might be a pose he'd perfected over the years – to win over female companions or probably a gullible wife.

'You're late!' she said accusingly. Playing his game perhaps?

The American raised both hands in apology. *'Your man Rees-Bramley,'* he offered in way of explanation. *'The guy's a workaholic. He never wants to go home.'*

Taylor nodded. *'He used to be my Chief Inspector in a previous life.'* Their waiter approached, unobtrusive, immaculately attired in the restaurant's livery of charcoal grey waistcoat, white shirt and black trousers. He bowed slightly, pulling out the American's chair for him. *'Welcome to Devignon's, Sir. My name is Eugene. I will be personally attending your table this evening.'*

Retrieving Thorburn's linen napkin the waiter shook out a series of elaborately folded pleats. He leant forward to place it across the American's lap. *'That's OK, Eugene.'* Lieutenant Thorburn didn't look entirely comfortable with the attention. He took the napkin from him. *'I'll handle it from here.'*

'Of course, Sir.' The waiter took a small notepad from his waistcoat pocket. *'And what are we having to complement our meal with this evening?'*

'I've no idea what you're having,' Thorburn grinned, *'but I'm about ready for a Jack Daniels over ice.'*

The waiter's fleeting smile was almost non-existent. He turned to the policewoman. *'And for yourself Madam?'*

Taylor indicated the already open bottle of Chablis. *'I'm enjoying my wine thank you.'*

'Does that fruit juice carry enough alcohol to lower a lady's resistance?' Thorburn asked her.

The policewoman regarded him from beneath her eyebrows. *'It has a tendency to make me feel drowsy. I then become bored with the company I'm keeping.'*

'Ouch!' The American's pained expression didn't suggest he was at all put out.

'Just a single Jack Daniels then, Sir?' the waiter enquired.

'Why not make it a large one,' Thorburn said.

'Why not indeed, Sir.' The waiter backed discreetly away from their table and made his way towards the restaurant's bar area.

Thorburn looked down at the regimented lines of cutlery set out neatly before him. *'You might have to give me a heads up on some of this hardware,'* he said to the policewoman.

Taylor nodded. *'I'm sure it would be perfectly acceptable to just use a fork if you're more comfortable with that.'*

The American laughed out loud. *'I love the English. They even make their insults sound polite.'*

'Something a New Yorker couldn't be accused of,' Taylor replied.

'Now that's stereotyping,' the lieutenant protested. *'We're not all of us loud and in your face. I'm a little further along the coast. Westchester County. We like to think of ourselves as up-state New York.'*

'Is that the same as up-market?' Taylor asked.

'And now you're mocking me.'

The policewoman smiled. *'I've heard it said that Westchester County fondly refers to itself as Old Colonial.'*

'You're very well informed, ma'am.'

Grace Taylor propped both elbows on the table and cupped her chin in one hand. *'And what are your views on that, lieutenant?'* she asked. *'Do you become misty-eyed and patriotic when you're referred to as Old Colonial American? Even though your ancestors were probably slave labour and imported from Africa's coastline.'*

Thorburn frowned. *'Have you had a bad day, Ms Taylor? Don't be too judgemental. British traders ferried black slaves to the colonies for over two hundred years.'*

'I've offended you, lieutenant.'

'No ma'am,' Thorburn replied. *'I'm black, American, and proud of it. I've accepted where history saw to deposit my ancestors. Our country's a great place to live.'* He leant back in his chair. *'Do you intend throwing any more darts at me this evening?'*

Taylor shook her head and smiled. *'I apologise. It's not your fault. Probably that bad day you were referring to.'*

'Anything you need to talk through?'

'Absolutely not,' Taylor said. *'It isn't your problem. Why don't we start again?'*

Thorburn nodded. *'That works for me. How about your background?'* he asked. *'Are you comfortable with your ancestral roots?'*

'I'm a third-generation Jamaican Brit,' the policewoman replied. *'My paternal grandfather emigrated to Birmingham in the late fifties.'*

'And does the Caribbean have a mystical pull on you?'

Taylor shook her head. *'I'm content enough in the UK. I leave pilgrimages and searching for one's inner self to those who find comfort in it.'*

'And have you always been with the West Midlands?' Thorburn asked.

'Joined after I finished college,' Taylor said. *'Ten years ago. How long have you been with NYPD?'*

'I enrolled with the Manhattan police academy after my graduation,' Thorburn replied. *'After eight months I was a rookie cop patrolling the Bronx. Made the grade to sergeant in my late twenties. Now I spend all day sitting behind a lieutenant's desk.'*

'Do you miss the streets?'

'Sometimes,' Thorburn said. *'A warm, comfortable office doesn't provide too many adrenalin rushes.'*

'And is there likely to be a captain's badge?'

'Maybe.' Thorburn shrugged. *'I've only just made lieutenant. How about yourself? Do you have plans to make sergeant?'*

'Promotion boards can't always spot potential,' Taylor said.

The American detected resentment and didn't pursue it. He looked up as a tumbler of *Jack Daniels* was placed in front of him. *'Are you ready to order, Sir?'* the waiter asked.

'I'm still catching up, Eugene,' the American replied. *'Ten minutes?'*

'Of course, Sir.' The waiter glided effortlessly away.

Thorburn turned to the policewoman. *'Have you eaten here before?'*

'Only when my date is on expenses,' Taylor answered.

Thorburn picked up his bourbon. *'A toast to Uncle Sam then.'* They touched glasses. The American swallowed a measure before standing up. *'You'll have to excuse me. The taxi took a while to get here. I think my driver caught the accent and added a few miles to our journey.'*

Taylor nodded. *'Your car passed the restaurant window on at least three occasions.'*

Thorburn grinned. *'I'll be right back.'*

Grace Taylor watched him negotiate his way across the restaurant. They'd met earlier that week, during the lieutenant's tour of Studley police station. He'd contacted her later that afternoon. Taylor was still unsure as to why she'd accepted the American's invitation to dinner. Was there a thought in the back of her mind that he might be able to help out with what she'd uncovered? Did she intend to use him in some way? Taylor shook her head. Maybe she was just attracted to him. Whatever the reason it was unprofessional behaviour, and Rees-Bramley would not be impressed if he found out they'd been on a dinner date. Perhaps that was her intention – to create even more embarrassment for the department. She picked up her menu again.

Thorburn returned to their table. *'Have you come to a decision yet?'* he asked.

'The Leek and Chestnut Risotto.' Taylor's smile was a little warmer.

The lieutenant picked up his menu. *'Sounds good to me.'* Thorburn turned to summon their waiter. He was already at the American's elbow, a notepad and pencil to hand. *'An excellent choice, Madam. And to start with?'*

'A mixed leaf Caesar Salad please.'

'Of course. And for you, Sir?'

'I like what the lady's having.'

'Of course, Sir.' The waiter finished jotting down their orders, before removing several items of cutlery and their menus from the

table. Thorburn was the first to speak after he'd left. *'You don't wear a wedding ring, Ms Taylor.'*

'Neither do you,' the policewoman responded. *'And now you're about to tell me that you're either separated or divorced.'*

Thorburn spread his hands. *'Which in this case might be true.'*

'I'm sure we can enjoy the evening without reviewing previous or current relationships.' Taylor said.

The lieutenant raised his glass. *'I don't have a problem with that.'*

Taylor waited for him to swallow another measure of bourbon. *'Is your exchange visit here proving beneficial?'* she asked.

'You never stop learning,' Thorburn replied. *'We like to think our procedures at NYPD nail down most eventualities. There's always something new just around the corner though.'*

'How do you find the UK itself?' Taylor enquired. *'Birmingham must be quite a culture shock after life in New York.'*

'I pretty much knew what to expect,' the American replied. *'It's my second exchange visit to Lloyd House.'*

The policewoman looked surprised. *'You were here before?'*

'About four years back,' Thorburn said. *'I was running a narcotics unit out of 41st Precinct in the Bronx. An opportunity came up to see how West Midlands drug enforcement operated.'*

Taylor frowned. *'Were you here when the Sixfields riot broke out?'*

'Reminded me of New York.' Thorburn tried to make light of it. *'The natives can get pretty restless during one of our heatwaves.'*

The policewoman sensed a hesitation. *'Sixfields' riots were bankrolled and engineered to gain control of the estate's drug supply.'* Taylor's brow furrowed. *'Were you aware of that during your time here?'*

Thorburn didn't look entirely uncomfortable. He signalled for another drink. Taylor wasn't about to let it go. *'We never quite established just how much our drugs squad knew about it at the time.'*

The American toyed with his cutlery. *'You know I can't discuss what particular strategies and procedures were in place back then.'*

'I know they offered very little assistance to CID during our six week investigation,' Taylor responded.

'Chrissake!' Thorburn's good humour seemed to have evaporated. *'Can we drop this? It was four years ago. Am I back on the witness stand here?'*

Taylor ignored him. *'And you must have been aware of the killings at Dryffed's Farm.'*

'Yes, ma'am.'

'Which were a direct consequence of what had taken place in Sixfields.'

'So I believe.'

'There were three survivors that afternoon,' Taylor said. *'I was lucky to be one of them.'*

The American didn't reply.

'My God!' Taylor looked directly at him. *'You bloody well knew I was at the farm.'*

Thorburn shook his head. *'I only found out about that earlier this week. Rees-Bramley filled me in during my tour of the Studfield station.'*

The policewoman didn't look totally convinced. Her recent, lone investigation had uncovered information about the missing drugs from *Dryffed's Farm* – and now here was someone sitting in front of her who not only admitted to being around at the time, but was actually on detached duty with West Midlands drugs enforcement. Is that why he'd asked her to dinner? Was it just a coincidence?

Thorburn attempted to retrieve the situation. *'Those riots cut short my secondment back then. I was sent home. How would I have known you were personally involved?'*

Taylor regarded the American. Was she being paranoid? If Thorburn did have additional information to what she'd already uncovered then the policewoman needed to know about it. *Dryffed's*

Farm and the missing drugs had already claimed at least two lives. Possibly more. *'Ignore me,'* Taylor said. *'I'm over reacting. I still get flashbacks about what happened at the farm.'*

'I was purely an observer,' Thorburn said. *'My role had no input to any operational decisions.'*

An awkward silence descended.

'I guess the evening just nose dived,' Thorburn eventually said.

'I don't know yet.' The policewoman leant back. *'That depends on how hard you work at winning me around.'* Taylor certainly didn't want to lose the opportunity of finding out what Thorburn might be keeping to himself. Their waiter re-materialised, expertly balancing two bowls of mixed salad leaves and another large *Jack Daniels.*

'How about it, Eugene?' the American asked. *'Do we Yanks have enough old fashioned charm to win back a lady's respect?'*

'Hollywood seems able to manage it well enough when there's a script involved,' the waiter replied. He placed the two small bowls of salad in front of them and made his way back towards the kitchen.

Thorburn arched both his eyebrows. *'What the hell did he mean by that?'*

Taylor smiled. *'It was certainly open to interpretation.'* She picked up her salad fork and speared two crisp, romaine lettuce leaves.

The meal continued. Thorburn was charm itself, employing everything he knew to re-capture the moment. Taylor had become pre-occupied however. Her mind elsewhere. She might need assistance to conclude her investigation and Lieutenant Bradley Thorburn could be the answer. If the telephone call she was expecting materialised within the next few hours then the American's presence and back-up could prove invaluable. Taylor had to be sure however – the policewoman wasn't totally convinced about him. Spending a night together would give her more time.

An hour later, after coffee had been served, the waiter returned to ask if they required a taxi. *'Well, I'll certainly need one,'* Thorburn replied. He looked across at the policewoman.

'What sort of living accommodation has Uncle Sam provided you with?'

'Private,' the American answered. *'Very comfortable.'*

'One taxi should suffice then,' Taylor said.

'I'll attend to it, Madam.' The waiter whisked their empty coffee cups onto a tray and left.

Grace Taylor pushed back her chair. *'And if there's a possibility of us waking up in the same bed tomorrow morning,'* she said to Thorburn, *'I think we ought to dispense with surnames.'*

'Yes ma'am.' Thorburn half-stood as the policewoman left their table. He followed the sway of Taylor's hips as she crossed to the ladies' rest room.

A folded card, embossed with Devignon's logo, appeared on the table in front of him. Thorburn didn't bother to look at the bill's detail. He reached into his jacket pocket. Opening a slim, black leather wallet, the American slid out an AmEx platinum card along with a crisp ten-pound note.

'You'll have a drink with my compliments, Eugene,' the lieutenant said. *'You've been lucky for me tonight.'*

'Thank you, Sir.' The waiter deftly palmed Thorburn's ten-pound note. *'I'm sure your expectations and good fortune will continue into the remainder of this evening.'*

The American shook his head. *'Why am I always having to interpret what you guys actually mean over here?'*

'Are you, Sir?'

'And why do you answer questions with a question of your own?'

'Do we, Sir?'

Thorburn smiled. *'Just see to my tab, Eugene.'* The waiter picked up Thorburn's AmEx card and made his way towards the restaurant's central station.

Ten minutes later, outside *Devignon's* front entrance, the American placed his hand lightly under Grace Taylor's arm. They negotiated half-a-dozen shallow, stone steps down to the pavement. A black taxi-cab edged forward from its holding bay and pulled up in front of the couple. Thorburn gave the driver his address and within minutes they were speeding along a dual-carriageway towards Birmingham's Ladywood district. Three large *Jack Daniels* had left the American in a relaxed and confident mood. He rested a hand on Grace Taylor's knee. *'Fuck's sake,'* the policewoman swore inwardly, but she allowed him to leave it there.

Towards the end of their journey Thorburn's hand transferred its attention to the inside of Taylor's thigh – where a certain amount of progress was allowed before she eventually brought it to a halt. The policewoman wondered who would have most regrets come tomorrow morning.

Their taxi pulled up outside Thorburn's accommodation. Grace Taylor's mobile ring tone sounded from the depths of her handbag as they both stepped out of the car. *'I'll need to take this,'* she said, moving a short distance away from him. *'I've been expecting an important call.'*

CHAPTER 17

Dartmoor is an area of natural, unspoilt beauty, covering more than three hundred square miles of the UK's south-west region. It is protected by National Park status and encompasses a variety of landscapes, including moorland, forests, rivers, waterfalls, rocky tor outcrops and deep rolling valleys. Bovey Tracey, a small town of Saxon origin, sits at Dartmoor's most easterly point – from where the open moor stretches across to Tavistock on its western fringes.

There's evidence that Dartmoor was inhabited and farmed during the Mesolithic period over ten thousand years ago – but it's tourism that underpins the area's economy now – an average of eleven million visitors accessing the park each year. Many of Dartmoor's old buildings, that would otherwise have collapsed into ruin, now provide accommodation for all those holidaymakers who prefer their vacations close to nature.

One such reprieved dwelling was a thirteenth-century farm labourer's cottage – *Leawater View* – four stone walls hewn from local granite, a roof constructed of Delabole slate. The farmhouse that it originally served had long since disappeared, but *Leawater View* somehow survived – tucked into one side of a shallow valley at nearly three hundred feet above sea level.

The remote cottage retained its original, small windows, restrictive openings that limited any daylight. On this late October morning, inside the cramped, single-storey dwelling, it was difficult to see properly. There had been attempts to alleviate the cottage's austere interior with items of tasteful furnishings, but a low, beamed ceiling and stone-flagged flooring made it feel sombre, inhospitable – even on the warmest of days there was a chill air that permeated throughout.

The cottage was currently occupied. A male figure, half-silhouetted, sat upright in one of the room's straight-backed wooden chairs. He was clearly agitated, his fingers drumming an irregular staccato on the table-top in front of him. The man cast frequent glances into a far corner, at an old iron bedstead. On its thin mattress someone lay huddled under grey blankets, a leg draped outside the bed's narrow confines. Shackled around the person's bare ankle a length of chain had been secured, its other end looped and padlocked to the bed's heavy frame. The chain's generous length allowed its tethered captive some freedom of movement, providing sufficient access to a nearby composting toilet.

Ten minutes passed. An impatient check of his watch caused the man to stand up. He crossed to the front door and unlatched it, stepping out into rugged, open moorland. A lone buzzard wheeled effortlessly overhead, quartering the ground below in search of prey. There was no other sign of life or habitation – *Leawater View's* closest neighbours were at least three miles away. The man lifted his face to an overcast sky and sniffed at the freshening breeze. A threat of rain in the air. He looked along the cottage's single-track access road, a narrow ribbon of flattened ground that wound its way through clumps of purple heather before disappearing into the far distance.

'*Affanculo!*' The man swore under his breath. '*Dove Sei?*' He began to pace. The silence was punctuated by sounds of distant gunfire coming from one of Dartmoor's three MOD firing ranges. Another ten minutes passed. The man's agitation increased. A distant speck of movement crawling along the access road caught his eye. As it progressed slowly towards him a 4x4 silver grey Mercedes-Benz gradually revealed itself – the vehicle eventually grinding to a bumpy halt in front of *Leawater View's* front door. There was a brief delay before Penny Zardelli stepped from her car. *Aquileia Catering's* executive director had dressed for autumn. She wore a chunky knit wool cardigan and roll-neck pullover, her tight-fitting, blue denim jeans tucked into knee-length boots. Despite the dull, overcast day a pair of large designer sunglasses hid most of the executive director's face. Her mood was prickly – the journey from Weymouth having taken over two hours. *'Any problems?'* she asked brusquely, removing a silk headscarf and shaking her short, dark hair into place.

'You leave me two nights, Signora,' Giorgio Messina replied. *'Is not comfortable here.'*

'You're descended from Sicilian peasant stock,' the woman said dismissively. *'It's five star luxury compared to what you grew up with.'*

The Italian didn't pursue it. Giorgio Messina had long since given up trying to gauge the mood of his employer's wife. *'We both stay here tonight, Signora?'* he asked.

'No we bloody well do not!' Penny Zardelli responded. *'Your rustic form of animal coupling has become rather tiresome of late.'* She looked towards the cottage. *'Are you ready to make a start?'*

'Is all in place, Signora.'

'Shall we get on with it then? This God forsaken place is already beginning to depress me.' Penny Zardelli collected a shoulder bag from the car before striding away from him, an expensive fragrance trailing in her wake. Messina quickly followed, hurrying past her to open the cottage's front door. She stepped inside, her eyes lighting on the iron bedstead. *'Jesus Christ!'* she said, holding the silk headscarf to her nose and mouth. *'It smells of animal excrement in here.'*

'The toilet is not good, Signora.'

Penny Zardelli kept the headscarf to her nose. *'It's perfectly adequate. You've obviously not been using it properly.'*

A public sewer connection was not the only mains service that *Leawater View* lacked – the National Grid system didn't supply gas or electric to the cottage either. Paraffin lamps lit the interior, heat came from a wood-burning stove, and an outside water tank provided occupants with all of their water requirements. Messina had other complaints but realised it would have been pointless to voice them.

Penny Zardelli had bought the cottage on a whim. She thought it would make an ideal retreat for both Enrico and herself – weekend breaks away – to relieve the stress of running their successful but time-consuming catering business. The cottage's purchase had been a mistake. She had immediately regretted it. *Aquileia's* executive director was used to bright lights and modern conveniences. Her first Dartmoor night had been unnerving – the impenetrable darkness – an alien silence and solitude. One weekend was more than enough. The experience hadn't been repeated. Dartmoor's rustic charm was left to those Mother Earth types who appreciated wide open spaces and a lack of human contact.

Aquileia's executive director turned her attention to the mound of grey blankets. *'Wake it!'* she instructed Messina.

The hulking Sicilian ambled across to the narrow bed. Bending his knees he grasped the bed's underside with both hands and tipped it completely over. A bewildered looking Sam Cavendish lay sprawled across the stone floor. He looked unkempt – make-up smeared all over his face – still in the same clothes and blonde wig he'd been wearing when taken from *St Mary's* old rectory house. The transvestite quickly recovered, glaring defiantly at *Aquileia's* executive director.

Penny Zardelli viewed him dispassionately. *'I thought the intention was to confuse and disorientate. Has it been blindfolded at regular intervals?'* she asked Messina.

'Si, Signora.'

'You assured me that he would be ready to talk.'

'The spirit is more strong in some.'

Penny Zardelli stepped closer to the transvestite. *'This needn't be difficult,'* she said to Cavendish. *'You tell me the current whereabouts of my daughter and your sister. We then return you to whatever institution is treating your condition.'*

No reply.

'What reason did you have for attacking Crosby in St Mary's rectory?'

Still no response.

'What do you know about the missing drugs?'

The same defiant look.

Penny Zardelli shook her head. *'So unnecessary.'* She turned to the chauffeur. *'I think we're ready to proceed.'*

'What you want me to use, Signora?' Messina asked.

'I don't care what you fucking use!' the woman snapped at him. *'I'm not here to assist. Just make sure he's talking when I question him again.'*

'Si, Signora.' Messina hesitated. *'You stay?'*

'Yes.'

The Italian looked unsure. *'It will not be pleasant.'*

'Just get on with it. I don't want to be here all bloody day.' Penny Zardelli retreated to a far corner and settled herself into the room's only easy chair. She took a pack of long, thin cigarillos from her shoulder bag and lit one up. Leaning back in her chair the executive director crossed her legs, exhaled a long plume of smoke, and motioned for Messina to proceed.

Cavendish was hauled to his feet. The transvestite struggled. He twisted his head and bit deep into Giorgio Messina's bare arm. The Italian didn't flinch. He balled one hand into a fist and drove his knuckles hard into the transvestite's lower spine, temporarily winding him.

Messina dragged a holdall from underneath the bed and dug out a roll of heavy-duty tape. He applied strips of it to Cavendish's mouth and bound both wrists, before throwing him onto the bed. A long, thin stiletto was used to slice away Cavendish's outer garments and underwear. *'Merda!'* the Italian said out loud.

'What is it?' Penny Zardelli looked up from the laptop she'd taken from her bag.

'You need to see, Signora.'

Aquileia's executive director sighed impatiently and crossed the room. Cavendish's naked body lay face up on the bed. There was a momentary silence. *'Is a woman,'* Messina said.

'Bravo, Giorgio.' Penny Zardelli's eyes remained fixed on their captive. *'Your powers of observation compensate for the lack of any intelligence. Remove the tape from her mouth.'*

Messina leant forward and slipped his knife beneath the layers of tape before slicing through them. He grasped the loose ends and tore them away, ripping thin slivers of skin from the woman's face.

'Stand her up,' Penny Zardelli instructed.

Messina hauled the naked woman to her feet. In contrast to her large frame and wide shoulders she was small breasted – a mass of wiry, dark pubic hair curled up towards the flat, hard stomach. She directed a look of undisguised hatred at *Aquileia's* executive director.

Penny Zardelli stepped forward to rip away the woman's wig. She studied her afresh. *'And how did you manage that, Giorgio? This is Rose Cavendish. We seem to have misplaced one oddity but gained another.'*

Messina looked confused. *'I don't know, Signora.'*

'Of course you don't bloody know!' Penny Zardelli snapped at him. *'You've only been living here for two fucking days with her.'*

The Sicilian looked distinctly unhappy. He wanted to point out they had both spent several hours with the woman on their journey here last Thursday afternoon. Messina thought it wise not to say anything.

'Something might have registered when she had to use the bloody toilet?'

'I not look, Signora.'

'I not fucking look, Signora!' Penny Zardelli wheeled away in exasperation. *'Jesus Christ!' Aquileia's* executive director began to pace the room. She turned back to Rose Cavendish, a look of disdain on her face. *'What in the hell was Lucy thinking of? Is there anything remotely attractive about you?'*

'Your daughter didn't seem too disappointed when I was screwing her.' Cavendish had found her voice.

Penny Zardelli's mouth hardened. *'Where's Lucy?'*

'Gone!'

'Gone where?'

'She didn't tell me.'

'I don't believe you.'

'That's your fucking problem!'

Penny Zardelli nodded. *'I think you'll find it's your problem.'*

A brief silence. Giorgio Messina's eyes darted between the two women.

'If it was possible,' Aquileia's executive director said, *'Lucy would have contacted me by now.'*

'No she wouldn't,' Cavendish replied. *'Your daughter doesn't want you. I look after her now.'*

'Although you appear to have parted company with her.' The lesbian's remark had clearly stung Penny Zardelli however.

'We had a disagreement,' Cavendish said.

'About the missing drugs?'

'What missing drugs?'

'About the child that was abducted?'

'What child?'

Penny Zardelli shook her head. *'All that male testosterone, Rose.'*

'Go fuck yourself!' Rose Cavendish spat directly into Zardelli's face. The executive director lashed out with the back of her hand. A large diamond sliced across the lesbian's cheek, leaving a narrow gash that began to drip blood.

Penny Zardelli's face was a mask. She snapped her fingers. The Sicilian passed a towel from his canvas holdall. Aquileia's executive director wiped away the saliva and tossed the towel back to him. *'I'll be outside,'* she said to Messina. *'Don't replace the tape. I want to hear her suffering.'* She crossed to the cottage door and wrenched it open.

Messina shrugged and stripped off his white t-shirt.

Leawater View Cottage: Saturday 29ᵗʰ October 2011: 12.00 p.m.

Penny Zardelli stepped from the Mercedes-Benz and lit up another of her cigarillos. It was now midday. She'd spent most of the last hour dealing with company business on her laptop. *Aquileia's* executive director glanced towards the cottage. She had quickly tired of listening to Rose Cavendish's interrogation earlier – a continuous cycle of shouting, swearing, low moans and the occasional high-pitched scream. It was quiet now, but Messina still hadn't emerged. She checked a thin, gold wrist-watch. The time concerned her. This was taking far too long. *Aquileia's* executive director ground out the cigarillo beneath the heel of her boot and walked across to the cottage's front door.

Inside *Leawater View*, Rose Cavendish lay full length on the bed. She looked comatose, semi-conscious, a bloodied swollen face, her naked body already showing signs of heavy bruising. Messina was stripped to the waist. An expanse of thick, coarse hair – almost fur-like in appearance – covered his torso, back and shoulders. It was damp and matted from his exertions.

'*Well?*' Penny Zardelli asked him.

'*I don't think she knows anything, Signora.*' The Italian was breathing heavily.

'*She knows.*'

'*Then it will take longer.*'

'*We don't have the time*,' *Aquileia's* executive director said. '*This is supposed to be your area of expertise.*'

The Sicilian hesitated before delving into his holdall. He pulled out a large cloth bag. '*Five minuti.*' Messina disappeared through the open doorway.

'Bloody hell!' Penny Zardelli lit up another thin cigarillo and resumed her seat in the easy chair. Cavendish continued to whimper intermittently. A few minutes later the Sicilian re-appeared. Penny Zardelli dropped her cigarillo to the stone flooring and ground it out. *'I try this, Signora,'* Messina held up the cloth bag. There was movement inside it.

'What the hell have you got in there?'

'I see a nest yesterday.' Messina opened up the bag for her to look inside. *Aquileia's* executive director recoiled. *'It's a fucking snake!'*

'Is a lizard,' Messina said. *'They have no legs. You call a slow worm.'*

'It looks like a bloody snake.' Penny Zardelli couldn't tear her eyes from the creature's frantic struggles. *'What do you intend doing with it?'*

'I have done once before.' Messina re-tied his bag and walked across to the bed. Rose Cavendish still had her eyes closed but was beginning to make small movements. She lay on her back, facing the ceiling. Her legs had been forced wide apart, both ankles tied to opposite ends of the bed-frame.

Messina put down his cloth bag, the slow-worm continuing to struggle and writhe inside it. The Italian retrieved what looked like a pot of grease from his holdall. He unscrewed the lid and scooped out a generous amount, working it in and around the lesbian's vaginal area with his fingers. Cavendish slowly recovered consciousness, lifting her head to see what Messina was doing. Penny Zardelli shook her head. *'What the hell are you playing at?'*

'I show you.' The Italian reached into his holdall for a pair of surgical gloves and snapped them on. *'I need firm hold, Signora.'* He untied the cloth bag and thrust a hand inside, pinching his thumb and forefinger behind the distressed creature's head. Once free of its confines, the lizard's thin, twenty-inch body curled itself frantically into figure-of-eight loops – flicking out a notched tongue as it struggled to escape.

'Is like a snake,' Messina said. 'It look for the nearest place to hide.' He lowered the slow-worm close to Cavendish's vagina.

Penny Zardelli looked on, her face a mixture of disgust and fascination. 'Are you intending to let that thing loose inside her?'

'Is an old form of torture,' the chauffeur replied. 'American soldiers sometime use in Vietnam.'

'No!' Cavendish was fully conscious now. She began to thrash around on the bed, both arms pulling against the restraining tape around her wrists. 'Bastards! You wouldn't!'

'I think he would, Rose,' Penny Zardelli answered. 'Bloody ingenious.'

'Please!' the lesbian pleaded, her voice no longer defiant. 'I don't know where Lucy is. She left in a hurry.'

'The schoolboy's abduction?'

'I'll tell you what happened.' Cavendish lifted her head up as far as it would go, eyes fixated on the struggling lizard. 'Just keep that fucking thing away from me.'

Penny Zardelli nodded at the Sicilian. Messina pulled back slightly. Cavendish spoke quickly. 'Lucy bought me a wig and clothes to kidnap the child. When I refused to do it she stormed out.'

'You haven't told me anything yet.'

'Lucy came back with the wrong kid,' Cavendish said. 'It seemed to send her over the edge. She didn't look right. Shouting and screaming at me, like someone possessed.'

Giorgio Messina looked across at Aquileia's executive director. It was the second time he'd heard someone refer to Lucy's mental state.

'I told her that Crosby would alert the police.' Cavendish was still speaking quickly. 'I managed to convince her we had to pack and leave straightaway. We broke into St Mary's old rectory and stayed the night there. Hid the car in its garage.'

'You still had the kid?'

'We dumped him next morning,' Cavendish replied. 'Lucy insisted on returning to the cottage. She'd left things behind.'

Penny Zardelli didn't look convinced. *'The police would have still been there.'*

'We could see them from the road above St Mary's.' Cavendish said. *'When I got out of the car to get a better view, Lucy just drove off and left me there. Took all my stuff with her.'*

The lizard began to struggle again, wrapping itself around Messina's forearm. Cavendish watched it closely as she continued talking. *'I went back to the rectory. Hid out there for a few days. There were biscuits and stuff left in the kitchen.'*

'You went back to the cottage at some point,' Penny Zardelli said. *'Crosby said he saw you there.'*

'The police had gone by then. I needed things.'

'There's something you're not telling me.'

'I swear it's the truth.'

Penny Zardelli shook her head. She nodded at the Italian. He leant down and prised the woman open with his thumb and forefinger. Holding onto the lizard's head with his other hand he touched the creature's head against Rose Cavendish's exposed vulva. She shouted and bucked her body. A knee jolted Messina's hand. It was enough to dislodge his grip. As he was still holding the woman open with his other hand the freed lizard slithered forward and disappeared inside her. The lesbian screamed. Her face turned puce. As she struggled to draw breath a sheen of perspiration broke out on her forehead. *'My chest!'* The cry died in her throat. Cavendish's head flopped to one side. She lay still, her eyes remaining wide open.

Penny Zardelli was momentarily stunned. *'What the fuck have you done?'*

Messina lifted the woman's wrist, trying to find a pulse. *'I think she had a heart attack.'* The Italian put his finger to Cavendish's neck. *'Her pulse is weak.'*

'Jesus Christ!' *Aquileia's* executive director seemed incapable of movement.

Messina touched the woman's neck again. He shook his head. *'I see someone like this. She is nearly gone.'*

'Shit!' Penny Zardelli had recovered from her initial shock. She stared down at the lesbian's near lifeless body. *'You'll need to smother her or something.'*

'Signora?'

'Fucking hell!' Penny Zardelli snapped at him. *'Just see to it. You said she's as good as dead.'*

'What will we do with her?'

Penny Zardelli slumped down into one of the straight-backed chairs. *'I need time to think.'*

'We bury the woman here, Signora?' Messina asked.

'No we fucking don't!'

The Sicilian stood and waited.

Aquileia's executive director sat for several minutes before looking at her wrist-watch. *'I'm not driving back through this bloody place in the dark,'* she said. *'I don't want a body in the boot of my car either. You'll have to come back tomorrow and collect her.'*

Messina didn't look happy about it. *'Where I take, Signora?'*

'I don't fucking care where you take her! Just make sure she's not found.' Penny Zardelli stood up.

'I finish this now, Signora?' the Italian asked.

'I'll wait in the car,' *Aquileia's* executive director said. *'Don't take all bloody day.'*

'Your husband,' Messina reminded her. *'He return from Italy on Monday. I have to get him from airport.'*

'Which makes it a long weekend for you,' the woman replied.

CHAPTER 18

He was outside the offices of *PB Investigations* again, after finally managing to make contact with the detective agency yesterday. Paul Berne had sounded harassed. *'Haven't got time today, Frank. Come and see me tomorrow morning.'* The call had been abruptly terminated.

Crosby pushed through the agency's outer door using his left hand. Although he hadn't broken a wrist during his fall at *St Mary's* rectory it was still bruised and sore. The small waiting room was empty, its reception desk unoccupied. He crossed to Paul Berne's office door and rapped it hard with his knuckles.

'Come!' The private investigator looked up from his laptop as Crosby opened the door and stepped inside. *'Didn't expect you this early, Frank.'* Berne sounded more subdued than the last time they'd met. He waved Crosby to a chair. *'You were right about Alcott by the way.'*

Crosby lowered himself into the chair. *'In what way?'*

'He came on too physical with our receptionist,' Berne replied. *'She resigned.'*

'You were warned. The man's a convicted rapist.'

'I had a ruck with him about it.' Berne shrugged. *'Now he's buggered off as well. I sent him out on a surveillance job five days ago and I've not seen him since.'*

'You must have a contact number?'

'It's diverting me to voicemail.'

'Where was he living?'

'Don't know exactly.' Berne turned down the corners of his mouth. *'It's probably for the best. Having to run this place on my own is a bloody nightmare though.'*

'I appreciate your situation, Paul.' Crosby didn't even try to sound sympathetic. *'You had something for me?'*

'It's not much. You're welcome to what I've got.' The private investigator looked uncomfortable. *'I want you to understand it was nothing personal, Frank.'* He spread his hands. *'I'm just trying to run a business here.'*

Crosby waited. Berne shifted in his seat. *'PB Investigations were engaged by two different clients. One of them wanted a detailed report on Dryffed's Farm. Anything I could find out about the place. Previous history. Owners and tenants.'* The private investigator reached down into an open drawer and pulled out a thin, manilla folder. *'They also wanted personal stuff about you and DC Taylor. Whatever I could lay my hands on.'* Berne shuffled through the file's loose pages. *'The other client's instructions were to have you followed on a daily basis.'*

'They weren't connected in any way?'

'I don't believe so.'

The ex-detective leant forward in his chair. *'Who were they, Paul?'*

Berne puffed out his cheeks. *'That's where it gets tricky.'*

'What's bloody tricky? And don't give me any bollocks about client confidentiality.'

'It's nothing to do with that.' Berne looked down at his folder again. *'I never met them face to face. One client was dealt with on-line. The other passed instructions through a Post Office box number.'*

'You have contact details then?'

'That's where it becomes a problem.' Berne tapped his file. *'Our on-line client opened an account with us using false details. The email address disappeared into the ether after I sent through my first report and invoice. It's all in here.'*

'And the PO box number?'

'That's been closed down as well,' Berne said. 'I can't trace the originator.'

'You didn't think to confirm details before accepting either of these jobs?'

'We're a small outfit,' the private investigator replied. 'I didn't get around to it. I've had staff issues.'

'You're lying.'

'It's the truth.'

'And this is how you run a business?'

'I take what I can get,' Berne said. 'You're not the only one who's been screwed over this.'

'Don't compare your bloody situation to mine,' Crosby snapped back at him. 'My family's under threat from these people.'

'Fair comment.' Berne closed the folder and tossed it across the desk. 'You're welcome to what's in there.'

Crosby picked the folder up. 'Have you included your reports?'

'Both of them.'

'Did you manage to uncover anything new about the farm?'

'Nothing that hadn't been reported before.'

Crosby stood. 'If I find out you're keeping anything from me.'

'I'm not.'

Crosby paused in the doorway. 'Did you attach a tracking device to the underside of my car?'

Paul Berne shook his head. 'Nothing to do with us.'

'If either of these clients get in touch again I want to know.'

The private investigator nodded. 'My word on it.'

Crosby left Paul Berne sitting at his desk.

Back inside his car the ex-detective flicked through Berne's folder. It was thin on detail. He needed to get in contact with Penny Zardelli again; find out what information she'd elicited from Rose Cavendish's brother.

CHAPTER 19

The UK's promised, late Indian summer had finally arrived. A warm November morning saw Crosby in his shirtsleeves, peering through *Endwell Cottage's* rear kitchen window. The room looked neat and orderly – everything tidied away – nothing to suggest it had been in use recently.

'What's your fucking game then, sunshine?'

Crosby stepped back from the window. A short, thickset individual stood in front of him, feet planted wide apart, long straggly grey hair framing his weather-beaten face. He wore a thick denim shirt and faded brown corduroys, the trousers hoisted up and held in place with a wide, leather belt. Crosby wondered what thought processes had been engaged to imagine that a loosely knotted tie would somehow complete his outfit.

'Heel!' the man instructed. A black and white border collie sidled into view from around the corner. It moved low on its haunches, a pair of pale blue eyes fixed firmly on the ex-detective. Another sharp command. The dog dropped to its stomach.

'Well?' the man demanded. Crosby reached into a jacket pocket and briefly presented his fake warrant card.

'Jesus Christ!' the man snorted. *'Are you lot still scratching around? I've seen headless chickens make more progress.'*

Crosby recognised someone who was about to inflict a personal rant and point of view on him. *'All this bloody technology,'* the man continued, *'and you still haven't got a clue where they are. Waste of time and taxpayer's money. They've long gone, Sherlock. Poking around the back of an empty house won't find them.'*

'You know the house is empty, Sir?'

'Course I know it's sodding empty. I own the place.' He waved a hand at the adjoining fields. 'I own all that lot as well.'

'Your tenants haven't been in touch then?' Crosby asked.

The man snorted. His ruddy face became even more suffused. 'How many more bloody times? If they turn up here I'll contact you.'

'And who am I speaking to, Sir?'

'Jack Carter! The same Jack bloody Carter that spoke to your lot last week.'

'It was just a routine call this morning, Sir,' Crosby said. 'There are several other lines of enquiry we are pursuing.'

'Oh Aye,' the man replied. 'And when do you plan on catching up with these lines of enquiry you're pursuing?' Carter laughed out loud, amused by his own humour. It startled the dog, who barked and rose to its feet.

'Sit!' The animal settled into a low crouch again, re-focusing its attention on Crosby. The ex-detective made to leave. 'You'll be extremely busy no doubt. I'll let you get on with your day, Mr Carter.'

'Aye. And it'll be a bloody sight more productive than yours.'

The border collie emitted a low warning growl, not bothering to move aside as Crosby carefully skirted around it. On returning to the front of *Endwell Cottage* he found a large Massey Ferguson tractor taking up most of the road's width. Crosby three-point turned his Mondeo and headed back through the village. His intention was to head straight for the south coast and Weymouth. Penny Zardelli still hadn't been in touch – and Rose Cavendish's brother had been taken from the old rectory house four days ago. A telephone call to *Aquileia Catering* yesterday afternoon had resulted in the receptionist telling him that Penny Zardelli was on a short break and wouldn't be in office for five days. He was being fobbed off. *'Please leave a message on her desk that Frank Crosby called,'* he'd said to the receptionist, *'and that I'll call in when she returns.'*

As Crosby exited the village he noticed a 4x4, black metallic Land Rover Discovery in *St Mary's* church car park. A sudden impulse saw him swing hard left. He pulled up alongside the vehicle and glanced inside. It was empty. Crosby sat for a few seconds. Something had caused him to stop. The detective in him wouldn't be happy until he'd looked around. Crosby opened his glove compartment to pull out the *Walther PPK*. *'Shit!'* He'd left the handgun's silencer back at Hawthorne Crescent. He thought twice about arming the *Walther* before snapping a loaded ammunition clip into place. Crosby opened his car door and stepped outside. He kept his jacket on. Although the Mondeo's read-out screen indicated an outside temperature of twenty degrees Celsius, he needed a large enough pocket to conceal the handgun.

A brief check of his immediate surroundings revealed nothing untoward. There was no sign of the Land Rover's driver. Crosby locked his car and made his way up *St Mary's* cobbled pathway. Inside the church's main entrance porch he was faced with a heavily studded oak door and an oversized cast-iron ring handle. Years of constant use had left the ring handle's surface shiny, smooth to the touch. Crosby needed both hands to twist it. The handle resisted. He wasn't surprised; gone were the days when a church could leave its doors open for passers-by to just drop in.

He re-traced his steps of five days ago to the building's rear. A shallow recess, set into the church wall, offered some shade against a strong November sun. The ex-detective lit up one of his small cigars and leant a shoulder against the wall's cool, grey stone – waiting for something to happen. Tom Dedberry's task from last week had been completed – rough clods of excavated earth piled high along one side of the open grave. A narrow carpet of bright green, artificial grass partly covered the earthy mound. Dedberry's small mechanical excavator was no longer in evidence.

Crosby turned to look at *St Mary's* rectory. Despite being bathed in direct sunlight the old house still looked bleak and unwelcoming. At least there was no one at a bedroom window trying to attract his attention this morning. He continued to monitor the house for several minutes. His eyes were eventually drawn towards the distant rising ground and Oxley's ancient hanging gallows – starkly silhouetted against the sky line – beyond a field of un-harvested maize corn. Guy Fawkes was still suspended from the gibbet's crossbar.

Crosby's eye-line continued to follow the horizon along – mostly open farmland – a number of wooded copses. Something caused him to turn his head back towards the old gallows. Guy Fawkes looked different. The suspended dummy had acquired a slightly different outline – more rounded than last time – its head slanted at a different angle. Crosby pushed himself away from the wall and walked across to a low wooden style, set into the church's perimeter fence. Once over the style he found himself looking up at a nine-foot high wall of maize corn. Crosby knew of the plant's reputation for rapid growth but hadn't realised it was capable of reaching such heights.

Directly opposite him there was a narrow mud-flattened path, running through the un-harvested maize, its sloping gradient rising up towards Oxley's distant gallows. Crosby hesitated before committing himself. A dozen steps into the maize and its high leafy stalks had completely enveloped him. He was able to stretch out both arms and touch the solid bank of foliage on either side.

Crosby continued further into the plantation. He could no longer see the entrance behind him. At irregular intervals the plant's tasselled tops had grown completely over to form a high ceiling. Beneath his feet the baked earth showed signs of cracking. Dry conditions and a crop thirsty for rainwater had resulted in all available moisture being sucked from the ground.

He was now deep into a narrow, claustrophobic tunnel. It became gloomy, the heat stifling – glimpses of blue sky directly above him provided a sporadic light. It was also becoming uncomfortable to breathe, small clouds of maize pollen dust floating in the air, catching in his throat.

A T-junction loomed ahead. Crosby opted for the left fork. Now he could only see a few yards in front and behind him. The ex-detective pushed on, small beads of perspiration breaking out on his forehead. A gentle breeze sprang up. It swept across the whole field. Thousands of plants began to sway rhythmically as one – producing a dry rustling sound – the noise amplified inside his enclosed corridor. It brought Crosby to a halt. He couldn't hear properly. As the breeze gradually abated, so did the rustling.

Crosby slid a hand across his brow, the rising ground and prickly heat taking its toll. To his left there was more rustling. This time it was isolated, and at ground level. Crosby sensed someone or something moving parallel with him. Probably ten feet away. He tried to peer through the curtain of thick stalks, but they were tightly-knit, packed closely together. The ex-detective stopped. So did the rustling. *'Who's there?'* Crosby immediately felt foolish for calling out. He reached into his jacket pocket for the handgun, de-activated its safety mechanism and stripped a cartridge from the magazine clip. Another movement. The ex-detective remained where he was, looking into deep shadow, seeing shapes and outlines that weren't there.

Crosby felt suddenly trapped, threatened. He turned, intending to re-trace his original route. Several minutes later and he still hadn't found the path's T-junction from earlier. Crosby was now completely disorientated. When the rustling began again it came directly towards him – moving at speed. He lifted the *Walther*, gradually increasing his pressure on the trigger. *'I have a gun!'* the ex-detective shouted. It was almost upon him. Crosby fired skywards, a deafening reverberation that echoed along the enclosed corridors of maize. Whatever was about to burst through suddenly veered sharp left, going away from him, its noise gradually decreasing.

The ex-detective's pulse rate had risen sharply. It took several minutes of deep breathing to slow his heartbeat. He began to move forward again – wandering aimlessly – one stretch of enclosed corridor looking exactly like all the others before it. He'd also forgotten to pick up the empty shell casing. A mistake. Had the cornfield's thick foliage deadened the noise of his gun being discharged? Crosby was still climbing, unable to find a downward gradient that would take him back towards the church.

Another blind corner approached. Crosby edged his way around it, unsure as to what might lie beyond. He stepped out into bright sunlight, suddenly free of the maize crop. It confused him temporarily, He halted, his eyes taking a few seconds to make the adjustment. Oxley's ancient hanging gallows were fifty yards away, directly in front of him on top of a grassy knoll. Guy Fawkes looked eerily realistic. Crosby put his gun away and scanned the cornfield's line of plantation, waiting for something or someone to emerge. Nothing stirred. No sign of any movement.

He started up the incline. As a welcoming breeze dried the perspiration on his forehead there was frenzied activity in front of him. A colony of wild rabbits had taken flight, their jerky, zig-zag scampering taking them towards a warren of burrows carved into the grassy hillside. One by one their bobbing rumps disappeared. A large buck remained above ground, standing upright, resting on his powerful hind-feet. He continued to monitor the intruder, nose twitching furiously, standing guard until all of his harem and extended family were safely back underground.

An angry whine zipped past Crosby's ear, thudding into the buck rabbit's head. It flopped over – a trickle of blood staining the thick, grey-brown fur. Two large, glassy eyes stared sightlessly in Crosby's direction. The ex-detective wheeled around. Tom Dedberry sauntered nonchalantly towards him. He had an air-rifle balanced in the crook of one arm, a large haversack slung over his shoulder.

'What the fuck are you playing at?' Crosby's nerves were already stretched taut after his journey through the maize field.

'Just rabbitin' mister.' Dedberry seemed oblivious to the ex-detective's anger.

'I'm not talking about the fucking rabbits!' Crosby snapped at him. *'That pellet came close to taking my ear off.'*

'I had to get a shot in quick,' the gravedigger replied. *'That bugger was about to make a run for it.'* He ambled past Crosby and raised his rifle butt, slamming it down with some considerable force against the dead rabbit's head. There was a sharp crack as the animal's tiny skull completely disintegrated. The needless act angered Crosby. *'Was that bloody necessary?'*

Dedberry prodded the motionless body with his foot and smirked. *'Didn't want the bugger jumpin' out of me bag did I?'* He lifted a blood-stained flap on his haversack and stuffed the dead carcass inside.

Crosby walked across to him. *'And I told you last time not to point that bloody gun in my direction.'*

'You were safe enough.' The youth shrugged. *'Our mam said there'd be no tea for us if I came home with nothin' for the pot.'*

Crosby didn't pursue it. He gestured at the wall of maize. *'Do you get any deer wandering around in there? I may have heard one earlier.'*

Dedberry shook his head. *'Can't go shootin' deer. That'd be against the law.'*

'Not what I bloody asked is it, Tom? But then we played this same game last week.'

Dedberry looked blank. *'You sounds upset, Mister.'* He narrowed his eyes. *'What you doin' up here anyway?'*

The gravedigger's appearance had caused Crosby to forget why he'd made his way through the field of maize. He turned and walked the short distance up to Oxley's old gallows. A small raised plinth alongside the ancient monument outlined its gory history. The suspended Guy Fawkes didn't look that lifelike on closer inspection – tattered remnants of clothing hung loose around its straw body – a Halloween mask and wellington boots completed the ensemble.

'I told you about that last week,' the gravedigger shouted up to him.

Crosby made his way back down the slope. *'Have you finished decimating the wildlife around here?'*

'Eh?'

'Are you done with shooting rabbits?'

The youth looked around him. 'Reckon so. Buggers have all disappeared.'

'I'll follow you back to the churchyard then.'

Dedberry turned towards the maize field. 'You worried about gettin' lost then, Mister? Or frightened of what you might find in there?' There was a hint of mischief in the gravedigger's voice.

'Just drop the bloody comedy routine and take me back,' Crosby said impatiently.

They entered the maize at a different point to where Crosby had exited from earlier. The ex-detective kept close to Dedberry, his hand on the *Walther*, listening for any sounds of movement around them. 'This bugger's heavy,' the gravedigger said, transferring his canvas haversack to another shoulder. 'Plenty of meat on him though. Do you want some dinner at our place? I can ask our mam.'

'Another time.' The ex-detective dismissed an image of Dedberry's mother skinning their blood-stained rabbit.

'Suit yourself.' The youth sounded put out. 'There'll only be our mam and sister there. Dad lives with his girlfriend now. He comes back to see me though. Stays the night sometimes.'

'Does he,' Crosby said.

Dedberry continued to ramble on. 'He has to sleep with our mam though. We only got the two bedrooms.'

'Fascinating.' Crosby didn't enquire as to what the sister's sleeping arrangements were when their father stayed overnight.

'They're cousins you know,' Dedberry volunteered.

'Who are?'

'Our Mam and Dad. Married each other when they were both sixteen.'

'Explains a lot,' Crosby replied.

The gravedigger continued to chatter about his family and their domestic arrangements as they progressed through the maize. Crosby switched him off. The pair of them finally emerged at a point where they both had to straddle a length of barbed wire fence in order to enter the churchyard. Crosby suspected this may have been done on purpose.

'You OK from here?' Dedberry asked.

Crosby nodded. *'I'll let you get back to the communal cooking pot.'*

They passed the open grave that had been prepared last week. Crosby stopped. It had been half-filled. There was a hand protruding through the loose earth. It looked human. The ex-detective leant forward to take a closer look. *'That's a hand buried in there.'*

Dedberry nodded. *'I saw it earlier.'*

Crosby spun around to face him. *'You're really trying my patience now. Is this another of your sick jokes?'*

The youth shook his head. *'It looks real enough.'*

'Then why the hell didn't you alert someone?'

'I already have.' Dedberry pulled a mobile phone from one of his overall pockets and held it up. *'They should be here soon.'* As if to confirm his actions a siren wailed in the distance. Crosby listened to it getting closer. He swore under his breath. If it was a dead body then the whole churchyard would shortly become a crime scene – and he was currently in possession of an unlicensed firearm and a fake warrant card. *'Jesus Christ!'* They had to be concealed. He might be searched. His first instinct warned him this was no prank, which meant the place would soon be overrun with police. What Crosby really needed to do was get into his car and leave. That wouldn't be possible now. The wailing siren was almost upon them.

Dedberry gestured at the open grave. *'Old Stan Blewett won't be best pleased. They was puttin' him in that one tomorrow.'*

'Fuck's sake!' Crosby's mind was elsewhere, working out his options. He walked swiftly towards the church. As he rounded its far corner, the familiar yellow and blue check livery of a West Midlands squad car screeched into the church car park. Crosby stood and watched – the wailing siren and blue flashing lights evoking a string of

memories from his recent past. Two police officers in bright yellow tabards exited their five-series BMW saloon and hurried up the church's cobbled pathway. Crosby's hand instinctively went to the flap of his jacket pocket, checking the semi-automatic pistol was hidden from view.

One of the policemen hurried past. The other pulled up in front of him. *'PC Lawrence, Sir. West Midlands Police. We are responding to an emergency call. I will require you to remain on-site until further investigations have been carried out.'*

Crosby nodded. *'I know the routine. I'm an ex-detective.'*

The young policeman hesitated.

'Detective Inspector Crosby. Studwell CID,' he added.

PC Lawrence took out his pocketbook and jotted down the details. *'Was it you who made the call, Sir?'*

The ex-detective was about to respond when PC Lawrence's colleague re-appeared. *'John!'* he shouted. *'We could have a dead body in the graveyard.'* Crosby might have found the remark amusing under different circumstances.

'You'll need to seal off that car park entrance,' the officer instructed PC Lawrence. *'I'll let Central know what's happening.'* He angled his head down towards the radio attached to his tabard.

PC Lawrence put away his pocketbook. He turned to Crosby. *'I'll wait here,'* the ex-detective reassured him. *'You'll be needing a statement at some point.'*

The young police officer turned on his heel and broke into a half-run, heading back towards the car park. Crosby followed him along the gravelled side-path, his focus on a nearby grave and its weathered stone urn. The ex-detective glanced around him before crossing to the urn, dropping his *Walther* and fake-id into it. Without breaking stride he moved along to a weathered bench that overlooked the car park. Crosby sat down. His pulse gradually slowed as he waited. A procession of emergency service vehicles began to arrive – PC

Lawrence directing them briskly and efficiently into position along the roadside's grass verge.

A Rapid Response Ambulance car was the first to park-up. Two paramedics in dark green uniforms exited their vehicle and hurried up the church's cobbled path – one of them carrying a lightweight medical bag strapped to his back. A Mercedes *'Sprinter'* transit van drew up. After the van's rear doors had been opened, both driver and passenger donned white protective overalls, before loading a large, reinforced case with various items of forensic equipment.

An unmarked car arrived. Crosby instinctively knew it was CID. Three suited individuals stepped out. He straightened. One of them was an old colleague. Barry Watson would be in his late-thirties now, a solidly built, shaven-headed Welshman whom Crosby had worked with over ten years ago. They were quite friendly back then. Often drank together. A transfer to another station and the passage of time had caused them to lose touch with each other.

The CID officers stood in conversation with PC Lawrence, occasionally glancing up to where Crosby was sitting. The ex-detective leant back. He had to gather his thoughts, run through the statement he'd be making. Barry Watson and his CID colleagues eventually left the car park, passing Crosby on their way through to the church's rear graveyard. Watson nodded in recognition but didn't stop.

Another two squad cars arrived. More uniformed PCs piled out. A nondescript Laguna Estate cruised slowly into view and parked on the fringes. Its occupant was grey-haired, distinguished looking, his movements unhurried. He opened the boot of his vehicle and began to don items similar to the Scenes-of-Crime officers who had arrived before him. The appearance of a forensic pathologist on-site completed the set, confirming the initial stages of a murder investigation. What did surprise Crosby was the arrival of all key services and personnel at virtually the same time, as if they'd been expecting an emergency call.

The forensic pathologist picked up his bag and stepped over a length of blue and white barrier warning tape stretched across the car park entrance. He flipped an id-wallet at PC Lawrence before continuing on up towards the church. A friendly, *'Good Morning,'* was aimed in Crosby's direction as the pathologist strolled past.

Crosby slowly eased himself up from the bench. He watched PC Lawrence waving a Citroen Relay ambulance van into place before making his way back along *St Mary's* south-facing wall. Individual scenes of well-ordered activity greeted him as he rounded the church's rear corner. A three-sided, lightweight crime-scene tent had been erected over the open grave. Outside the tent a green-uniformed paramedic was in the process of zipping up his medical bag. A roll of yellow and black plastic warning tape – bearing the legend 'CRIME SCENE DO NOT ENTER' – had been wound around several adjacent gravestones to form a circular barrier. There were intermittent camera flashes in and around the churchyard as Scenes-of-Crime officers recorded initial images for the investigation team to study. A number of uniformed officers were already on their hands and knees, carrying out a detailed search of the surrounding area.

The forensic pathologist was in deep conversation with a dark-suited, portly-looking individual who'd arrived with Barry Watson. Crosby presumed this was the Senior CID Investigating Officer. He watched as both detective and pathologist moved across to the three-sided tent.

A small group had gathered some distance from the grave under investigation. Standing among them was Tom Dedberry – currently being questioned by Crosby's former colleague Barry Watson. The CID Officer was scribbling copious notes into his pocketbook. Crosby walked along the gravelled surround to another bench, this one sited in front of *St Mary's* old rectory. He sat down. Above him the autumn sun had continued into early afternoon. Crosby let it warm his face as he watched ongoing, familiar procedures that had dominated his life for over thirty years. The ex-detective felt a small pang of resentment against those going efficiently about their work.

His attention strayed back to Tom Dedberry – still in the process of being interviewed by Crosby's former colleague. The young gravedigger looked excitable, waving his arms around and talking a lot. At one stage he pointed across to Crosby. The ex-detective watched and waited, monitoring the search party's progress, concerned it would extend around towards his fake-id and handgun before he had an opportunity to retrieve them. The local and national press would also be here soon, scrambling for the most advantageous photo-shoot positions. Oxley's ancient gallows – with a Guy Fawkes dummy swinging from its noose – would be manna from heaven for them. A perfect visual backdrop to accompany their reports.

Barry Watson eventually detached himself from Tom Dedberry's animated ramblings and walked across to where the ex-detective was sitting. Watson didn't appear to have altered a great deal over the years, his trademark shaven-head still prominent, the solution to a receding hairline in his early twenties. Some might have described the detective's chiselled features as hard, even cruel. Crosby recalled a short-fused temper – which the Welshman used to blame on his Celtic origins.

Both men shook hands, the CID officer sitting himself down next to Crosby. *'Didn't expect to come across you here,'* the Welshman said. *'It's been a while. PC Lawrence was telling me in the car park that you're retired.'*

'Three years ago,' Crosby replied. *'I'm assuming you've made detective sergeant?'*

Watson nodded. *'A year back.'* He paused. *'How's Doreen?'*

'She's fine.' Crosby didn't want to invite further small talk about his family.

The Welshman looked slightly uncomfortable. *'Jean and I heard about Dryffed's Farm. We should have contacted you.'*

'Doesn't matter,' Crosby answered. *'People lose touch.'*

'Even so.'

'Forget about it.'

'I have to ask a few questions.' Watson sounded apologetic.

Crosby nodded. 'Is it a murder enquiry?'

'Looks likely.' Watson glanced over his shoulder. 'We're just waiting for the Home Office pathologist to conclude his on-site examination.'

'I was impressed at how quickly all of this was mobilised,' Crosby said.

The detective sergeant shrugged. 'We already had someone here.'

'How do you mean?'

'The young gravedigger,' Watson replied. 'He's one of ours. PC Brandon.'

Crosby had spent a good many years at not showing any reaction to the unexpected. He wasn't sure if he'd managed it on this occasion. Watson didn't appear to have noticed anything. 'PC Brandon's been working undercover here,' he continued. 'His team are anxious to speak with two Oxley residents about a recent child abduction.'

'I heard about that,' Crosby replied.

'That particular operation's been screwed now,' Watson said. 'Oxley is about to come under the microscope.'

'Is there a connection?' Crosby asked.

'Christ knows,' Watson replied. 'We need to identify the body first. Are you ready for these questions?'

Crosby nodded. The detective sergeant took a pocketbook and pencil from his jacket pocket. He flipped through several pages before looking up. 'PC Brandon has described your behaviour here as eccentric.'

Crosby raised his eyebrows and laughed out loud. 'I'd be more concerned about his over-acting.'

'He said you've been here on two occasions recently.'

'My wife and I have been tracing our family tree.' Crosby waved his hand at a row of old gravestones running adjacent to the church's east wall. 'There's a line on her mother's side here in Oxley. I can email you a copy of what we've been compiling if it helps.'

Watson made a note in his pocketbook. *'Doreen not with you on this occasion?'*

'She's away on a short break with my daughter-in-law.'

Watson indicated the plantation of maize to their left. *'Apparently you were wandering around in there earlier.'*

'A detective's instinct.' Crosby jerked his head towards Guy Fawkes, the effigy still dangling from its noose. *'Old habits die hard.'*

The Welshman looked up towards the old gallows. *'It's unfortunate that you've been caught up in all of this.'*

Crosby shrugged. *'Your victim's the unfortunate one.'* He glanced at the activity continuing around him. *'It livened up another routine day for me. There's not much to get excited about when you're retired.'*

'What time did you arrive this morning?'

'About nine-thirty.'

'No one else around?'

Crosby shook his head. *'There was a black metallic 4x4 Land Rover Discovery in the car park. No sign of a driver.'*

'That's very precise.'

'I used to do it for a living.'

Watson managed a thin smile. *'It's still there. We're checking an address.'* The detective sergeant consulted his pocketbook again. *'Did you hear a firearm being discharged near the church this morning?'*

'I certainly experienced PC Brandon's air rifle,' Crosby replied. *'One of his pellets nearly took my ear off. I'd be seriously concerned about his behaviour and actions here.'*

'Anything specific?'

'Come on, Barry,' Crosby replied. *'As a police officer he should have been securing the crime scene, not stalking me through a bloody cornfield.'*

'He claims you had to be kept under observation.'

230

'*Why not detain me in the churchyard,*' Crosby argued, '*instead of acting like a bloody film extra on location. It was irresponsible. He wants the book thrown at him.*'

'*I'm not disagreeing,*' the Welshman said, '*but I'll still have to carry out a body search. You OK with that?*'

Crosby smiled. '*Are you hoping to find this gun?*'

Watson put his pocketbook away. '*Come on, Frank. You know how it works.*'

Crosby stood up and spread his arms. He was treading a thin line. What if the unidentified body had been shot and they wanted to test him for traces of gunshot residue. PC Brandon looked across at the ex-detective as he was being searched.

'*Is this undercover policeman aware that I'm a retired detective inspector?*' Crosby asked.

'*He is now.*'

'*Seemed to be having a lot to say for himself.*'

The CID officer nodded. '*Between you and me he's a cocky little bastard.*' Watson completed his search. '*Someone who enjoys being the centre of attention.*'

'*I presume my car is off limits until forensics have processed it?*' Crosby asked.

'*It could be a while,*' Watson replied. '*We'll have to make the 4x4 a priority. Can you make other arrangements?*'

'*I'll ring someone.*' Crosby just wanted to retrieve his handgun and put some distance between himself and the churchyard.

'*We'll just need an address and a telephone number then.*'

Someone standing behind them cleared their throat. They turned. The individual stood a respectful ten yards away. His suit looked new, at least one size too large on a tall, willowy frame. '*Detective Constable Tilson,*' the Welshman said in way of introduction. '*A member of our investigation team.*'

The young CID officer stepped forward. *'I've had a good nose around, Sarge.'* Tilson sounded more confident than he looked. *'There's nothing immediately obvious.'*

Crosby winced.

'Nothing immediately obvious is it?' The Welshman glared at DC Tilson from beneath dark eyebrows. *'I hadn't realised our investigation had stalled already.'*

The young detective flushed up, regretting his remark.

'You've not managed to locate the 4x4 driver then?' Watson asked.

DC Tilson looked even more uncertain. *'I'd assumed the dead body...'*

'...could be almost anybody,' his senior officer finished for him. *'What have they found inside the church?'*

'I believe it's locked, Sir.'

'Has the key holder been contacted?'

'I'm not sure, Sir.'

'Then I suggest you bloody well find out!' the Welshman snapped at him.

Crosby looked the other away. Watson's temper hadn't improved any during the intervening years. DC Tilson hesitated, as if wanting to clarify his instructions. He obviously thought better of it and turned smartly away. *'You'll need access to the rectory as well,'* Watson called after him. *'It doesn't look occupied.'*

Crosby watched Tilson's slight frame as it disappeared around the church's near corner. *'That takes me back. I see your patience hasn't improved any.'*

'Public school would you believe.' Watson sniffed. *'They manage to stuff their heads full of everything apart from common sense.'* He looked across at the crime-scene tent as his Senior Investigating Officer emerged from it. *'I'll need to get across there and see what DI Kingston's turned up. Maybe the deceased was just trying to cut out the middle man and save on funeral costs.'* Watson's comment was

232

delivered without humour. He stood up. *'We'll have to get together for a drink, Frank. Do some catching up.'*

'I'd like that,' Crosby felt obliged to add.

Watson nodded. Both men shook hands before the detective sergeant made his way across to where DI Kingston was waiting for him. Crosby needed to leave, retrieve the handgun and get off-site. It was only a short walk into the village, where he could arrange for a taxi to collect him.

The ex-detective vacated his bench and strolled casually away from it. Someone fell into step beside him. *'CID tell me you're a retired detective inspector.'* PC Brandon was still wearing his mud-caked blue overalls. The local accent and affected manner had disappeared however. Crosby's focus was on retrieving the gun. He certainly didn't need the undercover policeman attached to him.

'Are you familiar with the name Lucy Roberts?' Brandon asked.

'What!'

'Rose Cavendish?'

The ex-detective stopped. PC Brandon was managing to annoy him all over again. *'Are you a member of the investigating team here?'*

'Not this one,' Brandon replied.

Crosby measured his words. *'I've just given my statement to DS Watson. Have you been asked to clarify anything in that statement?'*

'It was a simple enough question.'

'I'll give you some simple advice then.' Crosby started walking again. *'Don't leave a major crime scene unattended without good reason.'*

'You were behaving suspiciously.'

'Whereas your impersonation of the village idiot was near faultless,' Crosby replied, *'a complete natural. Now piss off!'* The ex-detective increased his pace – not entirely sure whether his anger was due to PC Brandon himself or because he'd been so easily duped by the policeman's undercover role. What Crosby also wanted to point out was the presence of Rose Cavendish's brother in the old rectory – right

under Brandon's nose. That in itself raised another question. Had the undercover policeman seen Crosby visiting *Endwell Cottage* at some point? Also nagging away at the back of Crosby's mind was the thought that this morning's discovery might have a connection with the *Dryffed's Farm* missing drugs haul – and that was a reminder his family remained stranded – still unaware of what was happening. They'd left for the Isle of Wight ten days ago, and during that time Crosby had only risked the one message to his contact there.

He made his way back along *St Mary's* south-facing wall again. PC Brandon hadn't followed him. He looked around. It was clear at the moment – all activity still confined to the rear of the church. Crosby moved across to the stone urn and lifted out its contents, dropping them into his jacket pocket. He continued on past the church's main entrance and down its cobbled pathway, towards the car park. Crosby increased his pace, expecting someone to challenge him. Nearly there. Just a few more steps and he'd be off-site and on his way into the village.

PC Lawrence was still stationed in front of the barrier warning tape, directing vehicles past a melee of traffic camped along the grass verge. Another car nosed its way through – a familiar-looking Jaguar XJ6 coupé. *'I don't fucking believe it!'* Crosby mouthed to himself. He sensed his day was about to take another nose-dive.

The maroon-coloured Jaguar parked-up and out stepped Superintendent Oliver Rees-Bramley. Crosby's old boss allowed PC Lawrence the briefest glimpse of a warrant card before striding through the car park.

Crosby stood transfixed. There was nowhere to go. The last person he would want to see at this moment in time was his former DCI. Although both men had formed a tolerable working relationship in the past they had never been particularly comfortable in each other's company. Their parting had been somewhat acrimonious, a lack of trust on both sides. Rees-Bramley had accused Crosby of becoming personally and emotionally involved in the investigation which led to

Dryffed's Farm and its bloody climax. There'd been no contact between the two men since Crosby's retirement.

The detective superintendent's brisk staccato footsteps had already carried him up to where Crosby was standing. Rees-Bramley was, as ever, immaculately groomed. Nothing had changed in that respect – a sharply tailored three-piece suit – black leather brogues buffed to a mirror shine – the dark blue Oxford University tie announcing his background and profile.

'*Frank!*' Rees-Bramley looked genuinely surprised.

Crosby was unsure as to how he should address his former boss. It had always been *'Sir'* in the past. He certainly wouldn't be calling him Oliver. Crosby settled on using neither. '*It's good to see you,*' he said. '*I understand you've been promoted to detective superintendent since my retirement.*'

Rees-Bramley dismissed it with a wave of his hand. '*Not entirely unexpected. What are you doing here? Didn't you attend enough crime scenes during your time with CID?*'

'*I happened to be on-site when a body was discovered.*' Crosby was acutely aware that his former DCI viewed all coincidence with suspicion.

The slightest of pauses. '*That was unfortunate. You visit churchyards in your retirement?*'

'*My wife and I study genealogy.*'

Rees-Bramley made a point of looking around. '*Your wife didn't accompany you?*'

The comment annoyed Crosby. '*Not today.*'

'*Have you given a statement?*' Rees-Bramley had never been one to waste time on preliminaries.

'*Yes.*'

'*There's a 4x4 in the car park. Did you see it arrive?*' the superintendent asked.

'*It was already here.*'

'*Any sign of the driver?*'

'Not while I've been here.'

Rees-Bramley pursed his lips. *'Something I'd like to discuss with you, Frank.'* The request was more of an instruction. *'I'm just about to be briefed by our Senior Investigating Officer. I'll see you back here in about ten minutes?'*

Crosby swore inwardly. He had little choice than to nod his agreement. The superintendent left. What the hell had persuaded Rees-Bramley down from his lofty perch in *Lloyd House?* As a detective superintendent he would be responsible for strategy and policy issues, not poking around a crime scene. Why was *St Mary's* on his radar? Crosby resigned himself to another wait, the discharged firearm back in his jacket pocket and little chance of an immediate escape. *'Shit!'* He moved across to his bench overlooking the car park.

Whilst Crosby sat and waited for Rees-Bramley's return, the detective superintendent was progressing smartly along the church's gravelled surround, crunching particles of stone fragments beneath his purposeful stride. DI Kingston saw him approaching. The Senior Investigating Officer's look was not one of welcome anticipation. He'd been warned of the superintendent's arrival. He was also aware of his reputation. Rees-Bramley showed DI Kingston his warrant card. He dispensed with any pleasantries. *'You have a partially buried body on-site.'*

'Yes, Sir.'

Rees-Bramley nodded towards *St Mary's* car park. *'The Land Rover Discovery. It's currently on hire to a Lieutenant Bradley Thorburn. He's an exchange officer from the New York Police Department.'*

The news that an NYPD officer might be involved did nothing to relax DI Kingston's body language. *'We do have an address, Sir. It's being checked out.'*

'He's not there,' the detective superintendent said. *'Lieutenant Thorburn hasn't been seen since the week-end. What do we have on this body here?'*

'Our pathologist confirms a deceased black male,' DI Kingston said. 'The cause of death has not yet been established.'

Rees-Bramley compressed his lips into a thin line. 'Is the body still clothed?'

'Yes, Sir.'

'You've found ID then?'

'It's proving difficult.'

'In what way?'

'I understand the pathologist is having to proceed with some caution,' Kingston replied. 'He thinks there may be evidence directly underneath the body.'

'Who is the pathologist?'

'Professor Endicott.'

The superintendent nodded. 'University of Birmingham. I've had previous dealings with him. He's slow. Does most of his work back at the morgue.' Rees-Bramley looked across at the crime-scene tent. 'Is the victim's face exposed? I want to carry out an immediate identification.'

DI Kingston hesitated. 'The body is lying face down.'

Rees-Bramley swore under his breath. 'Professor Endicott,' he said, 'will be persuaded to pull his bloody finger out. There are a number of departments and organisations impatient for answers. If the body is that of Lieutenant Thorburn then terrorist activities cannot be ruled out.'

DI Kingston nodded. The superintendent would be under a lot of pressure if he was responsible for Lieutenant Thorburn's welfare during his visit here.

'I am currently having to field calls and enquiries from a number of high-ranking officials,' Rees-Bramley continued. 'Interested parties include the US Embassy in London. The UK Ambassador in Washington. New York City Police Department. The US Secretary of State. The CIA. The FBI.' He paused. 'And our Chief Constable wants to know why we can't bloody well look after NYPD exchange officers entrusted to our care. Do we understand each other?'

'Yes, Sir.' DI Kingston would liked to have pointed out that it wasn't him who had mislaid the lieutenant.

Rees-Bramley viewed the ongoing activity around him. 'I have no wish to interfere with your investigation but there is a need for immediate haste. I suggest you insert some sort of explosive device into the professor's rear-end and detonate the bloody thing.'

DI Kingston saw his detective sergeant hovering nearby and immediately called him over. It was the opportunity he'd been looking for. Introductions were brief. 'DS Watson will bring you up to speed with what we have, Sir. I'll liaise further with Professor Endicott.' Kingston disappeared back inside the crime-scene tent with unseemly haste. Rees-Bramley turned to the detective sergeant. 'Before leaving Lloyd House I was told about an undercover PC on-site who found the body.'

'Yes, Sir. PC Brandon.'

'Point him out to me.'

Watson indicated a blue-overalled figure leaning casually against the church wall smoking a cigarette. It seemed to annoy Rees-Bramley. His eyes narrowed. 'I'm assuming this undercover role has been derailed?'

'Yes, Sir.'

'Then why is he still acting like a bloody labourer?' Rees-Bramley turned back to the detective sergeant. 'There was another witness on-site. A retired ex-detective.'

The Welshman nodded. 'Frank Crosby. I've just taken his statement.'

Rees-Bramley raised his eyebrows. 'You are on first name terms?'

'We worked together some years back,' Watson replied.

'What time did he arrive here this morning?' the superintendent asked.

'Nine-thirty.'

'You're happy with the statement he's given?'

'Yes, Sir.'

'This body,' Rees-Bramley said. 'It appeared overnight?'

Watson nodded. 'PC Brandon has confirmed the open grave was empty when he left here yesterday evening.'

Rees-Bramley glanced across at the undercover policeman again. 'I'll speak with him.' Turning on his heel he left abruptly. DS Watson was left to reflect on a briefing that had consisted of him answering questions. He watched the superintendent close in on an unsuspecting PC Brandon.

The undercover policeman was still lounging against the church wall as Rees-Bramley approached, blissfully unaware of the rude awakening heading his way. It came in the form of a very loud voice. 'Put that bloody cigarette out and stand up straight!'

PC Brandon turned. Rees-Bramley planted himself squarely in front of the young policeman. 'I am a detective superintendent from Lloyd House. Do I have your full attention?' The undercover policeman quickly dropped his cigarette and pushed himself upright.

'I'm told that you've been here for the past two weeks on surveillance duty,' Rees-Bramley barked at him.

'Yes.'

'You will address a senior officer as Sir!'

'Yes, Sir.' PC Brandon's feeling of self-importance was rapidly disappearing.

'I want details of all visitors to the churchyard during your time here,' Rees-Bramley instructed. 'You've presumably filed daily reports?'

'Not exactly, Sir.'

'Not exactly! You either have or you haven't.'

'I was initially monitoring a cottage in the village, Sir.' Brandon was now standing to attention, arms down by his side. 'In connection with the child abduction investigation.'

239

'I'm not interested in your bloody abduction case,' Rees-Bramley said impatiently. *'I want to know about specific visitors here to the church. Vehicle registration numbers for a start.'*

'I don't have that information, Sir.' PC Brandon stared straight ahead.

'What exactly was the point of you being here then?'

The undercover policeman cleared his throat. *'I was switched to the churchyard because someone reported seeing one of the suspects here. My reports are only of a general nature during this period.'*

'Inefficient and slovenly,' Rees-Bramley said. *'Incompetent. A disgrace to the uniform. Your senior officer will be informed. What about the Land Rover? Have you seen it here before?'*

'No, Sir.'

The detective superintendent regarded him, stony-faced. PC Brandon's day was about to deteriorate even further. *'I will outline your duties for the remainder of this afternoon,'* Rees-Bramley instructed. *'You will return the fancy dress costume to wherever it was hired from and introduce yourself to a police uniform again. You will then consult your memory. I want a detailed report on everything you have witnessed during your time here.'* A business card was produced. *'The report will arrive at my email address no later than seven o'clock this evening.'*

There was a short pause.

'Are you aware of what is required?' the superintendent asked.

'Yes, Sir.' PC Brandon took the card but remained where he was.

'Is there a problem with your mobility?' Rees-Bramley asked.

'No, Sir.'

'Then bloody well get on with it.'

PC Brandon left. He moved quickly – striving to keep ahead of Rees-Bramley as the detective superintendent followed closely behind him. Both men reached the bench where Crosby was sitting. PC Brandon hurried past. Rees-Bramley took a white handkerchief from his top pocket and flicked away a few slivers of loose, flaking wood before sitting down next to the ex-detective. Crosby was uncomfortably aware of the handgun's weight still in his jacket pocket.

'*Your initial appraisal of a crime scene was always very sound, Frank,*' Rees-Bramley said to him. '*Was there anything about this morning that caught your eye? It would appear that you were only one of two people on-site.*'

The question took Crosby by surprise. He shook his head. '*The undercover PC ought to be of more assistance. He's been here for several days.*'

'*You're aware of PC Brandon's role?*'

'*DS Watson referred to it when taking my statement.*'

The superintendent nodded. '*An ex-colleague. It must have seemed like a works reunion when I turned up as well.*'

Crosby wasn't sure whether the remark was intended to be light-hearted. Rees-Bramley had never been renowned for his sense of humour. It looked as if there was something further that he wanted to discuss. Crosby waited. Rees-Bramley stood abruptly. '*I've no doubt the investigation team will be in touch, Frank.*' He turned and left, making his way back towards the rear of the church. '*Odd,*' Crosby muttered to himself. He didn't dwell on it, anxious to leave.

Crosby moved smartly down *St Mary's* cobbled pathway and out through the car park. '*My car has to be processed by Scenes-of-Crime,*' he called out to PC Lawrence. '*I'll pick it up tomorrow.*' Crosby continued on without stopping.

'*I can get someone to give you a lift home,*' the policeman shouted after him.

'*No need.*' Crosby waved a hand. '*I'll get lunch at the village pub. Someone can pick me up from there.*' PC Lawrence turned his attention back to the congested mass of vehicles clogging up the narrow road.

Crosby had no intention of hanging around the village for lunch. He'd get a taxi to his son and daughter-in-law's home. Michael had left him keys to their house and his Volvo. The ex-detective quickened his stride.

CHAPTER 20

The door-bell rang at nine o'clock. Although Crosby had received a telephone call last night to say his car could be collected from *St Mary's,* he knew there'd be a visit from CID this morning. DS Watson and DC Tilson stood facing him as he opened the door.

'*Good Morning, Frank,*' the detective sergeant said. '*Not too early for you?*'

'*I'm always up by seven-thirty,*' Crosby replied. '*My wife insists it's the best time of day. She doesn't like me to miss any of it.*'

Watson managed a polite smile. '*Do you mind if we come in for a few minutes?*' he asked. '*It's just a routine follow-up from yesterday.*' The Welshman didn't have his social face on.

'*That has a familiar ring to it,*' the ex-detective said. '*Am I about to be read my rights?*'

There was little sign of a smile this time. Crosby stood to one side and ushered both detectives through the door. They stepped inside. He directed them into the lounge, indicating two armchairs. '*I'd imagine you didn't get home too early last night.*'

'*More like this morning,*' Watson replied.

'*Can I get you a coffee?*' Crosby asked.

The Welshman shook his head. '*We're on a tight schedule. We've three more calls to make before this afternoon.*' He looked towards the kitchen. '*Is it OK to talk?*'

'*Doreen's not here,*' Crosby answered. '*I did mention that she's away on a short break with my daughter-in-law.*'

Watson nodded. '*You did. I could do with a holiday myself after yesterday.*'

'*Are you making any headway?*'

'*There's been one or two unusual developments.*'

'*Oh?*' Crosby was instantly on his guard. He moved across to the settee and sat down. '*I did give my statement some thought overnight. There's nothing I can really add to what I've already told you.*'

'*It's not your statement.*' Watson gestured to DC Tilson. The young detective retrieved a notebook and pencil from his jacket pocket. Crosby thought he looked subdued.

'*There's a press conference arranged for later today,*' Watson continued. '*I can tell you that our graveyard victim from yesterday morning has been identified as one Lieutenant Bradley Thorburn. He was a serving police officer from the USA who was here on an exchange programme.*'

'*Which explains the presence of Detective Superintendent Rees-Bramley on-site,*' Crosby said. '*The man used to be my DCI. Has he tried to take over the investigation yet?*'

Watson nodded. '*He's been sniffing at DI Kingston's anal glands since yesterday afternoon. There's a lot of VIP heavyweights waiting for answers apparently.*'

'*I can imagine.*'

The Welshman hesitated. '*Lieutenant Thorburn wasn't the only body discovered in the churchyard yesterday.*'

It took Crosby by surprise. '*Two bodies?*'

'*Both of them in the same grave,*' Watson replied.

'*Bloody hell!*'

The Welshman nodded. '*It didn't improve Rees-Bramley's mood.*'

'*Has the other body been identified?*'

'*There's no easy way of telling you this,*' Watson said. '*I believe she used to be a member of your team. Detective Constable Grace Taylor?*'

Crosby sat bolt upright. '*No!*'

The detective sergeant allowed him a few moments.

'*Grace and I worked together for a number of years,*' Crosby eventually said. '*That was a shock.*'

'My bedside manner's not the best,' Watson offered in way of apology. *'I believe you kept in touch with DC Taylor after your retirement?'*

'We met up on occasions.'

'Just the two of you?'

'I think some sort of bond formed between us after Dryffed's Farm. We both nearly lost our lives there.' Crosby was aware of DC Tilson scribbling away in his pocketbook.

'Was your relationship a physical one?' Watson asked.

'No it bloody wasn't!' The question had jolted Crosby. Probably a guilty reaction. *'What's prompted that, Barry?'*

The Welshman raised his eyebrows. *'We have to examine every facet of her private life, Frank. You of all people should know that.'*

Crosby nodded. *'I'm finding it difficult to take all of this in.'*

'Had you seen her recently?' the detective sergeant asked casually.

It would have been pointless to deny it. Watson obviously knew they'd been in contact. *'I saw DC Taylor at the station about two weeks ago.'*

'An odd place to meet.'

'She couldn't get away.'

'The purpose of your visit?'

'Grace occasionally lent us DVDs.' Crosby felt on reasonably safe ground. It wasn't a lie. *'I was returning some of them. My wife can verify all of this if you need confirmation.'*

Watson waved it away. *'Where at the station did you meet DC Taylor?'*

'In the car park.'

'Date?'

'I'd have to check.'

'It'll keep.'

Crosby was still aware of DC Tilson noting the exchanges in his pocketbook. *'This is beginning to sound like an interrogation,'* he said. *'Am I considered a suspect?'*

Watson smiled and shook his head. *'You might be indirectly involved however. Did DC Taylor talk about any recent problems she might be having when you met?'*

'It was just small talk.'

'She didn't seem to have any concerns? Worries? Major developments in her life?'

'Nothing I can recall.'

'Did she act differently in any way from previous meetings?'

'Not that I noticed,' Crosby replied. *'We did agree to meet up when she wasn't so busy.'*

'Which didn't happen.'

'No.'

A pause. Watson changed tack. *'You've visited St Mary's on previous occasions.'*

'I told you yesterday,' Crosby said. *'My wife and I have been tracing our family trees. The Oxley notes are on my laptop if you want to check them.'*

'Did you see anyone else there on these previous visits?' the detective sergeant asked.

'No one in particular.' Crosby certainly didn't want to bring Penny Zardelli into the equation.

'Apparently,' Watson said, *'Robert Milner is buried at St Mary's.'*

Crosby nodded. *'We came across his grave on one of our visits.'*

'Would Grace Taylor have known he was buried at Oxley?'

'I've absolutely no idea.'

'It never came up in conversation over the years?'

'Why would it? Neither of us attended his funeral.'

'It does have a macabre twist,' Watson said.

'Does it?'

'*Four years ago,*' the detective sergeant pointed out, '*DC Taylor almost lost her life alongside Robert Milner. Then she ends up being murdered in the graveyard where he's buried.*'

'*You're saying it's not a coincidence.*'

'*It's a tenuous link,*' Watson said, '*but there is a connecting thread. Robert Milner's daughter was recently released from Foston Hall prison. She rented a cottage in Oxley village.*'

'*You've just told me her father's buried there,*' Crosby replied. '*The family must have had ties with the village at some point.*'

'*I'm only speculating here,*' Watson said, '*but Milner's daughter might have been harbouring a grudge against DC Taylor. She was present at Dryffed's Farm when Lucy's father and step-father lost their lives.*'

'*I was also there,*' Crosby felt obliged to add.

'*Exactly,*' the Welshman nodded. '*Does it concern you?*'

'*Well it does now.*'

'*There's also the child abduction we spoke of. He attended the same school as your grandson.*'

'*Yes.*'

'*Lucy Roberts has been linked with the abduction. I think there's good reason for your family to be vigilant.*'

'*I appreciate the warning,*' Crosby said. '*She'd certainly be capable of it. We know the Sixfields operation wouldn't have happened without her input.*'

Watson stood. '*We've taken enough of your time, Frank. I just wanted to give you a heads up. Apologies for the inquisition.*'

Crosby also stood. '*Are you able to say how Grace died?*'

'*A bullet to the back of her head.*'

'*Christ!*'

'*Lieutenant Thorburn was similarly despatched. It appears that he and DC Taylor spent the previous Friday night together.*' Watson gestured to DC Tilson that they were leaving. '*We have to go, Frank. Other calls to make. We'll get together for that drink.*'

Crosby nodded. *'I'll see you out.'*

After he'd had closed the front door behind them Crosby returned to his chair – still shaken by the news of Grace Taylor's death. He sat for half an hour trying to link yesterday's events. The ex-detective still wasn't sure whether Barry Watson had called to question him or pass on a warning. Surely Lucy wasn't carrying out some sort of revenge vendetta at the same time as trying to recover her missing drugs. It didn't make any sense.

Crosby went through to the kitchen. Several weeks of crockery were piled high in the sink and on all available work surfaces. The dishwasher needed unloading. It was ignored. He filled the kettle and set about making a flask of coffee for his journey to the south coast. Penny Zardelli still hadn't been in touch. This would be his third attempt to confront her since Rose Cavendish's brother had been taken from *St Mary's* rectory. His land line rang. He picked up the wall receiver. *'Yes!'*

'Frank?' Paul Berne's south London accent grated in Crosby's ear. *'Derek Alcott's re-surfaced. He's calling at the office this afternoon to collect some personal belongings. You might want a word with him.'*

'Does he know something?'

'I've no idea,' Berne replied. *'He's been tailing you for the past two weeks. It's worth a try.'*

'Have you asked him why he disappeared?'

'He's not telling me anything.'

'What makes you think I'll get anywhere with him?'

'What have you got to lose?'

Although Derek Alcott was unlikely to give him the time of day it had to be followed through. *'Why the sudden helping hand?'* he asked.

'I told you last time,' Berne replied. *'It was nothing personal.'*

Crosby wasn't convinced. *'What time are you expecting Alcott to call in?'*

'About three o'clock this afternoon.' Berne paused. *'I'd appreciate you approaching him after he's left the office.'*

'How did you get my telephone number?' Crosby asked.

'Christ's sake, Frank! I'm a private investigator.'

A loud click in Crosby's ear told him that Paul Berne had terminated their call. He glanced at the wall clock. It would be yet another aborted trip to the offices of *Aquileia Catering.* Crosby returned his flask to the cupboard.

Gower Street: Wednesday 2nd November 2011: 3.15 p.m.

A cool, grey afternoon saw Crosby outside *PB Investigations* in Gower Street once again. The ex-detective had parked-up thirty yards along from the agency's frosted-glass entrance door. He'd watched Derek Alcott enter the front office approximately ten minutes ago. The former Metropolitan traffic officer was presumably collecting little in the way of personal belongings having arrived on foot. Crosby waited in his car. Alcott emerged a few minutes later, carrying a small shoe-box tucked underneath his arm. The Londoner's body language didn't show any outward signs of concern or anxiety as he turned and headed away from Crosby's position.

Another movement caught the ex-detective's eye. Emma Devonshire appeared in the agency's doorway. She watched Alcott making his way along Gower Street, before closing the door and disappearing back inside. Paul Berne had told him the receptionist no longer worked there. Crosby didn't have time to dwell on it. He exited his car. Alcott had already put a hundred yards between them.

Crosby hurried to close the gap. Alcott must have sensed someone behind him and turned. He saw who it was and continued walking. The ex-detective drew level with him. *'What the fuck do you want?'* Alcott didn't slow his pace.

'Ten minutes of your time.'

'Piss off!'

Alcott was clean-shaven and well dressed, his obnoxious manner still intact. Crosby took a folded roll of notes from his jacket pocket and held them out. *'A few questions?'* Alcott slowed. He eyed the money. His aggression relaxed slightly. *'What do you want to know?'*

'Anything you can tell me about the investigation.'

Alcott took the folded roll of notes and tucked them into his trouser pocket. *'We'll do this while we're walking.'*

'Berne claims he doesn't know who wanted me followed,' Crosby said. *'Do you know who it was?'*

Alcott shook his head. *'Paul dealt with all that. I just took my instructions from him.'*

'Did anything unusual come to light whilst you were tailing me?'

'No.'

'Did anyone attract your attention?'

'No.'

'How can you be sure?'

'I'm an ex-fucking copper.'

'Why did you suddenly disappear?'

Alcott didn't immediately reply.

'Were you warned off?'

'Not exactly.' The former Metropolitan officer stopped and turned to face Crosby. *'You paid me so I'll tell you. I ran into some bother down on the south coast. Aquileia Catering. The owner's wife.'*

'Penny Zardelli?'

Alcott nodded.

'What sort of bother?'

'I called in to have a word with her after you left,' Alcott said.

'And?'

'She objected to my being there.' Alcott shrugged. *'We had a ruck. I may have got a little physical.'*

'You assaulted her?'

249

'Depends on your viewpoint. She was gagging for it.'

'You need help,' Crosby said.

'Save your moralising for someone who gives a shit.'

'She didn't call the police?'

Alcott shook his head. 'She came looking for me though.' The Londoner started walking again. 'Brought a half-witted gorilla along with her to teach me a lesson.'

'She had you beaten up?'

Alcott gave a hollow laugh. 'They threatened to kill me initially,' he said, 'but Ms Zardelli is very enterprising when it comes to getting her own back. She's one hard-nosed bitch. And I've met a few.'

'Is any of this relevant?' Crosby asked.

'It might be,' Alcott replied. 'She wanted to know what our investigation had turned up about Dryffed's Farm.'

'Was that it?'

'It's just a gut instinct,' Alcott said, 'but I think she knows something. Word of advice. Don't cross her. The minder will do anything she tells him.'

'Aquileia's chauffeur?'

'Another of his duties is to part Ms Zardelli's feathers for her.'

'How would you know that?'

'I know!'

'None of which explains why you left PB Investigations.'

'The bitch warned me off,' Alcott said. 'It did me favour. I'm done with this fucking place anyway. You can't walk anywhere here without a turban or sari coming in the opposite direction. I'm going back to London. Some of them still speak English there.'

Crosby slowed and let him go. He sensed there was little else that Alcott could help him with. The Londoner continued along Gower Street and disappeared around the next corner. He didn't bother to look back. Crosby turned and re-traced his steps back to the parked Mondeo. As he contemplated calling into PB Investigations something caught his eye – another sheet of folded notepaper tucked behind his windscreen wiper again. Crosby whipped around. There were few passers-by. No one suspicious. He looked along a line of nearby parked cars. All of them empty. Crosby pulled the scrap of paper free. Its brief, three-word message was handwritten, in large block capitals – 'HEADLE POINT. SATURDAY.' Crosby slipped it into his jacket pocket and crossed the road. He'd have to compare its handwriting with the note from last week.

Emma Devonshire looked up with a nervous start as the ex-detective stepped into *PB Investigations* reception office. She probably thought it was Derek Alcott returning. *'I'd heard that you left,'* Crosby said to her.

'Mr Berne asked me to come back.'

'Is he in?'

'Yes,' the girl replied. *'Would you like me to see if he's free?'*

'No need.' Crosby crossed to Paul Berne's door and pushed it open without knocking. The private detective looked up from his laptop. A shadow of annoyance crossed his face when he saw who it was. *'I've told you all I know about this, Frank. It's no longer any concern of mine.'*

'Well it's a bloody concern of mine!'

Berne sighed and closed the lid on his laptop. *'Did you speak with Alcott?'*

'I've not called in about him,' Crosby snapped. *'This is the second time that someone's shoved a note under my windscreen wiper outside your offices.'*

'Note?' Berne repeated. *'What sort of note?'*

'Well it wasn't somebody handing out bloody flyers!'

Berne rose from his chair. *'What the hell are you having a go at me for? I don't know anything about a fucking note!'*

'You're the only one who knew I'd be here this afternoon.' Crosby pointed a finger at him. *'You must have told someone I'd be calling in.'*

'I haven't spoken to anyone.' Berne's voice was also raised. *'You've obviously been followed here.'*

'It's your bloody organisation that's been doing the following.'

'You're not making any sense, Frank.' The private investigator remained on his feet. 'I already knew you were coming here. Why the hell would I have you followed to my own offices?'

Crosby backed off. He wasn't thinking straight, probably just wanting to lash out at someone. Both men stood facing each other. Berne was the first to speak. 'What did the note say?'

'As you pointed out,' Crosby answered, 'it's not your bloody concern any longer.' He turned and left the office, slamming Berne's door behind him. Emma Devonshire was sitting bolt upright, wearing a look that suggested her decision to return might have been somewhat premature. The ex-detective pushed through the outer door with some force. By the time he'd reached his car Crosby had calmed down. He recognised the increasing stress levels – something had to give – and if this wasn't over soon his health would suffer.

An hour later and Crosby was back home at Hawthorne Rise, tapping *Headle Point* into his software's search engine. When all of the necessary server connections had been made he was pointed in the direction of *Andlebury House*. Crosby clicked on its web-site. The home page blurb waxed lyrical about a large stately home and nine hundred acres of parkland. The estate's many features included award winning gardens, a well-stocked lake, an eighteen-hole championship golf course and a recently opened safari park. *Headle Point* itself was an area of high ground beyond the lake. It apparently served as a natural viewing platform to look across at the house opposite.

Andlebury House had been the Wendlethorpe family seat for over eight hundred years – on land originally bequeathed by Richard I for services rendered during the Crusades. *Andlebury's* third, and current, house was sixteenth century – a fine example of Elizabethan architecture according to the web-site. Its three-storey, rectangular block stood over two hundred feet tall and boasted more than one hundred and fifty rooms. National Trust ownership of *Andlebury* had been assumed ten years after the Second World War – its acquisition a direct result of crippling death duties legislation. The current Earl and his family still retained private apartments in the building's west wing.

An associated web-page link indicated a calendar of events for the current year. Crosby clicked on its icon. *Andlebury's* planned event for this coming week-end was the staging of a scarecrow trail within its grounds – portraying well-known historical characters for visitors to locate and identify.

The house was only an hour's drive away. Crosby knew of its existence but had never been there. *'Somewhere else we didn't visit as a family because you were always working,'* he could hear his wife saying. Crosby paused for a moment. The sound of an empty house echoed around him. Despite their differences he wanted his wife back. It momentarily threatened to overwhelm him. He pushed the emotion aside.

Crosby picked up the two notes that had been tucked beneath his windscreen wiper and compared them again. Although the lettering on both looked similar there was little else to help him. He tossed them back onto his desk. Crosby was left with no option than to visit *Andlebury House* this coming Saturday.

CHAPTER 21

Lady Penelope's twenty-metre lightweight hull slid effortlessly through the flat, protected waters of Weymouth's inner harbour. It progressed slowly beneath the town's iconic 1930s road drawbridge. Over four hundred years ago a seventeen-arch timber construction had served as the harbour's first crossing – built to unite the separate ports of Weymouth and Melcombe Regis. There was very little activity on either quayside today. The town's holidaymakers had long since taken their leave of summer – and a grey, drizzly November morning ensured that local passers-by were at a minimum. *Lady Penolope's* pilot eased back on his throttle, not wanting to disturb the smaller craft moored alongside. Any excessive backwash was strictly against regulations and he didn't want to attract the harbour master's attention.

The luxury motor cruiser continued on through a narrow outer harbour, passing *Condor's* cross-channel ferry terminal and the town's *Pavilion* pier theatre. Once clear of the harbour's protective walls, *Lady Penelope* emerged out into open sea – the full force of a stiff south-westerly cutting across her starboard bow. It prompted Giorgio Messina to fully employ the eight hundred horse-power at his disposal. Opening up Volvo's state of the art twin diesel engine system he gradually increased rotation to both propellers – driving them through the English Channel's heavy swell. Messina allowed *Lady Penelope* to reach thirty knots before settling the craft back to its optimum planing speed.

The Italian's imposing physique stood in a protected, enclosed cockpit, both hands were wrapped around the power-assisted steering wheel, his muscled thighs braced against a pitching deck. He was comfortable at the helm of *Aquileia Catering's* ocean-going motor cruiser – an ability and expertise that stemmed from his roots. Raised in a fishing village on Sicily's north-west coastline he'd been sailing boats from an early age. Although *Lady Penelope* was larger and more technically equipped than small fishing boats, his ability to handle any type of vessel came from a natural affinity with the sea.

When the luxury motor yacht had been purchased two years ago it was intended for both recreation and business use. Enrico Zardelli, having already established commercial links with hotels across the channel, planned to entertain clients on board his company's latest acquisition. An ocean backdrop would be a persuasive factor in securing the next lucrative contract.

Aquileia Catering's owner had named the boat after his new wife, and he'd immediately enrolled Giorgio Messina on a basic RYA Helmsman course. The fisherman's son proved himself best in class when it came to executing practical tutorials on the water and further courses followed. Another year of training saw the chauffeur complete enough days at sea to undergo an RYA/MCA advanced power boat examination – its International Certificate of Competence award giving him licence to sail the inland and coastal waters of other countries.

Messina watched the Isle of Portland and its distinctive lighthouse clear *Lady Penelope's* starboard side. He glanced down at the motor cruiser's instrument panel to confirm his GPS and compass bearings for the channel island port of Saint Helier. Although comfortable enough with new technology he only used it as back-up. Messina still sailed by instinct, able to read the sea and its shifting patterns without a need for electronic navigational aids.

The Sicilian was travelling alone on this occasion – personally tasked with delivering orders urgently required by catering outlets in Jersey. He was familiar with the routine crossing and its procedures. His sailing plans had been lodged with the Maritime and Coastguard Agency two days ago – a hire van would be waiting for him in Saint Helier's harbour car park after he'd safely berthed the power cruiser.

Messina took a last look back at Weymouth's fast disappearing crescent-shaped bay – its beach line dominated by *Sea Life's* fifty-metre high observational tower. Messina's next planned sighting of the tower was scheduled for tomorrow afternoon – he'd allowed himself a one night stop-over in Jersey that would include an evening of personal recreation and female company. As *Lady Penelope's* advanced engineering system began to eat up the sea miles he cleared his mind to focus on the task ahead. The outward leg of his journey to Saint Helier would take in excess of two hours.

After approximately one hour's sailing time the motor cruiser passed a Met Office weather station – an automatic light vessel that had been sited in mid-channel. Messina scanned around him for signs of other shipping. There were three distant smudges on the horizon. Switching *Lady Penelope's* engines to idle he stepped down from his cockpit into the craft's main salon, moving quickly across to a two-wheeled handcart trolley standing upright in the far corner. A black plastic coverall covered the heavy-looking, bulky load that had been balanced on its lifting forks.

Messina unzipped and removed the plastic coverall to reveal a naked Rose Cavendish. Thin lengths of cord had been tied around the trolley and Cavendish's lifeless body to maintain her in an upright, standing position. The woman looked straight ahead, dead eyes staring directly into Messina's face. Cavendish's deceased state and early signs of decomposition had no effect on him – his family back in Sicily kept livestock to supplement their income – he was all too familiar with the practice of wringing a chicken's neck or razoring open a pig's throat. Rose Cavendish was just another carcass to be disposed of.

Alongside the trolley was a cast-iron ball – two metres of shackled chain embedded into it. Messina dragged ball and chain onto the trolley's lifting forks, placing both of them between Cavendish's feet. It wasn't particularly warm inside the salon but Messina was perspiring heavily – expending a lot of nervous energy. He dropped down onto one knee, securing the chain's shackle around Cavendish's bare ankles. The Italian stood up and leant the trolley back, pushing it towards a set of double-doors at the boat's stern. Opening both doors he wheeled Cavendish's body out onto *Lady Penelope's* exterior lowering platform – exposing himself to the full force of the elements.

Thin curtains of salt-water spray whipped at his face as he activated the transom's electro-hydraulic mechanism and lowered its platform down to sea level. Messina stopped it just above the water-line. He produced a switchblade from his pocket to slice away the restraining cord from around Cavendish's body. Once free of the upright trolley she fell forward into his arms. In one continuous movement he swivelled and heaved her dead weight over the platform's edge. Momentarily she lay afloat – the two-metre length of chain acting like an umbilical cord. Messina grasped the cast iron ball with both hands and rolled it into the sea after her.

Rose Cavendish's descent through the dark, channel waters was swift. After a three hundred feet downward journey the cast iron ball embedded itself into a sea-bed of shifting sand and gravel sediment. Cavendish's white, naked body floated in an upright position, both feet chained firmly to the cast-iron ball below her. A flat, grey monkfish finned its way lazily past – two unblinking eyes showing a somewhat bored reaction to the surreal spectacle. After a few minutes, Cavendish's translucent form began to take on the appearance of a slow-moving sculpture – deep underwater currents lifting and dropping both her arms – the body swaying to and fro in a synchronised rhythmic dance.

Visibility at this depth was limited. Only twenty metres away the lone monkfish had settled itself flat on the sea-bed. It could no longer see Rose Cavendish's puppet-like movements that she, and eventually her skeletal remains, would be forced to perform in perpetuity.

Three hundred feet above Cavendish's watery grave the Sicilian had returned to his position at *Lady Penelope's* helm. He re-engaged both engines. With the body no longer on board a great weight had lifted from his shoulders. He jabbed a button on his control panel. As the cockpit roof slid back he tilted his face skyward, embracing the cold, filling his lungs with sea air. It was almost a physical release.

There'd been no assistance from Penny Zardelli. She'd had minimal contact with him since the interrogation at *Leawater View* cottage – his employer's wife making it all too clear that Messina was solely responsible for ensuring that Rose Cavendish disappeared completely. St Helier's cross-channel trip had arrived at an opportune time – the dead woman's body having been stored in one of *Aquileia's* freezer storage units for several days.

Messina sucked in another lungful of sea air. He could relax now – the body disposed of – his brief liaison with Penny Zardelli over. The Italian wasn't sorry it had been terminated. When she'd told him that his services were no longer required it was also pointed out what would happen if Enrico Zardelli ever became aware of their relationship. Messina didn't doubt that Penny Zardelli's subtle manipulation of her husband would only have one outcome. The woman was calculating and dangerous. She put him in mind of a female black widow spider – who would often devour her mate after he'd completed his mating duties.

Messina counted himself lucky. Now the Sicilian could look forward to his overnight stay in Jersey without the double spectre of Rose Cavendish and Penny Zardelli hanging over him. He allowed his mind to wander. Messina's companion for the evening would be one Gabriella Carvalho – a twenty-year-old single mother of Portuguese descent from Rio de Janeiro. She waited on tables at one of the hotels served by *Aquileia Catering*. Ms Carvalho forwarded most of her wages to a grandmother in Brazil, who'd been tasked with raising the waitress's two-year-old daughter. Gabriella Carvalho was more than a match for Messina's voracious sexual appetite – their meeting a fortuitous one for the Sicilian. Although he accepted the woman's energies were probably fuelled by the need to supplement her limited income, it was an arrangement that suited both parties. Messina recalled a previous night spent in the woman's company. Memories of her innovative performance triggered an immediate reaction. He emitted a low-throated growl at the faint stirrings of an imminent erection.

Messina checked the time. Another forty-five minutes before *Lady Penelope* would be safely berthed and tethered within the confines of St Helier's super-yacht marina. His tension had completely evaporated. He was almost there.

CHAPTER 22

Andlebury's stone-carved, high vaulted archway had been in-situ since the beginning of England's *Renaissance Period*. At the time of its construction, Elizabeth I's reign was into a thirtieth year – and Tudor warships had recently sailed out from their base in Plymouth Harbour to see off the Spanish Armada. Perched on top of the vaulted arch were three, weathered stone gryphons – mythical guardians of their domain – fixing all those who approached them with sculptured, sightless eyes. The gryphons had initially been commissioned by *Andlebury's* seventh Earl to impress visitors entering his estate. He had also incorporated the creatures into his family's coat of arms and heraldic crest.

Crosby eased his Mondeo over twentieth-century speed humps. All three gryphons stared disapprovingly down at him. He continued on through the entrance – a comfortable access for modern-day traffic – the generous width of twenty-one feet across had originally been intended for a team of coach and horses to pass safely through.

It didn't take long for his progress to slow – the car becoming trapped in a queue of vehicles. Although *Andlebury's* scarecrow competition trail was obviously a popular event in the estate's autumn calendar he presumed there'd be no fireworks display. A safari park in close proximity would mean today's visitors having to celebrate the demise of *Guy Fawkes* at another location.

The slow moving vehicles gave Crosby time to appreciate *Andlebury's* long, sweeping carriage drive – an approach road that wound its way down from high ground through a lightly wooded valley. When the trees eventually thinned out they revealed acres of open parkland, a rolling terrain that stretched away into the distance. A road branched off to Crosby's left, its rustic, wooden signpost indicating the direction of *Andlebury's* championship golf course. He glanced across at tightly mown fairways and immaculate greens, just visible through a line of grassy hillocks that ran alongside.

The traffic ahead of him continued at a slow pace. Crosby estimated he'd been travelling inside the estate for almost a mile now and the house was still not in view. When his Mondeo reached another junction, several cars turned right for the Safari Park entrance. Crosby continued straight on. A brief spasm of tension knotted his stomach – its involuntary contraction reminding him of why he was here today.

He automatically dropped the Mondeo down into second gear as it encountered a steep climb. Upon cresting the rise, *Andlebury House* made a spectacular appearance. Crosby was immediately struck by the perfect symmetry of its columns, turrets and spires. According to *Andlebury's* web-site the house was a masterpiece of classical Palladian styling – the sandstone coloured, three-storey central block a testament to the architect's vision and design. Its construction at the base of a shallow valley faced east, to catch the light from a rising sun – and because all incoming traffic had to approach the building from a slight angle its undeniable grandeur was enhanced even further.

Crosby re-focused. He indicated left, turning off the main route onto a narrow gravel track. According to a map of the estate it led to an adjacent, concealed parking area – from where the public could access certain areas of *Andlebury* land to walk their dogs. There were only three other vehicles in the car park. None of them occupied. Crosby cut the Mondeo's engine but didn't immediately get out – monitoring activity in the main parking area down below him. A handful of energetic, fluorescent jacketed marshals waved drivers into designated parking slots – arranging their vehicles into neat patterns of straight lines and sharp angles. It all looked very routine. Nothing attracted his attention. Crosby opened the car door. If any contact was to be made it would be within the grounds, up on *Headle Point.*

He took a high circular route – avoiding the main car park to scan his surrounding area again. *Andlebury's* ticket booth entrances were probably half-a-mile away from his current position. What the ex-detective didn't notice was a tall, dark-suited figure standing among the ranks of massed vehicles – monitoring Crosby's progress through a pair of small binoculars.

The man was foreign-looking, lightly tanned, with hawk-like features. Alongside him, leaning against the side of their light-grey Citroen saloon, was a young woman – severely cropped hair, jet black in colour. She wasn't following Crosby's movements, her green, almond-shaped eyes fixed firmly on the man's face, as if waiting for him to issue instructions. He continued to track the ex-detective's progress, only lowering his binoculars when Crosby reached the ticket booths and entrance gate. The man nodded to his female companion. She pointed a key at their vehicle's central locking system. There was no conversation between them as they headed across towards the ex-detective – who had by now joined one of several long queues.

Crosby waited patiently, his own queue particularly slow-moving. It was another fifteen minutes before the ex-detective gained entry – finally able to make his way along a bark-chip path towards the house and gardens. He looked skyward. The high ceiling of light-grey cloud looked non-threatening. A dry day had been promised. Although an autumnal air had introduced itself into recent weather patterns the temperatures remained unseasonably high for November. Crosby drifted slowly along the chip-bark path, in amongst several knots of chattering visitors. After the path had eventually run its course he rounded a final corner to find himself standing in front of *Andlebury House.*

The building's impressive, double-fronted entrance doors sat above a semi-circular cascade of shallow stone steps, leading down to an extended area of paved terracing. The terracing boasted a large, ornamental fountain – an eye-catching centrepiece among the rows of neat, regimented flower beds. A number of wooden benches had been arranged at several points along criss-cross gravelled walkways for visitors to sit and appreciate the house and its gardens. A discreet, informative plaque outlined the finer points of Capability Brown's 18th century parkland design and layout. Crosby turned his attention to the faces of passers-by. No one seemed particularly interested in him. He found a vacant bench and sat down to monitor the stretch of high ground beyond *Andlebury's* nearby lake.

Ten minutes passed – groups of excitable children clutching half-completed competition forms ran aimlessly around him. Parents trailed slowly in their wake, studying small laminated maps that pinpointed where the various scarecrow exhibits had been positioned. Most adults appeared to be taking the event far more seriously than their offspring – who were keen to find the next scarecrow but impatient to move on without identifying it. One particular exhibit stood alongside a low wall, close to where Crosby was sitting. The stuffed caricature of *Adolf Hitler* came complete with toothbrush moustache, slicked-down black hair, and swastika armbands. A small group of older teenagers amused themselves by goose-stepping their way around the terrace whilst throwing extravagant Nazi salutes. Crosby silently congratulated the organisers for pairing a family fun day with *Herr Hitler*.

'Dad!' A voice called out from somewhere behind him. Crosby turned to watch the young girl approach another scarecrow exhibit. This one was female. It wore a blonde wig and flimsy white dress – which had been arranged to look as if its hem was ballooning up in a strong wind. *'Who is it, Dad?'* the girl asked. Her father looked unsure, continuing to study what were several obvious clues.

'Christ's sake!' Crosby mouthed to himself. He felt tempted to shout out the answer but his eye-line had continued on past them. Ian Brown was sitting on a bench facing him. Both men spotted each other at the same time. Although there was thirty yards between them he could tell that Brown was not happy to see him. The Scenes-of-Crime officer walked quickly across to Crosby's bench. He looked nervous and agitated. *'What the fuck's going on, Frank? What are we both doing here?'*

'It's probably not a coincidence,' was the best that Crosby could come up with. *'I presume you've been invited to Headle Point?'*

'Well, I'm not here by fucking choice. I don't do happy clappy, family fun days.'

Ian Brown's language was attracting attention. 'You need to keep your voice down,' Crosby said to him. 'Do you have any idea who it was that contacted you?'

'Oh aye! They also left their fucking address and telephone number.'

'We've obviously been seen together at some point.'

'No shit, Frank!' The Scot remained standing, his voice low, angry.

'Why turn up here if you knew what it was about?'

'I was told what would happen if I didn't.' Brown slumped down next to the ex-detective. 'You need to tell them I know fuck all about these missing drugs, Frank.'

'Which isn't strictly true,' Crosby reminded him.

The Scenes-of-Crime officer straightened. 'You bastard! Why do you need to implicate me? I'm the one who's been helping you out.'

'So how do we approach this then?'

'We?' Brown hissed. 'There is no fucking we!'

'There is at the moment,' Crosby said. 'They obviously want to speak with both of us.'

The Scot became even more irate. 'Jesus Christ! You fucking speak to them. I'm leaving.' Brown stood abruptly. 'It's not my problem.'

'Sit down, Ian,' Crosby said to him. 'It's become your problem. If you leave now it won't help. You'll be looking over your shoulder tomorrow.'

The Scot swore several times, but eventually sat back down. 'We need to see it through,' Crosby said to him. 'I've been chasing shadows since this started. It's the first opportunity to speak with someone directly.'

'I don't fucking need this.'

'Neither of us do.'

'*And why here?*' Brown asked.

'*I don't know.*'

'*I'll fucking tell you why,*' the Scot said. '*They want to kill us in a place that'll get headlines. Send out a message.*'

'*They'd have done it before now. It's the drugs they're interested in.*'

'*You don't know where the fucking drugs are!*'

'*I can tell them what I've found out.*' Crosby stood up. '*Shall we do this?*' He headed for a flight of stone steps that led down into *Andlebury's* open parkland. The Scot reluctantly followed. It took them ten minutes to reach a wooden-slatted bridge in front of the lake. A scarecrow tableau, featuring Henry VIII and one of his six wives, had been arranged near a waterside bench. '*Fuck's sake!*' Brown said to no one in particular. He trailed Crosby across the bridge, following a sign that pointed them up towards *Headle Point*.

Thin, manicured fingers lightly adjusted a small pair of binoculars, bringing both figures on the bridge into sharp focus. '*Do we have everything?*'

'*Yes.*' The woman's voice was deep, heavily accented.

Her companion lowered the binoculars. '*We'll follow from a distance.*'

Crosby and Brown made good progress up one of several inclines – rugged, uncultivated terrain – rising up towards a narrow grassed ridgeway. *Headle Point* didn't appear to be a popular feature with *Andlebury's* day trippers, the area on this side of the lake seemingly devoid of visitors.

Both men reached the narrow ridgeway. Several lengths of protective railing and a number of warning signs had been put in place where the land fell steeply away on either side. They stopped to rest. Ian Brown in particular was breathing heavily. He ignored the view of *Andlebury House* from their vantage point and removed his sweater – a light sheen of perspiration glistening wet across his forehead. The Scot continued to look edgy and nervous. Crosby was wearing a lightweight jacket but didn't take it off – the weight in one of his zipped pockets reassuring. He'd brought along the *Walther PPK,* its silencer, and a clip of ammunition.

Crosby looked along the narrow grassed track, towards another incline. An adjacent sign indicated that *Headle Point* was still somewhere above them. He turned to the Scenes-of-Crime officer. *'You ready?'*

Ian Brown muttered but moved forward again. Crosby's mobile rang. It startled the Scot. *'Jesus Christ! Can't you put that fucking thing on silent?'*

Crosby retrieved the phone from his trouser pocket and jabbed the receive button. *'Yes!'*

'Frank Crosby?' a remote voice enquired.

The ex-detective's antenna twitched. *'Who is this?'*

'I'm ringing on behalf of a client who has information for you,' the voice said in his ear. *'This conversation will last no longer than thirty seconds.'* Crosby signalled for Ian Brown to wait. The ex-detective walked away towards a length of wooden railing that flanked one side of their pathway. *'Who is your client?'* Crosby kept his voice low.

The enquiry was ignored. *'You are familiar with the name Sam Cavendish?'*

'What about him?'

'He doesn't exist,' the voice said. *'My client's enquiries have identified the person in question as a woman. Her name is Rose Cavendish. The partner of Lucy Roberts.'*

'That's not possible.' Crosby was momentarily confused. *'I had someone run a check. My contact confirmed that Rose Cavendish has a twin brother.'*

'A twin brother does exist,' the voice continued. *'A more thorough investigation of the facts would have revealed they were separated at birth and adopted by different families. She was raised in Rochdale. He remained in Scotland until the age of twenty-five. They*

266

were re-united with each other recently. This information has been checked through two reliable sources.'

Crosby experienced a twinge of unease.

The disembodied voice maintained its monosyllabic, one-dimensional tone. *'My client has positively identified the male twin. He is currently working as a Scenes-of-Crime officer for the West Midlands Police. His name is Ian Brown.'*

Crosby's mind scrambled. Ian Brown was Rose Cavendish's brother? There wasn't time to work out the implications. It took all of Crosby's will power not to react, acutely aware that Brown was standing behind him, approximately twenty yards away. *'This information,'* the voice concluded, *'has been passed on the understanding that you will make no further attempts to contact my client.'*

A click. The call was terminated. Crosby was still leant against the wooden rail, looking down at a sloping drop of well over one hundred feet. The ex-detective turned slowly, trying to keep his face neutral, impassive. Ian Brown was watching him closely – the small ginger moustache above his thin, colourless, lips twitching furiously. *'Anything important?'* he asked.

Crosby waved the enquiry away. *'Nothing that can't wait.'* He pocketed his mobile. The caller's client had to be Penny Zardelli. What else had been uncovered during Rose Cavendish's interrogation? And what had they done with her? Where was Lucy? And why had Penny Zardelli taken the trouble to contact him? Too many questions. Now wasn't the time to dwell on them.

Ahead of him Brown had started the final climb up to *Headle Point.* He looked back. *'Are we doing this or what?'* Crosby followed. A half-formed theory nagged at him. If there was any substance to it he was in imminent danger.

The ex-detective hung back. Ian Brown knew that Crosby possessed a handgun, and would have surely catered for the possibility that he was carrying it. A muted voice drifted up from below. Someone climbing the hill behind them. It was not the excitable chatter that Crosby would have associated with *Andlebury's* day trippers.

Brown disappeared around a sharp corner in front of him. Another muffled noise from below. Closer this time. Crosby pulled the zipper on his jacket pocket. *'Shit!'* It wouldn't release. The metal teeth had jammed. He tried to rip the pocket apart. No time. They were almost upon him.

Crosby ducked underneath a length of railing and looked over the side. There was a line of bushes thirty feet below him. He stepped out onto the incline – testing his weight against a layer of shale and loose earth. His leather-bottomed shoes offered little grip on its unstable surface and he allowed himself to slide down towards the bushes.

There was an angry shout from above. Crosby didn't look up, trying to maintain his balance. When the moving ground gave way beneath him he was thrown onto his back – shards of debris ripping at his clothes as he gathered momentum and continued to slide.

There were half-submerged boulders in his path now, embedded deep into the ground. Crosby instinctively wrapped both arms around his head as he bounced over them. When the line of bushes came rushing up to meet him he made an instinctive grab for them – skinning both palms as the thin branches slid through his hands.

Ian Brown's angry tirade continued from above. *'I can't see the bastard!'* he shouted. *'You'll have to go down there. He disappeared into those bushes.'*

There was another voice, quiet, authoritative. Crosby could only make out certain words. *'Not within our remit... armed... unnecessary risk.'*

'You've been paid to do a fucking job.' Ian Brown was still shouting. *'Send the fucking woman down after him.'*

As Crosby tried to focus on the continuing disagreement above him he started to slide again. The bushes that he'd come to a halt in were slowly giving way under his weight. Crosby made a vain attempt to grip the thin branches but couldn't hold onto them – his shredded

268

palms too painful. The voices grew fainter as he slid headlong down another section of steep gradient. One of the half-buried boulders caught him a glancing blow to his forehead. A fleeting image, before he blacked out, was of careering at speed into a wall of thick, dense foliage.

It must have been several hours later when consciousness returned because his surroundings were pitch black. He remembered exactly what had happened. A good sign. Crosby automatically reached for his police radio to call for backup. *'Fuck!'* Obviously not in that good a shape. Crosby slowly flexed all of his limbs – nothing seemed to be broken – just stiffness and bruising. Another good sign. His only concern was the deep throbbing pain to his forehead. He lifted a hand to explore an egg-shaped swelling. There didn't seem to be any blood. The only other discomfort came from inside both hands – where he'd grabbed at the bush's sharp branches. An arc of light cascaded briefly above him. A series of short, sharp explosions popped faintly in the far distance. Crosby's confused state took several moments to register that it was a fireworks display.

He must have drifted again. His next recollection was looking up at a full moon – patchy light cloud moving slowly across clearing skies. It wasn't particularly cold. Crosby took in his surroundings. The moon's reflected light showed him laid out full-length in an area of grassy clumps and thick foliage. He had to move. It was a slow and painful process, but Crosby eventually regained his feet. The ex-detective waited for any signs of dizziness or nausea. He felt reasonably intact – and the throbbing forehead had subsided to a dull ache. Crosby manoeuvred himself gingerly down a final, bush-covered slope – the moon providing enough light for him to see several steps ahead. As he continued to cover more ground the soreness eased, his movement became easier.

After several minutes he stepped out from the line of bushes onto a narrow strip of clear ground. In front of him, stretching away both left and right, was a thick, wire-mesh fence. Crosby had no idea where he was in relation to the house. His instinct told him to keep moving left. He progressed slowly – the narrow strip of ground between fence and undergrowth was rutted, uneven. A sudden dip caused him to lurch sideways. As Crosby stretched out his hand it made contact with the wire-mesh fence. A powerful jolt ran up his arm and threw him bodily into the air. It took a few seconds for the ex-detective to realise he'd been thrown backwards into the undergrowth. Crosby didn't immediately get up, allowing time for the after-effects to wear off. When he started walking again it was well away from the electrified fencing – presumably a perimeter barrier around *Andlebury's* safari park.

Crosby stumbled once more. *'Focus!'* the ex-detective remonstrated with himself. He remembered a small torch built into his mobile. Crosby retrieved the phone from a trouser pocket and made several attempts to switch it on. The screen remained blank. *'Shit!'* If his *Walther* was also damaged it might have consequences later. Crosby tugged at the zipper on his jacket pocket. It was still jammed. He lost patience, reaching inside his jacket to rip open its flimsy lining. Crosby tore the gun free. Sliding back its loading mechanism he pulled the trigger on an empty chamber. A loud click suggested it was still in working order. He unzipped his other pocket to retrieve ammunition and silencer – taking a few seconds to assemble the additional parts.

Crosby stiffened. Something moving to his right – a low, threatening growl from behind the fence – only ten yards away. He raised his gun, pointing it into deep shadow beyond the wire-mesh. An electrified fence between him and the animal didn't stop his pulse racing. Crosby waited until he was sure there was nothing about to launch an attack on him before moving forward again.

The low growling kept pace alongside him. Crosby caught glimpses of a dark shape every so often as it padded through shadows inside the fence's perimeter. As he contemplated firing a silenced round above the animal's head it suddenly veered away. Crosby stopped to look back. The fence had squared off at right angles. A pair of unblinking, yellow eyes monitored him from behind an upright concrete stanchion. Crosby moved on. After another fifty yards the dense foliage on his left-hand side began to thin out, eventually giving way to an uninterrupted vista of flat, open ground. He stopped to get his bearings.

Crosby had emerged further along the lake, looking out on a moonlit terrain, silhouetted trees casting long shadows across *Andlebury's* open parkland. Several costumed scarecrows remained from yesterday, bizarre additions to an eerie landscape. The house seemed to be some distance away – a dark, rectangular block, illuminated by tiny squares of orange light in several of its windows. He continued to follow the lake along its shore-line. On reaching a narrow stone bridge he stopped to look across the stretch of water – his sixth sense telling him someone was out there beyond it. A light wind sprang up, creating some movement in the bushes and trees. *Andlebury's* scarecrows also seemed to be on the move – their light, flimsy costumes flapping in the breeze. A bank of dark cloud suddenly blocked out the moonlight, plunging everything into darkness. Crosby took advantage of it, quickly crossing the bridge. He found a small clump of trees and waited under their cover.

The cloud passed. *Andlebury's* landscape re-appeared. Crosby remained out of sight, continuing to monitor his immediate surroundings. Several minutes passed. The ex-detective flexed both arms and legs. He felt surprisingly alert after his fall – probably due to the adrenalin coursing through him. Approximately thirty yards away his peripheral vision picked up someone or something edging towards the cover of a large oak tree. Crosby lifted the *Walther*. His thumb and forefinger snapped back the handgun's top slider – automatically slotting a round of ammunition into the weapon's firing chamber. It sounded noisy. A metallic echo in the stillness.

'*I knew you'd show up sooner or later, Frank.*' Ian Brown's voice, his unmistakable, grating Glaswegian cutting through the night air. '*Are you still carrying that unlicensed semi-automatic around?*'

'You've just heard me loading it.'

'I'm not armed,' Brown called across to him.

'Step out into the open then.'

There was a short silence before the Scot replied. *'Why didn't you phone someone, Frank? Problems with your mobile? You can't be feeling too good after that fall.'*

'It was a soft landing.'

'We need to talk this through, Frank,' the Scot said.

'What's to discuss,' Crosby replied. *'I've already worked most of it out.'*

'You know fuck all, laddie!'

'I know that Rose Cavendish is your twin sister.'

A longer silence.

'I also know,' Crosby said, *'that you were both responsible for lifting the drugs from Dryffed's Farm. It all made sense after the phone call earlier.'*

'And who was that from?'

'Didn't say. Keen to put your name forward though.'

'And what else have you managed to work out Sherlock?'

'There's a body count of at least four,' the ex-detective said. *'That doesn't include Lucy Roberts or your Scenes-of-Crime colleague John Hendry.'* Crosby paused. *'How am I doing?'*

'Too fucking sharp for your own good, Inspector.' The Scot sounded impatient. *'Are we going to stand here all night reminiscing?'*

'I'm in no hurry.'

'You might have trouble explaining away that handgun in the morning.'

'I'm quite happy for you to call the police.'

'Don't get too fucking smart, Frank. The others made that mistake.'

'Grace Taylor for one?'

'She was after a cut of the money.'

'I don't believe that.'

'Believe what you fucking like!'

'You must have had help for dealing with both her and the American. Was that your hired contract killer?'

Brown didn't reply. Crosby's eyes remained fixed on the oak tree, looking for any signs of movement. He didn't want the Scot circling around behind him. *'Terry Halloran wasn't a threat though. Why did you kill her?'*

'She was making a bloody nuisance of herself.' The Scot's voice carried sharply across to him. *'Stupid bitch came into the office after you'd seen her. Asking questions about Hendry.'*

'Killing her wasn't a problem then,' Crosby said. *'If a reward's large enough the conscience shrinks to accommodate it.'*

Brown laughed out loud. *'Don't play psychological fucking mind games with me, Frank. I sleep well enough.'*

'And then there's Lucy,' Crosby said. *'She told your sister about the hidden drugs during their time together at Foston Hall.'*

'We're wasting time, Frank.'

'But then Rose made the mistake of telling you.'

'All I did was remind her of Lucy's track record,' Brown replied. *'The woman would have ended their relationship after being released. I had to make sure that Rose didn't miss out on a share of the money.'*

'Not to mention your share.'

'You might be happy to exist on a shit pension,' the Scot said. *'I had the chance to supplement mine.'*

'At some stage,' Crosby said, *'Lucy would have realised that you and Rose were responsible for hoisting the drugs. Was it always your intention to get rid of her at some point?'*

'She'd have wanted the whole fucking lot for herself.'

'Technically speaking they did belong to her.'

'Well, they don't now,' Brown shouted across. *'It's all been sold on. And it was me taking the risks.'*

'And the profits.'

'Are we done with this now, Frank?'

'Not quite,' the ex-detective replied. '*John Hendry was enlisted at some stage. He carried out the forensic investigation at Dryffed's Farm. No doubt his knowledge of its layout helped recover the drugs.*' Crosby paused. '*How am I doing so far, Ian?*'

'*Boring me shitless, laddie.*'

'*But then I became a problem,*' Crosby continued. '*When Lucy accused me of stealing the heroin it would have been a concern that I'd discover who was responsible. You had to feed me stuff about Hendry to divert attention.*'

'*We can easily sort this, Frank.*'

'*And how do you propose doing that? I'm in the way.*'

'*It needn't be a problem. There's always a solution.*'

'*What's the plan then? Do I disappear as well?*'

'*Come on, Frank,*' the Scot replied too quickly. '*I couldn't do that to you.*'

'*Maybe not personally,*' Crosby said, '*but your hired contract killer wouldn't have had a problem with it up on Headle Point.*'

There was a lengthy pause. '*I've got a proposition for us,*' the Scot eventually said.

'*Us?*' Crosby replied. '*Are we partners now?*'

'*We could be if you'd shut the fuck up and listen,*' Brown said. '*I can make you a wealthy man. It's been a decent interval since the drugs were sold on. We kept some of the money back but I can start releasing the bulk of it now.*'

'*And you're offering me a share?*'

'*I'm able to do that. And we're in a position to trust each other now.*'

'*Is it the same trust that John Hendry placed in you.*'

'*Hendry wanted all of his cut straightaway,*' the Scot said. '*He couldn't wait. I told him it would attract attention.*'

Crosby couldn't keep up this pointless cat-and-mouse charade for too much longer. The adrenalin caused by their encounter had worn off. He was beginning to feel the after-effects of his fall now. Brown would know that. Crosby would have to act soon.

'Is your sister agreeable to handing over a share of this money?' the ex-detective asked.

'Rose will do what I tell her.'

'Is she still around then?'

A slight hesitation. *'Why the fuck wouldn't she be?'*

The Scot's reaction suggested there was a question mark concerning Rose Cavendish's whereabouts.

'Do you want a share of this fucking money or not?' Ian Brown was angry now. Crosby had obviously touched a nerve. The Scot continued to shout abuse and threats across the space between them. It had to be now, whilst Brown was distracted. Crosby began to circle around the Scenes-of-Crime officer in a wide arc – using nearby hedging and shrubbery as cover. *Andlebury's* thick parkland turf allowed him to move noiselessly into position behind the large oak.

'What's it to be?' the Scot shouted out. *'Final call.'*

Ian Brown was clearly visible now, his back to the ex-detective.

'I didn't want to do this, Frank, but we've fucked around long enough.'

Crosby inched slowly forward, holding the *Walther* at hip level. He froze. The Scot wasn't on his own. There was someone standing in the shadows alongside him. Brown pushed a small, silhouetted figure out into the open. Crosby's stomach spasmed. *'Christ's sake!'* He knew immediately who it was – even with the boy's back to him he could tell it was his grandson. Ian Brown reached out and loosened a gag from around the five-year-old's mouth but remained alongside him. Crosby could see that Jack was blindfolded, a handgun pointed at his head.

'Gramps! Where are you?'

The ex-detective bit down on a natural instinct to call out and reassure his grandson.

'We've been monitoring your family's house.' Brown was still shouting across towards Crosby's original position. *'They turned up yesterday. Weren't enjoying their unscheduled holiday presumably.'*

'I can't see you, Gramps,' Jack called out.

'Your grandson's here as a little extra insurance.' Brown pushed the barrel of his gun against the boy's head. *'In case you wouldn't see reason.'*

The Scot remained directly in Crosby's eye-line, still facing the other way, about twenty paces between them. *'Come on out, Frank,'* Brown shouted. *'I'm not fucking around here.'*

Crosby raised his *Walther,* its safety mechanism still de-activated.

'On a count of three,' Brown called out. *'I will blow the kid's head away.'*

Crosby fully extended his arms, holding the gun steady with both hands. He aimed at the back of Brown's head.

'One!'

Crosby's forefinger took up the slack on his trigger. He began to gently squeeze it.

'Two!'

'Gramps!' his grandson shouted.

Gunfire can only be muffled to a certain degree. Even through a silencer, the energy needed to release and propel a bullet at over nine hundred miles-an-hour can still sound very loud. The lethal projectile pitched Ian Brown forward onto his face. He made several involuntary twitching movements before lying completely still. It was over in a matter of seconds – silence quickly returning to *Andlebury's* wide open spaces.

The gun used to kill Ian Brown was now pressed firmly into the back of Crosby's neck. He could feel its silencer warm against his skin – a combination of hot explosive gases and spent gunpowder heating the thin, metallic tube.

'It would be wise to relinquish your weapon,' a man's voice advised.

The ex-detective let his *Walther* fall to the ground. A leather-gloved hand reached down to pick up the discarded firearm.

'It's doubtful the intended kill would have been successful. Your hands were unsteady and the aiming point too high.' A calm, authoritative voice – the same voice that Crosby had heard arguing with Ian Brown up on *Headle Point. 'Your grandson appears to be in some distress,'* the voice continued. *'You may remove his blindfold.'*

Crosby wasted no time in crossing to where Jack was standing. *'It's gramps,'* he whispered in the boy's ear, gently removing his blindfold. *'You're safe now.'* The five-year-old was shaking. Crosby drew him in close. He turned back around.

In front of him stood a tall man of slim build. His features were sharp, angular, dominated by a prominent, hawk-like nose. Crosby knew it had to be Ian Brown's hired contract killer. He also recognised him as being with his daughter-in-law outside Jack's school. The gunman moved across to Ian Brown's lifeless, outstretched figure and stooped over him. His eyes didn't once leave Crosby's face. He removed a glove. The man's long, thin index finger touched Ian Brown's neck, searching for a pulse. *'Mr Brown seems reluctant to leave us.'* The hired gunman's perfect English carried just a trace of foreign accent. He stood back up. *'I suggest you remove your grandson from the immediate area and wait for me.'*

Jack was still clinging tightly to his grandfather. Crosby found the boy's hand and began walking towards a nearby gravel path. There was another muffled gunshot. Jack flinched. They continued walking. The hired contract killer materialised in front of them, still carrying his firearm. *'I think we can safely leave your former colleague to enjoy his own company. He no longer poses a threat to us.'* Crosby turned to look behind him, but could see nothing through the clump of trees.

The ex-detective had yet to suffer any reaction – his emotions numbed by the speed of events. Now an after-shock set in and he began to tremble slightly. Jack felt it – burying his face deep into Crosby's midriff. They remained huddled together as the gunman appraised them. Crosby's prime concern was Jack's safety and he momentarily thought about trying to rush the hired contract killer.

'That would be unwise,' the man warned him, closing to within three paces. They stood facing each other. Crosby held his gaze.

'And now we have business to conclude,' the man said.

'Business?'

'I would introduce myself,' the contract killer offered, *'but having just listened to your exchanges with the recently deceased Mr Brown you will no doubt be aware of who I am.'*

'You kill people for money,' Crosby replied.

The hired gunman laughed out loud. *'I take exception to your terminology, Inspector. My skills are respected and sought after in many parts of the world. A profession that stretches back hundreds of years.'*

'Not dissimilar to prostitution,' Crosby replied.

A look of annoyance crossed the man's face. It quickly disappeared. *'My services offer a permanent solution. Whores can only ever provide temporary relief.'*

Crosby nodded in the direction of Ian Brown's body. *'Is it usual to murder those who hire you?'*

The hired gunman shrugged. *'Unfortunate but necessary in this instance. If it could have been dealt with in any...'*

Crosby cut across him. *'I need to know that my grandson's life is not in danger.'*

'Why would it be?' the man replied. *'Once we have concluded our business here you are both free to leave.'*

'Jack shouldn't be here,' Crosby persisted. *'I'll take him home to his parents. We can continue this elsewhere.'*

'All in good time,' the hired gunman replied. *'You're both perfectly safe.'* Crosby watched as the contract killer openly and deliberately put his handgun away. It made the ex-detective feel a little easier.

'There is an alternative to your ex-colleague's earlier proposal,' the hired gunman continued. 'It would prove beneficial for both of us.'

'I have nothing to offer,' the ex-detective said to him.

'I have something to offer you, Inspector.'

'It's Mr Crosby. I retired three years ago.'

The man shrugged. 'I prefer to use your police rank, Inspector. A small courtesy that is commonplace in my homeland. We recognise those who have served their community.'

Crosby cut him short. 'You had a proposal?'

'As you wish,' the hired gunman said. 'I control a small, hand-picked team. During our short association with your ex-colleague we were able to ascertain the extent of his wealth and how he obtained it.'

'Why would you do that?'

'My operations can sometimes extend into other areas.'

'Such as?'

'One of them might be described as stripping a company's assets.'

'Ian Brown's assets,' Crosby said.

'Quite.' The man smiled, his teeth white against a dark skin. 'I am an opportunist, Inspector Crosby. My enquiries suggested the possibility of being able to secure your ex-colleague's considerable wealth.'

'Which I had nothing to do with.'

'I'm aware of that now.' The contract gunman waved a hand. 'Initially of course you had to be part of our investigation. Your meetings with Ian Brown suggested a role in his operation. We had to identify who had control of the laundered drugs money.'

'I saw you at the school. With my daughter-in-law.'

The man nodded. 'We would have considered the possibility of kidnapping your grandson.'

'You weren't responsible for the abduction?'

The hired gun smiled. 'My team doesn't make mistakes. We wouldn't have taken the wrong child.'

'And that's supposed to reassure me that we're both safe.'

'You are no longer a concern to us,' the man said. *'We have established where the money is deposited. It's being held in an overseas account under the name of John Hendry. Mr Brown was obviously concerned about it being traced directly to him.'*

'Why would he hire you to eliminate Hendry then?'

The man shrugged. *'Mr Brown was in possession of all necessary access data to assume ownership of the account at a time of his choosing. It also meant one less shareholder of course.'*

'How do you know all this?'

'It's what I do for a living.'

'You're in a position to assume this account?'

The hired gunman nodded. *'In today's world of computerised banking it doesn't require masked gunmen with sawn-off shotguns to secure another person's assets. I received confirmation an hour ago that a safety deposit box has been traced and is now in our possession. It contains everything we require, including encrypted electronic data and original documentation identifying John Hendry.'*

'Then why did you need to help Ian Brown take my grandson as a hostage?' Crosby asked.

'That was unfortunate,' the man spread his hands, *'but Mr Brown's safety deposit box hadn't been recovered at the time and we were still in the employ of your ex-colleague. If we had refused his request it would have caused him to be suspicious. We didn't want to compromise our operation at that stage.'*

Crosby's grandson suddenly spoke out, his face still buried in the ex-detective's midriff. *'I want to go home, Gramps.'* Crosby pulled him in close. *'Won't be long now, Jack.'* He turned back to the hired gunman. *'I don't know why I'm being told all of this. What is it you want from me?'*

'Very little, Inspector,' the man replied. *'I require you to just walk away. Go back to your family. Enjoy the retirement you've worked for.'*

Crosby was wary. His CID career had taught him to accept nothing at face value. He nodded in the direction of Ian Brown. *'How is that to be dealt with?'*

'Mr Brown's vehicle has already been taken care of.' The man folded his arms. *'His current residence is being prepared to suggest that he's moved on. I suspect your ex-colleague's disappearance will raise no more than a short-lived ripple of interest.'*

'And why am I being excluded from your clean-up program?'

'Any number of valid operational reasons,' the hired gunman said. *'You have close dependants. The sudden disappearance of a grandfather and his grandson would raise far too much interest in the public domain.'* He paused. *'Besides, three bodies are more difficult to recycle than just the one.'*

'And if it wasn't for that?'

The hired gunman smiled. *'We'll not dwell on it, Inspector. Simplicity is the key to a successful operation. Any complications are to be avoided.'*

'What's to stop me informing the police about all of this?'

The man shook his head. *'I'm a good judge of people's character. You know that a police enquiry would only prolong the trauma your family is currently experiencing. And what would it achieve anyway? I don't exist. The authorities would be chasing shadows.'* He retrieved Crosby's *Walther* from his jacket pocket and offered it to the ex-detective. *'I also understand that an investigation into recent events would prove to be very awkward for you personally.'*

Crosby reached out and took his handgun.

'It's still a good light,' the hired gunman said. *'This path will take you back to where your car was left yesterday afternoon.'* Crosby's hand automatically went to his pocket. The car-keys were still there.

'There are two members of my team currently safeguarding your family.' The hired contract killer moved to one side. *'By tomorrow afternoon I will have confirmation that all monies have been*

successfully transferred into my ownership. Only then will my associates vacate your son's house.'

'Which would indicate you're not totally sure of my intentions,' Crosby said.

'You are not a concern,' the man replied. *'It is your family that might decide to act in haste. Once my associates have left the premises our operation here in the UK is concluded. How matters proceed after that is entirely up to you.'*

'I doubt my family would agree.'

'You have a window of opportunity in which to persuade them otherwise,' the man said. *'I suggest you use it wisely.'*

Crosby picked up his grandson and started walking. He didn't look back. His only thought now was to put distance between himself and the contract killer. *'I want my mum,'* Jack said. He wrapped both arms around his grandfather's neck. The ex-detective forced himself to sound more upbeat than he felt. *'She's waiting at home for you. We'll be there soon.'*

The path continued on. When they reached a steep incline he had to put his grandson down. *'Can you walk from here, Jack?'* The five-year-old nodded. *'I think so.'* Crosby looked about him. Although the moon continued to light their way he still wasn't entirely sure of his exact position. A few minutes later they topped the rising ground and looked down on *Andlebury's* main parking area and entrance booths. *'Nearly there, Jack,'* he said reassuringly.

They kept to the high ground. When the gravelled path ended abruptly it was opposite a side entrance to the dog-walking car park. His Mondeo was where he'd left it. Crosby checked behind, to make sure no one was following. Was that a figure in the distance? He blinked – re-focused – just his eyes playing tricks. Crosby waited a few moments in nearby shadow, looking for signs of movement in the car park. *'What's up, Gramps?'* his grandson asked.

'It's OK, Jack.' Crosby thumbed his key's remote to de-activate the car's security system. Amber lights flashed, and the doors

automatically unlocked – a solid clunk of noise, amplified within their enclosed parking area. Crosby slowly approached the car. There was no one inside. He ushered Jack around to the Mondeo's front passenger door, hurriedly opened it, lifted the boy inside. An absurd thought crossed his mind that Jack ought to be sitting in his booster seat. He secured the boy's seat belt and ruffled his hair. *'Soon be home now.'* Crosby moved back around the car, anxious to get away, still expecting someone to stop him. Once inside he quickly fired up the engine and gunned its accelerator – spitting up shards of loose gravel as he engaged the clutch and moved sharply away.

The headlights of his Mondeo cut through *Andlebury's* darkness as the moon slid behind another bank of dark cloud. Crosby forced himself to slow down through a series of tight bends along the estate's exit route. He glanced across at his grandson who was sitting bolt upright, staring directly ahead. Jack had lapsed into silence. Crosby was worried about the boy's state of mind. He needed some sort of reaction. A normal conversation would be impossible. He tried. *'How was the Isle of Wight?'*

'I didn't like it.' The reply was muted. *'They were shouting at each other.'*

'Who were?'

'Mum and Dad.'

'Why did you come home?'

The boy didn't answer it. He looked across at his grandfather. *'That man had a gun.'*

'He was helping us.'

'Did he shoot the other man?'

'An accident. We'll talk about it tomorrow.'

'Are we safe now?'

'Yes.'

Jack closed his eyes. The ex-detective's vision blurred. He blinked away pinpricks of half-formed tears. Crosby couldn't imagine what effect this experience would have on the boy. His injured forehead began to throb again. He took a deep breath and re-focused, concentrating on the narrow ribbon of tarmac stretched out ahead of him.

His Mondeo passed beneath *Andlebury's* stone archway – its three brooding gryphons seeing him off the premises. Crosby had to think about what came next. Whatever the hired gunman had told him he couldn't be sure about what he'd find back at his son's house. Were the family being held at gunpoint? Had they been murdered? Crosby pushed that thought to the back of his mind. There was little time in which to act. Should he drive immediately to the nearest police station? What would that achieve? Would it put his family in more danger? What about Jack? The boy ought to be taken somewhere safe – but that would cause even more panic if Crosby returned home without him. The ex-detective looked across at his grandson. He'd fallen asleep.

By the time Crosby had run through his options several times over he found himself five minutes away from Jack's home. The contract killer had known exactly what he would do. Nothing at all. And if his family were safe and unharmed that's where he would probably leave it.

Crosby's Mondeo approached the small, rural hamlet of Little Wintermore. Michael and Angela's four-bedroom detached was not an isolated property, but neither was it close to neighbouring houses. There were three cars parked on their double driveway. Crosby didn't recognise a light-grey Citroen saloon. He pulled up behind his son's Volvo. An exterior security lamp angled towards the drive didn't activate – and there were no lights or movement in any of the windows that faced him. If the house was occupied, those inside would have heard him arrive. Crosby cut his engine and switched off the Mondeo's headlights. He sat for a moment, looking across at his grandson. Still asleep. Crosby quietly opened the car door and stepped outside. He took a few seconds to check his immediate area before moving up to the house.

Crosby could see the front door had been left ajar. He pushed it open and stepped cautiously inside. There was a switch on the wall to his left. He pressed it, flooding the long narrow hallway with light. One hand remained on the handgun in his jacket pocket. The ex-detective caught sight of himself in a nearby wall mirror. It was a shock – his chalk white face covered in scratches – the bruise to his forehead a raised, purple weal. There were traces of dried blood showing on both hands, his clothes ripped and soiled.

Crosby advanced further along the hallway, hesitating outside the half-open lounge door. His pulse quickened as he pushed against it, allowing the door to swing slowly inwards.

A woman dressed completely in black stood in the far corner. She wore a thin roll-neck sweater, loose-fitting combat trousers tucked into a pair of lightweight military-style boots. High slanting cheek-bones and green, almond-shaped eyes were set into a face that Crosby would recognise again. The pistol pointing directly at his chest looked too heavy for the woman's child-like hand. A mobile phone she'd been holding in her other hand was shoved into a pocket of her combat trousers.

Standing alongside her, dressed in similar attire, was a solid, squat individual. His long arms and flat, elongated skull gave Crosby the impression of early prehistoric man. He was holding what looked like a *Kalashnikov* semi-automatic rifle, its carrying-strap slung casually over his shoulder. A pair of dull, close-set eyes zeroed in on Crosby's arrival. The permanent lop-sided idiot grin directed at the ex-detective didn't look particularly friendly. No words were spoken. The woman lowered her gun and waved Crosby inside.

He stepped further into the room. Michael, Angela, and Crosby's wife were sitting on a couch to his left. All three of them half-rose from their seats as they took in his appearance. Crosby walked across to them. *'Are you all OK?'*

His wife's response was hostile. *'Does it bloody well look as if we're OK! What the hell's going on, Frank? Who are these people?'*

Angela stood up. *'Where's Jack?'* Her voice was high-pitched, close to hysterical. She looked ashen-faced, eyes red and swollen from crying.

'He's asleep in the car.'

'Has he been harmed?'

'He's fine.'

'I have to fetch him,' Angela said.

'Sit down!' the woman instructed. She turned to Crosby. *'You fetch the boy.'*

He left immediately. The woman's accomplice followed him outside. Crosby's relief at finding his family unharmed reassured him that the hired gunman hadn't lied. If his associates left, as he said they would, then Crosby had already made the decision not to pursue it further. There'd be just a small matter of convincing his family that the police shouldn't be involved. He reached the car. His grandson was still asleep. Crosby unclipped Jack's seat belt and lifted him out. The five-year-old didn't stir.

On re-entering the lounge his daughter-in-law was quickly out of her seat to take Jack from him. The armed woman motioned Crosby towards an armchair with her handgun. *'You sit now!'* He wondered why the *Walther* hadn't been taken from him. She must have been told it was in his possession.

Michael spoke for the first time. *'We can't take much more of this, dad.'*

'It's over now,' the ex-detective said. *'They'll be leaving in a few hours.'*

'What are they waiting for?'

'A telephone call.'

'A telephone call about what?'

'Now isn't the time. We'll talk about it when they've gone.'

Michael nodded at his father's head injury. *'That needs looking at.'*

'It'll keep.'

The ex-detective avoided direct eye contact with his wife as she glowered across the room at him. Doreen Crosby turned her attention to the armed woman. *'My grandson needs to be in his own bed. I'll take him upstairs.'*

The woman's eyes flashed. *'You will be quiet. No more talk.'*

'There's no point in antagonising them,' Crosby said to his wife. *'It won't achieve anything.'*

'Don't bloody well tell me what I can and cannot do,' she hissed at him. *'I want them out of this house.'*

'This isn't helping,' Michael said.

Doreen Crosby wouldn't leave it alone. *'Aren't you able to do anything?'* she said to her husband.

'I already have,' the ex-detective answered tersely. *'They'll be leaving shortly.'*

'I want them out now!'

The armed woman moved in front of Doreen Crosby. *'Is enough from you.'* She produced a gag from her pocket. *'I will use.'*

'Don't you know when to shut up for Christ's sake!' the ex-detective snapped at his wife. Doreen Crosby shot the woman a look before slumping back in her seat.

A lengthy silence ensued. It stretched into twenty minutes. The male accomplice continued to fix Crosby with his idiot grin. It was preferable to the hostile glances from his wife. He looked across at his daughter-in-law who had contributed very little. She sat quietly gently rocking Jack in her arms.

'If you're able to sleep,' Crosby said, *'I'll wake you when they've left.'*

'Sleep!' his wife shot back at him. *'How the bloody hell are we supposed to sleep?'*

The lounge remained warm – a combination of the central heating and several people gathered in one room. An hour later everyone had fallen asleep apart from Crosby and his two armed guards. The ex-detective felt his eyelids begin to droop. He tried to fight it.

CHAPTER 23

The hydrogen-powered, municipal street cleaning vehicle had been hard at work since first light – its twin circular brushes scrubbing at kerbside road surfaces that were already presented in immaculate order. Zurich's reputation as being one of the cleanest cities in the world had not been achieved by accident, and the revolutionary, cell-powered MPV was a small example of the measures in place to maintain that status.

The street cleaning utility vehicle continued its slow, relentless progress along a stretch of Zurich's *Bahnhofstrasse*, one of the world's most expensive and exclusive shopping thoroughfares. At one and a half kilometres in length the iconic street was also home to many of Switzerland's financial institutions – a range of private and retail banks residing within the much sought after *Bahnhofstrasse* post-code.

On this particular Sunday morning the street had already been busy for two hours – a never-ending stream of tourists filling it with noise, colour and movement. The tall, slim, figure, in a tailored full-length coat and black homburg hat, paid them no attention. He certainly didn't look like a tourist. The thin leather attaché case chained to his wrist suggested a man engaged on more serious business. He briefly lifted his gaze to the far horizon – a bitingly cold, clear day had manufactured ideal conditions in which to view the distant, snow-capped Alps. The man didn't dwell on them. A quick check of his watch told him it was now 11.30 a.m. – exactly one hour ahead of Greenwich Mean Time in mainland UK. He waited for the street cleaning vehicle to pass in front of him before making his way across the road towards a nondescript two-storey building identified as *'AVZ Schweiz Privatbank'* – the name picked out in gold lettering across a smoked glass frontage.

In general terms the Swiss banking sector can be broadly divided into two categories, either private or retail. *'AVZ Schweiz Privatbank'* was family-owned – a private bank – requiring at least $1,000,000 to secure an account there. The man had reached a large circular bell-push incorporated into the bank's facing wall. He pressed it. After a short delay two glass doors slid smoothly open – even though a small, discreet wall plaque indicated the bank's opening hours were from Monday through to Friday. A middle-aged, grey-suited bank official stood just inside the open doorway. He arranged his smooth, plump features into a welcoming, business-like smile. *'Mr Hendry?'*

'Yes.'

As they shook hands the bank official executed a slight, well-practiced bow. *'My name is Herr Grütten,'* he said. *'I will be personally attending to all of your requirements this morning.'*

Although Grütten's spoken English was clear and precise, his accented delivery identified a Swiss-German background. He ushered the man who called himself Hendry into a thickly carpeted and subtly lit interior. Its modern, open lounge had been fitted with tasteful, minimalistic furnishings, creating an aroma of wealth that permeated throughout. The man called Hendry sniffed appreciatively. *'It was considerate of the bank to transact our business outside your normal trading hours,'* he said, a Southern Irish lilt clearly evident in his voice.

Grütten respectfully bowed his head again. *'We are always able to accommodate the requirements of valued customers.'*

'An account in excess of three hundred million pounds sterling always helps of course,' the Irishman murmured under his breath.

Herr Grütten crossed to a small, rectangular control panel and punched in a sequence of numbers via its keypad. The two exterior glass doors slid together with a muted hiss. Grütten turned back to his valued account holder. *'Can I offer you some refreshment?'* he asked. *'Coffee? Tea? Perhaps something more fortifying after your journey. A Schnapps?'*

The man called Hendry shook his head. *'I'm booked on a late afternoon flight to London. I would appreciate an early conclusion to our business.'*

'Of course,' Herr Grütten said. *'There is much we have to deal with. I understand your assets are to be broken down into smaller, manageable portfolios and transferred to other accounts.'*

The Irishman nodded. *'That is correct.'*

'A robust and thorough security check will be necessary,' Herr Grütten said. *'You have all the necessary accreditation?'*

'Of course.' The Irishman raised his leather attaché case. *'It would be a major embarrassment for someone to walk in off the street and fraudulently access one of your accounts.'*

'Quite,' the bank official agreed. *'Shall we proceed then?'* Grütten extended an arm, ushering his customer into an adjoining anteroom. *'May I take your hat and coat?'*

'It's not necessary,' the Irishman replied.

'As you wish.' Herr Grütten indicated a chair in front of the anteroom's solid oak desk. The Irishman sat down, placing his black homburg hat and attaché case on top of the desk. Grütten's unhurried movements took him around the desk and into a chair opposite his visitor. A built-in computer terminal – already activated – flashed images to its VDU screen. The bank official's soft, nimble fingers danced effortlessly around his computer keyboard – opening the first of several security clearance applications. *'I will first require your passport, Sir.'* Grütten's voice had assumed a more efficient, business-like tone.

The man called Hendry opened his attaché case – retrieving both a *United Kingdom* and *Eire* passport. He placed them on the desk.

'You have dual nationality,' Herr Grütten remarked.

'My mother was born in Dublin. She married from across the border.'

Grütten raised his eyebrows.

'My father came from Belfast,' the Irishman said. 'An ongoing, uncomfortable divide.'

'A troubled region,' Grütten acknowledged.

The Irishman smiled. 'I was possibly referring to my parents' relationship.'

'Indeed.' Herr Grütten didn't appear amused by the Irishman's humorous aside. He picked up the burgundy-coloured *Eire* passport and began to flick through it. 'You were born and raised in Dublin?'

The man called Hendry nodded. 'Yes.'

'A beautiful part of the world.' Herr Grütten glanced up. 'I very much admire your country's magnificent Giant's Causeway. One of nature's most natural wonders.'

The Irishman smiled again. 'I'm presuming the Giant's Causeway is still resident in Northern Ireland. I trust that wasn't an initial security check.'

'My apologies.' Grütten turned his attention to processing the electronic form displayed on his computer screen. The man called John Hendry re-focused.

Two hours later the Irishman emerged from *AVZ's* glass-fronted doors. He stepped out onto the pavement, drawing cold air deep into his lungs, releasing pent-up tension. Several knots of slow-moving tourists passed in front of him. The Irishman joined them as they progressed along the thoroughfare. At *Bahnhofstrasse's* first intersection he peeled away from the main route to retrieve a mobile phone from within his attaché case. The number he had committed to memory was answered on the third ring.

'Yes?'

'The mother lode has been dispersed.'

A click. His call was disconnected without reply.

Five hundred miles away in mainland UK the call's recipient activated a keyed-in number on his other cell-phone.

Inside Michael and Angela's home at Little Wintermore no one had yet woken. It was 12.30 p.m. The armed woman and her accomplice had left the house some hours ago.

CHAPTER 24

Crosby's eyes snapped open, slowly adjusting to the semi-darkness. They focused on an empty wall in front of him. The ex-detective frowned. There was obviously something significant about it. The fog gradually lifted – a dawning realisation that the armed woman who'd been standing there had gone.

As the events of last night gradually filtered back through to him he turned to look around – a severely stiff neck restricting his head movement. Although the room's curtains had been pulled together they didn't quite meet, allowing a thin sliver of daylight to show itself through the narrow gap. Michael and Angela were asleep – sprawled across the settee – Jack wedged in-between them. Crosby's wife slept upright in one of the armchairs, her features pinched and angry, as if re-living what she'd had to endure the previous night.

A nearby table clock told him it was approaching one o'clock. Several attempts to stand were unsuccessful – every part of his body protesting at the effort required. Crosby inched forward to the edge of his chair, slowly hauling himself upright. He allowed the dizziness and pain level to subside before shuffling unsteadily towards the lounge door. His wife stirred but didn't wake. Crosby paused. He didn't want to disturb anyone just yet – not until he'd made sure that the woman and her accomplice had left.

As he went through into the kitchen his progress became more co-ordinated, the discomfort and stiffness easing. A length of thin metal slats at the front window hadn't been closed, allowing him to look out onto the driveway. There were three cars in view. The light-grey Citroen saloon wasn't one of them. He turned, intending to check upstairs. His wife stood in the doorway. She didn't look well – the past two weeks had obviously taken its toll.

'They've gone,' Crosby said.

His wife took in the ex-detective's appearance, her eyes flat, unsympathetic. *'Have you contacted the police yet?'*

'No.'

'Why not?'

'I've only just woken.'

'I'll do it then.'

Doreen Crosby made a point of deliberately brushing past him to reach the kitchen wall telephone. He stopped her from picking it up. She wheeled around. *'What the hell do you think you're doing?'*

'Involving the police at this stage will have implications.'

His wife reached for the phone again. *'You'll get out of my way.'*

Crosby grabbed her wrist. *'Michael and Angela have a right to be consulted.'*

She tried to pull away. *'You're hurting me.'*

'I'm not hurting you. Stop playing the wounded bloody martyr.' Crosby took his hand away but placed it over the telephone's wall mounting. *'This has to be discussed.'*

'Bastard!' His wife glowered at him. She also massaged her wrist for good measure.

'And how do you think this will help?' Michael had entered the kitchen. *'Angela's close to breaking down and you two are at each other's throats already.'*

'We need to check all the bedrooms,' Crosby said.

'I've looked,' his son replied. *'There's no one here.'*

'I tried to call the police.' Doreen Crosby gestured towards her husband. *'He wouldn't let me.'*

Michael looked across at his father.

'You need to be aware of the consequences,' Crosby said. *'I'll tell you what's happened and we can decide after that.'*

'I know what's happened,' Doreen Crosby shot back, *'and I know who's bloody responsible.'*

Michael put an arm around his mother's shoulders. *'We should hear what he has to say.'*

The arm was shrugged away. Doreen Crosby shot her husband another venomous look, stalking past him as she left the room. Michael turned to his father. *'Well?'*

'This family's safety has been my sole concern for over three weeks,' Crosby answered. *'It still is.'*

'And why haven't you contacted the police?'

'There's good reason.'

'Which is?'

'I'd rather everyone was told about it at the same time.'

'It had better be good.' His son turned and left. Crosby followed him back to the lounge.

The room's curtains had been drawn. Crosby's wife stood at the window, stony-faced, her arms folded. Angela was obsessively tidying cushions – arranging and re-arranging them. Michael had to sit her down. *'Jack needs to be in his bed.'* She looked across at their son, still asleep on the couch. *'We can't stay here. It's not safe.'*

Crosby could see she was close to the edge. Michael took his wife's hand. *'They're not coming back. It's over now. We'll talk about it after you've taken Jack upstairs.'* Angela stood abruptly. She picked up her son and carried him from the room.

'See what you've done?' Doreen Crosby hissed at her husband.

He didn't answer. Their relationship seemed to have completely broken down. There was no sign of support from Michael or Angela either. Crosby should have felt angry, but his current physical and mental state had left him with very little fight. There was only so many times he could say that it wasn't his fault.

Michael filled a silent void. *'I suggest we talk this through over some breakfast.'*

Doreen Crosby was quickly to her feet. *'I'll see to it.'* She left the room. Michael remained behind. He crossed to the lounge window and looked out, as if deliberately facing away from his father. *'Are you sure that Jack wasn't harmed last night?'*

'Not physically.'

'What the hell's that supposed to mean?'

There seemed little point in concealing what the five-year-old would later tell his father. *'He witnessed a gun being fired.'*

'Christ alive! The boy's five years old.'

Crosby didn't respond.

'Why was he taken?' his son asked.

'Insurance,' Crosby replied. *'They knew I wouldn't put him at risk.'*

'Who are they?'

'It's complicated.'

'Angela was out of her mind with worry.'

'I can imagine.'

'No you bloody well can't!' Michael looked as if he had more questions but crossed to the lounge door and left. Crosby let him go. He needed to focus, pick his way through the past few weeks. If his family were to be dissuaded from calling the police then a number of events would have to be altered, incidents omitted. It had to remain simple. Ian Brown's name couldn't be mentioned in the re-telling. Crosby's previous working association with the Scenes-of-Crime officer would cause his family to be suspicious. There could be no reference to Grace Taylor's death, hired contract killers, or murdered prostitutes either.

He ran through his sanitised version of events again. Something out of synch. Not quite right. A weariness washed over the ex-detective. He sat down. It would be very easy to call the police and tell them what had actually taken place – but that would put him at the centre of six related murder cases, a fake id, and the un-licenced *Walther*. And could he rely on Paul Berne or Penny Zardelli to back him? Probably not. There was also the document that Lucy Roberts had referred to – accusing him of knowing where the drugs had been stored at *Dryffed's Farm*. What if that turned-up during the course of an investigation? He attempted to address the various options again. They blurred and ran into each other. Probably sleep deprivation. The matter had to be somehow buried this morning. Its logic remained stubbornly out of reach.

'*Breakfast!*' his wife shouted from the kitchen.

Too late now.

Crosby struggled to push himself upright. Angela was coming downstairs as he reached the lounge doorway. She hesitated. Crosby could see that his daughter-in-law had something she wanted to tell him. It was probably about the hired contract killer who Crosby had seen getting into her car outside Jack's school. She would have realised by now that he had a connection with what had taken place. Angela eventually dropped her eyes and continued on past him. She wasn't ready yet. Crosby didn't call her back. It might have to be used as a lever over breakfast.

His wife had set four places around the kitchen's oval pine table. There were two large plates of buttered toast at its centre. Crosby lowered himself into an empty chair and picked up the large mug in front of him. Strong tea. He added two spoonfuls of sugar and emptied the mug in seconds. It helped to revive him. The earlier panic attack had passed and he didn't feel so lightheaded. '*Is there another?*' Crosby asked his wife.

'*You're not an invalid!*' she replied sharply.

'*Christ's sake.*' Michael pushed his mug across to Crosby.

The ex-detective drained half its contents before reaching for the toast. He was hungry. His appetite had returned. It wasn't until his third slice that Crosby realised no one else was eating. They sat in silence, waiting for him to finish. He took a few extra minutes.

'*We need to make a start,*' Michael said.

Crosby couldn't delay it any longer. '*The threat we talked about before you left for the Isle of Wight no longer exists.*'

'Well that's a relief,' his wife was quick to answer. *'I can just forget about the inbreds who were holding me at gunpoint last night.'*

'If you'd remained in the safe house,' Crosby shot back at her, *'it wouldn't have happened.'*

'That's enough,' Michael warned them both. *'We're wasting time.'*

Doreen Crosby sat back, arms folded, her features rigid.

'The heroin that disappeared from Dryffed's Farm,' Crosby said, *'was essentially down to just one person. A former prison officer by the name of Rose Cavendish.'*

It didn't draw any comment.

'She worked at Foston Hall,' the ex-detective continued. *'It's where Lucy Roberts served out her custodial sentence. Rose protected her from the prison mafia and they eventually became lovers. At some point Lucy must have told Cavendish about the hidden cache of narcotics.'*

'Lovers!' Doreen Crosby's face suggested an obscene act had been committed. *'Are you saying this woman entered into physical relations with a female prisoner under her charge? It's your association with these sort of people over the years that caused our home life to suffer.'*

Crosby ignored it. *'Lucy was extremely vulnerable,'* he said. *'She became totally dependent on her prison warder. Their relationship changed however. Once Rose Cavendish became aware of the hidden drugs, her only interest was to recover them for herself.'*

'If they'd become that close,' Michael said, *'why didn't she just wait until Lucy's release?'*

Crosby shook his head. *'Cavendish's fear was that the relationship wouldn't continue outside of prison.'*

'She was solely responsible for recovering the drugs?'

'Yes.'

Michael frowned. *'Surely Lucy must have considered the possibility that Cavendish was responsible?'*

'Not at the time of her release,' Crosby replied. 'I became Lucy's prime suspect after she found a document among Henry Roberts' personal effects.'

'The one that suggested you knew about heroin being stored at Dryffed's Farm,' Michael said.

Crosby's head lifted sharply. 'We've already had this conversation. The document's irrelevant.'

'It doesn't sound irrelevant.' Doreen Crosby had been following the exchanges. 'What is this document? Why wasn't I told anything about it before we had to leave?'

'There wasn't time to tell you anything,' Crosby said.

Michael interrupted them. 'Why did Cavendish go along with this charade of you being a suspect?'

'She was buying time. It was always her intention that Lucy would eventually disappear.'

Crosby's wife muttered something inaudible.

'You told me about a drugs syndicate before we left for the Isle of Wight,' Michael said. 'They hadn't been paid for the original shipment.'

'Yes.' Crosby had to focus now – about to weave several more half-truths and omissions into his story – bury himself a little deeper into the hole he was digging. 'Cavendish was playing a dangerous game, aware that the syndicate were waiting for Lucy to recover their investment.'

'Is that who was here?'

Crosby nodded. 'They lost patience and picked all of us up last night. Two of the syndicate remained here with you.'

Michael didn't look convinced. 'Why you?'

'They'd have seen me with the two women,' Crosby replied. 'Lucy probably told them I was responsible for lifting the drugs.'

'But they let you and Jack go.'

'Rose Cavendish broke down under interrogation,' Crosby said. 'She was taking them to where the heroin had been relocated.'

'You said there was a shot fired.'

'That was to frighten Cavendish.'

'And that's it?'

The ex-detective nodded. *'Those two leaving this morning would confirm the drugs have been recovered.'* Crosby had reached the stage where he was starting to believe his own spin. He glanced at the faces around him. Michael still didn't look convinced. His wife's body language remained hostile. Angela hadn't spoken. Tears were beginning to run down his daughter-in-law's face again. She continued to sit bolt upright, white-faced, twisting a damp handkerchief between her fingers. Michael was first to break the extended silence. *'So where are Lucy Roberts and Rose Cavendish now?'*

'I don't know.'

'But you're here,' Michael said.

'They knew I wouldn't go to the police.'

'Why the hell not?' Doreen Crosby's interruption was angry and vocal. *'They're no threat to us now.'* She turned to her son. *'What are you waiting for?'*

'Why can't we call the police, dad?' Michael asked his father.

Crosby shifted in his seat. *'I've had to employ certain practices during the past three weeks that were not strictly legal. A police investigation would be awkward for me personally.'*

'How awkward?' Michael asked.

'It might involve a custodial sentence.'

'Best place for you,' Doreen Crosby muttered. *'I don't know why we're still discussing this.'*

'Is there anything else?' Michael asked.

Crosby had only one more argument to put forward. He always knew it would have to be used at some point. It needed his daughter-in-law's support. *'A police enquiry,'* he said, *'would disrupt this family for months. If it reached the public domain then all of us as individuals would be under the media microscope. Every facet of our private lives, including casual relationships, would be closely examined.'*

Crosby hoped it would be enough. He waited for a reaction from his daughter-in-law. Angela hesitated before standing. *'I don't want the police here.'* Both hands were clenched, her knuckles showing white. *'This ends now. I want our family back to normal.'* She turned to her husband. *'I mean it. We've suffered enough.'*

Michael raised his eyebrows at the outburst. *'OK. We'll talk about it.'*

'No!' Angela snapped at him. *'We won't bloody well talk about it. I've told you what I want. Just do it!'*

Michael watched his wife leave the room. *'It's been traumatic for her,'* Doreen Crosby said. *'She'll feel differently after a night's sleep.'*

'I don't know.' Michael shook his head. *'I'm worried about her state of mind. She's close to a breakdown. We ought to respect what she wants.'*

Doreen Crosby didn't reply.

'You know this is over?' Michael asked his father.

'Yes.'

Michael turned to his mother. *'I don't think that Angela would cope with the aggravation of a police investigation and intrusive reporters. We have to think of her well being.'*

'You're prepared to just forget about it?'

'Yes.'

'Well, I'm not.'

'You will. We all have to be in agreement.'

Doreen Crosby wheeled on her husband. *'This bloody mess is entirely your fault.'* She pointed a finger at him. *'If my grandson has been affected by what he endured last night then this marriage is over.'*

Crosby didn't reply.

Michael stood up and left the room.

Crosby waited a few seconds. *'I need to go back home,'* he said to his wife. *'Are you coming with me?'*

'No!'

The ex-detective nodded. *'When do you intend returning?'*

'*I don't want to be in the same room as you,*' his wife answered, '*let alone the same house.*'

'*Not any time soon then.*' The remark was unnecessary. He immediately regretted it.

Doreen Crosby pushed her chair back and stood up. '*I hope your flippancy will be company for you,*' she said. '*Enjoy it. I'll be staying here indefinitely.*'

The ex-detective sat back in his chair – beginning to wilt again – last night's events catching up with him. He reached for his half-finished mug of tea. Had he managed to cover everything? It was close enough to the truth. Would it suffice? Only time would tell. Crosby grimaced as he took a swallow of his tea. It was stone-cold.

CHAPTER 25

The northern pike's long, sleek, mottled-green body held a stationary position just above the river bed, perfectly camouflaged within the dense weed and vegetation. It waited, a skilful hunter with the ability to ambush and swallow other fish up to a third of its own length. This particular specimen was in excess of four feet, a female, weighing approximately ten pounds. At this time of year she was only interested in the feeding cycle, having spawned her fertilised mass of over one hundred thousand eggs back in early spring.

The predator's patient endeavours were not being rewarded however – a distinct lack of suitable passing prey for the pike's needle-like teeth to immobilise. She moved away in search of more favourable hunting grounds, a languid snake-like action, propelling her through the river's murky depths.

After the pike had settled into a new location she was rewarded by agitated movement directly above her. The hunter didn't immediately attack – continuing to monitor the spinning earthworm with some suspicion. It didn't look completely natural. The pike waited. She eventually pointed an alligator-shaped snout towards the surface – ascending slowly into lighter waters. Twelve years of patrolling this particular stretch of river had taught the predator to investigate further before committing itself.

She allowed her snout to break through a calm, flat surface – her cold reptilian eyes sweeping the riverbank. There was a dark shape visible, not completely immobile. It confirmed the pike's suspicions. A flick of her tail and she submerged into deeper waters.

Crosby caught a flash of soft, yellow underbelly as the pike twisted and dived away. It barely registered with him. Although he'd been camped at his favourite stretch on the *River Blythe* for over two hours now he couldn't settle – automatically casting and re-casting his lines – just going through the motions.

The ex-detective tossed another handful of ground-bait into a sluggish current. It was the sort of day that Crosby would normally have relished – an abundance of fish – his battered old stainless steel thermos – enough sandwiches to see him through until late afternoon.

Recent events were still dominating his thoughts however – keeping him awake at night – the solitude of a deserted river bank only serving to underline his present state. Although it had been three weeks since the family's return, his wife remained at Little Wintermore, her contact irregular. She showed no interest in returning home, and there was little he could do about it. Crosby shrugged deeper into his waterproof fishing jacket, the depression taking a firmer hold.

His other worry was the police. He'd only received one further visit from them in regard to Grace Taylor and Lieutenant Thorburn's ongoing murder investigation. An examination of the ex-detective's logged mobile calls should have raised a lot more questions for him to answer. Maybe his old colleague DS Watson was returning a favour after their previous, close working relationship. Crosby wasn't convinced. There were too many loose ends for him to have escaped the net entirely. In retrospect, his actions after leaving *Andlebury Park* were probably wrong. Maybe the police should have been informed that night – but he hadn't been thinking clearly back then – a physical and mental tiredness overwhelming him. And it was too late now.

He retrieved a tin of small cigars from the pocket of his waterproof and lit one up. Alongside him, in an open plastic container, a seething mass of earthworms continued to twist and squirm – his preferred choice of bait to land Chub or Perch. Crosby's heart wasn't in it though. And when the balsa-wood float from one of his two lines suddenly disappeared below the surface he didn't even notice, allowing the reel on his fishing pole to spin aimlessly.

'Call yourself a detective?' The familiar Glaswegian growl came from behind him. *'When was the last time you let anyone off the hook?'*

Crosby spun around. *'What the...!'*

'Hello, laddie.' Ian Brown manoeuvred himself down the sloping, grassy bank, to where Crosby was sat on his canvas stool.

The ex-detective could only stare at him.

'You can close your mouth, Frank. I'm not a fucking ghost!'

'You were shot.' Crosby was struggling to accept Ian Brown's presence. *'I saw it happen.'*

'Aye.' The Scot nodded. *'Bloody convincing wasn't it. Smoke and mirrors. A round of blank ammunition.'*

The ex-detective couldn't take his eyes off Brown. *'What the hell's going on, Ian?'*

'That's a fucking good question.' Brown sat himself down alongside Crosby, on top of the ex-detective's fishing box. *'It's not exactly what I planned.'*

'You arranged to have me killed up on Headle Point.'

The Scot shook his head. *'Andlebury House was a set up to fake my own death. But you decided to throw yourself down the side of a hill. We had to wait until you re-appeared.'*

'You're lying!' Crosby was still having a problem accepting the Scot's appearance, his mind working overtime, not exactly sure what was happening.

'You were close to finding out I was responsible for Lucy's missing heroin,' Brown continued. *'I had to ensure that you witnessed me being shot.'*

'You're not making any sense.'

'After what I put your family through,' Brown said, *'you'd have come looking for me if I was still out there. You had to be convinced I was no longer alive.'*

Crosby didn't trust what Brown was telling him. *'Why didn't you just get your hired gun to kill me off along with all the others?'*

'Your murder would have caused too many complications.' The Scot shrugged. *'Or maybe I didn't give a toss about what happened to the others. You were as close to a friend as it gets.'*

'That's bollocks! You're telling me the whole charade was for my benefit?'

'And mine,' Ian Brown said. *'I wanted to enjoy my windfall without having to look over my shoulder every day.'*

'The hired killer claimed he'd taken control of your assets.'

'All part of the set-up to convince you,' Brown replied. *'He couldn't assume the account. I had safeguards in place. And there was already someone earmarked to impersonate John Hendry in Zurich.'*

'Who was that?'

'A business associate. Someone I could trust.'

'Obviously not that trustworthy,' Crosby said. *'What went wrong?'*

'Nothing in that respect. I have access to a great deal of money.'

'What game are we playing now, Ian?'

'It's no fucking game, laddie.'

'I witnessed your death,' Crosby pointed out. *'You could have disappeared a rich man. What are you doing sat here?'*

'Because he forgot about me,' a voice said from behind.

Crosby turned. Lucy Roberts stood on the bank above them holding a small revolver, pointed directly at the ex-detective. She cut a desperate looking figure – the face thin, almost skeletal – dark roots showing through her matted bleached hair. She looked grubby, unkempt, her clothes creased, heavily soiled. It was the eyes that had Crosby's attention though, small black marbles, intense, slightly unfocused. He'd seen them four years ago in the face of her father – at a point when Robert Milner had lost his mental strength and crossed the boundary that passes for civilised normality. *'Face the front!'* she instructed.

Ian Brown hadn't reacted at all, continuing to look out over the river. *'She insisted that I drive her over here to see you,'* the Scot said.

'It's difficult to refuse when there's a gun being waved in your face.'

Crosby's lack of surprise at Lucy's presence was probably due to an already surreal situation. *'How did she know where to find us?'*

Brown shook his head. *'Fuck knows!'*

'You told me she was no longer alive.'

'I didn't. You assumed it.'

Crosby half-turned his head. *'We have to keep her talking.'*

'Good luck with that,' Brown said. *'Her fucking mind's gone.'*

Crosby attempted to stand.

'Sit down!' the woman ordered.

Crosby remained seated, twisting himself around to face her. *'You must know by now that Rose helped to recover the drugs from Dryffed's Farm after you told her about them.'*

'Shut the fuck up!' Lucy shifted the gun's aim towards Ian Brown's back. *'I know who was responsible.'*

The ex-detective edged towards his fishing rucksack. Somewhere inside was the *Walther.* He had intended to throw it into the river at some point that morning. *'Do you accept Rose's part in all of this?'* Crosby needed to keep her talking, divert her attention.

Lucy shook her head, continuing to point the gun at Ian Brown's back. *'We loved each other. This bastard turned her against me.'*

'Did you know he was Rose's brother?'

Crosby's remark seemed to confuse her. *'I had a brother.'* Lucy's brow furrowed. *'I can't remember his name.'*

'It was Stephen,' Crosby said to her.

'Yes.' Lucy sounded vague. *'I had to shoot him. Why was that?'* She paused, as if searching her memory. *'My father was also shot. You were responsible.'*

'He committed suicide.' Crosby was watching her closely.

'It was your fault.'

Ian Brown leant in towards the ex-detective. *'She's fucking rambling. We could rush her.'*

'She's too unstable,' Crosby murmured. *'We keep her talking. Did*

307

you find out where she's been for the last two weeks?'

'Christ's sake!' Brown hissed. *'I didn't think to fucking ask. I was more concerned about a gun rammed into the back of my neck.'*

'No more talking!' Lucy said sharply. Crosby sensed her moving down the slope towards them. He shifted a little closer to his rucksack.

'Face the front!'

'Your money's safe, Lucy,' Crosby said. *'He can get it for you.'*

'Shut up!'

The ex-detective felt her standing directly behind. He held his breath, conscious of the gun almost touching his head. Seconds ticked by. *'Where's Rose?'* Lucy eventually asked.

Crosby slowly exhaled. *'We can help you look for her.'* He risked another slight shift towards his rucksack. Lucy didn't seem to notice. *'When I had to stay with my father in Sixfields,'* she said, *'he would tell me all about the late night visitors who used to call on him.'*

Crosby knew all about Robert Milner's late night visitors – shadows and demons who eventually took control of a tortured mind. He really needed to retrieve the *Walther* from his rucksack.

'My father had no other friends,' Lucy said. *'They were company for him.'*

Crosby needed the woman in his eye-line.

'My father was quite insane of course.' Lucy laughed. It was loud, high-pitched. *'But his friends were real enough. They're here with us now.'*

Ian Brown swore softly. *'Fucking hell!'*

Lucy began to circle slowly around the two men. Crosby's peripheral vision tracked her. His rucksack was almost in touching distance. When she stood directly in front of the ex-detective he looked up into eyes that had completely glazed over. *'I've been talking with my father's old companions,'* she said. *'As you're both responsible for the misfortune I've suffered they've told me what I have to do.'* Lucy continued to pace about in front of the two men, agitated movements, muttering to herself. *'You've stolen three hundred million pounds from me. I've lost my father and my brother. I have no family left.'*

'You still have your mother.'

'I don't have a fucking mother!'

Crosby finally manoeuvred himself next to the rucksack. He needed a distraction. Lucy stopped pacing. She extended the gun towards them. *'Lower your heads!'*

'Jesus Christ!' Ian Brown attempted to stand up. *'She's going to execute us.'*

Out on the river, Crosby's second float was being tugged underwater. *'I have to get this, Lucy,'* he shouted. A distraction. It was all he had. The loudness of his voice seemed to jolt her. Crosby lifted his fishing pole from its mounting. He expected her to stop him. She didn't – turning to watch the fish as it was reeled in – seemingly mesmerised by the creature's frenzied attempts to free itself.

The ex-detective lay down his rod and reached over into the rucksack. *'I need my landing-net.'* His eyes never left her. Lucy seemed oblivious to what he was doing. Crosby located the handgun.

Lucy's attention was still fixated on the hooked fish. She began to recite an old nursery rhyme in a small, childlike voice. *'One, two, three, four, five, once I caught a fish alive.'*

Ian Brown watched Crosby pull the handgun clear of his rucksack.

'Six, seven, eight, nine, ten, then I let it go again.'

The fish continued to struggle and flap about on the river's surface.

'Why did I let it go?' Lucy turned back towards the ex-detective, her eyes flat, the gun hanging down by her side. *'Because it bit my finger so.'*

A surge of adrenalin pumped through Crosby as Lucy slowly raised her gun. He didn't have time to consider the consequences. At this precise moment it seemed a perfectly logical solution – but then he too might have slipped across the line that separates normal behaviour from irrational action. Crosby snapped back the *Walther's* top-loader, extended his arm, and pointed the gun barrel directly at Lucy's upper chest. He pulled the trigger.

Although much of the gun's loud report was contained within their sheltered confine it still caused disturbance; two moorhens paddling quickly away from the river bank, a kingfisher's rapid exit from nearby alder trees – its colour a vivid flash of blue and orange against the grey sky.

Ian Brown climbed slowly to his feet. *'And I'd say that just about fucks up everything, laddie.'*

CHAPTER 26

Ellendene Heights offered ten acres of tranquil seclusion to both its long-term residents and casual day visitors alike. The well-kept formal gardens boasted wide stretches of manicured lawns and sharply cut borders. These had been filled with colourful winter bedding plants – violas, cyclamen, polyanthus – to alleviate the site's sombre reputation.

Positioned centrally within the grounds was a single-storey building of red brick and dark wood, the structure blending discreetly into *Ellendene's* landscaped surroundings. On this particular day there were several knots of people standing in front of the red-bricked building. They all wore dark attire and spoke in hushed tones, occasionally breaking off to check the site's distant roadside entrance.

At eleven o'clock precisely, two sleek black limousines turned into the grounds. A respectful hush fell over *Ellendene's* invited gathering – all eyes following the sedate progress of both vehicles. There was an extended silence. The two cars eventually pulled up in front of *Ellendene's* main entrance. A tall thin figure, dressed in Victorian frock coat and black top hat, stepped theatrically from the first limousine. With what looked like a well-rehearsed gesture the man removed his hat – directing an extended low bow towards a wreath-covered coffin in the vehicle's rear section. As family members began to emerge from limousine number two, those mourners waiting outside slowly drifted towards the building's open double-doors.

A discreet signal from the frock-coated funeral director saw half-a-dozen dark-suited figures materialise around the first limousine's raised tail-gate. They worked together briskly and efficiently, lifting the coffin out and up onto their shoulders with practiced ease. A final check was made to ensure the casket's tapered end pointed forwards – those about to embark on their final journey are traditionally carried feet first into the church or crematorium.

Another curt nod from the funeral director prompted his pall-bearers to shuffle slowly forward. They were closely followed by family members of the deceased. Waiting for them at *Ellendene's* entrance doors was the Reverend Edwin Traherne – resplendent in a white linen surplice worn over his ankle-length purple cassock. The Church of England minister arranged his benign, genial features into a sympathetic smile as the family approached. He turned and led them inside.

An excerpt from Elgar's *Enigma Variations* accompanied the funeral cortege as it moved slowly along a wide central aisle. The haunting music faded into a respectful silence – coinciding with the coffin being carefully lowered onto a raised catafalque. Reverend Traherne settled himself behind his lectern, waiting for the six pall-bearers to back discreetly away. His sympathetic smile remained firmly in place as family members located their places among the front row of chairs. A last minute arrival slipped into the crematorium's chapel. Detective Superintendent Oliver Rees-Bramley's short, slim, frame was, as always, immaculately attired – a sharply cut dark suit, double knotted black tie and white shirt.

The senior CID officer found a seat in the chapel's back row, picking up his copy of a thin, four-page pamphlet that itemised the committal's order of service. On the pamphlet's front cover a young, relaxed looking Frank Crosby smiled back at him. Beneath the ex-detective's colour image was a bold line of black print, indicating the dateline 1952 – 2011. Reverend Traherne began to address his congregation.

Rees-Bramley looked up to check out those in attendance – finding Detective Sergeant Barry Watson several chairs to his left in an otherwise empty row. Watson had already noted the superintendent's arrival. He groaned inwardly as Rees-Bramley stood up and moved along the row towards him.

'A surprisingly small turn-out sergeant.' Rees-Bramley hitched

up his trousers a fraction before lowering himself into the chair next to Watson. *'I always imagined that Frank Crosby would have a wider circle of friends and acquaintances.'*

'The nature of our work, Sir,' Watson replied. *'Week-ends and night shifts play havoc with your social life.'*

'Quite.' The detective superintendent's tone was clipped, unsympathetic. *'We all have that particular cross to bear.'*

A short pause. Reverend Traherne's monotone voice continued in the background. *'Did you know Frank well?'* Watson asked.

'He was my DI three years ago,' Rees-Bramley answered curtly. *'I'm just here to represent the Department. Was your relationship with him a long standing one?'*

'We worked together a few years back. Our families used to see a lot of each other.' The Welshman shrugged. *'We lost touch.'*

A young boy's voice reverberated around the chapel's hushed interior. *'Where's Gramps?'* Both detectives lifted their heads. In the front row Crosby's five-year-old grandson had been swept up in his grandmother's embrace. Watson and Rees-Bramley resumed their conversation. *'It's a strange affair though,'* the superintendent said.

Watson groaned inwardly. *'Is it, Sir?'* He sensed that Rees-Bramley was keen to move away from polite small talk.

The superintendent's voice remained low. *'A dog-walker found the woman Roberts sat alongside Crosby's body.'* He paused. *'She was rocking to and fro apparently. Reciting an old nursery rhyme.'*

'I understand that Lucy Roberts has underlying mental health issues.'

'And there were two unlicensed handguns found at the crime scene,' Rees-Bramley said. *'Crosby was shot clean through the forehead with one of them.'*

'So I believe.'

'He was still holding his handgun,' Rees-Bramley continued. *'Apparently its firing mechanism had jammed. What the hell was Frank Crosby doing with an unlicensed firearm?'*

The detective sergeant shook his head. *'It's not my investigation, Sir.'*

'They still haven't found out how the woman got to him either,' Rees-Bramley added. *'It's an isolated spot. Crosby's vehicle was the only one around.'*

'Perhaps Lucy travelled there with him.'

The superintendent raised his eyebrows. *'I'm told she's not talking.'*

'I understand she's incapable of saying anything coherent.'

There was a brief respite for the Welshman as both detectives stood up to join *Ellendene's* congregation in their rendition of *The Rugged Cross.* Watson mouthed his way silently through the hymn's words, aware that his own investigation would be next on the superintendent's agenda. He knew that Rees-Bramley had been keeping a close eye on it – the murders of both DC Taylor and Lt Thorburn were still causing huge embarrassment to West Midlands Police Force.

The Rugged Cross reached a half-hearted conclusion, allowing *Ellendene's* small gathering to resume their seats. *'Your investigation regarding the murders of DC Taylor and Lieutenant Thorburn,'* Rees-Bramley said. *'I'm hearing little in the way of progress.'*

'That's because there is no fucking progress!' the Welshman muttered to himself.

Rees-Bramley leant back and steepled his fingers together. *'I'm inclined towards a possible connection between the two investigations.'*

'Are you, Sir?'

'I believe it was also a line of enquiry that you were following?'

'One of several, Sir.'

'You sound sceptical sergeant,' Rees-Bramley said.

'Ballistic tests indicate the handgun used against Frank Crosby was of a different calibre to the one used at St Mary's.'

Rees-Bramley arched his eyebrows. *'Which shouldn't rule out the* possibility that Lucy Roberts used a different gun to murder DC Taylor. Wouldn't her deranged mind be looking for some form of revenge after what happened at Dryffed's Farm?'

'We were of a similar opinion initially, Sir,' Watson replied. 'Subsequent enquiries have been unable to link either of the incidents.'

'It is also significant,' Rees-Bramley added, 'that DC Taylor's body was found in the cemetery where Lucy Roberts' father was buried.'

'That could have been done to deliberately implicate her,' Watson said. 'We know that both Taylor and Thorburn's bodies were taken to St Mary's after they'd been shot.' The Welshman was becoming annoyed at Rees-Bramley's persistence. This was neither the time nor the place.

The detective superintendent didn't look convinced. 'Our American connections want it dealt with,' he sniffed. 'The tabloid press are still having a field day with Thorburn's involvement in all of this.'

Watson nodded. 'I understand the headline 'Cock Happy Yank' was particularly embarrassing for them, Sir.' The Welshman's tone remained neutral, his face expressionless.

Rees-Bramley's mouth compressed into a thin line. 'My only concern is how all of this reflects on our Department. Are you satisfied with the current direction of this investigation?'

'DI Kingston is an experienced senior officer, Sir,' Watson replied. The Welshman certainly didn't want to get into a discussion about his team leader's ability and qualities. The two detectives were once again interrupted by *Ellendene's* resident organist as she launched herself enthusiastically into the opening chords of *Abide With Me*. Both men stood. Watson glanced through the pamphlet's order of service. He was anxious to part company with the superintendent. Rees-Bramley resumed his seat before the final chorus had faded away. 'We should also consider the fact that Frank Crosby remained on friendly terms with DC Taylor after his retirement.'

'Should we, Sir?'

'His presence at St Mary's is suspicious in itself,' the detective superintendent added.

'There was a perfectly reasonable explanation for him being there,' Watson replied.

'And is there a reasonable explanation for him being in possession of a handgun?' Rees-Bramley asked.

'The Walther wasn't used to murder either Taylor or Thorburn.'

'It still requires an explanation,' Rees-Bramley said. *'I take it there's still nothing from any of your informants?'*

'No, Sir.'

'Which would seem to confirm someone acting alone,' the detective superintendent pointed out. *'And that takes us right back to Lucy Roberts.'*

Watson didn't bother replying. There was movement at the front as Crosby's son stood up and made his way across to the lectern. Reverend Traherne stepped aside for him. Michael Crosby unfolded a single sheet of notepaper and began reading aloud from it. Rees-Bramley and Watson listened in silence. The tribute to Frank Crosby was short and unemotional. Crosby's son returned to his seat five minutes later. Both detectives bowed their heads as Reverend Traherne moved smoothly into the Lord's Prayer. At its conclusion Rees-Bramley was quickly to his feet. *'Amen,'* he said. Watson also stood as the Reverend embarked on the Final Commendation and Committal.

All eyes switched to the raised catafalque as it was remotely lowered to floor level. A slow-moving conveyor track moved the highly polished oak coffin towards a pair of dark-red brocade curtains. When the curtains finally closed behind Frank Crosby the congregation climbed to their feet, suppressed whispers humming quietly around the room. Both detectives edged sideways along their row of empty chairs to stand in *Ellendene's* central aisle. The detective superintendent checked his watch. *'I have a meeting at two o'clock. You'll pass on my condolences to the family.'*

316

'*Of course, Sir,*' the Welshman replied with some relief. He watched Rees-Bramley exit the chapel through its main entrance doors before joining the congregation's slow-moving tail as mourners exited through a side door of the chapel. It took a while for the queue to shorten – sympathetic, concerned faces stopping to exchange words with Crosby's family as they waited outside. When the Welshman finally reached Doreen Crosby she smiled in recognition, brushing her cheek lightly against his. '*It's good to see you, Barry. Frank would have appreciated it.*'

'*I'm sorry for your loss,*' Watson offered lamely.

'*We should have kept in touch.*' Doreen Crosby's eyes were red-rimmed and swollen. She wore very little make-up. '*How are Jean and the children?*'

'*They're fine,*' Watson replied. '*Jean's away in Scotland at the moment. She apologises for not being here.*'

'*It would be good to see her again.*'

'*You must come and stay,*' Watson offered. '*When you feel the time is right.*'

Doreen Crosby's attention slid to her left. Reverend Traherne had exited the chapel's side-door and was heading in their direction. After a brief, final embrace the detective sergeant moved across to speak with Crosby's son and daughter-in-law. Their responses were detached, monotone. Watson continued on past them, stopping alongside a small display of wreaths and flowers propped against the facing wall. He scanned their handwritten cards for anything that might be of assistance to his ongoing investigation. One of the cards he looked at caused him to lean forward and re-read it. Minutes later the Welshman was hurrying across *Ellendene's* car park, speaking urgently into his mobile.